HOUR OF THE DOG

The Hour of the Dog—twilight by the ancient Chinese clock—epitomizes Hong Kong during the Japanese occupation from Christmas 1941 until August 1945. For the British and Chinese population, herded into military or civilian camps, it was a time of danger, suffering and humiliation. Some, however, made their escape through the enemy lines into the hinterland, and though many died en route, a few survived to reach Chungking, headquarters of Chiang Kai-Shek in a China rent by civil war and Japanese invasion.

Among the survivors was Vincent Stafford, grandson of Old Ross who founded the princely house of Stafford and McMurtrie in *The Pagoda Tree* and son of Bard Stafford whose adventures enlivened *The Midnight Gun*. Another was Shivka, the beautiful White Russian who lived on borrowed time and worked for Allied Intelligence. This is the story of their lonely, dangerous war, and of those who worked with them: of 'Raucous', the British Tommy left behind in the Hong Kong Military Prison by mistake, and of Aggie, his Chinese girl-friend; of the Misses Willis who defied the Japs and maintained their Cheltenham standards to the end; of Long John Silberstein, the one-legged American ex-naval convict; of Percy Kwan, Chinese-Australian professor of archaeology; and many, many more.

Berkely Mather served throughout the Burma and Far East campaign and was in Hong Kong in the immediate post-war period. He has drawn on his personal knowledge of places and people to create this third chronicle of the Stafford family.

BERKELY MATHER

Hour of the Dog

COLLINS
St James's Place, London
1982

William Collins Sons & Co. Ltd
London · Glasgow · Sydney · Auckland
Toronto · Johannesburg

British Library Cataloguing in Publication Data

Mather, Berkely
　Hour of the dog.
I. Title
823 [F]　PR9619.3.M3 / 18

First published 1982
© Berkely Mather 1982

ISBN 0 00 222670 7

Photoset in Baskerville
Made and Printed in Great Britain by
William Collins Sons & Co. Ltd Glasgow

The Hour of the Dog—
Sunset by the Ancient Chinese Clock

To Fred Jones, of Shanghai, Hong Kong and Sydney, who survived the rigours of the Gatehouse; and to his sister-in-law Zena, originally of Leningrad—which she still calls St Petersburg—and her husband 'Poppin', who managed to stay outside but aided those inside at enormous risk to himself; and lastly to B.C., who for cogent reasons would not wish to be more positively identified, who came out through the wire, swam the Whangpo on two sealed biscuit tins, and reached India after many vicissitudes—mostly on foot.

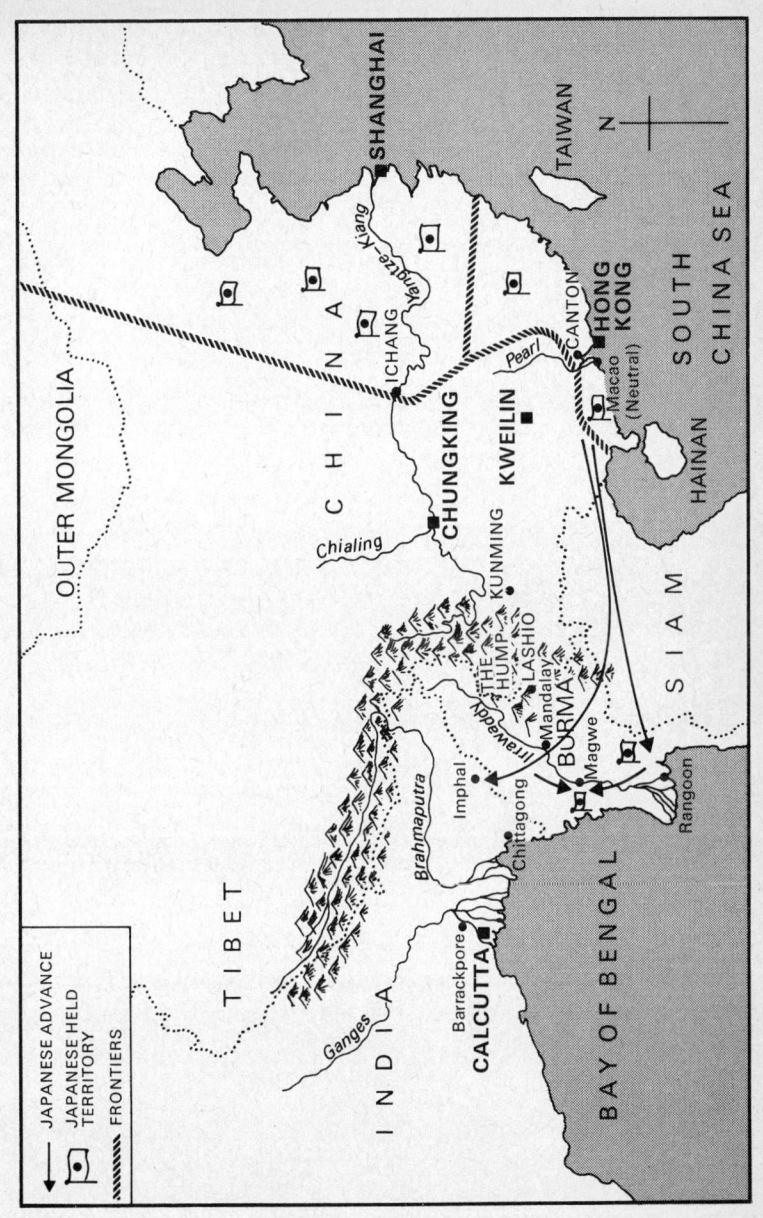

Chapter One

1

I stopped the car at the end of Conduit Road and looked north across the harbour to Kowloon. Except for a column of smoke rising lazily into the evening air towards the far end of Nathan Road there was little sign of yesterday's air raid, if it could be called that. The Jap Zero had skimmed in over the hills and dropped three small anti-personnel bombs, waggled its wings, probably as an earnest of more to come, and departed, inspiring our English-language newspaper to come out next morning with banner headlines proclaiming that 'Hong Kong could take it,' and now proudly stood in line with London, Coventry and Liverpool, blitzed but unbowed.

'Propaganda purposes only,' Intelligence has said profoundly. 'That's just to stampede the Chinese. Wait until the reinforcements arrive from Singapore—you won't see the Nips for dust then.' Intelligence, in our case, was embodied in Pemberton, one of my under-managers, whose keenness and impeccable turnout had won him a no doubt well-deserved captaincy in our local Defence Force in which I wore, blushingly, the single pip of a hopelessly inefficient second-lieutenant.

'They're on their last legs in Singapore,' Laird said glumly. 'We'll not be getting reinforcements from there, or anywhere else.'

'Defeatist talk,' Pemberton said sternly. 'There's a war on, and you're supposed to be an officer.'

'Out of this fancy dress I'm Chief Accountant, and your boss,' Laird reminded him. 'The war won't last forever, so just watch it, Captain—*sir*.' He was a lieutenant, Scotch and dour like most of our seniors—a tradition going back to the Founders of our princely house, my grandfather Ross Stafford and his partner, Old Jock McMurtrie—now both long dead—so Laird, also, was my superior in this topsy-turvey military world into which I had been sworn, enlisted and commissioned all in one day a month earlier. I has asked diffidently to be allowed to start a little lower down the ladder, but the adjutant, Regular and very pukkha, had explained that there was nothing lower than a Volunteer second-lieutenant, and handed me over to the regimental sergeant-major, also Regular and even more pukkha, who took me, solo and in camera, behind the Mess, through the intricacies of saluting and foot drill. 'That'll have to do, Mr Stafford sir,' he had said at the end of an hour, adding under his breath thanks to the Almighty that we still had a navy. But in this he had spoken too soon because the *Repulse* and the *Prince of Wales*, the two biggest warships in our Far Eastern fleet, had since gone to the bottom off the Malayan coast.

I sat on for some minutes looking down at the city which stretched ribbonlike along the narrow shelf of flat land beneath the Peak. There was supposed to be a blackout, but lights were beginning to twinkle along Hennessey Road towards Wanchai and I could even see a doubledecker tram lumbering past the racecourse at Happy Valley. Yes, things looked much the same as usual except for a paucity of shipping in the roadstead. The last two small coasters of our own Line had managed to sneak out of Shanghai and were now anchored off Stanley on the south side of the island, ready to take on evacuee women and children, my own among them. There had been a devil of a row about this, of course.

'I'm staying,' Helen had said flatly. 'Like every other wife worth her salt. My place is by your side.'

'How the hell could you be by my side?' I asked her wearily. 'I'm supposed to man a machine-gun when the balloon goes up—and I don't known which end of the bloody thing makes a noise. Get out, Helen, for God's sake, while there's still time.'

'Phyllis Carpenter-Bryant is staying.'

'She has no children, and if you're thinking that I'm likely to be hopping into bed with her you can forget it. She's not my type.'

'Now you're being vulgar.'

'I always am, according to you. Locally educated with the Pongs and the Portuguese, remember?'

And so it had gone on far into the night until the matter was resolved by the GOC, who finally declared martial law and ordered the stiff-upper-lip brigade out willy-nilly, women with children being placed at the top of the list, and I had delivered her thankfully with the two children to the assembly point at the barnlike China Fleet Club.

'You're going to Australia,' I told her.

'I haven't brought any warm clothes—'

'You won't need any. December is their midsummer.'

'Or money—'

'Or money either. Our Sydney office will let you have whatever you want. Stop making difficulties where none exist.'

'Passports and my jewel case,' she had wailed. 'In the safe at home—'

She had a point there. She'd need the former, although I was cursing her stupid obstinacy in not bringing such obvious necessities with her in the first place, and now I was on my way back to the house at the eastern extremity of the island to collect them.

I started up again and was actually moving forward when the patrol came out of a patch of undergrowth between two villas and dropped down on to the road in front of me, and I felt my mouth go dry because they were dressed in a different type of khaki to the one I was familiar with—smarter and more an olive green colour—then I saw with relief that they were white men, a corporal and three privates in field service order, carrying Sten guns. I stopped abruptly as they level-led the wretched things at me. The corporal came up to the car and held out his hand, checking a salute as he noticed my solitary pip. I said, 'Good evening,' affably. He said, 'Papers, mac,' shortly. I fumbled through my pockets and realized that once again I had left my identity card on the table in my billet. I was always doing it.

'I'm sorry,' I said foolishly. 'I don't seem to have it with me. My name is Stafford—'

'Get out,' he snapped.

'By all means,' I said, obeying with alacrity because the others were cocking their guns. 'But I assure you that I am an officer—'

'In a private car? No papers?'

'The car's my own—'

'All private cars have been commandeered.'

'Yes, I know that, but I've had special permission to use this one.'

'Sure, sure, sure—tell it all to the captain. Take him down, Pierre, and blow his goddam head off if he gives any trouble.'

'Ah, oui,' said one of the others, and smiled nastily. Can-adians, I realized—newly arrived in the Colony and already making their presence felt.

'For God's sake,' I said angrily. 'Do I look like a Jap?'

'Maybe not,' he conceded grudgingly. 'But then I ain't seen many Japs—yet.'

'Could be goddam Doukhobor,' Pierre suggested, and the corporal brightened visibly.

'Could be,' he agreed. 'Russian stoolpigeoning for the Nips like the captain was telling us about. Fifth Column, they call it.'

'Shoot the son of a bitch,' one of the others grunted and raised his Sten. 'It'll save having to walk him all the way to Li Mun.'

'Look here,' I said desperately. 'I assure you my name is Vincent Ross Stafford. I'm the managing director of Stafford & McMurtrie. You must have heard of us. We're one of the biggest concerns in Hong Kong. Dammit, we've even got an office in *your* country—Vancouver—'

'Wouldn't be knowing,' the corporal said. 'I'm from Ottawa myself. Anyhow, if you're such a big wheel what the hell are you doing dressed like a second-looie? That's for the boys. You must be all of fifty.'

'Thirty-eight,' I said with dignity, and only then did I realize that all four of them were laughing at me, and I went stiff with resentment. 'All right—take me to your captain—'

'Okay, mac,' he grinned and waved me on. 'Only don't forget your ID card next time.'

'Don't you salute officers in your army?' I inquired, administering in my relief my very first military reproof to anybody.

'Sure, if we like the guy,' the corporal said. 'You got any cigarettes we'll like *you*. We're fresh out.'

It was Helen's car, which meant there was the better part of a full carton of Camels in the glovebox. I handed them over and they saluted flamboyantly. Pierre even bowed from the waist, but they were all grinning broadly nevertheless.

I was still shaking with reaction when I reached the gate to Annandale. This was Stafford country—our Mount Olympus—and I had been ridiculed and humiliated by a group of common soldiers. I wondered how my father, the now legendary Bard Stafford, decorated in the Boer War and again before being killed on the Somme in 1917, would have coped with the situation. Damn it all! My mother, Abigail, would have had those four monkeys standing stiffly to attention with one direct look, while I, Lord High Panjandrum of our princely house, even with the added bonus of an officer's commission, had come out of it like a frightened coolie.

There were more Canadians here, establishing a strongpoint at the head of the path that led up the cliff from the foreshore, but Dhanrah Bahadur, one of our corps of Gurkha pensioner watchmen, was with them, sniffing powder from afar like the old warhorse he was, and he was able to vouch for me. A heavily preoccupied officer, a second-lieutenant like myself, waved me on into the house when I explained my mission.

'Help yourself,' he invited. 'If the Nips set up a couple of field guns across the channel there they're going to knock this place and the Li Mun barracks flat anyhow. Look what they've given me to defend the whole area with.' He waved his hand round in the darkness. 'Cooks, clurks and convalescents, and a couple of bums out of the stockade. All our first line men are across in the New Territories with your guys, waiting for the little bastards to come in from the north.'

I never had much love for the huge Victorian monstrosity my grandfather had built nearly a hundred years earlier, but I felt a pang as I went through the hall to the wide staircase. It was now quite dark outside but they had covered the windows with heavy curtains and ripped-up carpets, and indoors all the lights were blazing and the whole place was in as Augean a state as only soldiers could achieve in so short a period. At this time yesterday Helen and the children had been decorating the Christmas tree that was now stripped and trampled underfoot, and the furniture, a heterogeneous mixture of imported mahogany and priceless Sung ebony, marble and jadestone, was piled into the windows to form breastworks. The brocade hanging had been ripped from my study wall, uncovering the safe, which somebody had evidently been trying unsuccessfully to force.

I twiddled the combination and cleared the contents into my haversack—two passports, my own and Helen's, on which both the children were entered, her small morocco jewel-case and a folder of mixed currency—British, American and local. I looked into the drink cabinet hoping to find more cigarettes and a few bottles to take back to the Mess, but there the new occupants had been more successful and the cupboard was bare, so I bundled some clothes—hers and the children's—into a suitcase and left.

I went round to the servants' quarters behind the house, intending to give each of the eleven of them half a year's pay and to tell them to find their respective ways to 'country-more-far' as they call their homes, and lie low until the storm had passed, but they had already decamped, and only Dhanrah Bahadur remained. He, of course, being a Gurkha, was an institution rather than a servant. I asked him what he intended to do, and he told me angrily that he had tried to re-enlist in the Defence Force, but that the dam' bastards had told him that at seventy he was too old, so he would remain here and look after the family home until we all returned. I tried to persuade him to come with me to some place a little less precarious than this, but he would have none of it, nor would he take a cent more than his current month's pay, so I left him honing his already razorsharp kukri, and drove out on to the Sheko road.

I looked at my watch. It was now just after eight o'clock, and the families convoy was due to leave the assembly point at eight-thirty. It was only about six miles from here, but if I happened to be stopped again by patrols I might easily miss them, so I decided to make direct for Stanley by the back road through Magazine Gap. Once over the ridge-back and screened by the Peak I could risk using my headlights—

I heard the first shell just as I got to the crest. It came from behind and passed obliquely over my head, a shrill rising sound that reached a climax directly above me, and then rapidly receded, and I thought that it was a low-flying aircraft that had cut its engine, until it burst on the higher slopes of Mount Austin where the Navy had its main signalling station. It achieved in the space of less than a minute what the newly formed volunteer corps of air raid wardens had failed to get into our thick heads in the three weeks that had passed since Pearl Harbor, because the lights in various scattered houses up the hairpin road before me snapped out as though controlled by one switch, and, turning to look back down the mountain to the city, I saw that the same thing had happened there. Hong Kong, for the first time in its hundred-year history, was in total darkness. It was a weird and frightening experience—intensified by the stunned silence that followed the explosion. I slammed the brakes on and sat

15

and gaped into the darkness, then I heard the second shell coming. This one, also, seemed to pass directly overhead, but it burst more to my left. The third was well ahead of me—the fourth a scant hundred yards behind, and smack on a small white house that I knew to be the entrance lodge to the Carmelite convent. I hoped the nuns were still helping with the families down at the assembly point. A good place to be out of, I decided hurriedly. There seemed to be something horribly personal about this attack, as if the entire Imperial Japanese artillery was concentrating on my insignificant hide.

I swtiched off the dimmed parking lights on which I had been running and moved on as fast as I dared, the road before me being a slightly lighter ribbon between the pitch-black monsoon ditches that flanked it on either side. Of course, had I been a soldier of not quite so recent vintage, I would have realized that this was merely a little harassing fire on previously selected targets well clear of the city itself, and I was here through sheer mischance. I was, in fact, starting to tell myself that when the shelling stopped on this sector and moved east on to the Sheko road which I had just left. It accorded with the Intelligence prognosis Pemberton had passed on to us, that the Japs, hopeful of taking over the Colony intact and largely undamaged, would only be putting down a token strafing, and that on the outskirts. A comforting thought—more comforting still once I had the solid bulk of the Peak between my back and the guns, which I judged to be located somewhere to the north of Kowloon.

I could see the dark crestline now that the summit of the ridge was making against the marginally lighter night sky. Another few hundred yards and I would be over it, and momentarily safe. My foot came down a shade heavier on the gas as I heard the approaching whine of the next shell, and the inevitable happened, and I overshot at the next bend, left the road and was into the monsoon ditch. They are exaggerated gutters, six feet wide and about four deep, of solid concrete, made, as their name indicates, to carry off the

16

terrific rainfall that turns the slopes of the Peak into a veritable Niagara for the three months of the rainy season.

I climbed out and puttered round the wretched car miserably. It was seesawing on the edge of the ditch, the front wheels on the bottom and the rear ones a good two feet clear of the ground—and I saw that I hadn't a hope in hell of getting it on to an even keel unaided, so I retrieved the suitcase from the back, hoisted it on to my shoulder and set off on the seven mile slog to Stanley. Behind me I could hear the bombardment increasing, which served to quicken my pace more than somewhat, so that I reached the waterfront by the side of the big prison in something just over two hours, but the families had already embarked although I could make out the dark bulk of the two ships still anchored out in the fairway, and there was a motor-launch moored at the end of the long jetty.

Fate relented a little then because I saw Wilkinson, one of our coast pursers, in the light of a hurricane lamp, and I grabbed his arm as he started to climb down into the boat, and asked him if he had seen my wife and the children. He said wearily, 'Have a heart, old man. There are five hundred and forty of them. How the hell do you expect me to know one from t'other?' Then he recognized me and stammered, 'Oh Gawd! Mr Vincent—Sorry, sir. I've been on the go for forty-eight hours. Yes, they're aboard the *K'aisang*, safe and sound. I've just left a letter for you from your mother—it's with the Movement Control people,' and I felt a measure of relief because this had been something I had been pushing to the back of my mind for three weeks, trying to persuade myself that she would turn up, cool and unperturbed as usual, on the train from Shanghai, which had been running uninterruptedly right up until yesterday.

'Where did you see her? How was she?' I asked quickly.

'Still at the hotel, thank God,' he chuckled. 'It was her who fixed our clearance papers—complete with the Jap port commandant's stamp. Don't ask me how. They got us down-river all right. We were the last two out.'

'Why on earth didn't you bring her with you?' I demanded angrily.

'You don't think for one moment we didn't try, do you, sir?' he answered. 'Make the Dowager Empress—sorry—Mrs Stafford senior—do something she didn't want? What a hope! She just told us to mind our own business, gave the skipper this letter to you, with a duplicate to Captain Saunders on the *Failoo* in case one of us didn't make it, and went back to her office. She was quite nice about it, of course. She always is.'

'Of course,' I agreed. 'I understand. Thank you all for trying, anyhow.' I passed him the suitcase and haversack. 'Give these to my wife and tell her I'm all right—and she's not to worry.'

'But aren't you coming with us?' he asked.

'I'm afraid not,' I said regretfully. 'I'm in the army now.'

'So are a hell of a lot of high-ups who *are* sailing with us,' he said. 'Indispensable to the war effort—live to fight another day, and all that. I've had my balls chewed off by a brigadier because he's got to share a cabin with a major, and a colonel's memsahib is going to report the skipper direct to the War Office because he wouldn't let her bring her piano aboard. Bechstein grand, she says. Didn't half make a splash when we pushed it over the side.'

'Good for him,' I said. 'Give him my compliments and tell him I'll double his bonus when this lot is over. I'm not supposed to ask you, but where are you making for?'

'Sealed orders until we're twelve miles out,' he told me, 'but the buzz is Sydney.'

'Good. Take my wife to the office when you get in, and introduce her to Mr Matthews. Tell him she's to have full drawing powers on my personal account, and tell her I'll write as soon as I can. Bon voyage and the best of luck, Wilkers.' I hadn't called him that since I was sweeping out the proverbial stockroom and he was a junior writer on one of our smaller ships.

18

He gulped and gagged a bit because we had always been very much a family concern, and said, 'Come aboard, for Christ's sake, Vince. You can run the show properly from that side. The Japs will be swarming all over this damned place in a few hours, and what use will you be then?'

'Not a lot,' I agreed glumly, 'but that's the way it's got to be, I'm afraid.' And make no mistake; if I could have run into a reasonably senior officer at that juncture, to whom I could have put a sensible case and received from him permission to embark, I'd have been off like a shot from a gun, because there had been an awful lot of 'indispensable to the war effort', or ITWE as we called it, going on both here and in other places the Japs were in process of overrunning. There were an awful lot doing the other thing also—insisting on remaining when they had been offered an exeat—but I was not of that bulldog breed. I stayed because I hadn't the courage to run without express permission. People could be shot for that, I reflected with a shiver.

I went to seek a lift back to Force HQ then as I had only asked Pemberton for two hours' leave and I had now been away nearly six. The trucks that had brought the families across had all returned to town, but I managed to beg my way on to a returning ambulance that had just left some wounded at the military hospital near the prison. The Volunteer driver was a senior civil servant from the legal department, a chap called Swanley, with whom I had played the occasional game of golf at Fanling on the mainland. Had he been a professional he wouldn't have been so damned keen. As it was, he kept going when we neared the crest, and the barrage, which had stilled for a couple of hours, opened up again, in earnest this time. They were bursting all along the skyline, with a proportion of overcarries that were lobbing frighteningly close to the road as we came to Magazine Gap.

I said nervously, 'You're not going through this lot, are you?'

'My dear chap,' he said in tones of chilling reproof. 'They need every one of us down there—' And that is all I remember.

2

It was getting light when I came to. The shelling had stopped but the ambulance was on its side in the monsoon ditch and there was a stink of burnt cordite hanging heavily on the dawn mist that was drying my mouth and throat and making my eyes smart. I moved each limb tentatively. Nothing seemed to be broken, so I crawled out from under the debris that covered me and looked around for Swanley. He was still in the driving seat, held in position by the steering-column which had transfixed him like a spear, and he was very dead. I kept repeating '—they need every one of us down there,' and giggling foolishly, then I was violently sick.

I pulled myself together after a time and walked unsteadily to the top of the gap and looked down the sheer slope to the city. Nothing seemed changed down there, certainly not in the streets, although there was now more activity in the harbour and along the waterfront. Barges and motor junks crowded with antlike figures were crossing from Kowloon on the mainland, disgorging, and returning empty for more. I saw troops drawn up in Statue Square, the Murray Barracks parade ground, and even on the sacred turf of the Cricket Ground, that hallowed acre in the middle of the city where hitherto even the horse that pulled the mowing-machine wore felt overshoes. Then I knew Hong Kong had fallen, and that the battle, if it had come at all, had passed me by—and I was still alive, with every intention of staying that way. And it was Christmas morning.

I sat by the roadside for some time, trying to think

coherently. It was not easy, because my hearing kept switching off and then returning, like a faulty radio, and I was also troubled with recurring double vision, all of which, no doubt, was the result of concussion. But at last the symptoms passed, and I decided that, whether the city was occupied or not, the only course left open to me was to find my way to HQ and report to somebody, as my present status was that of straggler—or even deserter. I shivered again, got up and continued on my way down the Peak road.

I had been walking for about ten minutes when I ran into the patrol. There were half a dozen or so of them, and they were as surprised as I as we came face to face round a bend in the road. My first, and lasting, impression of them was of short men in baggy pants, filthy shirts and canvas sneakers, with absurdly long rifles which, with their fixed bayonets, seemed of considerably greater length than the soldiers who carried them. Some of them were smoking, all of them were laughing, and two of them were carrying out bayonet practice on the sagging, blood-soaked body of a man propped against a tree-trunk.

The road at this point clung to the slope, the sides rising cliff-like on the one hand and dropping sheerly into a gulch on the other. I chose the latter. I didn't even think. I just jumped. The drop must have been all of thirty feet, with thick undergrowth at the bottom, and it was that which saved me, because I crashed through it and it closed again over me, and I landed on a cushion of fallen leaves and slid into a tiny stream, and because every vestige of breath was knocked out of me, I lay still. There was a ragged fusillade and a lot of shouting from above, and bullets smacked and spattered against rocks the other side of the stream, but I was protected by the bank under which I cowered.

I waited, paralysed with fright, expecting them to climb down to search for me, but the sheerness of the drop must have taken the edge off their keenness, because after a lot of arguing I heard their voices receding as they continued on their way up the road down which I had been coming.

Then a hoarse voice said, 'Jesus! You was lucky, mate. They're bayoneting everybody they catch with a gun.'

I turned and peered in the direction of the voice, and saw a dirty unshaven face framed by the undergrowth not two feet away from my own.

'I was a bit lucky myself,' the man went on. 'I come down here to fill a waterbottle, and the bastards caught my officer up there still carrying his revolver, poor bugger.' He noticed the solitary star on my epaulette then, and said, 'Huh—you're an officer too, are you? You'd better get rid of that peashooter of yours then, unless you want 'em to make a bleeding pincushion out of you.'

I said, 'Can you tell me what's been happening? Since last night, I mean?'

He shrugged. 'Should be the other way round, shouldn't it? What the hell do you expect a member of the depressed classes to know? Yesterday you was all telling us to do the last-man-and-the-last-bullet act—this morning you tell us to pack it in and lay down our arms and not give the Nips no trouble or it will make it uncomfortable for everybody—that's some of you. Others have been saying that it's every man for himself, and that if we think we can make an escape we're free to do so — but where the hell to, nobody seems to know. Swim to bloody Australia maybe—unless the Nips have take that over too.'

'So as far as you know, Hong Kong has surrendered?' I said bleakly.

'Far as I know.'

'But *you* haven't?'

'No—trusting bugger, me. My officer was a decent little bloke—decent enough to come and get me out of the moosh, that is—'

'The moosh?'

'The nick, the glasshouse—the little hostelry next door to Murray Barracks, where they send the bad boys—'

'Oh, the military prison?'

'That's right. I was doing a hundred and twelve days for telling a frigging lance-corporal to—well, never mind. Our little Mister Wheeler comes and signs for me and says he's going to try and pinch a boat and make it to Macao—Portuguese and neutral—'

'But not for long, I'm afraid,' I said. 'The Japs don't give a damn for *anybody's* neutrality. It might be worth trying, though. But if you contemplated stealing a boat, what were you doing up here on the Peak?'

'Making our way to the south side of the island. There's not a chance of knocking one off in the harbour. There's Nip guards elbow-to-elbow all the way along the waterfront.'

'Yes, I see your point. Stanley or Aberdeen, or in fact any of the little fishing villages in between would be you best bet.'

'No good now, though. Mr Wheeler was doing a language course here. He could talk proper Chinese—'

'So can I,' I told him, suddenly making up my mind. 'I've also got a little money. If you care to join up with me we might have a slim chance of making it.'

'OK by me,' he said. 'I'm not risking moving in daylight, though—not any more. There's patrols over all the roads, rounding up the strays. We heard that over the loudspeakers down below. Some joker was yelling in pidgin English that if we came in with out hands on our heads and filed into the compounds in an orderly manner we'd be all right—treated as "onnalable plis'nors of woah"—the flat-faced little yellow bastard—but if we were caught trying to scram we'd get it in the guts. Simple as that. Mr Wheeler said the hell with it, you can't trust any of 'em, let's get out of it. We did—' he jerked his thumb over his shoulder—'you seen what happened to him. So no more daylight promenades for me, mate—sorry, *sir*.'

'No need to apologize,' I told him. 'I'm not a real officer, I'm afraid.'

'You don't have to tell *me* that.' He grinned sardonically.

'A volunteer Saturday-afternooner, I should say—same as Mr Wheeler. He was a bank clurk before he got called up. A real gent though, which is more than I can say for some of our pukkha Percies. Business bloke, are you?'

'In a sort of way. My name is Vincent Stafford.' I put out my hand. He hesitated for a moment as if summing me up, then shrugged noncommittally and shook it limply.

'Mine's Rawcliffe—one-seven-nine-three-two-five—Private, J.H., C Company, Royal Herts, usually called Raucous by me friends.'

'Does that include me?'

'Please yourself. That'll make two of you. OK—what do you suggest we do now?'

'First of all we'd better move from here. That poor chap's body will be marking the spot where I made my dive and there's always a chance that they might send somebody down to look for me later.'

He nodded. 'Makes sense,' he conceded. 'Which way?'

'Up this nullah we're in,' I said. 'There's a culvert about three hundred yards above us, and a path from there right over the top, missing Magazine Gap, which they'll undoubtedly have picketed. We can hole up there until dark.'

'Know you way about then?'

'I ought to. I've lived here all my life.'

'Poor sod. Five years, me—which is four years and eleven months too long. I'd have been going Home this week if it hadn't been for this bloody war—and being in the nick. Still, lucky in a sort of a way, I suppose. Might have got sent to North Africa or somewhere worse.'

'That's right, Raucous,' I said heartily, doing my duty as an officer. 'There's always somewhere worse, isn't there?'

'It's all bloody worse,' he grunted. 'Only some is more worse than others. We better get going hadn't we?'

We crawled up the watercourse, shielded from observation from above most of the way, although there was a nasty open bit just before we reached the culvert, but we managed to make it safely, and we found a dry shelf some few yards inside it.

At the risk of prolixity I had better give an idea of the topography of Hong Kong island at this point. It is really the top of a mountain sticking up out of the sea a mile off the mainland. It is nine miles long from east to west and six from north to south, an asymmetrical pyramid with its apex, the Peak, considerably closer to the north shore than the south, so that the slope we were now on was much steeper than the one the other side. Both slopes were covered with dense scrub and stunted trees growing out of crevices in the rocky surface. A zigzag road runs up from the city of Victoria, which lies along the narrow shelf of the north shore, and it crosses the eastern shoulder of the Peak at Magazine Gap, then it continues on down the gentler incline to Stanley on the southern coast. There are shelves on the northern side, some natural, some manmade, some a combination of both, and on them some of the 'taipans', as we, the so-called 'merchant princes' are known, have built their mansions, high above the heat and smells of the crowded town. Small winding drives take off from the main road to the houses which are, for the most part, set in exquisite jewels of gardens. A few of us, my own family for one, have apostatized from these Elysian Fields, and staked our claims along the coast. In our case my grandfather, Ross, built Annandale at the eastern tip of the island, overlooking Li Mun Channel, which leads into the harbour. It was an architectural nightmare of bastard baroque on early victorian—huge, sprawling, turreted and battlemented like a London railway terminus, but it was redeemed by the gardens—fifty-five acres of lovingly tended lawns, beds, shrubberies and follies. As a family we loved it—with the exception of my mother, Abigail. She loathed every square inch of it, and spent as little time there as she possibly could after the death of my father, whom she worshipped, which was why she had taken up permanent residence in Shanghai.

How was she faring now, I wondered?

We spent the long day peering down at the city which hummed with activity, although the distance was too great for us to see exactly what was happening. Squads of soldiers moved about, theirs and ours, the former distinguishable only by flashes of sunlight from their bayonets, because the uniforms of both armies were much the same colour at that range. Our people were being ferried across to Kowloon for the most part, but civilians were being brought to this side in the returning barges and herded on to the Cricket Ground. There was something antlike, sinister, and unbearably depressing about the whole scene. A huge red and white flag was flying over Government House—the Rising Sun of Japan—and during the day others appeared over the Law Courts, Army HQ and the naval dockyard as the surrender proceeded.

There was a lot of activity on the road above us, with small patrols like the one we had already encountered moving up and down and fanning out through the scrub like beaters at a pheasant shoot, and on several occasions the sound of smallarms fire came to us as fugitives were flushed out into the open. We saw one incident in a clearing immediately below our position, where the little stream ran across an open space before dropping in a waterfall over the edge. Three khaki figures broke from cover as a line of Japs overran them. They halted at the waterfall, turned and held up their hands. One man was frantically waving a white handkerchief, but it availed him nothing. There was a burst of automatic fire and one figure went over the edge. The other two lay twitching, and the Japs advanced on them and their ghastly bayonets came into play like hayforks in a harvesting field, stabbing, hacking, ripping, and finally, after going through their pockets, tossing the torn bodies down into the ravine.

I sat hunched in the semi-darkness, my head sunk between my knees, my eyes tightly closed, fighting down the nausea that was threatening to overwhelm me. Raucous said savagely, 'You haven't chucked your pistol away, have you?'

'No, I mumbled, 'and I'm not going to.'

'That's right. If the bastards shove their heads up this spout let 'em have it right between the eyes, but keep two rounds for ourselves. I don't fancy them bayonets. I'll take the gun over from you if you like.'

It was a sensible suggestion and he no doubt meant it kindly, but it gave rise to a stab of resentment in me which developed into an upsurge of pseudo courage akin to that of a cornered rat. 'You won't,' I said curtly. 'Stay here. I'm going to keep watch from the entrance,' and, surprisingly, he said, 'Yessir.'

I lay flat in the mouth of the culvert, peering down through the curtain of grass that partially masked it. The Japs were squatting in a circle examining their booty and arguing over a couple of wristwatches. They had found some hardtack rations in the haversacks of the dead men and I shuddered afresh as I saw them opening tins of bully beef with the very bayonets they had been using just minutes before and which they had hardly bothered to wipe clean. It certainly stilled the hunger pangs of which I had become increasingly aware over the last few hours.

They mixed up the rations with some stuff of their own which looked like dried seaweed, and made a scratch meal, then they lay around in the sun with their equipment loosened, belching and snoring, for about an hour until the NCO in charge got up and kicked them back on to their feet. He stood in front of the squad and turned slowly in a circle, studying the ground all round, and my heart missed several beats as his eyes came to rest on our position. He could undoubtedly see the entrance to the culvert, which was no more than a hundred yards from where he was standing, and it was a natural hiding-place. Had he been a corporal of the same mould as Napoleon or Hitler he would have searched it. Thank God he wasn't, but he did send one of his men up. I wriggled into reverse, hissing to Raucous to move further back into the darkness, and hauled out my gun. It was a Browning .38, my own property, and it held eight rounds, with two spare clips—twenty-four rounds in all. I was thinking clearly—sheer, ice-cold fear sometimes has that effect, providing panic doesn't supervene. I could get this fellow before he knew what had hit him, immediately he blocked the entrance. That would, of course, bring the others up but they would hardly be foolish enough to come crowding in on an unseen, armed enemy. I might possibly get a snapshot or two more off at them unless, of course, they tossed a grenade in first—

The man's head appeared blackly against the light, then the whole of his body. I took aim, trying desperately to control my shaking hand, then I pressed the trigger—and nothing happened, because I had forgotten to release the safety-catch. It was an omission which saved our lives—all three of us—because in that split second, before I could recock the action, the Jap calmly unbuttoned his trousers, squatted down, and defecated. Behind me I heard Raucous expel breath in a sigh of relief that was almost a sob.

The fellow completed the function without so much as a glance into the culvert, adjusted his dress and slid down the hill to rejoin his comrades, who were now straggling back to the road. And Raucous called me 'sir' again, and probably meant it this time.

He said admiringly, 'Blimey, sir. Cool as a cucumber you was. I'd have lost me head and blinded off at him right away. Phew! Jesus! That was close.'

'Er—yes, it was rather, wasn't it?' I said modestly when I had got my vocal cords under control again.

Darkness had fallen completely when we emerged from our rathole a couple of hours later. We were both ravenously hungry as by now neither of us had eaten for over twenty-four hours, and I knew that we would have to find food before tackling the very rough march ahead of us to the southern coast. As the crow flies it was only a little more than five miles, or perhaps twice that distance by the zigzag road over the crest and down the other side, but as I proposed to do it—up the densely scrub-covered and pathless slope, over outcropping boulders and across deep ravines in pitch darkness—it was going to be testing to say the least.

We had been climbing for half an hour when we came to the first house. It stood on a rocky spur that jutted out from the hillside, whitepainted as most of them were, and set in a terraced garden. I tried to identify it in my memory in order to check my bearings, but without success. There were over a hundred taipans' mansions on the northern side of the Peak, with possibly fifty the other side, and although we were a very tight social community, all on visiting terms with each other, I just couldn't place this one. It was in complete darkness and I wondered if the residents were still here lying low, or whether we would be answered by a Jap patrol if we inquired. We sat and debated the point in whispers for a long time before I managed to screw up my courage to a point necessary to investigate further.

'It would be stupid for us both to be taken,' I told Raucous. 'You wait here. If I don't come back or you hear a rumpus you had better push off on your own.' I had been hoping that he would volunteer to go himself, as the more experienced warrior, but he just said 'Yessir' again, very respectfully, so, with my scalp prickling, I crept up through the shrubbery and across a smooth, dew-soaked lawn until I came to a pergola running along the side of the house. I felt my way round the wall, pausing to listen at each window as I passed, and made a complete circuit of the house. There were three doors—a glass one opening into a conservatory, a heavy studded teak one that obviously led to the kitchen area, and finally the big, porticoed front entrance. All were locked, and on the last was a notice which I couldn't read in the dark, and as I gently tried the wrought-iron handle my fingers cane in contact with a strip of tape connecting a pair of lead seals each side of the centre crack. I retraced my steps then and found that the other doors were also sealed, which at least told me that the house was unoccupied, so I went back and collected a very relieved Raucous, and we broke one of the windows and climbed in. It made a hell of a noise and it scared both of us badly, but after listening for some minutes and giving our jangled nerves time to settle again, we felt our way across a large room and into a hallway where, shielded from outer windows, I risked striking matches until we found ourselves in the kitchen, and here we made a lucky find in a candle stick in its own grease on a table. We lit it and explored further.

The whole house was a shambles of overturned furniture and opened cupboards with their contents strewn about the floor, although there did not seem to be a great deal of wanton vandalism. It was more as if a hasty search had been made of the place than a looting operation, and although broken bottles and jars made a sticky mess underfoot in the large pantry adjoining the kitchen, there were still cans of food on the shelves—both European and Chinese—salmon, cheese, bean and bamboo shoots, corned beef and various vegetables. We didn't risk staying to eat there, but we filled an empty potato sack with a selection of cans and went out again through the broken window, and I risked a quick look in the light of the candle at the notice on the front door. There was a Jap rising sun at the top, and two rows of ideographs, one in Japanese, which I couldn't read, the other in Mandarin, which I could. It said that the premises had been requisitioned by the Imperial Nipponese Army and that trespassing would be punishable by death.

The pattern of things was becoming clear. They were systematically clearing the Colony of both soldiers and civilians and taking over property as it stood for their own occupation, which was obviously why they were not destroying anything.

'What do we do now, sir?' Raucous asked as we continued our climb to the crest.

'Press on until just before daylight, then hole up again like today,' I said. 'We should be over the top in an hour or so. Can you tighten your belt until then?'

'Wouldn't it be better to hole up this side?' he suggested. 'We know the little bastards have searched up as far as here.' And I looked at him with a new respect.

'You're absolutely right,' I agreed. 'We'll go back to the culvert. We've got water there, and a good field of view down the road to the city.'

So that is what we did, and we spent the second day much as the first, lying prone behind the grass screen and watching the passing scene. There was more traffic on the road now—staff cars for the most part, still with British markings on the side panels but with the eternal rising sun fluttering above them—filled with important little men gravely acknowledging the salutes of passing Jap soldiers on foot. But, thankfully, there were no more search parties beating the undergrowth, nor sounds of smallarms fire, so it looked as if this side of the Peak had, as we had surmised, been toothcombed.

But one incident upset us badly and had Raucous screaming and sobbing with rage. A party of British prisoners came down the road, marching towards the city. There were about fifty of them, escorted by half a dozen Japs strung out along the column. Noticeable among them was an exceptionally tall man with a bandaged head, who was limping badly.

'Jesus!' exclaimed Raucous. 'That's Lofty John, our drum-major—all six-foot-four-and-a-half of him. Decent bloke, for an NCO. Looks as if he's been through the mill, poor bastard.'

A staff car came sweeping up the road at that moment, preceded by a pair of motor-cyclists and followed by two more. There were two officers in the back and a larger than usual rising sun fluttered overall. The guards hurriedly halted the column, turned inwards and not only saluted, but bowed deeply from the waist. The car jerked to a stop in a cloud of dust, and both officers leapt to their feet, and we could see them gesticulating angrily. One of the guards came out in front of the squad and started to bow rapidly again, as if demonstrating, while the rest of them ran up and down

31

through the ranks, prodding and punching the prisoners with their rifle butts. The quicker thinkers bowed immediately the meaning of the Japs' screamed orders became clear, and the rest followed suit, with the exception of the tall man who stood immobile, staring ahead of him, obviously dazed. One of the officers in the car pointed to him and shouted something to the NCO in charge of the party, who unslung his rifle, and pushed his way through the ranks. He halted in front of the tall man, measured the interval between then and bayoneted him in the stomach. Two of the other prisoners darted forward towards the NCO, and the rest of the guards started to shoot into the thick of the crowd wildly. It was all over in a minute or so. Five bodies lay in the road, two still and the others thrashing about wounded. These were despatched and all were rolled into the monsoon ditch. The staff car continued on its way uphill, and the sad cavalcade on foot resumed its march downhill.

Raucous said dully, 'Can't we do something? *Anything?*'

'Like what?' I asked.

'Like I said—*anything*? Come on, for Christ's sake—I don't care whether you're a pukkha officer or a bleeding pen-pusher, you're an educated man, aren't you? We've *got* to do something. Think—*think*, blast you!' He had a double handful of my shirt and was shaking me, and I realized he was about to go what the French call *avoir le diable au corps*, which is not merely frenzied, but homicidally so. I had seen it happen often enough among the Chinese—patient, dumbly suffering coolies, normally as docile as sheep, suddenly breaking under strain and running amok with knife, axe or club, killing and maiming any living creature they could reach—but this was the first time I had seen it in a white man. It was very, *very* frightening, because I knew that a wrong move on my part then would have sent him screaming down the road after the marching squad which was still in sight, so I went insane with him and yelled, 'Yes, let's get the bastards! All of them—' and hauled out my pistol, then, as he released me and stooped to dash out of the culvert I slammed it down on the back of his neck with all my force in a vicious rabbit-chop. He lurched forward, his head cracked sickeningly against the concrete wall, and he lay still.

He was out to the wide for an hour, which happened to be just the length of time it took me to get over my own shakes. He sat up and looked at me blankly, moving his head slowly from side to side like a stunned ox, but to my relief the madness seemed to have passed. He groaned and felt the back of his neck gingerly. 'What the hell happened'? he asked.

'There was a bit of trouble on the road,' I told him tactfully. 'You started to dash out, and banged your head on the side of the culvert.'

'Yes—yes, I remember now,' he said. 'They stuck poor old Lofty John and then shot some of the blokes. They weren't all dead, were they? The ones they shovelled into the ditch, I mean?'

'I don't know,' I said gently. 'When it's a bit darker we'll go across and see. It wouldn't help anybody if we went out in the light, would it?'

'No—no, I suppose not,' he muttered and his dirty, battered face creased in a grimace, and I saw that he was crying, so I became interested in the view down the slope.

He was his own man again in a few minutes, and I kept him busy opening cans of food with his claspknife and we made a second cold, greasy but filling meal, and packed the remainder in his haversack. His infantryman's training asserted itself then, and he took his boots and socks off and meticulously washed his feet in the stream, and insisted that I did the same, then he produced a thing he called a 'housewife' from somewhere—a small cloth folder containing needles, cotton and yarn—and neatly darned some holes that had appeared in his socks and mine.

'Can't be too careful,' he told me solemnly. 'Next to his rifle a soldier's best friend is his feet. Spuds in your almond rocks can bugger your dogs in a lance-jack's waltz.'

'Sorry,' I said. 'I don't understand—'

33

'You wouldn't,' he said kindly. 'You're not a soldier, see? "Spuds" is potatoes—another name for holes in your "almond rocks", which is army socks—"dogs", feet— "lance-jack's waltz", the five paces a junior NCO takes from the serrefile to the left flank before moving off in column of route—a short march in other words. Got it?'

'Er—yes,' I said uncertainly.

'Ah, you got a lot to learn,' he told me. 'Take last night, for instance. I was just following you. You might have known the way, but I seen damn soon that you knew sweet Florence Arkenshaw about marching—'

'Who is she?' I asked, now completely mystified.

'Nobody, for Chri'sake. That's just SFA—another way of saying sweet nothing. Anyhow, tonight it's going to be done proper. We march fifty minutes in the hour and rest for ten. We change our socks every third halt—'

'I've only got one pair.'

'So have I. You change the right one to the left foot, and the left one to the right. That's to stop the darns rubbing the same spot for too long, and causing blisters. When we finally halt in the morning you wash your socks first thing, then shove a bloody great rock inside to stop them shrinking, and stick 'em somewhere to dry ready for the next march. Yers,' he went on reflectively, 'you can get lousy, dirty, wet, hungry and dog-bloody-tired, but keep your feet clean and the old almonds darned and you can slog on for ever.'

'Thank you, Raucous,' I said. 'As you remarked, I've a lot to learn.'

'But there's a lot I can learn off you,' he conceded generously. 'You stick to the officer's tack, and leave the old sweat's bits to me, and we'll rub along fine—only when you got to give an order, give it quick and snappy, and I'll jump to it without thinking, which is the proper way. Start humming and hawing and asking my opinion, and I'll start arguing as like as not, and we'll finish up shit creek without paddles. Got it?'

'Got it,' I confirmed.

34

'Good.' He squinted out of the entrance. 'Nobody on the road as far as I can tell. I think it's dark enough to go and have a look at those blokes, don't you?'

'I think so,' I said, although I had been dreading this. 'Follow me—only keep a grip on yourself this time. No blowing your top, Raucous, or we *will* finish up the creek.'

"Don't worry," he muttered. 'It won't happen again.' But I was having my doubts as we ran quickly across the road to the edge of the ditch the other side.

I prefer not to dwell on the next few minutes. They were piled one on the other, and we had to pull them apart like so many sacks of wheat in order to feel their hearts. All were dead, thank God, because I really do not know what we would have done had any been alive. I had heard from members of a party that had escaped from Shanghai that orders had been given that hopelessly wounded troops who obviously couldn't be carried had to be put out of their misery rather than be left to the 'mercy' of the advancing enemy. But I just could not have done it myself—not at that stage.

We came back without a word and continued on our way up the hill, moving quicker this time than the night before because we were now more familiar with the route. The house we had burgled had a dim light in one of the windows and we could hear the crackling of a radio playing eastern music, so we gave it a wide berth, and eventually came out between the big naval hospital on the ridge and the upper terminus of the Peak tramway, a funicular which climbs the two thousand feet from the city at a uniform forty-five degrees the whole way. The endless cable which pulls one passenger car up and lets its companion down in compensation was now stilled, but the little station at the top was being used as a guard post, and we could see a sentry outside in the light of a hurricane lantern, and there were other troops in bivouac along the broad carriageway that runs up to the radio masts on the actual summit of the Peak itself, a further hundred feet higher.

There were houses the other side of this road, facing the hospital, which normally accommodated the medical staff and nurses—large and detached, but fairly close together, and many of them seemed to be occupied because we could see lights in some of the windows. We lay in the monsoon ditch and studied the position for a long time while I tried to remember the layout of the place.

I said, 'I think the easiest route is between a couple of the houses and down through their gardens at the back, which shelve fairly gradually. Unfortunately there is a sheer drop at either end of the row which would be difficult to climb down in daylight let alone at night. It's going to be pretty tricky, I'm afraid, but we'll have to risk the gardens. The white gate directly opposite—can you see the one I mean?' He grunted an affirmative, so I went on, 'I'll go first. Count five, then follow—straight down between the two houses. Right!'

I darted across the road and opened the gate, which creaked abominably, and nipped through and down a flag-ged path on to a lawn at the back. I crossed this, crashed through a bed of very thorny standard roses which tore at my thin drill trousers and scarified my thighs, and then came smack up against a high wire-netting fence which pinged and vibrated like a bank of concert harps, and Raucous crashed into my back.

'Bloody tennis courts!' I raged. 'I'd forgotten the wretched things. This way—' I turned left and hurried along, hoping to come to the end of a single court, but there were six of them, end to end, because there was insufficient width on the razorback to place them side by side, and the fence was common to them all, without a break in its entire length. There were gates in them, of course, but every single one of them was secured with a chain and padlock. I remembered then playing up there in the past with Curly Durlock, the Fleet chief surgeon. They were always locked at night, he had told me, as a safeguard against thieves sneaking up from the valley through the dark.

36

We came to the end at last only to find yet another gate at the head of a path, but this one was open. We sped down it, myself still in the lead, and ran smack into a man coming up the other way.

He let out a muffled yelp and chattered in terror, and I had enough Japanese to understand that he was excusing himself and swearing that the sergeant-san had sent him to steal the fruit and he wasn't taking it for himself, then there was a cascade of round objects about my feet as he released the skirt of his baggy tunic which he had been holding in front of him like a woman holds an apron.

'Jap soldier pinching lychees from the orchard at the bottom,' I muttered to Raucous. 'He doesn't realize who we are, and he's frightened silly.'

'Hold his throat—tight,' snapped Raucous, and because it was a command, delivered as such, I obeyed without hesitation and slid my hands up the Jap's neck. It was as skinny as a pipestem and I could feel the muscles twitching under the skin. I squeezed hard and he started to struggle violently.

'Move to your left a little,' Raucous said. 'Right—that will do. Don't let go, in case he hollers.' He punched past me lightly once, twice—three times—and the struggling ceased and the man went limp. Raucous stooped and wiped his claspknife on the Jap's tunic before snapping it closed. 'I hope he enjoys his fucking lychees,' he said drily. 'What'll we do with the bastard?'

And so it was over to me again. We were at the end of the terraced gardens now, where the sheer precipice started, and the path we were on clung to the face of it. I couldn't see what was at the bottom, but I hoped it was the usual thick undergrowth that filled these ravines. 'Heave him over,' I said, and we took the sagging bundle by wrists and ankles and slung it into space like a sack. It was a long drop and there was a commensurate interval before we heard faint crashing through the trees from below.

We went on then, down through the orchard and over a wall the other side, and once more we were on the rough,

37

boulder-strewn slopes. Then, suddenly, a ring of lights like a string of jewels appeared below us—and then there were more above us—and far to the south-east we saw another patch—and then another to the south-west—and we heard a faint burst of cheering in the distance.

'Bloody hell! What's happening?' Raucous breathed, then it came to us both simultaneously. The huge power station on the mainland, with its satellites here on the island, all of which had been shut down, were now back in business. We had apparently crossed the Rubicon on the ridge just in the nick of time, because the roadway past the naval hospital was normally lighted like a ballroom and had we been a bit later we'd have been caught full in the glare.

'Just shows you, doesn't it?' sniffed Raucous. 'There was supposed to be a blackout here ever since Pearl Harbor, but the bloody taipans didn't take any notice until the current was cut off. It might have spoiled their dinner parties. The sods. Sorry—you're one, aren't you?'

'Not at the moment,' I said. 'But why pick on the taipans alone? Aren't we all in the same boat now?'

'Yers, I suppose so,' he grunted. 'The blackout don't seem to be worrying the Nips either, not that it makes any difference one way or the other. We've got no flogging aeroplanes anyhow, and I suppose they know it.'

'Raucous, listen to me,' I said sharply. 'I intend getting away from here, don't you?'

'Of course I do.'

'Good. Then suppose we stop bitching and binding at each other—and at the taipans—and the army and the air force—and just concentrate on that. Let's get out and carry on the fight, eh? You've just had one smack back at them, why not have another—and another—and another?'

'Yes, turn up for the books, that, wasn't it?' he said, his tone brightening. 'I wouldn't have thought I could do it—not a few days ago. Shoot a bloke from a distance, yes, if I was ordered to—but not stick him in the guts with a jack-knife. It was what we seen yesterday and today that done it. I don't think I'd feel the same about a Jerry or an Eye-ti. But these bastards? Ugh!'

We moved on downwards, making good time since I could now orientate on the distant lights, and we reached the cliffs above Aberdeen as dawn was breaking. It is an entirely Chinese fishing village which lies on the shores of a small sheltered harbour. Its proper name is Applichau and nobody seems to know when, or by whom, it was Caledonianized. Three or four demasted junks lay permanently anchored in the bay, opium dens in the old unregenerate days, it is said, but now they are restaurants, and serve some of the best seafood in the world. They only came to life at sundown, and the women, who filleted and salted huge mounds of fish all day, used to leave this task and run a taxi service to and from the shore in small sampans which they handled with amazing skill, sculling with a single oar over the stern. I knew one of them—a Hakka whose husband had been one of our company boatmen, and when he was drowned in an accident on the harbour, we set up his widow in business as a fishwife. It was her, Ho Yee, I was thinking of then. If she was still here, and the place wasn't overrun with Japs, I felt sure she would help us, because, traditionally, the Chinese never forget a benefaction. I was telling Raucous about her as we lay in the long grass at the top of the cliff and watched the sun come up over the offshore Po Toi islands.

'There's none of 'em about now,' he said, peering down at the cluster of huts, each with its netdraped drying frame in front. 'Oh, oh, I spoke too soon—' He pointed along the coast road as an army truck appeared. We watched it pull up in the village square and disgorge a dozen Jap soldiers who ran round the huts hammering on doors with their rifle butts. They were obviously a foraging party and they seemed already to have established a drill, because the inhabitants came out into the open immediately, as if expecting the visit, dragging baskets of fish behind them. The NCO in charge was apparently not satisfied with the initial contribution, because several of the women were beaten up and kicked.

Some more baskets appeared then, and they loaded the truck to capacity and moved off in the direction of Stanley.

We climbed down the cliff and slipped across the road into the shelter of the huts just as another Jap convoy of six trucks came round the bend into sight, and we crouched under a festoon of drying nets cursing ourselves for not waiting until nightfall, but this time they didn't stop, so I knocked softly on Ho Yee's door. It was a long time before she opened it, and then only by the merest crack, but she recognized me immediately and let us in.

She bowed and said in Hakka, 'The tide of misfortune is high, master, and the monkey people are all around us like stinkweed in the rice paddies.' The Hakkas love parables. They are a rough, tough race, fisherfolk and coastwise farmers for the most part, and even in these modern times not averse to a spot of piracy when the opportunity occurs. They speak an archaic form of Mandarin which bears about the same relationship to the generally spoken Cantonese of Hong Kong as, for instance, Chaucer's English would to present day Cockney. Ho Yee was a middle-aged woman, short, stocky and as wind-and-sun-weathered as a baulk of teak—and as sound—dressed in the universal black cotton jumper and trousers that all the coast people, of both sexes, wear.

'It is not right that we should bring danger to you, Ho Yee,' I said. 'If you could help us to find a boat we will go our way as soon as it is dark.'

'Danger?' she shrugged. 'Fleas upon a dog—always with us— the police, the Customs, the Triad, and now the monkey people. One takes sensible precautions against it, then accepts it. Boats? All fifty-three of them are still here, but they can't be removed.'

'Could one be stolen, and the owner paid?' I asked.

She shook her head. 'They have taken all the men and boys to Stanley to work. Only the women are left here, to fish at night in the Lamma Channel. We have to hand the catch over each morning. They have made lists and told us that if

40

one boat is ever missing, ten of our men will be *sak ma tao*—'
She made a chopping sign on the back of her neck with the
edge of her palm.

'I see,' I said sadly. 'I am sorry, Ho Yee. We will leave
immediately.'

Her craggy face split in a grin. 'I said fleas upon a dog,
master. There are many ways of killing fleas without putting
one's neck under the axe. We can set you ashore on the
mainland without difficulty.'

'How?' I asked, my hopes rising, though very slightly.

'Smokee-smokee makee two boat one light,' she answered,
lapsing into pidgin, the grin widening, and I began to understand.

'What the hell is she chunnering about?' Raucous growled, because all the foregoing conversation had been so much
Greek to him.

'Shut up,' I told him. I returned Ho Yee's grin and
shook my finger at her chidingly. 'You're a bad woman,' I
said. 'You were settled here to make an honest living, not
ride the dragon.'

'Me—ride the dragon? Never,' she cackled. 'I know how it
is done though. But now sit—eat—drink tea—' She busied
herself with a kettle over a charcoal brazier while Raucous
and I settled ourselves where we could watch the road
through the hut's single window.

'We can't take a boat from here,' I explained to him. 'The
Japs have checked them all and they will behead ten men
from the village if one goes missing. That rules Macao out.'

'So what do we do?'

'She'll put us ashore on the mainland.'

'*She* will?'

'An old smugglers' trick. These people are keelung fish-
ers—that's a thing like a mackerel that they net at night,
with a bright acetylene lamp over the bow of the boat. The
police and customs can check the number of boats out at any
one time by the lights. If one goes dark they get suspicious,
and pounce on them all when they come back to harbour,

just in case one has made a quick run to the mainland to pick up opium. It's strictly forbidden on the island itself, but there's a lot of it sculling around on the Kowloon side.'

'So?'

'So they sometimes go out doublebanked—a second boat lashed alongside the one that's carrying the lamp. "Makee two boat one light" as they call it. It's the second one that does the actual run, blacked out—then it makes its way back to its partner before daylight.'

'That sounds easy enough.'

'It isn't. It's extremely dangerous. You've got to know the coast and the terrific currents you get round these parts, like the palm of your hand *in the dark*. Only the Hakkas would ever attempt it.'

'Hm, a bit hairy like?'

'It's hairy all right,' I told him.

'I see. Okay, so the old girl gets us put ashore on the Kowloon side? What happens then?'

'One step at a time, Raucous. It will be sufficient for the moment just to get off this island in one piece and find our way through the *cordon sanitaire*.'

'What's that?'

'The strip of land round the coast of China held by the Japs. It varies. They hold Shanghai—and now this place—and probably a few other ports—Amoy, Swatow, Foochow and places like that, but they couldn't possible hold the entire coastline in strength—it would take literally millions of men. We'll no doubt find garrisons here and there, and we'll just have to find our way between them.'

'And finish up in the middle of China somewhere?'

'And out the other side, I hope,' I said. 'It's only a matter of a few thousand miles. You just have to wash your feet every night and keep your socks darned. You told me that yourself, didn't you?'

'Jesus,' he said, appalled. 'A few thousand miles! How long is that going to take?'

'How the hell do I know?' I said, my patience suddenly

42

snapping. 'We've got to take things as they come, and keep slogging on—unless you happen to have any better suggestions?'

'Me? Not me, cocker—er—*sir*. You're the officer. Suggestions is *your* job. Orders would be better, of course.'

'I quite agree,' I told him. 'Here's our tea coming—and here's your first order. Drink it and belt up—and then keep your eye on the road while I have a further talk to our hostess. After that I'll relieve you for a couple of hours, and you can get some sleep.'

'That's better,' he said happily. 'A bloke knows where he stands when he has orders. See if the old biddy can rake up some tallow, will you? Nothing like tallow inside your almond rocks on a really long march.'

Chapter Two

1

'To the squirrel, nuts—to the Hakka, tidings,' is a Chinese proverb, and it is very apt. They certainly have the knack of collecting news almost as it happens—and it *is* news, never rumour, because they sort the grain from the chaff unerringly. They lie, like any other race, when it suits their purpose but they never exaggerate or embroider for the sake of sensation, so that which Ho Yee told me during the course of the long morning while Raucous slept, I had to accept as the unvarnished truth, and I was sick with the horror of it. Nurses who had volunteered to remain with the wounded in Stanley Hospital had been raped and murdered. The figure of Christ had been torn from the lifesize calvary outside the Portuguese church, and a British officer crucified in its place. A whole company of Canadians who had fought like tigers while their ammunition lasted, had finally surrendered on the promise of honourable treatment, only to be mown down as they came in under the white flag. There was a strict curfew throughout the Colony and anybody caught on the streets after sunset was bayoneted on the spot—man, woman or child.

'You must get away, master—far, and fast,' she warned. 'It is the taipans they look for, people like yourself. They know you. They have lists of names made ready by their spies and traitors. They know that there was much gold here that you had not time to send out, and they are torturing to find where it has been hidden. Chien-re Foy, the Mandarin banker, was hung by his ankles head downward over a charcoal fire and then disembowelled. British, and Chinese known to be partners of the British, they are hunting you down—' And so it went on until I could take no more, and I begged her to stop, and I thanked whatever gods were left to us that I had managed to get Helen and the children out, and that my mother had not been here—and that reminded me of the letter Wilkinson had given me, and which I had stuffed into my pocket and forgotten.

I took it out and opened it. It was terse and to the point, dated December 18. 'Don't worry about me,' she had written. 'I am leaving for "the other place" immediately. You and the family must get out, because yours will be the job of rebuilding when this madness is over. Get word to me through L.B. Love, A.'

Damn her, I thought angrily. Why had't she got out while she had the chance? 'The other place' was, of course, Chungking, in the very heart of China, over a thousand miles up the Yangtse-kiang from Shanghai. What guarantee had she that the ramshackle capital of the discredited Kuomintang would hold out against the Japanese any more than the rest? Those wretched hotels of hers—But at this point I think I had better put in a word of explanation.

Old Ross, my grandfather, married twice. His second wife was my father's mother. She was a woman of great beauty, intelligence and business acumen in an age when the two latter qualities were not considered seemly in the weaker sex. She was considerably younger than her husband, and was blessed with a superabundance of vitality. It was therefore inevitable that two such strong personalities should clash, and although it shocked the Victorian community of those days, it came as no great surprise when she skipped with a handsome young veterinary officer from one of the cavalry regiments. His army career was at an end, of course, and they had little or no money, certainly not enough to pay their passages to England, so they went upcoast to Shanghai, where they lived precariously but happily enough at first on what he could pick up in veterinary fees round the newly opened racecourse. It didn't last for very long though,

45

because he was drowned one night in the Whangpo on his way home, royally drunk, from the Jockey Club, so it was said, and she was left penniless in the large, semi-derelict villa they had rented on the outskirts of the International Concession.

It's a long story, which has no place here, but she took in boarders—fed them well and housed them cleanly, and charged them accordingly, and thereby made money hand over fist. The boarding-house graduated to hotel status and flourished, and her business activities widened. She played the ever bullish Shanghai stock exchange shrewdly, but never gambled, because anything she put money into was a preordained copper-bottomed certainty. She underwrote insurance, bought a moribund shipping line and sold it again at a thousand per cent profit within twelve months—and so on and on. She was, in short, the legendary Mrs Kempton, a name to which she had no legal entitlement, but which was almost as sound on a bill of exchange as that of our own princely house.

It would have been a picturesque ending to the story had she and my grandfather become reconciled in their old age, but that didn't come about, because he never forgave her for abandoning her year-old baby, my father, when she skipped the ancestral home, although she more than made up for that later when she helped him out of a hell of a predicament many years later—but that, also, is another story.* Suffice it to say here that when she died she left the Hotel Kempton in Shanghai, and the Cathay Palace Hotel in Chungking, to my mother, Abigail, a great favourite of hers. Mother, like her mother-in-law, couldn't stand Old Ross, so, after my father was killed in the Great War, she spent less and less time in Hong Kong, and devoted all her energies to managing these two glittering establishments, thereby obstinately maintaining her complete independence of Stafford & McMurtrie. Me? I was neutral. I was fond of my mother, but we were never very close. She was a one-man woman, and my father

* see *The Midnight Gun*.

46

had been her all, and she regarded me, I think, as the epitome of our Princely House—an embryo Ross. 'You're as stuffy and pompous as the old devil himself,' she had once charged me. Perhaps I was; after all, Annandale was the only home I had ever known, my grandfather was my mentor, and his daughter by his first marriage, Aunt Anne, a true-blue Stafford, had largely taken my mother's place.

The Cathay Palace was an idea of Abigail's. An American missionary's ward, albeit a highly unconventional one, who in moments of stress was prone to swear like a longshoreman, she was born and raised on the Yangtse-kiang, spoke half a dozen Chinese dialects and, under her mother-in-law's tutelage, had learned to tap and interpret the undercurrents of Chinese politics like a jade-button mandarin. She had foreseen the Japanese occupation of Mongolia long before it actually occurred in 1937, and she had persuaded Mrs Kempton, a very old but anything but geriatric lady by this time, to put some of her eggs in another basket by building a first class hotel a thousand miles upriver from Shanghai, which latter would obviously be their first objective when the real invasion came.

I remembered her discussing it with Old Ross when I was a very young man. 'A hotel in Chungking' A modern one?' my grandfather had scoffed. 'You're mad. It's nothing but a filthy, muddy village.'

'It's going to be Chiang Kai-shek's headquarters,' she answered quietly.

'I doubt it.'

'I *know*.'

'Very well then—assuming you're right, which I'm damned certain you're not—if the Japs occupy Shanghai what's to prevent their swarming upriver and doing the same in Chungking?'

'Distance—a thousand miles of it. When the balloon does go up they'll have their work cut out to take this place and Shanghai, and other coastal centres, and hold them against the British and Americans. They certainly won't have the troops to spare on inland adventures.'

47

'British and Americans? What the devil are you talking about? We're not at war with the Japs.'

'We will be by then.'

'You're mad,' he snorted again. 'You and that ex-wife of mine—the both of you. Well, go ahead. *Your* money, not mine, thank God. Who on earth would want to stay in your wretched hotel anyway?'

'When Chiang settles there it will be the *de facto* capital of China, because if Shanghai, the *commercial* capital, goes, then Peking will go also. All right: that means the legations and embassies will move to Chungking; then the business concerns will open up there—'

'*This* business concern won't, I assure you.'

'You want to bet?'

'No, I don't gamble with women.'

'Please yourself. But there'll be plenty of people staying there when it's finished, my dear Pa-in-law. I'll have a suite permanently reserved for you, but it won't be on the house. You'll pay—like any other travelling salesman.' And I remember her winking at me as the old man turned purple round the gills.

2

Ho Yee was shaking me. 'Time to go now, master,' she said. 'Boat ready. There is some fighting along the coast. Listen.'

I sat up and looked at my watch. I had slept for six hours and now it was pitch dark outside. Faintly in the distance I could hear the staccato chatter of machine-guns. So it seemed that the surrender was not complete.

'Some soldiers have gone into the big hotel at Repulse Bay', she told me. 'They put up a white flag and the monkey people told them to come out holding their hands up, but when they did they started to kill them with their bayonets, so the soldiers went back and continued to fight. But it will not be for long now. There were few soldiers and many, many monkey people—'

Even as she spoke, the firing died down except for single sporadic shots.

'How do you know this?' I asked.

She shrugged. 'I know,' she said simply. 'Our people have been watching all day from Applichau. Many business taipans and their ladies gathered in the hotel. They surrendered and were made to march over the hills to the city—old men, old ladies—the monkey people that were left found much whisky, beer, wine, and got drunk. Some British and Canadian soldiers on the hillside then tried to break through to the shore, and there was a fight, and they took shelter in the hotel—'

Raucous demanded, 'What's she saying? For Christ's sake, what's she saying? What's going on? Hasn't there been a surrender?'

'In the city, yes,' I said wearily. 'We saw it ourselves, didn't we? The Japanese flags going up as ours came down. It seems that the word hasn't reached some parties though, and there's been isolated fighting going on in the hills.'

'And we're pissing off, and leaving them to it?' he said bitterly.

'What were your last orders?' I asked him. 'From your own officer, I mean?'

'Every man for himself. If you think you can get away anywhere, then bugger off.'

'They still stand. You don't have to stay with me if you don't want to,' I told him.

'What are you going to do?' he asked in an agony of indecision.

'What you just said. I'm buggering off, for the simple reason that I know that there's not a thing I can do to help those people along there—and the Japs are slaughtering prisoners. You can please yourself.' I turned as Ho Yee jerked at my sleeve.

'Take these soldier clothes off, master,' she said. 'Put on

Hakka clothes.' And I saw that she had a bundle of black slacks and smocks over her arm.

'I'll come with you,' Raucous broke in sullenly.

'Very good,' I told him. 'But let's have no more of this "pissing off" business. You're not going to ease your military conscience by trying to make *me* feel guilty, my lad. You've been wailing for orders—well, now you've got them, for the second time: belt up, and do as you're told. Get those clothes off and put these on.'

'All right,' he said, unbuttoning his shirt.

'All right what?' I snapped.

'Sir.'

'That's better, Just keep it that way.' And once again he appeared to brighten visibly as the iron claw took over from the velvet glove.

We put on the bombazine clothes, with bandanna handkerchiefs worn pirate fashion on our heads, and Ho Yee even had two big coolie hats as they are wrongly called—the sensible Hakka straw headdress as wide and round as a cartwheel, which shields from the sun and is also an umbrella when it rains. She studied us for some moments critically, then she got a handful of charcoal from a cold brazier and rubbed it on our faces, and the effect was remarkable, because now clothes and skin merged into dark neutrality.

'That is better,' she said. 'Even in daylight you would not be noticed unless someone comes very close to you. Remember to walk like this, master.' She slumped her shoulders and bent her knees and shuffled her feet along flat-soled for a few paces, then she made us do it two or three times before she was satisfied. I tried to give her some money, but she shook her head.

'All right,' I said. 'When we come back I shall give you a new boat, Ho Yee.'

'Good,' she said practically. 'A number one Ning Po sampan with a put-put motah.' I didn't thank her. Among the Hakkas you only thank when you do not intend to keep a promise.

She took us down to the stone jetty then and we boarded a sampan to which another was lashed, catamaran-fashion. 'They take you to Castle Peak. That is the best place, but it is still very dangerous, master,' she told me. 'There are monkey people all the way along the coast from Gin-drinkers Bay to Kowloon. You will not be safe from them until you are fifty miles north of Canton, and even then there will still be danger from the Hung-hu-tse. They say the monkey people will pay a thousand dollars for all escapers who are handed back to them.'

We pushed off into the darkness then, without another word, because farewells and good wishes come into the same category as thanks.

The Hung-hu-tse, she had said. Literally 'Redbeard', the term has a number of connotations—mercenaries, irregulars, freebooters, and just plain bandits. Some supported Generalissimo Chiang Kai-shek, others the newly risen Communist leader, Mao Tse-tung, still others were fifth-columning for the Japanese. But whoever they were owing their transient allegiance to at any one time, their methods and motivation remained constant. If one fell into their hands one could count with absolute certainty on being robbed, held to ransom or, if there seemed no profit in the latter, having one's throat cut. A thousand dollars bounty on escapers? That would be big money to them. Oh well, yet another bridge to be crossed when one came to it. I had travelled extensively in the Chinese hinterland but had never been troubled by them, for the simple reason that the Company, in common with all the other princely houses, paid lavish protection money to whichever authority held at the time, amban, mandarin or warlord, all of whom maintained private armies for just this very purpose. But now we were on our own.

We came out into the Lamma Channel, which runs along the southern coast of the island, and the hissing acetylene lamps were being lit that threw a ray of white light down into the depths and attracted the fish. There were nine boats altogether, strung out in line abreast over a frontage of

51

perhaps half a mile, each of us supporting a portion of the heavy rope which held the huge curtain net that swept a good thirty feet below us. We were third from the shoreward end, in the twin boat that was lampless, and they cast us loose immediately we came into the open fairway, and we bobbed motionless on the dark water for about twenty minutes as the line of lights moved forward and away from us, then our crew hoisted a slatted lugsail and bore out into the centre of the channel. There were two of them, an old man and a boy, and Raucous was muttering nervously.

I said, 'What's wrong?'

'The bloody crew,' he complained. 'An old geezer about a hundred, and a perishing kid. I hope they know what they're about.'

'They do,' I told him. 'Don't worry.' But I must admit that I was feeling a little fidgety myself, because I thought the old man was bearing too far to the west towards Lantao and away from Castle Peak. He knew what he was doing though, because after a time he made a long sweep to starboard and I could see the loom of Tai Mo Shan, the high mountain on the mainland behind Kowloon, faintly against the dark northern sky, and I realized that he was taking every tithe of advantage from currents and wind with an instinct that these people share only with the fish and the seabirds, and that now we were bowling smartly along towards Stonecutters Island at the western entrance to the harbour, and that from there a turn to the north-west would bring us in a dead straight line to Castle Peak. I did the sensible thing then and settled down and tried to sleep, because it would be at least an hour before we would fetch up on the beach, and possibly twice that if the tide turned against us.

The light woke me—a long stabbing pencil of it that came out of the surrounding darkness and held us transfixed like a pin through a butterfly—an apt simile, because it picked out the multicoloured patches on our gently fluttering sail prettily for a long paralysing moment before moving on and losing us. It swept back again, but whoever was handling it was hamfisted, because it failed to lock on to us, and the old man, chattering like an angry parrot, had an instant in which to put his helm hard over and run before the wind which had now risen considerably. A machine-gun cut loose then, but it was firing wildly and we were really moving, and the old man was jinking sharply from side to side. The light was searching for us and I could hear the beat of an engine, but the wily old devil had now brought us round and was bearing away closehauled, so that the newcomers were looking in the exact opposite direction to the way we were heading. It was as neat a bit of evasion as I ever hope to see, but it had one cardinal disadvantage. We were driving head on through the harbour entrance between two blockships that had been sunk each side of the narrow channel, and we had no room to turn, and, to make matters worse, our pursuers had realized their mistake and had swung round and were on our track again.

Raucous said, 'Oh Jesus—there's another of them in front of us.' And there was, because a second searchlight was sweeping from side to side dead ahead of us, and I guessed that they were in radio communication with the first boat.

We were now between two fires, literally, because both boats were closing on us and their machine-guns were blazing and the water all round looked as if it was boiling, but, like the searchlight handlers, the gunners were not very accurate and, except for one nasty moment when splinters flew from our bow, we were not hit. It could only be a matter of minutes, though, before we became grain between the millstones, and the old man realized it, so he went hard aport out of the narrowing path of light and suddenly there was an almighty crash and we stopped as dead as if we had hit a stone wall—which is exactly what we had done, because at that moment the searchlight licked along a red and white hoarding high above us and I saw the two Chinese characters that spell Coca-Cola. We had hit the stone abutment beside the Jordan Road traffic ferry on the Kowloon side, that was marked by a huge billboard, and the old man and the boy were out of the sinking sampan and up the sloping ramp like a brace of hares, and Raucous and I were hard on their heels. From behind us there came a rending crash and a babble of yelling as our two pursuers rammed each other head on. One searchlight remained alight for a few moments and we saw that they were a pair of motor junks with the now sickeningly familiar white rectangle and red circle and rays of the Rising Sun painted on their sides. Then there was a flicker of flame from amidships of one of them and a muffled boom from the other and in a split second they were both beautifully ablaze from stem to stern, and screaming figures, some of them with their clothes on fire, were leaping into the water.

Raucous said, in tones of deep content, 'Lovely grub! A couple of boatloads of Nips in the crap, and we're only two jumps and a spit from Homuntin Alley.'

'What's Homuntin Alley got to do with it?' I asked.

'That's where me downhomer lives—if she hasn't shifted in the last couple of days.'

'Your what?'

'Downhomer—girl-friend—name of Aggie Tong.'

'You're surely not thinking of calling on the lady now, are you?'

'Why not? It's going to be light soon, and we don't want to be seen on the streets, do we?'

'Not if we can help it,' I said thoughtfully. This was a situation I hadn't envisaged, being caught in a highly populated area like this. 'But your—er—girl-friend—can she be trusted?'

'I should hope so.' He sounded hurt. 'You trusted the old fisherwoman, didn't you?'

'Yes, but then—well, I've known her quite a long time.'

'So've I known Aggie—nearly two years now. Blimey! Doesn't time fly?'

'But what is she exactly? I mean—'

'Is she on the batter? Well, yes, I suppose—in a sort of a

54

way. She's got to live, like anybody else, and *I* couldn't keep her fulltime on three bob a day. She has the odd bloke in when I'm not around, but she damn soon sees them on their way when I do show up, even if she's got to give them their money back.'

'Yes, but what I mean to say is—what if she's got a visitor at the moment?'

'Like I said, she'd see him off. Anyhow, it's only an idea. If you've got a better one, just say the word and we'll push on.'

I looked around the dark parking area the other side of the ferry building. There wasn't a sign of life—the old man and the boy had just vanished—but between us and open country the other side of Kowloon lay Nathan Road, a wide thoroughfare over two miles long, with not a bolthole or a modicum of cover for its entire length, and probably there would be Jap patrols lurking in the shadows waiting to pounce on the unwary. Ho Yee had said that they were bayoneting curfew-breakers . . .

'I haven't got a better one,' I told him. 'Lead on—that's if you don't mind my butting in.'

'Friend of the family,' he said, grinning. 'She'll be tickled stiff. I don't think she's ever met an officer.'

'For Christ's sake don't tell her I am one,' I said urgently. 'Ho Yee told me that they are on the look-out for us, especially ones that have business interests here in the Colony.'

'I won't,' he assured me. 'Although you needn't worry about me old downhomer. Safe as houses.'

'Why do you call her that?'

'Downhomer? Just a name we blokes have for our steadies. If you're not on duty in barracks you go "down home" for the night, see? Come on—this way.'

We padded along in the shadows, up Jordan Road for two blocks and then into a narrow lane that led down to the waterfront between rickety tenement buildings, and in all that way we saw not a single thing that moved, with the exception of a skinny black cat that crossed our path and

55

made me nearly jump out of my skin. Raucous stopped finally in front of a shuttered apothecary's shop, beside which a covered alleyway opened. We turned into this and he whispered a warning to me about where to put my feet, which seemed a little futile as it was totally dark and ankledeep in filth. The alley ended in a tiny open courtyard where a crumbling flight of steps led up the side of one of the surrounding houses to a sagging balcony.

Raucous said, 'Wait a minute,' and stood on tiptoe and fumbled in a small recess in the brickwork under the steps. 'All clear,' he said happily. 'She's in and there's nobody with her.'

'How do you know that?' I asked.

'If the coast is clear so's that little hole. If she's got a john with her she puts a cotton-reel in it. If she's out she puts Sai Loo there—'

'Sai Loo is a dragon,' I said.

'That's right. She's got a little carved wood one. He guards the joint till she gets back. Funny buggers, the Chinks.'

We climbed to the balcony, which creaked ominously as we put our combined weight on it. 'Stand close to the wall,' Raucous advised. 'This lot is going to give way one of these days.'

He tapped softly but distinctly on a door—three times—then a pause—then three again—another pause—and then twice—slightly louder—and I heard movement the other side. 'Open up allee same, chop-chop,' he muttered, his mouth close to the crack of the door, and bolts were withdrawn, the door opened and we stepped inside into total darkness. '*Lorkas!*' a woman's voice said ecstatically. 'Where you been, bloody man? Allee time I looksee, this side, that side—'

She closed and rebolted the door, struck a match and lit a lamp on a table and I looked first at her, then around the room. Chinese share one essential characteristic with pigs, in that they can exist in filth that would kill most other races, but give them basic facilities and they are the most incredibly fastidious creatures on earth. The room was about twelve feet square, furnished with one table, two chairs, a native bedstead, a rope across a corner supporting some neatly hung clothes, a tiny clay charcoal stove and two gleaming copper cooking pots. Ten dollars would no doubt have bought the entire contents, but I never remember seeing a safer, more comfortable or cleaner place in my life. Raucous, looking sideways at me in the dim lamplight, seemed to read my thoughts.

'See what I mean by "down home"?' he said. I did see. As occasional surcease from the agora of the barrack-room, this must have been pure bliss.

The woman, clad like ourselves in the universal black jumper and slacks, was looking from one to the other of us, plainly put out at the presence of a stranger, her initial joy at seeing Raucous cut short. He grinned broadly and shoved his haversack forwards towards her.

'Here you are, me old dutch,' he said. 'Catchee number one vellee good chow, chop-chop. This feller flend belong me—half-section, see? We makee lun flom Japs allee same quick-one-time, savvee?' Her nervousness seemed to be transferring itself to him in the form of awkward shyness. 'Sorry about this,' he said to me. 'She don't talk English too good, but we manage to get along all right except when there's anybody else around. Come on,' he said turning to her. 'Don't stand there allee same no-talk monkey. Say how's-your-father or *some* bloody thing.'

She smiled uncertainly but still seemed unable to find words, so to ease matters I slid my hands up opposite sleeves and bobbed three times swiftly—the peasant greeting rather than the formal bow—and said in Cantonese, 'We ask you to excuse us. We need somewhere to rest during daylight, but we will not stay if you do not wish us to.'

She said simply, 'My unworthy house is yours for as long as you wish.'

'That's better,' Raucous said, relieved. 'I don't know what

you said to her, but it did the trick. I thought the cat had got her tongue.'

He continued to talk to her thereafter in execrable pidgin and I sat on one of the chairs, gratefully, and was able to study her as she busied herself in rooting through the haversack and unpacking the supplies with suppressed shrieks of sheer delight. She was not young—perhaps twenty-four or five, which for the peasant women is verging on early middle age—nor was she particularly pretty, certainly not in the fragile mould of so many of the Hong Kong girls; at the same time she hadn't the heavy cast of features of the Hakka. Inland, Southern Central Provinces, I guessed—Hunan or Kiangsi—the dirt-farmers who scratch a living from some of the poorest soil on earth, two or three acres per family, battened upon by the petty mandarins, robbed and pillaged by the warlords and the Hung-hu-tse and now, if that were not enough, with the Japanese to contend with. She was well formed and her movements were lithe, as would be expected of who who had no doubt wielded a scythe from the time she was able to stand, and even in the lamplight her smooth olive skin seemed positively to glow with health and well-soaped cleanliness, and her thick black hair looked as if it received its daily meed of grooming with the heavy pig-bristle brushes that they make in those parts as their sole cottage industry. Yes, I decided that Aggie Tong was rather a nice person, now that the ice was broken and she was chattering freely, in pidgin to Raucous and Cantonese to me.

I asked her how long she had been in Hong-Kong and she told me two years.

'My father sold me to a travelling hide merchant,' she explained. 'Not in marriage but as servant maid to his Number One wife. She did not travel with him but remained on their farm outside Amoy. The work was hard both in the house and also the rice paddies, but she was kind to me and I was well fed. But then she died, and I passed to Number Two wife who was *not* kind, because now I was in my eleventh year and she thought that her husband would soon be taking

58

me to his bed, which would mean that she would be dropping to Number Three Wife, and would lose face, so after a bad beating I ran away in Canton and hid myself in a junk and reached Macao, where I worked in a godown making fireworks, then after that in a teahouse for four or five, or it may have been six years—I have lost count— and I was still a virgin because, of course, I had no dowry so who would wish to marry me?'

'What the bloody hell is she chunnering about?' Raucous asked irritably.

'She's giving me a lot of information about what the Japs are doing,' I lied. 'Shut up, Raucous. All this is most interesting.'

He mumbled complainingly and then went to sleep on the bed, so she continued her story while she set about preparing a meal. And it *was* interesting, to me, and I have no doubt to her, because she had probably never before met anybody eccentric enough to want to hear the lifestory of such an unimportant microcosm of humanity as herself, and in the telling of it she was enjoying a totally new experience. And in it all was not a single word of complaint. This was just life as she knew it.

'But then all that ended when I was spoiled,' she went on.

'Spoiled?'

'Yes. There was a foreign devil ship in harbour with sick engines, so it was anchored for a long time, and two sailors took me one night tied in a quilt and with my mouth filled with rags, and they kept me in a locked cabin and many, many of them had me, and I did not like it. So I managed to get out and I stole much money from them while they slept—nearly fifty dollars—then I swam ashore, and I had trouble hiding for some days because the Portuguese police looked for me. That would have meant two years in São Agostino prison if I had been caught, for stealing and making lovee-lovee with sailors without a licence.'

'But they took you against you will,' I said, and she laughed merrily.

59

'That would make no difference,' she answered. 'The sailors would have told *their* story, so who would believe *me*? I had been on the ship and I had stolen money. The police would want twenty-five dollars for the licence and half of whatever the sailors said I stole, and there would have been a beating in any case. So I left Macao in another junk and went to Swatow and worked in other teahouses and kept out of trouble, and after two more years I had saved enough money to get into Hong Kong "allee-samee-softlee-softlee-back-door" as the soldiers say, which means two hundred dollars squeeze-pidgin to the Immigration Control. I got work this time in Tommee Beer Kitchen, where all the British soldiers get drunk on pay night. There I met him—' she smiled fondly at the sleeping Raucous. 'He is a good man,' she said. 'When a corporal wanted me one night I refused, because Lorkas was there. The corporal insisted, so Lorkas hit him, then the military police came and Lorkas made a great fight and was taken to prison.' She sighed contentedly. 'But now he is out. I am very happy. You are his friend?'

'I am his friend,' I assured her.

'Where did you learn to speak our language so well?'

'I was born in this country,' I told her, which sufficed although it was not strictly true. I was a year old when Bard and Abigail brought me here from South Africa.

'Ma'tse?' she asked. That means locally born poor white and is applied in the main to the descendants of the large colony of White Russians which settled in China after the Bolshevik revolution of 1917—and *it* sufficed also, or so I thought, I nodded, and her face clouded.

'Many of the Ma'tse work for the Japanese,' she said. 'They have been selling British soldiers to the Kempitei.'

'I am not one of those,' I said hastily. 'I am a British soldier myself.'

'Some Ma'tse have taken the British rice,' she conceded, but I could see she was still troubled. 'It is to them that the Japanese officer in the motor-car spoke with the Big Tongue—'

60

'Loudspeaker?' I translated. 'What did he say?'

'Ma'tse who declared themselves as such would receive good treatment even if they had taken the British rice and wore their uniform. Those who betrayed British soldiers in hiding would receive one thousand dollars. Those who helped them would be beheaded." She looked at me very directly. 'If I thought you meant to harm Lorcas I would sell *you* to the Japanese—or kill you myself.'

I took a very deep breath, and expelled it slowly. 'I lied to you,' I confessed.

'I know,' she said. 'Do you think I do not know how the Ma'tse speak? It is with the coolie tongue—like mine. Yours is jade button—mandarin speech.'

I had enjoyed the two years at Peking University to which old Grandpa Ross had sent me in preference to Cambridge, which he always averred had been the ruination of my father, but I could have done without it at that moment.

'I am not lying now,' I said. 'I mean no harm to Lorkas. I am British, or rather half British, half America—' which was literally true, because Abigail had never relinquished her American nationality '—the same as Winston Churchill,' I added hopefully, but that meant nothing to her, and I felt that the more I tried to explain, the more doubts I was engendering in her. To one who like Aggie had been balanced since birth on the very razor edge of bare existence, suspicion was a natural and constant state. The warmth seemed to be leaving that little room and I was cursing myself inwardly. Things had been going so well until that first stupid lie of mine. If I had told her the truth in the first place she would most probably have accepted it without question, but then, of course, I had wanted to keep my real identity dark. They were looking especially for taipans, so Ho Yee had said—

She was still searching my face, her own now hardened, cold, calculating.

'Why did you say you were Ma'tse?' she demanded sharply.

'You asked *me*,' I reminded her. 'It was easier to say yes then to try to explain, and I was—I *am*—tired. Now I give you the truth once again. I am British, I am Lorkas's friend, we try to escape together—'

'And where did you learn to speak as you do?'

'Peking. The College of the Mandarins.'

'Then you must be rich.'

'I am rich.'

Behind her a pot of noodles was boiling over and hissing on the little charcoal stove. She moved it off the heat, then turned back again to me. In her hand was a small delicately painted rice bowl. She held it out to me, her eyebrows raised questioningly. I nodded and took the bowl, then picked up a few grains of rice from the table and dropped them into it. I lifted the bowl to mouth level, touched my lips to it and then brought it down sharply and broke it on the edge of the table. Raucous, catnapping on the bed, sat up and stared at me.

'Hey! Go easy on the crockery,' he said. 'What the hell do you think you're doing?'

'Your lady friend is under the impression that I'm a Mig,' I told him. 'Mig' is an abbreviation for 'émigré', which is what the White Russians call themselves rather than the pejorative 'Ma'tse'. 'I'm trying to convince her that I'm not.'

'Mig?' he roared at her. 'You number one, topside, big piecee silly cow. What thing makee talk like so? This master number one Peakside top taipan, makee 'longside London. Mig my bloody arse. Getchee chow, chop-chop—we're hungry.'

And that succeeded much quicker than the broken rice bowl, which to the Chinese, be they Confucian, Buddhist, Tao, Christian, Jew, Moslem or animist, is the most binding oath they can ever take.

Aggie smiled sweetly and said meekly in pidgin, 'Yes, Lorkas—will do,' then she reached out both her clasped hands and touched each of mine in turn, and, knowing these people, I accepted her trust as she was accepting mine: rather more completely than I would have taken a signed, stamped and sealed bond on 'Change from a hell of a lot of people I had met in the sacred purlieus of the Hong Kong Club.

We spent most of that long day peering through a crack in the shuttered window which commanded a view across intervening roofs of a section of Jordan Road. It was heartbreaking. They were ferrying the defeated British troops over from the island, herded like cattle on lighters, gaunt, ragged and filthy, many of them wounded and wearing dirty, bloodstained field dressings, some limping painfully and trying to avoid the pricking bayonet points of their guards. The Japs were really making a gala of it, and extracting full propaganda value from the spectacle for the benefit of the Chinese crowd that lined the route.

A military band arrived at mid-morning and formed up by the ferry building. They opened the programme with their national anthem, the dreary 'Empress of the Eastern seas, Brightest star of mystic skies' that I had so often heard in the past when any of their shoguns were here on courtesy visits. The column that was actually disembarking at the time was halted, and the guards presented arms. Some of the weary prisoners sat down on the ground, and paid for it when the dirge ended and the guards got among them with boots and bayonets. The bandmaster, a little fat man, all teeth, flashing hornrimmed glasses and samurai sword, turned on his soapbox and started to shriek angrily, and to my amazement a white man in the smart blue winter uniform of the Hong Kong police pushed his way through to the front of the crowd and shouted in English through a megaphone.

'Listen, you men! You have just had the honour of hearing the Imperial anthem played by the band of the 29th Infantry Regiment, by kind consent of Colonel Timatu, the commanding officer. Whenever you hear it again you will stop whatever you are doing and stand rigidly to attention. When it is finished you will bow from the waist—*really* bow—like this—' he demonstrated—'three times—or by God you'll regret it.' He repeated it in very good Cantonese for the

63

benefit of the crowd, then saluted and bowed to the band-master who returned the compliments punctiliously. They then went into a spirited but rather off-key rendering of 'Colonel Bogey'.

Raucous gasped, 'But—but—he's one of ours—a copper, but still one of *ours*. What the hell goes on?'

'Inspector Kordakov,' Aggie said in pidgin. 'Ma'tse.' She tapped herself under the chin with her fingertips, making the sign that means 'no face', then rubbed her thumb and fore-finger together. 'Takee plentee squeeze-pidgin us girls, opium man, shop man, washee amah—all people. Damn bastard—no good.'

'Yes,' I said. 'I recognize him now.' The last time I had seen him he had saluted me at the gateway to Government House.

'Bloody coppers,' Raucous swore indignantly. 'Can you beat that?' He pointed. 'And there's more of the sods.'

A file of blue-turbaned Sikh constables had marched into our view. They wheeled smartly and came up into line in front of the inspector, and a sergeant came forward and saluted and they went into close colloquy.

'Blitish policeman go in plison camp allee same soldiers,' Aggie explained. 'Ma'tse policeman go along Jap side.'

'What about Chinee policeman? I asked.

'Take off policeman clothes, lun like hell,' she answered. 'Chinee policeman catchee plentee savvee.'

That put things in focus for me. The Hong Kong Police Force, highly efficient though regrettably bedevilled by cor-ruption in the lower cadres, was European officered from the rank of sub-inspector upward, almost entirely British but with a sprinkling of Russians and Portuguese. The sergeants and constables were largely Chinese, but with a strong con-tingent of Coast Indians, Sikhs and Bengalis in the main, the descendants of immigrants who had been settled in the Colony for many generations. They retained their Indian culture, customs and religion, though few of them had ever seen their original homeland. Those who had managed to obtain an education entered Government service as clerks, or 'babus', which was the generic term, and many more were small shopkeepers—but the bulk of them went into the police force, retiring in the fullness of time as very rich men indeed by local standards.

The group we were watching seemed to be working smoothly under new management, controlling the crowds, directing traffic and, with zeal and evident satisfaction, helping the Japanese guards to speed up the disembarkation of the prisoners, both military and civilian.

'Soldier go to Shamsuipo,' Aggie informed us. 'Vellee big camp, vellee bad—no food, no water. Other people go to Argyle Street. That vellee bad same like.'

'How do you know all this?' I asked her in Cantonese as Raucous sat with his eyes glued to the crack, growling in the back of his throat as he recognized some of his pals in the column.

'It has been going on for four days now,' she informed me. 'I have been out many times to try and buy food and have seen and heard much in the crowds.'

'Do you know how closely the streets are patrolled at night?'

'Here, Jordan Road, Nathan Road, Chatham Road, the railway station and Peninsular, very closely. The top end of town, where the Castle Peak and Fanling roads divide, not so closely.'

'You mean you have been as far as that—after the curfew?'

'Yes, twice. I am going again tonight—finally this time—north to the Shumchun River, avoiding Lowu and To Kat, and up past Canton, where the Japs finish.'

'But why? I mean you, the Chinese, are in no immediate danger here.'

'The Comfort Battalion,' she said. 'I have no wish to join it.'

'The Comfort Battalion?'

'The Japanese soldiers' brothel. They are rounding up us girls, the unattached ones without husbands or families, and drafting us there. I prefer to choose my own men—and I do not want the Disease. Fut Sui, a girl I know, came from Shanghai, where the Japs have been for five years, and she told me what it is like. I go with you.'

'But—er—' I began, badly startled.

'Do not worry,' she said calmly. 'I will not stay with you longer than you wish me to, and I can show you a way out of Kowloon that you would not be able to find yourselves.'

'Aggie wants to come with us,' I said to Raucous.

'Bloody good show,' he said, without turning from the window. 'Her cooking's lovely. The *bastards*—they just kicked a bloke on crutches.'

3

We left after dark, not without a certain amount of disputation, because she wanted to bring along some cherished household chattels, the fruits of God knows what saving and contriving over the years, but we managed to separate her from the weightier objects in the end and she settled for a rice bowl, a set of chopsticks, a knife and spoon each, and one of the smaller cooking pots.

We came down into the small courtyard and she whispered to us to wait while she went ahead to reconnoitre, then she melted silently into the darkness. A fine drizzle, that curse of the otherwise quite agreeable Hong Kong winter, was falling and we were soaked and chilled in a matter of minutes, but I took comfort from the fact that it would help to keep the opposition under cover.

She came back and led us out into the alley and turned left, away from Jordan Road, and down to the waterfront. I thought I knew every nook, cranny and byway of both the Hong Kong side and Kowloon, but I soon realized that I had a lot to learn from this strange girl, because she moved ahead of us at a swift, mile-eating trot that had both Raucous and me sweating, then steaming and finally gasping in an incredibly short time, and never once did she come out into an open street. She just dived into one narrow alley after another without a check or a moment's hesitation. Hong Kong, under normal circumstances—if anything can ever be normal in Hong Kong—never sleeps. There is always an effulgence of coloured neon over the central part of both cities, and even in the outskirts naked electric bulbs are plentifully festooned, and the street-traders' stalls that do business right round the clock are usually lighted with naphtha flares. And noise never dies completely—the cries of nightwatchmen, the honking of prowling taxis, rickshaw bells, the rattling of mahjong tiles, all blend into an eternal insomniac cacophony. But now there was not a glimmer of light anywhere. Behind us, across the harbour, the Peak was a black, menacing, formless bulk against the moonless sky. And there was a pall of silence over everything, broken only by the dripping rain and the rhythmic scuffing of our felt-soled slippers on the wet flagstones.

Then, when I felt I could not go another step without a rest, I smelt cedarwood strongly on the moist air, and I realized that we had reached the Tailan Pencil factory, which incidentally was one of my company's smaller holdings, and I hailed it with joy—not because of any pride of ownership, but purely for the reason that it stood at the bifurcation of the Castle Peak and Fanling roads, which meant that we were now out of Kowloon and at the start of the open countryside of the New Territories.

I called, 'Makee stop, one time, Aggie,' in pidgin for the benefit of Raucous, who was wheezing and blowing behind me like a busted bellows, and he grunted, 'Thank Christ for that! I'm just about knackered.'

She wheeled on us and positively spat in a sibilant whisper: 'Two piecee copulating fool! Jap guard on road here,' and I remember the old-maidish shock I felt, because, of course, she used the universal soldier's adjective—the first woman I have ever heard do so. It even shocked Raucous, because he said sternly. 'Here, that's enough of *that* sort of language, thank you.'

But how right she was, because a challenge came out of the darkness then and a door was opened and I saw the glow of a brazier. Left to myself, I think I would have run for it, but behind me Raucous breathed, 'Freeze—look downwards,' and I instinctively obeyed. Aggie didn't need telling. She was completely immobile. There was a gabble of Japanese among them but, fortunately, a marked unwillingness on the part of the soldiery to come out into the rain. One, presumably an NCO, did make a few token sweeps with an electric torch, then contented himself with belting the sentry round the ears with it before going back inside.

Aggie touched me on the arm and led off the road through a flooded ditch that put the coping stone on my misery, and we crept up a muddy slope through stunted bushes in a wide detour until we rejoined the road a few hundred yards further along. She halted again then and I heard a muffled giggle, which didn't of necessity mean that she was amused. Chinese are prone to laugh in moments of fear or anxiety. She said in Cantonese, 'Pi Lung, the rain-in-the-night god, showed mercy then. Had you called one half-minute later we would have been right beside the sentry, and nothing could have saved us.'

'I am sorry,' I said contritely.

'It was my fault,' she said generously. 'I should have warned you, but I did not realize that we had come so far. Even now I am uncertain, because I did not reach this point when I was spying out the route,' which gave me the opportunity of recovering a little of my amour propre, since this was very much home territory to me.

'That was the pencil factory,' I told her. 'It is a building which stands alone in otherwise open country. There are no more houses until we reach the outskirts of Fanling. We are now about six miles from the Shumchun. When we cross that we have left British Territory and are in China proper. There is barbed wire there and British army and police posts which now will be occupied by the Japanese.'

'Yes . . . yes . . .' she said uncertainly, and I could sense that she was desperately tired, and I felt that it was time that someone took over from her.

'We must find somewhere to hide, Aggie,' I said. 'A point from which we can see the road when it is light again.'

'What the hell are you two talking about?' Raucous asked querulously. It always seemed to worry him when we spoke Chinese for any length of time.

'Just discussing the route,' I said. 'We've got to get under cover before daylight.'

'Suits me,' he said. 'I'm creased. But it had better be somewhere out of the rain or we'll be stiff and shagged out when it's time to move on again.'

'A counsel of perfection,' I said sourly.

'A what?'

'Never mind. Yes, I agree, but how the hell are we going to find somewhere out of the rain in the dark? A clump of bushes to dump down in is the best we can hope for.'

'This is Bird Hill on our right, isn't it?' he said surprisingly, because visibility was down to zero.

'It is, but how did you know that?'

'I've done every last lousy inch of it on manoeuvres, in daylight and dark, pissing rain and blinding bleeding sun that would take the hide off a Jerusalem canary—Twice a year for the last five. Christ! Do I know Bird Hill!'

'Then why didn't you say so earlier?'

'You didn't bloody well ask, did you? You and her between you—you know the sodding lot.'

'Stop that!' I told him. 'This is getting us nowhere. Do you know of any shelter on this hill.?'

'Yeah,' sullenly.

'Don't play the fool, Rawcliffe,' I said, now thoroughly angry. 'What is it? And where?'

'A foxhole in the side facing north. A sort of cave, like.'

'Hm. In that case the Japs might have occupied it by now,' I said doubtfully.

'They'd have to be lucky. Every officer and NCO in the batallion has looked for that little hidey-hole. Me and old Jacko Nicolas used to hole up in it and watch 'em. Not a chance.' His mood lightened at the memory of it and he chuckled mordantly. 'We used to sneak into it when we got browned off with traipsing over the landscape on practice patrols, and watch the other mugs wearing their feet out.'

'Could you find you way there now?'

'Of course I could. Haven't I been telling you?'

'Well, stop blethering, and lead us to it.'

'Just like an officer,' he grumbled as he moved off the road and started to climb the slope. 'You get a bollocking for not talking, then when you do open your trap you get told to shut up.'

The going was difficult—steep, muddy and broken by outcropping rocks and clumps of she-oak, but he never hesitated for a moment. He climbed steadily for about half a hour, pausing only twice when I swore at him and made him wait for Aggie, who was now making heavy weather of it. Then we lost him. One moment he was just ahead of us, an amorphous lump in the dark, the next he had disappeared. I halted, cursing sulphurously—one can in Chinese.

'He is a man of evil intent,' I snarled to Aggie.

'He is not,' she said loyally. 'We have lost him for the moment because we are weak and stupid.'

And then his voice came to us seemingly out of the bowels of the earth, right underfoot, scaring the daylights out of both of us.

'Come on. Don't stand out there chunnering in Chink again,' he said irritably, and a hand gripped my ankle. 'Down here—don't disturb the bushes more than you can help—duck down under the rock—pull Aggie in—mind you heads, for Christ's sake. There! What did I tell you, eh?'

I was conscious only of the merciful fact that, although we were soaked to the skin, we were at least out of that horrible

70

rain and chilling wind, and I knew overwhelming relief and was commensurately grateful.

'Yes, you told us,' I mumbled. 'Clever bloke. Now shut up—I'm going to sleep.'

4

There was a sickly greenish light coming from somewhere, and I sat up to investigate further, and cracked my head on the roof. The others were still asleep, Aggie in the middle, and Raucous the other side. We were packed into a rectangular space about eight feet by six, and as I had discovered, with not quite enough height in which to sit upright. The dawn light was coming through a screen of leaves that covered the hole through which we had entered, and since I urgently required a couple of minutes in decent privacy I wriggled out through it, and saw immediately that Raucous and not been exaggerating. It would have been virtually impossible to unearth this covert—certainly without a dog. It wasn't a cave in the exact meaning of the word. It was just a space under an overhanging boulder, one of some hundreds of identical ones which dotted the long, sloping hillside that swept down to a fjord that I recognized as Santoy Inlet—a twisting saltwater gut through the hills that came out into the open sea some ten miles north-east of Hong Kong Harbour—and there at my feet, a sloping half-mile away, was Rutland House on its two-acre island at the end of the short causeway that linked it with the shore. I was facing north. To my right the sun was rising over the Mirs Bay headland; to my left, westward, I could see the New Territory Road that we had been coming along when we left it to climb this hill. The side-road that led off it to connect with the causeway was in plain sight, perhaps a mile away, and I could see that a roadblock has been set up at the junction. There was a lot of activity, with wheeled traffic and marching men moving in both directions.

Behind me there was a rustling in the bushes that over-grew the hole, and Raucous, looking like a dirty hedgehog, wriggled out and pushed past me. He stood with his back turned to me, communing with nature. 'Huh!' he sighed with deep relief. 'I needed that. Me radiator was just about boiling. What do you think of me hidey-hole?'

'It is everything you claimed for it,' I conceded, 'but it's no good for permanent habitation. We'll have to push on as soon as it's dark.' I wriggled uncomfortably in my wet clothes. 'We need to dry out and get some hot food into us, and we can't do that here.'

The sun had now inched up over the headland and its rays were striking across the fjord, lighting up the house on the island below us and throwing up the garden plots surround-ing it into a glorious patchwork of colours.

'Lovely, isn't it?' Raucous said sorrowfully. 'Poor old dears. I wonder what's happened to them?'

'The two Willis ladies? You know them?' I asked.

'You bet. Many a meal me and old Jacko scrounged off of them. We used to help with those chrysanths, weeding and watering and that.'

'I hope to God they got off in one of the evacuee ships—' I began, and then I stared down at the house unbelievingly. 'Look!'

Two figures had come out into the open from the house, foreshortened under wide straw hats, but unmistakably English, in skirts instead of the universal Chinese trousers. They moved into the flower-beds and started to cut blooms.

'Oh Jesus!' Raucous groaned. 'Poor old dabs. Nobody could of told 'em. They don't know the bloody place has fallen—and they'll get done in by the Nips.'

'They must have been warned,' I said. 'All Europeans were—days ago—and the women were ordered to the Assembly points. They probably just decided to say put.'

'Let's go down, anyhow,' Raucous said. 'We can't just push off and leave them.'

'All right,' I agreed reluctantly, 'but I don't see what we

can do for them. Getting out is going to be touch-and-go for us as it is. Two elderly ladies couldn't hope to make it. Personally I think it would be advisable for them to stay where they are, and hope for the best.'

'Yes, that's the easiest way out, isn't it?' he said nastily

'What other way is there?' I asked him. 'Come on, Rawcliffe, just forget the snide remarks for once, and suggest something constructive.'

'Well—er—'

'Well, what?'

'We ought to tell 'em at least. Just in case they don't know the Nips are only a few hundred yards away.'

'All right then, if it eases your conscience—although I'm damned if I can see what good it can do.'

'Maybe none at all, but I'd feel better if we had at least warned 'em. It'll be on our way, anyhow.' He grinned slyly. 'And there's always the chance of a hot drink and a warm by the kitchen fire.'

'Oh no you don't,' I said firmly. 'Two harmless old ladies on their own might possibly be left in peace, but if they were caught sheltering British troops there wouldn't be a hope for them. No, we tell them in passing tonight, and then scoot.'

We sat on the ledge outside the cave for the rest of that day, warmed by the sun but bedevilled by thirst because in the misery of the previous night's march we had forgotten to fill out waterbottles, a point I determined to note well in future. The two old ladies down below worked steadily right through to sunset, except for a short break at midday. There was something at once ridiculous and heroic about it. Blood counts, so they say—and if whispered gossip was to be believed, theirs was of the best.

Nobody knew the exact age of the twin Misses Sophie and Susan Willis. Guesses ranged between seventy-five and eight-five. There were a few oldtimers who claimed to remember their mother, the widow of a P & O skipper who had invested wisely and settled out here, building an exact replica of the house he would have erected on the damper

73

shores of Plymouth Sound had it not been for his rheumatism. Others shook their heads and said there never was a husband, and that 'Mrs' Willis had been the pretty lady's maid of the wife of a long defunct Governor of the Colony, and that Edward VII, while still Prince of Wales, had paid a State visit here in the late 1860s. Be that as it may, these two old ladies had made this droplet of land off the coast of South China a corner that was forever England—except for the chrysanthemums. Their income, no doubt adequate in late Victorian days, whether issuing from the estate of a comfortably placed retired sea-captain or through the backdoor of the Household Chamberlain's office, was probably less now in terms than I paid a junior clerk in my company, so for many years they had been supplementing it from their garden, sending sheafs of glorious blooms twice a week into the two flower markets of Hong Kong to the south, and Fanling to the north. Chrysanthemums are an autumn flower in most parts of the world, but some quirk of climate and soil condition enables them to be grown all the year round in this exactly defined area. But only the Misses Sophie and Susan cultivated them, the local farmers and horticulturists being exclusively concerned with food production.

'Where the hell are their Chink garden boys?' Raucous asked. 'They had about six of them.'

'Obviously made off for their homes,' I said.

'Windy bastards,' he said disgustedly.

'Not at all. We were told at Defence Headquarters that Chinese servants working for Europeans were likely to have a hard time when the Japs came. I paid all mine off and sent them packing. Most people will have done the same.'

'A pity the army didn't,' he said ruefully. 'Fight to the last round, and the last man, they said.' He spat. 'For *what*?'

'It's no good getting your tail down now,' I said. 'You can bellyache all you like *after* we get out. Come on, get off your arse. It's nearly dark enough to start moving down.'

'Getting to be a real NCO, aren't you?' he gibed, rising and stretching. 'Officers—pukkha officers—don't use rude

74

language to us lower classes. 'Sergeant, instruct that man to move a little faster,' they'd say in a posh voice, and the sergeant hollers, 'C'mon—move your fuggin self, you idle sunnervabitch. You heard what the gentleman said, didn't you?' Oh Gawd, why did I ever enlist?'

The tide was at full ebb when we reached the shore, and we were able to wade kneedeep out to the little island without having to risk crossing the causeway. The short twilight had faded to a dim afterglow by the time we climbed over the high surrounding garden wall, and the old ladies had long gone inside. We halted at the edge of the beautifully tended flower-beds and surveyed the gaunt house. It was as incongruous an edifice as one could have found the length and breadth of the Far East. Imagine a typical South Kensington villa, complete with basement, ground floor, two upper storeys and finally a mansard-windowed attic, topped by massive chimneys lifted complete from a quiet square off the Cromwell Road and set down here, and you have it.

I had never been this close to it before—few Hong Kong residents had. It wasn't snootiness on our part, nor were the Misses Willis recluses. It was just that they didn't entertain. They were on the Government House visiting list—List B, to be exact, which meant that they would be invited once or twice a year to a garden-party—and they never missed a function at the cathedral, which they kept supplied with generously donated flowers, but that was the full extent of their social activities. Yet everybody knew them, and they knew everybody, and they were much loved, by Chinese as well as by us foreign devils.

We could see a chink of light in one of the lower windows, but otherwise the place was dark and wrapped in a silence broken only by the faint lapping of wavelets on the foreshore.

'What about it?' Raucous asked. 'You or me? They know me quite well.'

'As a reasonably respectable soldier, no doubt,' I said, 'But if you go barging up to the front door in that get-up you'll scare the day-lights out of them.'

'What about yourself?' he retorted. 'You look like busted

rickshaw wallah. Anyhow, I wouldn't go to the front door. I know me place. Tradesmen's entrance, me.'

'All right,' I said. 'You'd better go. But, Raucous—no hanging about on the scrounge, do you understand? Just tell them where the Japs are, if they don't know already, and ask them if there's anything in reason we can do to help them, then come away.'

'Sure, sure, sure,' he agreed, too readily, and melted into the shadows.

He was gone about ten minutes, and I was beginning to worry, when he returned.

'You took your time,' I said sourly.

'Blimey!' he exclaimed. 'You never heard anything like it. They've got a hell of a lot of news. You'd better come in and listen.' He was quivering with excitement.

'No', I said sharply. 'I've already given you your orders. You can either obey them, or push off on your own.'

'All right—er—sir, but I'm telling you the truth. They're really insisting that you come in. Here you are—here's one of 'em to tell you herself.' He broke off as a woman approached over the dewy lawn.

'Good evening,' she said conversationally. 'Have we perhaps met? Mr Rawcliffe said you were a businessman in Hong Kong.' She was peering closely at me through the darkness.

'Good evening, Miss Willis,' I said. 'Yes, I've had the pleasure of meeting you both— I mean you and your sister—but of course, I could never—'

'Tell one of us from the other?' She giggled like a schoolgirl. 'We take advantage of it. Naughty of us. I'm Susan. You are—?'

'My name is Stafford.'

'Not—?'

'Vincent Stafford. We met last at Church House—a sale of work, I think it was. I was picking my wife up.'

'*Mr Stafford*!' she said breathlessly. 'Oh, please—*please* come in.'

'I don't think it advisable, Miss Willis,' I said firmly. 'I don't want to alarm you, but if the Japs *should* pay a surprise visit and find us on the premises, the consequences would be serious, to say the least. Believe me, I am only thinking of *you*.'

'The Japs will not come before morning,' she said positively. 'I know what I'm talking about. Please, Mr Stafford, you *must* come in. It's really most important—' She became aware of Aggie standing some distance behind me in the darkness. 'Oh, there's somebody else here?' She sounded a little alarmed.

'A Chinese woman,' I said.

'Who is she?' she demanded sharply her tone changing.

'Her name is Aggie Tong,' I said somewhat awkwardly. 'She's travelling with us.'

'Just a moment, please,' Miss Susan said coldly, then she addressed Aggie in fluent Cantonese. 'Who are you, and what is your condition?'

'I am the concubine of this soldier,' Aggie replied with devastating frankness. 'I have no desire to be a whore for the monkey people, so I leave with him and this master, who will speak for me.'

'I *can* speak for her,' I said in the same language. 'She is of good character.'

'How long have you known her?' Miss Susan asked, reverting to English.

'Only for the last couple of days,' I said. 'But Rawcliffe assures me—'

'Then how can you speak for her?' Miss Susan said. 'I'm sorry, but one cannot be too careful. These women, well, you know—'

I felt my patience fraying I hadn't wanted to come here in the first place, and now I was being catechized by this stupid old creature while the inoffensive Aggie was being gratuitously insulted. 'No, I *don't* know, Miss Willis,' I said. 'I think we should be moving on. I hope things go well for you. Good night.' I turned away from her but she caught my arm.

'Now I've offended you,' she said almost tearfully. 'I'm so sorry—I didn't mean to. My sister will be furious with me. She's the sensible one, you know. Please, Mr Stafford, do forgive me—and come in, if only for a moment. Sophie has something she *must* pass on to you.'

So what could I do? We followed her into a darkened doorway, with Aggie, well aware that she was a subject of contention, following us, bristling with resentment. Miss Susan led us through a clinically clean, tidy and very English kitchen, along a dark corridor and into a drawing-room that could have been transposed in its entirety from a Tunbridge Wells or Cheltenham of half a century earlier—a mixture of mahogany and chintz with a wild miscellany of porcelain vases and shepherdesses. There was huge gilt-framed lithograph of Queen Victoria over the mantelshelf, with smaller ones of all the reigning monarchs and their spouses since ranged on occasional tables and what-nots. Even the un-crowned Edward VIII was there, though I looked in vain for Mrs Simpson. Two big ornamental oil lamps lighted the place, which looked warm, comfortable and, improbably enough, safe.

'There,' said Miss Susan hospitably. 'Now do please make yourselves comfortable.' She waved us to chairs. 'What can I get you? Sherry? Gin? No, how stupid of me—whisky for men, of course.'

'We'd better not sit down,' I said. 'We're filthy.'

'Nonsense. Chair covers can be washed,' she trilled. You should see Sophie and me sometimes when we come in from the gardens. Mud from head to foot.'

Moving in a dream, I perched gingerly on the edge of a chair, and Raucous, looking exceeding ill at ease, followed suit, but Aggie stood glowering by the door. Susan bowed to her and murmured the formal phrase which translates roughly as 'Honour my unworthy abode by being seated,' which has to be complied with unless the one so invited wishes deliberately to give offence and so cause loss of face.

Aggie returned the bow and slid down and sat on the floor. Miss Susan went to a cabinet and produced decanters and glasses—and I forgave her the slight contretemps outside, because never did neat scotch taste so good.

'That's better,' she beamed. 'Sophie won't be long, then we'll see about getting you some supper.'

I sighed and stood up. The prospect of a civilized meal in these surroundings was enchanting, but this was rank folly. 'Miss Willis,' I said firmly, 'the Japs are less than half a mile away. They have a guardpost on the main road—'

'I know,' she said happily. 'Just where our private road leads off it. The young lieutenant posted them there to see that we weren't disturbed again. He has been *most* courteous. They're not *all* bad, you know. This one is a graduate of the University of Southern California. He's an engineer. He's promised to get our little electric generator working for us again, so the pumps can supply the sprinklers in the gardens, and we'll have proper lights in here once more.'

Raucous said hollowly. 'Gawd Almighty! Tell her, sir, for Christ's sake—'

'Mr Rawcliffe,' Miss Susan said severely. 'I've asked you before not to blaspheme.'

'Sorry, ma'am,' Raucous said. 'I don't want to scare you, but we've seen these bas—these *soldiers* in action, haven't we, sir? Shooting, bayoneting—and, well—you know—men, women, children—'

'Shut up, Rawcliffe,' I said. 'I'm afraid he's right, though, Miss Willis, you may have met the exception that proves the rule, but you can't trust them. They've been doing some terrible things—'

'I know,' she said regretfully. 'We've heard. Those poor nurses—and the wounded men in the Salesian Mission Hospital—all slaughtered. And the nurses—worse.'

'How have you heard?' I asked sharply.

'Oh, er—it must have been by telephone,' she said vaguely.

79

'Is it still working?'

'No, not recently, but you know how news travels out here.'

'Yes, by chattering tongues very often,' a voice said behind her, and her twin entered. 'Susan, you talk too much. These gentlemen are tired, and I'm sure hungry. Go and get supper started, there's a good girl.' She made a slight bow towards Aggie and said in Cantonese, 'You are welcome, and if you would help my sister prepare a meal for all of us we would be most grateful.' She waited until they had gone, then she came towards us, her hand outstretched. 'How do you do, Mr Stafford?' she said. 'I'm delighted you're safe—and this rascal too. Let me freshen your drinks.'

'*No*,' I said explosively. 'Miss Willis, I've been trying to make your sister understand—'

She eased our glasses out of our hands and topped them up generously.

'A little difficult at times, isn't it?' She smiled mischievously. 'Poor Susan, she means well, but she does run on so.' The likeness between them was remarkable, but there seemed a little more ballast to this one. They were both short, rotund and chubby as little robins, with dancing blue eyes with heavy bags beneath, small, rather pursey mouths, double chins, and grey hair pulled back severely into buns. I had, of course, seen them on many occasions and it had always worried me. They resembled somebody I thought I knew, but for the life of me I couldn't think exactly who. Now, as Miss Sophie stood in front of the fireplace beneath the lithograph, it fairly leapt at me. Of course! Queen Victoria. I wondered if this was the source of the Prince of Wales legend. The old girl's granddaughters, with a touch of their royal papa's spice? It certainly seemed to fit.

'You're very tired, aren't you?' she said sympathetically, and I realized that she had been speaking while I was woolgathering.

'You're right,' I agreed. 'But we can't stay here a moment longer, Miss Willis. It's far too dangerous—for you two, I

80

mean. If you have managed to get on the right side of an apparently decent Jap officer, that's all to the good; but if we were found here, nothing could save you.'

'They will not be here until morning,' she assured me. 'They come at eight o'clock each day, and you can be well on your way by then. They bring fresh milk, eggs, chickens and things, and the officer has given me his word that the farmer who supplies them is paid a proper price; then they collect their chrysanthemums—'

'Chrysanthemums—?'

'Of course. That's how it all started. Chrysanthemums are sacred to them. They have a shrine—Shinto or Buddhist or something—and they are delighted to get fresh blooms each day, and as luck would have it, it happened to be General Sakai's birthday a couple of days ago—that's their comman-der-in-chief—and they sent him an enormous sheaf of them—a sort of apple for the teacher,' she chuckled. 'Everybody is most happy about it, except perhaps the serge-ant, poor man. He got the most terrible thrashing, and lost his stripes.'

'I'd have liked to have seen that,' murmured Raucous wistfully. 'Any sergeant at all, but particularly a Nip one.'

'I'm sorry,' I said. 'I just don't follow.'

'The day they arrived,' she explained. 'They came tearing over the causeway shrieking "Banzai!"—a dozen of them led by the sergeant—and dashed straight across a bed of double Golden Empresses. It was heartbreaking. It was too much for Susan—the Empresses are her particular pets—and she screamed at them and smacked the sergeant's face, really hard. He started at her, his mouth open and his eyes nearly popping out of his head. Then he let our a roar of rage and brought his horrible rifle and bayonet thing up, and my heart stopped beating and I thought that was the end, but then the officer arrived and wanted to know what was going on, and I begged his pardon and kowtowed and said poor Susan was a little simple and so on, in Cantonese, a bit of Hakka and the rest pidgin. He answered in perfect English, with a slight American accent, and it finished up with his begging *our* pardon and turning on the wretched sergeant and ripping his shoulder straps off and beating him unmercifully with a garden spade. It was really sickening to watch.'

'Wouldn't have been for me,' Raucous said ecstatically. '*Cor!*'

'Anyhow, since then they haven't been able to do enough for us,' Miss Sophie concluded. 'I hope they are not moved from here, but if they are they have promised to pass the word on to whichever unit relieves them. Apparently that particular sergeant was not awfully popular with them.'

'*La dame aux chrysanthèmes*,' I laughed. 'Well, thank God that turned out all right, but we can't afford to put too much of a strain on it.'

'You can at least stay for a decent meal and a few hours' rest, and we can let you have some of the servants' clothing to replace yours. Low tide is at five tomorrow morning and it will still be dark, so you can cross dryshod to the mainland and I can direct you to a safe hiding-place until I can arrange for a guide to take you over the frontier.'

I stared at her. 'You can arrange for a *what?*' I asked, the breath taken right out of me.

'A guide,' she repeated calmly. 'You are our first customers. Now I'm telling you no more than that until you've eaten— and I've been able to talk to somebody to arrange things the other side. I've just about got enough juice left in my last battery for one more transmission. I do so hope little Lieutenant Shigatu can get the generator going again quickly. It's our only means of battery charging since the electricity has been cut off from the mainland.'

Chapter Three

1

Raucous tapped softly at the bathroom door as I lay luxuriating in almost scalding water right up to my ears. 'Aggie says she'll give you a massage if you like,' he said in a hoarse whisper. 'Lovely, it is. Takes the stiffness right out of you.'

'I think not,' I said regretfully. 'It might shock the old ladies.'

'Please yourself,' he said. 'There's a pile of clean clothes outside here. They said to leave your dirty ones there—and grub will be ready in half an hour.'

I thanked him and took up my train of thought again, although it was leading me nowhere except deeper into a dense maze of bewilderment. Who on earth were they, these two that were as much a part of the everyday local scene as the statue of their speculative ancestor outside the Hong Kong Legislative Chamber? Radio? Guides? Orders from some shadowy source? It was like something from the pages of a spy thriller. I had tried to prise more details from Miss Sophie, but she had shut me up, very sweetly, but very, very firmly.

'I'm so sorry, dear Mr Stafford,' she had said. 'I know it all sounds terribly absurd, but there you are. They have a term for it—"need to know", they call it. I am permitted to tell you no more than the absolute minimum necessary to get you to the next staging-post. It's not that they don't trust the "customers", but there's such a thing as torture. That which you do not know, you can't disclose, can you?'

'Yes, I understand,' I agreed. 'But "they"? You can tell me who "they" are, can't you? I *am* an officer—of a sort.'

She shook her head. 'No, I couldn't tell you,' she said. 'Even if I knew—and strictly speaking, I don't. We get our orders and we carry them out to the best of our ability. I'm afraid I must ask you to do the same. There are one or two further things I must tell you, but they can wait until you are more rested.' She rose and smiled at me like a kindly kindergarten mistress dismissing a lovable but rather dim pupil. 'That's all for now, Horhay.'

'Horhay?'

'The Portuguese pronunciation of "George", dear. Their Gs are sounded as H, the same as Spanish, you know. That's your code name until you are officially debriefed. Under no circumstances are you to divulge your real identity from now on to any unauthorized person. Horhay Pereira, Portuguese sailor from the tramp steamer *Estrelita*, mined in the Lamma Channel. You're trying to find your way to Macao. You're confused and stupefied—'

'You can say that again.'

'I'm not saying *you* are, you wicked man. I'm just giving you the outline of your cover story. I'll fill in the details when you've bathed and have eaten.'

It was a wonderful meal—with pork, chicken and fish predominating—cooked fast, as the best Chinese food always is—in an incredibly short time by Miss Susan and Aggie, who served it straight from the wok and then sat and shared it with us round the big scrubbed kitchen table. Miss Sophie didn't join us, but she pulled me into another session as the others went off to bed. She looked as tired as I felt.

'We are sending you north-west,' she told me.

'Chungking?' I asked.

She shrugged. 'That's a long way off—well over a thousand miles, and certainly beyond *our* little parish. It could be eventually, of course, but you may be switched half a dozen times before then, debriefed and renamed. What's your present one? Come on—*quick!*'

'Horhay Pereira,' I said.

'Good boy. It's a pity that you don't speak a little Portuguese—'

84

'I do. Not very grammatically, but enough to get by on. I was in charge of our Macao branch in my earlier days.'

She brightened. 'Splendid! I didn't know that, of course. Technically the Portuguese are neutral, and they should not be interfered with by the Japanese, but we can't put too much reliance on that. Well now, let's get on with it. Your ship was sunk two days before Christmas, eight miles out. As far as we know there were no survivors, but your story will be that you were washed ashore. You would have been in a state of deep shock, naturally. I hope and pray that you won't be caught and interrogated, but if you are you must say that you were terribly afraid. You saw some dead Europeans and that frightened you further. You started to walk in what you thought was the general direction of Macao and you fell in with this soldier and the woman—'

'What are *their* code names, by the way?'

'They haven't any. They are just what they appear to be, a simple British Tommy and his small-piecee sing-sing girl. You stayed together for company. You bought your clothes from second-hand stalls off Nathan Road—a few are still functioning—and you *don't*, for heaven's sake, say you stole them. Looting is a capital offence. Any questions so far?'

'A thousand,' I told her, 'but you'd probably tell me I didn't "need to know" the answers.'

'You can try me, if anything is really worrying you.'

'One thing is. How on earth did you know we were coming here? We didn't ourselves until we saw you from the top of Bird Hill.'

'We didn't know either. That's what threw us into such a tizzy when you arrived. We were told that "customers" would be guided here through "the proper channels". Ready-prepared cover stories, clothes, guides, food, money, are to be allotted at our discretion to special category personnel—taipans, big businessmen such as yourself, senior officers and officials, a few technicians and so on. We're strictly forbidden to help little people—ordinary soldiers and civilians. Oh, I know that sounds horrible, but it's not class distinction. It's just that persons who are vital to the

85

war effort must take priority. Our facilities are pitifully small, and we don't know at this stage whether the scheme is going to work. You will be watched very closely because you are guinea pigs. I have had permission to include Rawcliffe and the girl as a special case—simply because they happen to be with you, and it would be dangerous to let them go off on their own. But remember, *you* will be held responsible for them.'

'I see,' I said thoughtfully. 'One more question—'

'*No* more questions.' She shook her head decisively. 'I have an uncomfortable feeling that I've said too much already. I have a few for you, though.'

'Go ahead,' I invited her.

'One. From where did you escape? And when?'

'I didn't actually escape. I just went adrift on Christmas Eve. I had leave to go to my house—'

'"Annandale?'

'Correct—to get some clothes, passports and money for my wife and family who were being evacuated on the last ship—'

'Which one?' she asked sharply.

'The *K'aisang*, one of our own company's vessels—from Stanley.'

'I see.' She was silent for a few moments, the she said, 'Have you had any news of her? The ship, I mean?'

'Not a word. How could I? I've been completely out of touch since that night. My car had been shot up in the shelling from the mainland, and I was returning to my unit in an ambulance—'

'You have been wounded?'

'No, not a scratch. I was just hitching a lift. We were clobbered at Magazine Gap and the driver was killed—a chap called Swanley—'

'J.R.D. Swanley?'

'Yes, I think those were his initials. He was certainly *John* Swanley, Legal Department—'

'Thank you. Go on.' She was not writing anything down,

but I felt that she was committing everything I was telling her to memory.

'I think I must have been badly concussed, because I don't remember anything between about midnight and dawn next morning. I was coming down the Peak road towards town when I ran into a Jap patrol bayoneting an officer. I jumped over the edge of a drop and took cover in the undergrowth. They fired but didn't chase me. Rawcliffe was already hiding in this gully. We teamed up.'

'Good. Two. How did you cross to the mainland?'

'We were helped by a—' I began, then stopped.

'By?' she prompted.

'If you don't mind, I think I'd rather keep that to myself for the moment,' I said awkwardly. 'You see—well, it involves somebody else who is still there, and I promised . . .'

She nodded approvingly. 'Quite right. That's a cardinal rule in this business. If you have any doubts you keep your mouth shut.'

'Oh, I have no doubts—not of you, I mean,' I said hastily.

'You should have. I could quite easily be a Ma'tse looking for just that very link,' she said.

'Damn it all, Miss Willis,' I protested. 'I've known you both all my life. What I meant was—'

'You have known us as a pair of old fuddy-duddies who grow flowers in the New Territories,' she snapped. 'I'm trying to put you on your guard against sleepers. This whole wretched colony is stiff with them.'

'Sleepers?' I shook my head in bewilderment. This was becoming a Mad Hatter's tea-party.

'Sleepers—Russians, Germans and Portuguese in the main—often established here in business for so long that their backgrounds and covers have become impeccable.' She shrugged and spread her hands. 'Like ours, for instance. You see, the Japanese, Chinese or any other Oriental race can't do their own spying in Occidental circles, so they've got to recruit Europeans to do it for them. Some are loyal to one master through genuine political conviction, others, usually the really dangerous ones, are freelances working for whoever is paying them at the time, with very often the threat of blackmail and murder hanging over them.' She shuddered slightly. 'Bribery, corruption, fear,' she said. 'The very atmosphere is polluted by it. Double, treble, sometimes quadruple spies—one's own right hand often not knowing what the left is doing. I'm sorry, I must be depressing you.'

'Not at all,' I assured her. 'I'm most grateful to you for warning me about all this.'

'All part of the service.' She smiled. 'I hope everything works out well for you. I fear things are very *ad hoc* in these opening stages, but our temporary rapport with this Japanese outpost has been a real turn-up for the books, as the racing people say. To bed now, Mr Stafford. You have six hours before your have to move. You know your room. Oh, one last thing, and I feel it is insulting even to mention it, but I must. This place: under no circumstances whatsoever do you tell anybody you have been here—*anybody at all*—either under interrogation or even in an official debriefing by our own people, certainly not at any of the staging-posts. Those who need to know will be aware of the route you've come by before you arrive. They might ask you where you've been, but that will merely be to test how well you have been briefed. You will react in those cases just as you did when I questioned you about your crossing from the island. *Do* impress that on the others. Good night. Sleep well. I'll see you before you leave.'

'Good night, Miss Sophie,' I said, 'and thank you.' It sounded very inadequate, so I kissed her hand.

2

It was pitch dark when we left. There was a chill wind blowing in off the sea, but the rain had stopped. Miss Susan handed us each a coarse fisherman's creel bag in place of the army haversacks we had been carrying.

'There's two days' food in each,' she told me. 'Do be careful of your gun, Mr Stafford. If there's the slightest risk of your being taken, do your best to get rid of it in time.'

'This is Ting Li,' Miss Sophie said, indicating a figure waiting in the shadows outside. 'You are under his orders—*strictly*—until he hands you over at the next post. Godspeed, my dears. We shall pray for you.'

They kissed all three of us on the cheek, the door closed softly behind us and we followed the guide through the garden plots, over the wall and down on to the rocks beneath.

'Number One top vellee good tai-tai missee,' Aggie murmured to Raucous appreciatively, and the guide hissed, also in pidgin, 'No makee bloodee fool talk. No puttee foot topside sand. Stay on rock same like my.' Hakka, I decided. 'Me' is always 'my' to them. It made good sense. Even though the incoming tide would obliterate them, footprints were always things to be avoided.

He led us across the inlet, zigzagging and hopping from one stone outcrop to another until we reached the mainland, then we climbed a low cliff and plunged into dense undergrowth, moving uphill the whole time.

It was light by the time we reached the top of the first slope, half an hour later. I paused and looked back. The false crest below us hid the house, but we could see the road away to our left. Even at this early hour there was much activity on it—motor traffic, ox-carts and strings of basketladen coolies.

'Just like ants, the horrible little bastards,' Raucous growled.

'I was thinking the same thing,' I said. 'I hope it stays that way. Ants stick to one route and don't go exploring.'

'A pair of real old cautions, them two, ain't they?' he chuckled. 'I knew we'd do all right once we made our number with them.' And I seized on the opening he had made.

89

'There were no such people,' I said. 'No house, nothing. Put the whole incident right out of your mind. Never mention them again, even to me. We were in Kowloon when the fighting ended, and we just met up. I'm a sailor, a Portuguese. My English is not too good and you don't even know my name. You are a soldier who got separated from his unit. You had no orders so you used your savvee. You picked up your girl-friend and just got the hell out of it. You had an idea that the British were still holding out somewhere in the north, and you were making in that direction. You have not made any contacts, you haven't seen or spoken to anybody except Aggie and me since we left Kowloon. Have you got all that?'

'Yes, sure—but who do I tell it to?'

'Nobody, I hope. That's just in case we're unlucky enough to be picked up. One other thing: we weren't on Hong Kong Island when we met, or they'll want to know how we crossed, and we don't want to drop anybody in the crap, do we?' I added a clincher. 'And if we weren't on the island we couldn't have had anything to do with that dead Nip on the Peak, could we?'

'No, see what you mean,' he said. 'Okay. We better get all that lot over to Aggie now, hadn't we?'

'Yes. Leave that to me. I'll brief her in Chinese,' I told him. And I did, needing far fewer words to make it clear to her.

We continued the march right through the day, Ting Li, a little, shrivelled, parchment-yellow greybeard, moving ahead of us in a swift, mile-consuming half-trot that had the rest of us sweat-soaked and panting by mid-morning, halting for a brief few minutes every two hours which he seemed to judge to the second by a quick squint back over his shoulder at the sun, because I never saw him consult a watch.

'How far do we go today?' I asked him during one such all-too-short rest, and regretted it immediately, because he cocked a rheumy old eye at me and said, 'The length of a piece of rope. You should not sit when we stop or you will stiffen. It is something I have difficulty in making the children of my children's children understand when we are smuggling.'

The New Territories, through which we were moving, are roughly circular, a saucer with a twenty-four-mile, very mountainous circumference, with the southernmost point—'six o'clock' on an imagined clock face—resting on the outskirts of Kowloon, and the Shumchun River, which is the frontier with China proper, running round the northern segment from say ten o'clock to two. The bulk of the area is flat, rich arable land divided into pocket-handkerchief-sized farms which grow some of the finest rice and vegetables in the world, manured, perhaps unfortunately, by the excrement of Hong Kong's teeming millions, which is brought out in huge and rather beautiful blue-glazed urns. The main strategic road runs right round the circumference at the foot of the encircling hills, and two minor ones cross it diametrically. Taipo Inlet lies, again to use the clock analogy, at about four o'clock. We were travelling north, just below the crestline of the hills and so roughly parallel with the main road which lay beneath us to our left, at a distance which varied from half to one mile. The slopes were fairly thickly covered with undergrowth, so we were in little danger from distant observation provided we were careful in crossing bare patches—and the old man's language was sulphurous if we were not.

We came abreast of Fanling late in the afternoon. It lay beneath us in a pleasant green valley, its nucleus of barracks, police post and farmers' cooperative recently enlarged by the racecourse, golf-links and club-house of Hong Kong's European community, now submerged in a sea of tents, vehicle and gun parks and animal transport lines, with the Rising Sun floating over all. Far in the distance I could see the International Bridge at Lowu, which carried the Canton & Kowloon railway over the Shumchun. If the main road to Hong Kong resembled a line of ants, this was the anthill itself. I looked to the north, into China, and shuddered. Here the Bad Lands began, as barren and inhospitable as a lunar landscape. Lacking an adequate rainfall the further they lay from the coast, and also access to the Colony's abundant supplies of their disgusting but potent fertilizer, agriculture was practically non-existent apart from patches of starved earth round a few scattered, isolated villages. Only one industry thrived here: banditry. Anybody or anything that had to cross this five-hundred-mile belt was grist to the mills of the locals even in what passed for peacetime. What would it be like now that the Japs were here, I wondered?

There was a grunting chuckle behind me, and turning I saw Ting Li grinning maliciously. 'To Kat,' he said pointing into the distance. 'The place our masters in Hong Kong gave to the monkey people.'

'That is foolishness, old one,' I said. 'To Kat is a village seven or eight miles north of the frontier, in China itself. How could Hong Kong give it to anybody?'

The grin vanished. He cleared his throat and spat. 'The big ships have been coming for over a year,' he said, 'bringing the Japanese soldiers up the Canton River—and you let them pass through Hong Kong waters. You saluted them with flags and big guns, and played bands and they saluted you in return, and laughed up their sleeves.'

'That is the custom,' I told him loftily. 'There was peace then, and the Canton River is an international waterway. We could not stop them.'

'You did not want to stop them,' he sneered. 'They came to fight Chiang Kai-shek, they said. That is good, you smiled. Fight whom you wish as long as you stay off our doorstep and leave our moneybags alone. So they built up their forces at To Kat, until they were ready. Then they struck, like hawks above the farmyard—and you ran, like the chickens therein.' He spat again, and I was silent, because I had no answer. I was a businessman, I told myself. This war had been no affair of mine, not until I was pitchforked into it. But it was worrying, because this ignorant old peasant was perilously close to the truth, and he was obviously hostile to us, the British—and we, the three of us, were entirely in his hands. He seemed to read my thoughts.

'Have no fear,' he went on. 'I am no friend of the British, nor of the Japanese, who are even more evil. I am *their* man—they who took me and my family in from the famine area across the river and fed us, and paid me a fair wage for my labour in their flower gardens, and raised me above the level of a beast of burden—and gave me dignity. I have broken my rice bowl in their service and you are safe in my hands, while you do as I tell you. Eat now, then sleep. We don't move again until after dark.' He turned away abruptly and grunted something to Aggie, who started to unpack food from the bags.

3

The town below us was ablaze when I awoke, with vehicle headlights and campfires extending along the river bank in both directions as far as the eye could see.

'The bloody Nips don't seem to have heard about blackouts,' Raucous grumbled. 'Don't ever seem to sleep either. How the hell are we going to cross to the other side with that lot going on?'

'We'll just have to leave it to the guide,' I said.

'Miserable old sod. He seems to have a down on everybody, including himself. I tried to ask him just now, and got a load of old buck back off him—in Chink. He talks pidgin as good as me when it suits him.'

'I wouldn't bother if I were you. Silence is golden in his job.' I rose and stretched stiffly, and the old man came across to us.

'You follow my,' he said in pidgin, which he always spoke when he wanted to include Raucous. Properly used, it is a regular and very expressive language in its own right. 'Softlee-softlee—putchee feet down ploper fashion—no

93

makee clash-bang same like bull-cow last time. No makee talk. Plentee Jap makee hear. Savvee?'

'My savvee,' I confirmed.

'Maybe *you* savvee,' he said sourly. 'This man savvee? Sing-sing girl savvee?'

There was an angry rumble from Aggie. 'Sing-sing' is a euphemism which has no connection with vocal prowess.

'All people savvee ploper fashion,' I told him sharply. 'Whyfor you makee bad talk this way?'

'Come,' he growled, and set off down the slope, straight towards the town at first, which made me jittery, but after a time he swung away obliquely round a buttress which brought us out directly over a pitch-black void where there was no sign of life whatsoever on either side of the darkly silver thread that marked the river.

'That's more like it,' Raucous said approvingly. 'The old bugger had me worried for a bit. I thought he was going to take us slap up High Street.'

But *I* was worrying now, because the warmer air was rising from the valley, bringing with it a subtle redolence, faint at first, but unmistakable to anyone knowing the seamier end of Fanling. And the significance of it hit Raucous at the same time.

'Oh *no*,' he said in deep dismay. 'He's not going to take us through *that*?'

Ting Li understood, because I heard him laugh gratingly. 'Jap no likee,' he said. 'No go.'

'I no likee either,' Raucous howled. '*I* no go.'

'Maskee daiman,' said Ting Li, which is a very insulting term for bandit or soldier, synonymous in China. 'Go different way all li'—get bloodee head chop off. My? Don't give one goddam.'

'Look here,' Raucous ground, 'if you think I'm—'

'Shut up, Rawcliffe,' I ordered. 'You'll do as you're told or go off on your own. "My" don't give one goddam either.'

We had reached the edge of the flat area now, and my

stomach was turning over at the very thought of what lay before us, but, I determined, if this was the only way to cross in reasonable safety, so be it. Fortunately, however, fate and Ting Li relented at the very last moment.

'Follow in my footsteps closely, master,' he instructed me in Hakka. 'First you, then the woman, then the maskee daiman. He is clumsy, as are most men of low intelligence, and if he departs from the path by one half pace and falls in the unpleasantness, it will not incommode us others.'

'You mean we can cross dryshod?' I asked, very relieved.

'If one is careful,' he answered. 'There are stepping-stones known only to the opium smugglers, over which the police and customs guards would never risk following. The unpleasantness is deeper than one would think. To drown in it would mean a great loss of face." Hakkas love under-statement.

I prefer not to dwell on the crossing of the sewage farm. It called on the part of Ting Li for the precision of a ballet-master combined with that of a Guards drill-sergeant. He would go forward a few steps, counting softly back over his shoulder to me, 'yih, urh, san, sze, woo, luh—straight ahead as we now face. Halt! Now to the left—yih, urh, san—again forward, yih, urh, san. Now to the right—', and I would have to translate this back through Aggie to Raucous: 'one, two, three, four, five—' and so on. How in the name of heaven the old devil remembered the hideously complicated layout of those stones, which were completely invisible in the dark, I cannot hazard a guess. But remember them he did, because never once did our questing feet miss a step until after a crawling eternity we reached a raised earth embankment, and the river was the other side.

Ice-cold though the water was, I wanted desperately to immerse myself in it, but Ting Li wouldn't hear of it. He made us follow him downstream for a few hundred yards, remove our shoes and trousers and then wade after him across a waist-deep ford until we came to the opposite bank,

95

along which ran a dense barbed-wire entanglement. But even this didn't deter him. He led us unerringly to a fallen tree-trunk over which the wire passed, and here he halted us.

'This was the British wire, master,' he explained to me in a whisper. 'It is the Jap wire now, but they have not found our runway beneath this tree. It calls for great caution because they patrol the bank constantly. Tell the soldier to be extra careful, and, above all, to keep his big mouth closed.'

I bowdlerized this to Raucous, then we resumed our clothes and Ting Li pulled a few strands of wire aside at ground level and nudged me forward into the resultant passage it made. It was easy enough, with the smooth trunk to one side of me and the wire arching over the top of it making a tunnel some eighteen inches in diameter for the first few feet, but it narrowed considerably as it neared the top of the sloping bank, and I found myself badly snagged on the barbs. I stopped and tried painfully to free myself, and it *was* painful, because some of the rusty points had gone right through my clothes and were ripping into my skin. Somebody behind me was tapping my ankle impatiently to get a move on, so there was no time for finesse. I took a deep breath, gritted my teeth, thought of yogis on their beds of nails, and shoved forward and upward with might and main—and a jangling bedlam broke loose above me, and I saw, outlined against the night sky, rows upon rows of the brass bells that Chinese hang in their hundreds round their temples and josshouses, all dancing madly on the top strands of the wire and making a hellish din. I struggled frantically to push through and, of course, only made matters worse, because I got hooked up further and made even more noise, and somewhere to my left I heard a shout and saw a lantern jiggling quickly towards me.

There was nothing for it now but to lie quiet and hope desperately for the best, if I had been capable of any thought processes at all. The jingle-jangle ceased, but then I realized that the ankle-tapper behind me was Raucous, and he was inquiring petulantly what the bloody 'ell was going on? I kicked back at him to try and shut him up, which set up more racket from the bells.

'*Quiet*! Japs,' I hissed, and, fortunately, the message got through.

They came on slowly, holding the lantern over the wire and searching with painstaking thoroughness. 'I'm stuck,' I whispered miserably. 'Get back into the river, and you may have a chance.'

But it was too late for any of us to make a move by this time. The questing lamp arrived above my position, and halted, and somebody said in very bad Cantonese, 'What is this black thing under the wire?'

'A tree-trunk, corporal-san,' an obsequious voice answered. 'Shall I get my policemen to shift it?'

'Where exactly were the alarm bells ringing?' the other asked.

'Along this whole section, corporal-san. You see, all the wire is connected. Anything at all could set them off, a stray cow or a goat or even a dog—'

'More likely your filthy opium runners—'

'Oh no, corporal-san. They would be far too frightened to operate now that the captain-san has so cleverly placed the bells—'

'Shut your mouth, fool. You talk too much. Come.'

They moved on and I tried to control my trembling limbs. Behind me Raucous was almost sobbing with relief. I watched the lamp move along the bank until it disappeared round a distant bend, and then I decided on desperate measures.

'I'm going through, and to hell with the noise,' I told Raucous urgently. 'Push through after me and help me hold the wire clear for the others.'

I made it at the expense of a few more square inches of hide, with the bells keeping up a ghastly racket that I thought must have been audible for miles on that still air, but at least we managed it quickly, and first Aggie, then Ting Li wriggled through the archway Raucous and I were able to make for them. Far to the left I saw the lamp making its way back towards us, steadily in a straight line and without pausing to explore the wire, and a whistle was sounding shrilly.

Ting Li took charge again. 'Thissee way,' he grunted. 'Follow my.' He ran straight ahead into the darkness, away from the river, in a quick shambling run over flat ground that didn't offer a vestige of cover, then suddenly he turned to the left and led us back towards the approaching light, which had now been joined from somewhere by another—a more powerful electric one that threw a concentrated and horribly bright beam that was sweeping from side to side. I was certain that it was going to pick us up, and I hissed a warning at him, thinking that his old eyes had become confused.

'No talkee bloodee fool,' he snarled, keeping to pidgin. 'Do same like my. *Now*! No move!' And he froze in this tracks at the last possible moment, and the light swept over us and continued on. It was all beyond me. I just didn't understand. But Raucous did, and I heard him grunt approvingly.

'The old bugger knows his stuff,' he muttered. 'We're on ground that they've covered now.

'Why the devil didn't he tell us to drop flat?' I asked angrily.

'Because he's using his head, that's why,' Raucous said. 'Four of us dropping together would have sent up a cloud of dust on this ground. When you're going to get a light on you, you just freeze—you've got a chance of getting away with it then. It's movement that attracts attention.'

More lights were coming from both directions and they were converging on the spot where we had come through, and I could hear above the babel of unintelligible Japanese a voice yelling in Cantonese, 'This is the place! See, the wire is raised and there is torn cloth and blood here!'

Yet more lamps had arrived, and this section was as light as a ballroom, and, to make matters worse, someone was organizing things intelligently. 'A line!' he was shouting. 'Form a line, you fools, and work outward from the river.

98

The captain-san says men have passed this way. Fifty dollars to whoever sees them first, or some heads on poles in the morning if they haven't been taken.'

They were fanning out now into a long irregular line and coming straight towards us, like beaters in the wild pig shoots the Fanling Club used to lay on in happier days—with hurricane lanterns, pitch torches and powerful flashlights, moving fast over ground that they knew, avoiding potholes and outcroppings of rock which they could see and we couldn't, and, curiously, I was no longer terrified. If I felt any emotion at all it was anger at the sheer inevitability of capture. And it needn't have been. If this old fool had not turned back towards the hunters and had kept going we might conceivably have made it.

I said to Raucous, 'Split up and make a run for it.' And I was actually on the point of taking off myself, when Ting Li snapped, 'No makee move. Sit! My come back, one time—chop-chop!' and he took to his heels obliquely across the advancing line, yelling at the top of his voice in Hakka, 'The Lowu path, my brothers!—*the Lowu path*—two men! This way!' And like a flock of sheep following the bellwether, the whole line wheeled half left and streamed off after him in full cry. It was close—*very* close—because I swear the van of the line was within ten yards of us when they checked and turned.

'Gawd perishing blimey!' Raucous gulped. 'That's as close to the chop as I ever want to get. What was it he said?'

'He's drawn them off towards Lowu.'

'Good. Then we better get the hell out of it the other way.'

'No, he said to wait here until he came back.'

'Um. I hope he knows what he's doing.'

'He's doing all right at the moment,' I said. 'We'll wait.'

Ting Li was back in ten minutes. 'They run like village curs after a bitch on heat,' he said, 'but soon it may dawn on the fools that there is no bitch, so let us move quickly.'

I shall never cease to wonder at the way that old man found his bearings in pitch darkness. He didn't hesitate.

99

He just stood for a moment, stock still, head raised like a questing animal, sniffing the air, then he chose his direction, grunted to us, and started out at his tireless, mile-consuming half-trot. Hour after hour we jogged on without a single halt—down shallow slopes to dry watercourses, up the corresponding inclines the other side, which invariably seemed much steeper, through patches of scrub and round outcroppings of rock, always coming back on to the original line once open ground was gained again. It was Aggie who cracked first. She was following Raucous, who was hard on Ting Li's heels, and I was now bringing up the rear, and she just went down in a heap, and I stumbled over her. I called a halt then and Raucous spat curses at the old man.

'You one piecee bloodee fool,' he swore. 'This one piecee woman, not goddam coolie same like you. Why for you not stop one time, two time?'

'We are on open ground here, master,' Ting Li told me, ignoring Raucous. 'To Kat is before us, to the left. Soon we will see the Japanese campfires. When daylight comes there will be much activity here, and much danger. One more hour brings us to a place of safety.'

I bent over Aggie, listening to her quick, shallow breathing. 'The woman is exhausted,' I said. 'We must rest, Ting Li.'

'We cannot,' he said urgently. 'We must reach this place before the sun comes up.'

'What's the silly old bastard saying?' Raucous demanded. 'He wants a bloody good thumping.'

'Shut up!' I snapped at him. 'Come on, get her on to her feet. One each side of her. *Up*!'

She rallied a little then and we moved forward, but at a painfully slow pace, with the old man raging at us and threatening to go on alone, and when the first streaks of dawn lightened the sky I saw the reason for his anxiety. We were a bare two hundred yards from the Canton & Kowloon railway on the one hand, and slightly less than that from the dusty motor road on the other. They run parallel for practically the whole hundred miles between the two places,

100

raised above this bare corridor on continuous manmade embankments twelve feet high.

Raucous was looking from side to side in angry amazement. 'Damned old goat,' he said. 'He's got the whole of bloody China to choose from and he brings us to this lousy gully. That's the railway on the left, isn't it?'

'Yes,' I said, 'and the main road on the right.'

'And not enough cover for a bleeding squirrel in between. If a Nip patrol comes along either of them they'll have us stone cold. Why the hell couldn't he have taken us along one side or the other?'

'Flooded rice paddies on both sides,' I explained. 'You can't see them from here, but I recognize the country now. I thought we were miles to the east.'

'*Down!*' Ting Li snapped, and dropped flat.

We hit the ground almost at the same moment and lay straining our eyes up at each embankment in turn, and I took it to be a false alarm, but then we heard the noise of an engine faintly in the distance, and we saw the gleam of headlights far ahead of us. The vehicle came on slowly, the lights swinging from side to side and I thought it was being done in order to search the slopes of the embankment, but then I remembered the axle-breaking potholes along this stretch and realized that the driver was picking his way with care. We were in no danger from it in this half-light, but it would be a different matter later. It passed us, a big five-ton Honda truck, and Ting Li was calling urgently again.

'Come,' he said. 'There will be others, and also the coolie gangs will arrive to work on the railway. Another mile, just a mile. If we fail I will lose face, and I am an old man with little time left in which to regain it. Come, just one little mile.'

And he kept it up, pleading, cajoling and cursing us in turn for what must have been another three miles at least, because it was broad daylight when we reached a culvert under the railway, and there was now an almost unbroken stream of traffic both ways on the road, and once a troop train rumbled slowly past from the north.

101

We crawled into the bricklined burrow just as we reached the limit of human endurance. Aggie, although she was bravely trying to keep up, had become a dead weight between us, my feet were giving out on me, and Raucous was on the verge of collapse. The three of us fell in a heap and lay inert. I had a burning thirst, but I was too far gone even to fumble for the waterbottle in my tackle bag.

Ting Li, as exhausted as the rest of us but still on his feet, was chattering angrily. 'Do not sleep! Do you hear me? *Do not sleep*. If you do it will be your last. The railway coolies use this place to shelter when they take their midday meal. There is a reward for such people as you. They will hand you over to the Japs. Listen to me—*listen to me!*' He had a handful of Raucous's shirt and was shaking him.

'Piss off,' Raucous mumbled, and struck at him feebly.

The old man turned to me, pleading tearfully, 'Master, I speak the truth—*please*—there is danger here. Just a little way more and my task is completed— I can leave you in a place of safety and go back.'

Somehow or other we managed it, and we followed him through the culvert and out the other side into a field of sugarcane. Then he went off and left us.

Coolies were working on the railway line above us. We could not see them from where we lay, but we could hear the clinking of their picks and shovels, and once or twice women came down and filled water jars at the ditch, but other than that we were not distrubed until mid-morning, when the carts arrived.

There were ten of them, each drawn by a pair of lumbering, slate-grey water buffaloes, driven by a coolie who sat hunched on the broad shaft that ran between them, and they halted, nose to tail, along the dirt road not five yards from where we crouched, and then, joined by another dozen coolies, the drivers got down with billhooks and started to cut the cane, moving in a long line towards us. They worked fast, with two practised strokes per cane, topping and tailing them and tossing them back over their shoulders to be

102

gathered up in bundles and carried to the road. We looked at each other in dismay, because, although the cane extended far into the distance the other side of the carts, behind us it only ran back fifty yards or so before ending at the edge of the open paddy fields—and we were in much the same position as rabbits in a cornfield surrounded by mowers, with our cover diminishing momentarily. Then, when things were getting really desperate, Tung Li returned.

'Follow me, master,' he said. 'Heads down, and do not speak. You first, then the woman and then the soldier.' He pushed back to the path and walked unhurriedly to the road, and I translated quickly to the others and followed him. We passed the line of cane-cutters quite openly, and not a single one of them so much as glanced in our direction. Ting Li was talking rapidly without looking back at us.

'The third, fifth and seventh carts,' he said. 'In that order, counting from the front—one of you into each. They have left a space in the middle. Lie flat, and they will pile bundles of cane above you. It is a long journey but you must remain still until someone comes to release you. You will pass checkpoints but the carts will not be searched because you will be escorted.'

'Escorted?' I said, startled.

'One Jap soldier. It is a daily duty, and they fill his waterbottle with rum at the sugar mill—squeeze-pidgin. He rides on the first cart. He sleeps in the shade at the end of this road now.' He halted us with upraised hand, and I passed the instructions back to the others, then he went forward and looked up and down the road. 'Right,' he called softly. 'One at a time. Hurry, but do not run. Good joss go with you—Now!'

'But you?' I asked as I passed him. 'Don't you come with us?'

He shook his head. 'Go,' he said. 'You are expected.'

I darted out of the cover of the canebrake, the first two lines of which remained standing, feeling as naked as a snail suddenly bereft of its shell, and walked to the third cart. It

103

was about four feet wide and perhaps twice that in length, and bundles of cane had already been loaded into it, piled up on each side. I climbed over the tailboard and flattened myself on the bare planks in the middle, and almost immediately two coolies appeared from the other side and dumped a couple of bundles on top of me, then followed it with a few more until I thought I was going to be crushed and I hunched like a camel until I realized with relief that two bundles had been placed crosswise, head and tail, in order to take some of the weight, but even so it was claustrophobic to say the least. The damned things were exuding sap and it was dripping down on me and I could feel the stickiness of it penetrating my clothes. I have an obsessive hatred of stickiness—even as a child a trace of jam on the handle of a spoon would send me into screaming tantrums—so I felt extremely unhappy, because I knew that we would not move until the cool of the evening. Water buffaloes, stronger than bullocks though they are, have a rooted objection to pulling heavy loads in the full heat of the sun, and are apt to demonstrate it by sitting down, chewing the cud and flatly refusing to budge.

The long afternoon wore on. I found that I had a certain amount of vision through chinks between the bundles and I watched the cane-cutters coming back to the road with maddening leisureliness, squatting in the shade, smoking, gossiping, spitting, scratching themselves and, worst of all, drinking. I hated them all, severally and collectively, because I could do none of those things except, perhaps, to spit, and I was too parched even to do that, because, like a fool I had left my waterbottle in the tacklebag, and that was at my feet and I had no room to turn and reach it. These people were Kwangsis—inland peasants lacking the sturdiness of the Hakkas and the industry of the Cantonese, but possessed in full of the craftiness of both. How many of them besides those who had covered us knew we were in the carts, I wondered? And, more to the point, how many could be trusted? How had Ting Li managed to make contact, and presumably a bargain, with them in so short a time? And, above all, what was that bargain? Where were we being taken? And when? What was the next stage to be, if any—or were we to be left to our own resources now that the old man had gone? I gave it up in the end, and dropped off into a sweaty, sticky, twitching and supremely uneasy sleep.

The sound of shrill and discordant singing woke me, and a solitary Jap soldier staggered past the cart. He differed not by one hair from those I had previously seen. They all seemed to have been cast from a single mould—undersized and skinny, wearing sloppy uniforms much too large for them, ridiculous little peaked caps, and canvas shoes with the big toes separated like the thumbs of gloves. Their rifles, on which their ghastly two-feet long, saw-edged bayonets were invariably fixed, always seemed too big for them. Fifty per cent of them wore huge round spectacles, most were buck-toothed—and all were indescribably filthy. This specimen halted a few yard from the cart and puked, took a swallow from his waterbottle and staggered on towards the head of the column, yelling in broken Cantonese for the buffaloes to be yoked in.

The shadows were lengthening as we plodded creakingly down the dirt track, under a railway bridge and up on to the main road the other side. The overall pace I judged to have been about three miles an hour at the very most, and we rumbled along for two hours before coming to the first checkpoint.

There was the usual knife-rest barrier across the road with a straw matting shelter beside it, and a number of soldiers were sitting round a fire in front of it. One of them rose and came forward with a lantern as the head of the column halted. He called up into the darkness as he reached the first cart, and receiving no reply he raised the lantern above his head and called again. In the light of the fire I could see two others going towards the barrier, obviously with the intention of moving it and letting the carts through, but the man with the lantern called out sharply and halted them. He

105

climbed up the side of the cart and I could hear an angry outburst, and he came down again into the light, dragging our escorting warrior by one ankle. He landed flat on his back, and when he tried to struggle to his feet he received the butt of a rifle in his face. All the others were gathered round now and one of them had snatched the escort's waterbottle and uncorked it and was holding it upside down to demonstrate its emptiness. I couldn't understand a word of the babble that was going on, but its meaning was perfectly clear. A Jap waterbottle holds a couple of quarts, and these clients had been hoping for a drink of rum, but our fellow had evidently hogged the lot and was sleeping if off on top of the cane. He was certainly paying for it now, because they were laying into him with verve and enthusiasm. Some of them pulled the coolie down also and started to dismantle the load and I could hear him shrieking in Cantonese and pidgin that only the soldier had had any rum and they would be in trouble at the mill if they were short of any cane on arrival. But the soldiery was incensed and was now mindlessly intent on destruction, and in a matter of minutes the whole cargo of the first cart was strewn on the ground and they were dragging armfuls of it to the fire—and then they turned their attention to other carts and I lay helplessly waiting for them to uncover me, and in fact a couple of them had leapfrogged the second and were actually starting on mine when Providence in the shape of an NCO intervened. He came bounding from the shelter wielding a length of sugar cane two-handed like a flail, bringing it down across backs, necks and heads with impartiality, and he had good order and military discipline restored in two minutes flat—and I started to breathe again.

They reloaded the carts, and the escort climbed painfully back to his perch, helped in his ascent by a hefty boot up the backside from the NCO, and we rolled forward again.

We came to To Kat shortly after that. It's a river town that was once of some consequence as an entrepôt for the area south of Canton itself, but it had lost a lot of its importance

106

with the opening of the railway, and we had closed our small office here some years previously. But now it had a new lease of life, because it was ablaze with paper lanterns and naphtha flares. and along the riverfront every second house seemed to be doing business as a teahouse, drinkshop, or denoted by a red lamp in each case, a brothel, and the sidewalks were crowded with Jap troops.

We creaked on through the town, past another checkpoint where the scrutiny was perfunctory, and came out into quiet country again the other side, and by this time I was in very bad shape indeed, tortured by thirst, cramped, and generally as miserable as a fly in treacle. I tried in my desperation to claw my way out, prepared to accept whatever consequence might follow, but it was now quite beyond my strength, because the jolting of the springless cart over the rough road had settled the load down immovably.

We turned off the road after another couple of hours. I could tell this by the increased jolting, and I could hear the coolie urging the tired buffaloes on and telling them that their stables were near and that much rice straw and unlimited water awaited them, and I could feel their pace increasing.

4

A hand was gripping my upper arm and someone was whispering in Cantonese, 'Careful—there are Japanese soldiers here. Take this bundle of cane on your left shoulder.'

I made a hash of it because my knees gave way under me as I rolled to the ground, and I finished on my back under the cart. The whisperer hauled me out and got me to my feet and somehow I managed to pull myself together sufficiently to take the bundle he was lifting for me, but I was taking it on my right shoulder, and he hissed angrily, 'Your *left* shoulder—now follow me.'

'The others—?' I croaked.

'They are coming. Don't speak again. Just follow.'

He took up a bundle himself and I stumbled after him through the darkness towards a group of lights, and we tailed on to a line of shadowy figures similarly laden, and filed through a gate in a high palisade. There was a table the other side with a lamp on it, and somebody was counting the bundles as we went through, and I saw the point of carrying the cane on my left shoulder, because it was between me and the checker, shielding my face. There was a long open shed in front of us, with a clanking steam-engine and a series of open cauldrons taking up the rest of the space, and a huge fire cast an inferno-like glow over groups of sweating coolies feeding cane into a crusher. We dumped our bundles in a long heap and then my guide pulled me aside into the darkness and through a gap in a fence, and after a few minutes we were joined by Raucous, Aggie and another dark figure. Then there was more walking over rough ground until, after what seemed hours we came to the muddy, reedy bank of the main river. Someone whistled softly and a small boat slid out of the reeds. They hustled the three of us into it, and one of the guides took the oars while the other melted away into the darkness.

It was a tight squeeze and a rough passage because the current was running strongly and we shipped a lot of water before grounding under some overhanging bushes. We stepped out into kneedeep mud and squelched to dry land. The guide gave a perfect curlew call, and it was answered from some way ahead of us. Then, God help us, there was more walking—endlessly along a narrow path through thick undergrowth beside the river until, against the now lightening sky, I saw the pale outline of a pagoda. We climbed a crumbling wall and went in through a doorway.

Somebody said out of the darkness, 'Goodo. First bit over. You must be just about flaked.' In English, with an Australian accent.

Chapter Four

1

There was just enough light for me to make out a gilded statue of the Buddha in front of us, perhaps twice lifesize and seated cross-legged in the lotus position, but I didn't see the speaker until he moved out of its shadow, and then only dimly as a short, slight figure in coolie clothes. He came up to me and took my wrist and drew me round the statue into an alcove behind it and I was blinded by the beam of an electric torch that was shone right into my face. He said 'What's your name and where have you come from?' again in English, and, of course, I fell straight into it and gave my own and followed it with 'Hong Kong.'

'Quite a walk,' he said conversationally, and directed the beam downward and I saw a square trap in the stone floor. 'Follow me, and mind your head. The roof is rather low.'

He led the way down a flight of about a dozen steps, and when we got to the bottom I heard a hollow thump as the trap was closed behind us. There was a tunnel before us, and he was right about the roof because Raucous banged his head hard on it and swore savagely and I heard Aggie giggle nervously. Bent almost double, we shuffled along for quite some distance. The air was cold and dank and the leader's torch glinted back off runnels of moisture trickling down the walls. I was conscious of a muted roar which I thought at first was some trick my ears were playing on me, but it got louder as we progressed until it was positively overpowering, then, dopplerlike, it receded and finally died altogether. We came to another flight of steps at the end of the tunnel, leading upwards, and I was expecting a trap-door similar to the first, but they continued on and I realized that they were spiralling and I became completely disorientated, and Aggie's giggle now had a rising note of panic in it and Raucous was cracking childish jokes in pidgin in order to steady her. I started to count the steps and got to a hundred and ten, but I must have missed a good fifty before that.

To keep some slight grip on reality I tried to work out the route we had taken since leaving the mill; a couple of miles across flat wasteland, then about the same distance through flooded paddy—then the river—muddy banks—small Buddhist pagoda—down some steps—a long walk through a narrow tunnel. Now this climb up a winding stair, two or three hundred feet. Damn it, it didn't make sense. I suppose it was a combination of exhaustion, fear and general bewilderment, but I was finding it impossible to think coherently. All I was conscious of was the dark figure of the man ahead of me silhouetted against the glow of his own torch, and Raucous's muttered encouragement to Aggie behind me as we climbed.

I don't remember coming to the end of it. A voice in the darkness said, 'Would you like a meal—something to drink?' and I grunted that I only wanted to sleep. The torch flicked on to a pile of padded quilts. I flopped on to them and passed out.

2

I sat up and looked around. Diffused sunlight was coming through a bamboo chick blind and making a slatted pattern across a rough stone floor. I was warm, comfortable and relaxed and I wanted to stay that way, so I tried to go to sleep again, but the spell was broken now and I was thirsty, so I crawled out from under the quilts and stood up. I was in a small, irregularly shaped room, and the light came through an embrasure in the wall. I crossed to it and looked out and saw only brilliant blue sky with a kitehawk poised motionless

on outstretched pinions a few feet away. I parted the slats
and looked downward and saw the river far below running
swiftly through a narrow gorge. The opposite bank appeared
to be a couple of hundred yards away. It was thickly wooded
along the actual verge, but behind a belt of undergrowth and
twisted casuarina trees a bare cliff rose sharply almost up to
the height at which I was standing, so that the effect was that
of looking out of a window in a tall building at other, not
quite so high buildings across a street. I squinted sideways
up and down the 'street' and made out a small white pagoda
on a spit of land jutting out from the opposite bank, and
memory came flooding back.

A voice behind me said in English, 'Recognize the spot?'

I turned and saw a Chinese who had just entered through
another bamboo curtain which screened an archway in the
rear wall. I said, 'We're somewhere on the Pearl River,
aren't we?'

'That's right.' He nodded. 'Looks quite peaceful from up
here, doesn't it? It's a fair bugger though when there's a bit of
a flood on, as you probably know. There's more wrecks along
this few mile stretch than there are on the Great Barrier
Reef.' He put out his hand. 'How are you, Sir Vincent? Sorry
about the stepmother's welcome when you arrived, but one
has to be certain. You'll be wanting a bath and some breakfast, I reckon. In that order, or would you rather reverse it?'

'Bath first, if I may,' I said, shaking hands. 'Of course,
you're Professor Kwan, aren't you?'

He smirked. 'Promotion yet,' he said. 'I don't get the
Chair until old Christie quits. You didn't run into him back
there by any chance, did you?'

'I'm afraid not. Things were a little confused when I left,' I
answered.

'Beats me how you made it at all. Which way did you
actually come out? Before you met up with the old girls?'

'Straight up Nathan Road, at night—' and only then did
warning bells start to ring. 'Which old girls do you mean?
We only have this woman with us.'

111

'Good.' He said, smiling. 'But you've got to watch it the whole time, especially when you're tuckered out on arrival. You gave your proper name when I asked you. You should have said—what?'

'Oh hell,' I said. 'Sorry—*Horhay*.'

'That's better— but too late now, I'm afraid. I've got your name *and* your code name. If I were working for the opposition I'd have you compomised and I'd be putting the heat on to find out who gave you the code name, and why. Ordinary escapers and evaders don't have them. No need.'

'I assure you that that's all I am,' I told him. 'A very ordinary escaper.'

'*Evader*,' he corrected. 'An escaper is one who has been in enemy hands and has broken out. An evader hasn't been captured.'

'A rose by any other name,' I said. 'I can't see that it matters much.' I was starting to prickle with annoyance and he sensed it immediately.

'My bloody oath it matters,' he said decisively. 'They have a sneaking admiration for a bloke who's trying to make it back to fight again, but one who has surrendered and then makes a run for it is outside bushido—that's their military code of chivalry— and is executed on recapture. Just remember that.' He strode back to the door, palpably angry.

'Sorry,' I said again. 'I'll remember it. That goes for the other two also. Neither of them has been in enemy hands. Er—how are they, by the way?'

'They're being looked after,' he said shortly. 'They shouldn't be here at all. They constitute a nuisance.'

Something snapped. 'If that's the way you feel,' I told him, 'we'll go *now*. They happen to be friends of mine.'

'You can't go *now*,' he mimicked. 'You're in the pipeline and you'll be sent forward at the proper time.'

I took a deep breath and screwed down hard on the safety-valve. 'I don't know who or what you are, Mr Kwan, other than a fairly junior member of the teaching staff of Hong Kong University, but you have no authority over me

112

whatsoever and I shall go when the hell I please, and what is more—' But he cut me short in full spate.

'I'll tell you who I am, *Second-lieutenant* Stafford,' he said. 'I am *Major* Percy Chung Kwan, Australian Imperial Forces, attached to Hong Kong Command, and as such, your superior officer. That good enough for you, or do you want to look it up in the bloody Army List?'

The choler went out of me like the air from a punctured pneumatic cushion when sat upon heavily, but I made a pathetic attempt to hold on to the tattered remnants of my dignity.

'That's good enough for the moment, sir,' I conceded lamely. 'I'll take a rain-check on the Army List, however.'

'I haven't got a copy,' he said, and grinned disarmingly 'It's dinkum, though. Sorry about all this. Nothing personal against the soldier and his bint. I should have said problem rather than nuisance. But that's what they are. They know too much to turn them loose, and I don't like the idea of liquidating them.'

'*Liquidating* them?' I stared at him in horror. 'You're surely not serious, are you?'

He didn't answer, because at that moment another Chinese looked through the door and make a sign to him. 'I'm afraid I'm going to be busy for the next hour or so,' Kwan said to me. 'I'll send some hot water and grub in to you in the meantime.'

I felt a rising tide of panic within me. 'Look here,' I shouted. 'I want to see those people—now—this instant. They're under my command. I'm answerable for them—'

'Don't worry,' he said over his shoulder. 'Nothing's going to happen to them—yet. I give you my word on that.' He went through the bamboo curtain and I tried to follow him, but there was a solid wooden door the other side and it was slammed in my face just as I reached it. I pounded on it with both fists, yelling threats after him futilely, then I leant against the wall, gasping and feeling sick. My eyes fell on my tacklebag on the floor near the pile of quilts. I pounced on it

113

and shook the contents out. Razor, soap, toothbrush and two cans of beansprouts were still there, but not the pistol.

I sat down and tried to marshal my thoughts into some sort of order. Who was this man? I had met him once only, shortly after his arrival in the Colony a year or so ago. Professor? Lecturer? Reader? in Chinese archaeology or some such thing. There had been lots of jokes about him. Anything but academic—pronounced Australian accent. Melbourne University and Rhodes Scholarship to Oxford, somebody had told me. Major in the Australian army? First I'd heard of that—and I only had his word for it anyhow. Hush-hush job—Intelligence, if he was telling the truth. But was he? He could just as easily be working for the other side. What had I told him? Only my name—but he knew who I was in any case—even to my brand new and in present circumstances rather absurd title. Nobody was supposed to know about that until the Honours List was published on New Year's Day—Good God! That would be today, wouldn't it? Or tomorrow? Or yesterday? I had lost count. Sir Vincent Stafford, Knight Commander of the British Empire. What absolute damned nonsense. Old Ross, my grandfather had been the first; Order of the Bath in his case. It had meant something in those days, no doubt. Just routine now because of the college we'd endowed and maintained at the university. Missed my father, who was probably the only one of the line who had done anything to deserve it—

I jumped to my feet as the door opened. Two coolies came in with a collapsible bath and a couple of cans of hot water. I tried to push past them through the door but there were two more outside, both with rifles and fixed bayonets. They didn't actually poke them at my belly, but they didn't salute either. They just looked at me very steadily. I went back.

Bathing, shaving and climbing into the clean clothes they had left kept my mind from squirreling for the next half-hour, and then they came back with hot food in covered bowls—rice, pork and noodles—good solid fare well cooked, but it did nothing to cheer me. My thoughts kept going back to the others. *Liquidate* them? In God's name why? Well, he

114

had answered that himself, hadn't he? 'They knew too much,' he had said. But what did they know? Two old ladies who were helping evaders? The mill? And now this place? Yes, I suppose that if they were captured by the enemy and put to the question they might break and talk. But wouldn't *I*? Wouldn't *anybody*? Including this wretched little Melbourne Chink. So where do we go from there? Do we liquidate anybody who may have information likely to be of use to the Japanese—just in case they are captured? What absolute rot.

But I had a chilling feeling that he meant just that, in which case, I reflected bleakly, I was a sure candidate for liquidation also. So what was the purpose of this pipeline, as he called it? An underground railway along which to pass individuals who might conceivably be useful to the war effort, obviously—with Major Kwan at a strategic point sorting the wheat from the chaff, the former being graciously permitted to proceed to the next station, and no doubt another Major Kwan, the latter—liquidated?

I gave it up through sheer weariness after a time and went and looked out through the embrasure. It's remarkable what a difference the angle of the sun can make to a landscape. It was high overhead now, casting its light straight down and dispelling the gloom at the bottom of the gorge for the first time. The stream coursing through it was wild and tur-bulent, but much narrower than I had thought at first sight. This surely could not be the Pearl River, which was nearly a mile wide all the way up to Canton even in the dry season, except—*of course*—except for the Boque, as we called it nowadays, the Boca Tigre, the Mouth of the Tiger! Then this land directly opposite was Kwai-ossu Island, a cigar-shaped break-off from the main eastern bank about seven miles long and a few hundred yards wide, rising to some five hundred feet and hiding the main river the other side. I was able now to pinpoint my location, and although I could see no material advantage in the discovery at this moment, for some reason it cheered me enormously.

Let me explain. The Pearl is not a river in its own right. It

115

is the confluence and estuary of several others, wide and shallow and broken by treacherous sandbanks but with a navigable channel for its entire eighty miles from the sea at Hong Kong up to Canton—always provided that one has a pilot who knows his job. All ships, large and small, have to keep to this channel, but very small junks and sampans can save a lot of distance, if they have the skill and nerve, by shooting the rapids in the Boque when travelling south. Nothing at all, however, could buck the current when going the other way. This was being demonstrated even as I looked, because a group of sampans came through, nose to tail, whirling along through white water like leaves in a flooded gutter. I was conscious in retrospect of a flutter at the base of my belly, because that was the way we had come last night, with the current, from the north—but we had landed on the right-hand bank. Then that must be the pagoda that I could see opposite, in which case the long passage we had traversed had come *under the stream*. Impossible. And yet . . . No, I was tired and confused. I must surely have been mistaken. And yet—that noise . . .?

I spun round as a hand touched me on the shoulder. 'Sorry,' said Kwan. 'I didn't mean to startle you. I've brought you a visitor,' and past him I saw Raucous standing in the doorway, shaven and spruce in clean clothes.

'Everything all right, Private Rawcliffe?' I asked him. I tried to sound curt and military, but there was a tremor of relief in my voice.

'Everything OK, sir,' he answered, playing it back incisively, but I thought he was looking a trifle relieved also. 'Any orders, sir?'

'Not at the moment,' I told him. 'How is Aggie?'

'Happy as a sandboy, sir. She's dhobi-ing our clothes. This gentleman has lent us these in the meantime.'

'Good,' I said, and ran out of steam. 'Er—well—er—carry on, Rawcliffe.'

'Very good, sir.' He tried unsuccessfully to click his bare heels, turned and went out.

Kwan said, 'A very good type, that chap—and so is the girl.'

'Certainly not for liquidating,' I said, and he laughed shortly.

'I never said they were. I said I wouldn't like to *have* to liquidate them.'

'It struck me as a very peculiar thing to *think* of, let alone say.'

'Some pretty peculiar things happen in wartime, Sir Vincent,' he answered.

'I wish you'd drop that,' I said irritably. 'I haven't assumed the title yet, and I don't suppose I ever will now.'

'Actually you have,' he told me. 'It's been gazetted in the London papers.'

'How do you know that?' I demanded.

'It came over the radio,' he said. 'The Japs already had you on their VIP list. Now there's a double reward for turning you in, so we'll have to be quadruply careful.'

'What possible use could I be to them?' I asked impatiently.

'Quite a lot, under certain circumstances,' he said. 'But to come back to the liquidation matter. I'm sorry if it shocked or annoyed you, but—well, let me try and explain. Have you ever heard of MI9?'

I shook my head.

'It's the branch of Military Intelligence that deals with escapers and evaders. It started very small, in Europe, now it's quite big business—shot down aircrew mainly. It takes six months and costs twenty thousand pounds to train a pilot or navigator, so getting them back is a matter of prime importance.'

'Not much scope for them out here,' I said bitterly. 'Our chaps were shot out of the sky in the first twenty-four hours, all six of them, in obsolete stringbags.'

'Regrettable, no doubt, but just skip the bitching, will you, until I've finished.' The rasp had come back into his voice. I looked at him curiously. It is said that Chinese faces are inscrutable to Europeans, but I have never been a subscriber to that view. There was a quality of command about this man that was unmistakable, and it stilled the rejoinder I was about to shoot at him.

'The escape routes, ratlines as they are sometimes called, run all over the Continent, from Germany itself across the occupied countries to a variety of outlets, some over the Pyrenees to neutral but unfriendly Spain, some into Switzerland, others across the Baltic to Sweden—to pick-up points on the French coast—to *ad hoc* temporary landing grounds. The escapers and evaders—let's call them "customers"—travel, sometimes singly, sometimes in parties, in plain clothes and on forged papers, from one safe house to the next, guided by couriers. The couriers come in various shapes and sizes. Some of them, men and women, are patriots pure and simple; let's call these the "amateurs", motivated solely by love of their respective countries. Others, mostly Communists, do it for political reasons, so we'll call them that—the "politicals". Then, lastly, we have the "professionals"—smugglers, pimps, prostitutes and various other types of petty criminal, who do it for reward on a *per capita* basis. Oh, I assure you, there's big money in it. The going rate for a pilot on the hoof safely landed into Allied hands is anything up to eight thousand pounds at the present moment. And the customers are not only airmen—there have been soldiers, officers and other ranks, and a couple of naval types who have made home runs. The biggest prize to date, though, was a Norwegian scientist, a high-powered explosives expert, who was wafted out of a laboratory in the Ruhr and delivered to London, at a cost of twenty-five thousand pounds. That was a purely professional job, of course. Have you got the drift of what I'm getting at?'

'More or less,' I said, 'though I'm afraid I can't see how any of it applies out here.'

'You'd be surprised at how closely conditions in both theatres run parallel,' he answered. 'Take the couriers, for instance. The amateurs here hate the Japs every bit as much as their European equivalents do the Germans, but they labour under the same disability: loads of patriotism but often little skill. The politicals? Equally anti-Jap but that doesn't of necessity make then pro-West. The Party comes first, last and always with Mao Tse-tung's boys, and devil take any customer in their hands if interests ever clash. The professionals?' He shrugged. 'The most efficient of the lot. The Triad, secret criminal societies, are tailormade for the job, but they are in it for the profit alone, and they would sell us out to the Opposition for the difference of one half-dollar in the take.'

'All of that is quite feasible,' I said, 'but isn't it a bit early to be so certain about the parallels? The war—*our* war—is only a few weeks old yet.'

'*Our* war started right back in 1937, when Japan invaded Mongolia,' he said.

'Hadn't we better define "our"? I meant Britain and now America on the one side, Japan on the other.'

' "Our" doesn't hold any complications for me, nationally or politically,' he said. 'I am an Australian subject, born, bred and largely educated there—which means British. Politics don't concern me, and although I am ethnically Chinese, only their archeology really interests me. You speak better Cantonese than I, and I understand that your Mandarin is impeccable. I only have a few polite phrases.'

'How do you know all this?'

'It was my job to know,' he said simply. 'But let me continue. I'm sorry to bore you—'

'You're not doing that,' I assured him. 'Only puzzling me.'

'Bear with me a little longer. There are some things you must know. To revert to couriers. All three categories have one thing in common. If taken by the opposite side they will talk—eventually. How long they hold out varies with the individual, but talk they will in the end. That is the reason why we must have inbuilt safeguards—the "need-to-know" syndrome, in other words.'

119

'I can quite see that,' I said. 'But isn't it carried to absurd lengths at times? I mean, you obviously knew who and what I was before I even arrived here, yet you put me through the third degree. Surely that wasn't necessary?'

'*Absolutely* necessary. It's when exceptions are made, short cuts taken and *bona fides* accepted without verification, that catastrophes result,' he said emphatically. 'Let me give you an example. One of the best-organized ratlines in the European theatre ran from Schubin, a town in German-occupied Poland, right across the Continent to Perpignan on the Franco/Spanish border, a thousand miles of it by road and rail, forest paths and canals, with over forty safe houses, each with a couple of alternatives in case any one of them ever came under suspicion. Each courier was "*en secteur-securement*", which meant that not one of them knew anything except the point where he or she had to pick up their customers, and the point where they had to hand them over, and these varied with each party. That meant if a courier was taken he could only blow *that* section of the line however much they tortured him—and that section could be "taken out", bypassed and replaced with another, so that the rest remained secure. Oh yes, a splendid line—the most secure of the lot. They got a hundred and thirty-seven customers out the whole way back to England before they were blown.'

'*How* were they blown?' I asked, interested now in spite of myself.

'By somebody who should have known better departing from the rules in one tiny detail,' he said. 'This line was for British personnel only. As you probably know, they have Poles, Czechs, French, Norwegians and even Russians in the RAF now, all of whom were forbidden customers for the simple reason that it was not always possible to vet them. You see, the system works this way; chaps would get out through the wire of different camps with the name and address of a contact which would be given to them by the camp escape officer. This contact, if he was satisfied, would put them in touch with one or other of the ratlines. They would then be lodged under cover until they had been six-pointed. Six-pointed means that all their service particulars—name, rank, number, age, physical details, body marks, next of kin, mother's maiden name, birthplace, etcetera, etcetera, had been checked by secret wireless with London. The purpose of all this is to guard against the enemy slipping a mole into the burrow, an agent who could travel the whole way and blow everything at the end of it.'

'But surely the others, the genuine people, would know if a stranger was put in among them?' I said.

He shook his head. 'Not of necessity. Parties of up to twelve, many from different camps—there might quite likely be an evader or two among them who had not been in a camp at all, and the first time they would all meet up together would be at the first safe house, at night, all very hush-hush. The mole would be a perfect English speaker, complete in many cases with a provincial accent and always with authentic RAF slang. Look, this is not supposition I'm giving you. It has happened—more than once—although it hasn't always been on the debit side. One or two moles have slipped up and aroused suspicions during the journey.'

'What happened then?' I asked.

'The word you took exception to—liquidated—damned fast. What else? But I was explaining what six-pointing meant. Service particulars in excess of name, rank and number could be collected by the enemy in the camps, by moles and by interrogation officers—from scraps of overheard conversation. That's not difficult for Intelligence-trained operators. To make a cast-iron certainty of a man's identity you need to be able to ask him a few questions that only he is likely to be able to answer in the ordinary course of events, so, from a serially numbered list of a hundred prepared by MI9, eight are shot at him at random. If he can't score a minimum of six correct and two "don't knows", he's in trouble. If he tries to bluff and gives wildly incorrect answers, he's in *dead* trouble—literally.'

121

'What sort of questions are they?'

'Very simple ones, like: what is your mother's maiden name? How many sisters has she? Married or single? If the former, what are their names now? How many sisters have *you*, the customer? Married names? Brothers? Ages? Occupations? Where were you at school in your thirteenth year? Name two of the masters there at that time. Name of your vicar? Where was your father educated? Your mother-in-law's christian name?'

'Do you mean to tell me that they send a bulky questionnaire like that over a secret radio, and that the War Office then chases round checking on it?' I said incredulously.

'No bother at all. All that the escape organization sends is the customer's service number followed by the question numbers. The questions are all of a type that can be verified by a telephone call to the customer's next of kin, or the vicar or his old schoolmaster, just as I've explained. But to revert to this particular case: the whole line was blown, over two hundred couriers and safe house-keepers were arrested, tortured and executed by the Gestapo, and a mixed bag of customers were shoved back behind the wire, all because somebody departed from the rules in one small particular. There was an Australian flight-sergeant in this party, a tail gunner in a Lancaster bomber. The MI9 check wasn't established in Australia at that time, so he should have been left out until he could have been vertified by a longer and rather more cumbersome method. But the rest of his crew, all of whom had been cleared, begged of the controller to let him stay—damn it all, they knew him, didn't they? Decent little bloke from Adelaide who happened to be in London when war broke out and had enlisted in the RAF without a moment's hesitation—volunteered for aircrew and had flown on three missions before being shot down. His skipper got really nasty about it. "If he doesn't come with us you can shove it," he said, "we'll find our own way back," and so on.

So they let him through, which was a pity, because although his old man was a naturalized Australian and Junior had been born and gone to school out there, they were still as German as sauerkraut under the skin.'

'You mean he was a spy?' I said.

'Exactly. A highly specialized one—a sleeper, which means he was "inert until activated" in Intelligence jargon. He would have been in possession of a foolproof set of papers and a genuine Australian passport at the time of his enlistment, with orders to do exactly nothing in the spying line until instructed. All he had to do was make himself known to the German interrogating officer at his first camp and he was under orders from then on.'

'How was he unmasked?'

'Well, the fact that every safe house on that line was busted simultaneously told us that it was an inside job which could only have been pulled by somebody who had been the whole way along it, so we *really* put every member of that party under the microscope and found the wild joker. He went back into the bag with the rest, completely unsuspected, as he thought, and the Huns were preparing to use him again—so we let them—and dealt with him after his party had got out the second time.'

'How?' I couldn't forbear to ask.

He looked at me expressionlessly. 'Just dealt with him,' he repeated. 'There's no need to go into details. The point I'm trying to make is the constant, never slackening need for one hundred per cent security. One cannot afford to take the slightest chance in this business—ever.'

'How do I stand now?' I asked him half jocularly.

'You're clear with me,' he answered seriously. 'But I'm not the only one concerned. There are still a few doubts to be settled before you go forward.' Which completely vitiated the jocularity.

'Look here, Kwan,' I said through clenched teeth. 'This has gone far enough. I accept the necessity for caution in

123

whatever you are doing, but I'm damned if I'm going to be insulted. You know perfectly well who I am, so why keep up this cloak and dagger nonsense?'

'*I* know who you are,' he agreed. 'So do the others—'

'*What* others?' I scoffed. 'Have you got a balloting committee hidden backstage?'

'Let me finish,' he said sharply. 'Of course we know who you are, but this is not a question of identity. It's *suitability* we're trying to determine.'

'Suitability for what?'

'Certain duties you might be asked to undertake.'

'Asked?'

'Asked. It's not the sort of job you'd be ordered into. You'd have the option of turning it down.'

'Well, suppose you tell me what it is, without all this bugaboo?'

'Isn't that what I'm trying to do? Shut up, for Christ's sake, Stafford, will you, and let me get on with it.'

I simmered down a little, and nodded.

'As you've probably guessed,' he went on, 'this is a rat-line—Hong Kong to Chungking, with two tributaries—feeder lines from Macao and Shanghai. I am in overall command, with two assistants to the north, either one of whom should be able to pinch-hit for me here when I have to be elsewhere. This is where we depart from the European system; each one of us has of necessity to know the whole line. With me so far?'

I nodded again.

'Good. Well, there's a break in the line—at Kweilin—Communist territory. Our man there has disappeared, and three safe houses have been blown. We want someone to set up a bypass round the break. Personally I think you're the man for the job. How would you feel about it?'

I blinked. 'That's a swift one,' I said. 'But if you really think I could be of use, well, you've only to tell me . . .' I tailed off.

'That's just the point. As I've already said, we wouldn't *tell* you to take it on,' he said.

'The one thing I've learned in my very short military service,' I told him, 'is never to volunteer for anything at all. Suppose you give me an order?'

He shook his head firmly. 'Sorry. Rule of the house. Take an hour or so to think it over if you wish.'

'What happens if I say no?'

'You just go forward as a passenger, on a need-to-know footing, as soon as we've been able to make some sort of an *ad hoc* arrangement round the break. On the other hand, if you care to take it on I'll brief you on the whole route.'

'If the answer's yes, what about Rawcliffe and the girl?'

'That would be entirely up to you. If you wanted them with you, I'd raise no objection.'

That settled it as far as I was concerned. 'The answer is yes,' I said, and started to regret the words even as I uttered them.

He didn't fall on my neck or wring my hand. He merely shrugged and said that he hoped I'd made the right decision, and not to blame him if I hadn't, but there was a perceptible easing of the atmosphere immediately.

'Right,' he said briskly. 'I'll start to give you the dope now. Do you know Kweilin?'

'Fairly well,' I answered. 'We have—*had* I suppose I should say now—an office and a godown there. Cinnamon mostly.'

'It's in the clear at present,' he said. 'The Japs haven't occupied it yet, and I don't think they are going to try until they have consolidated things rather more down at this end.'

'So there's no danger there at the moment?' I said, my spirits rising slightly.

'My bloody oath there is,' he said emphatically. 'The boss cocky there is a cove called General Tai Li, number two to Chiang Kai-shek, and more anti-British than the Japs themselves.'

"Nonsense. Chiang is firmly on our side.'

'For the time being, because we're feeding him supplies from India, over the Hump, and the Americans have given him an air force—the Flying Tigers, under Claire Chennault. If we've got to cut back on help to him, he's not going to love us the least little bit. Anyhow, Chiang doesn't come into it at the moment. It's his local commander-in-chief we're talking about, Tai Li—'

'I think he came to Hong Kong fairly recently,' I said. 'Yes, that's right—I remember now. He came for lease-lend munitions—'

'You're damn right he did,' Kwan said. 'And we not only turned him down on the munitions, but we stuck a *persona non grata* ticket on him and gave him the bum's rush out of the Colony because he was pulling a Mafia racket on some of the richer Chinese citizenry—"pay up, you bastards, or risk getting the chop when we've chased the British into the sea". He was supposed to be doing it on Chiang's behalf, though the Generalissimo looked shocked and disowned him, but didn't fire him either; just demoted him from Chungking to Kweilin. Tai Li lost a lot of face over it, and I don't need to tell you what that means to a Chinaman. He hated our guts before. He's rabid now.'

'Is it he who has blown—if that's the word—your safe house there?' I asked.

'God, I hope not,' Kwan said fervently. 'That could possibly mean a lead back to here—and this is the citadel for the whole line. You know where we are, of course?'

'I do now, although I didn't recognize it immediately. This is the Boque, isn't it?'

'That's right. The place itself could hardly be more secure, but the damned fools who set it up originally did the one thing that should be avoided at all costs. They made it a dual purpose station—escapers and agents—as mixable as oil and water.'

'Why should they be unmixable? They're all on our side, surely?'

'Two-way traffic,' he explained, shaking his head.

'Escapers and evaders going north, agents and saboteurs travelling south—not a good thing. Customers in a pipeline know where they've been, but they should never know where they are going. If the opposition knocks off a safe house with both categories in residence at any one time, they've got leads both ways, haven't they?'

'I suppose so,' I said, but I must have sounded doubtful, because he took a deep breath and expounded further.

'An evader going north arrives here in darkness, either downriver by boat, or on foot over the hills. Whichever way it is, he's pretty well bound to be knackered and he wouldn't be noticing much. He leaves in darkness also—downriver, which is in itself confusing because he's going back the way he came. By the time he's been swung round on to the northern route again he doesn't know whether it's Good Friday or Piccadilly Circus, so he couldn't give anything of value away however much they were leaning on him. Even if he could remember the route, and spilt it under torture, he could only blow *the place he had been*—not where he was *going*.

'But your Australian flight-sergeant?' I said. 'You told me he had blown the whole line.'

'That's just the point I'm trying to make,' he said with painful patience. 'He was an *agent*, a trained man. In his particular case, incidentally, they found a map and microscopic notes in pencil, on Red Cross toilet paper, on him when he was dealt with. He used to have a few minutes privacy in the loo on arrival in each safe house, while the route was still fresh in his mind. So there should be two ratlines—one for agents, who know the ropes and can take proper precautions against capture, doubly protected by really safe houses like this one, and another for escapers and evaders, as safe as one can make it but not of such prime importance as the agents' line. Run-of-the-mill safe houses—farms, teahouses, opium joints, brothels and bandits' encampments—can be established and disestablished, abandoned and bypassed in a matter of hours. This palce took five hundred years to set up. I'd hate to have it blown.'

'Five hundred years?' I said incredulously.

'It was a Buddhist monastery back in the days when Taoism was the official religion and all others were persecuted and had to keep underground. It's a system of caves that runs for miles through these hills, some of them natural, some manmade, but all interconnected. The monks lived here undisturbed for centuries until about three hundred years ago when they were almost entirely wiped out by a plague. The handful of them that survived moved south and set themselves up on Lantao Island, after putting a curse on this place that still holds today. The locals are terrified of it—they wouldn't come near it for a fortune. *Sun-lim-sho*. You know what that means, of course.?'

'Literally "into the ultimate void of nothingness",' I said. 'Taboo—not to be spoken of or even though of. Yes, I know what that means all right, but it can't be true in this case or *you* wouldn't be here. *Sun-lim-sho* holds for all Chinese—Taoists, Buddhists, Mohammedans and Christians. It's supposed to be completely leakproof, or so we're asked to believe.'

'Quite true, but there's an exception in this particular case. The secret is passed from one generation to the next. This is Paradise Lost to the Lantao monks—an Eden they were driven out of but hope to find again sometime in the future—like the Jews and their "next year in Jerusalem". The Sakya Lama, that's the chief abbot, of Lantao is the hereditary custodian of the secret. Each passes it on to his son—'

'Is an *abbot* supposed to have a son?' I asked with some flippancy.

'Yes, in this branch of the religion,' he answered seriously. 'He has to be a man "fulfilled in all respects" so he remains married until he begets a son, and only then does he enter the monastery and take vows of celibacy. When the time is ripe he passes the secret on to the son, and so it goes on.'

'If it's as tight as all that how did you get hold of it?'

He shrugged. 'Simply because my old man happened to

128

be the Sakya Lama,' he said. 'He passed it on to me before he died.'

'You're pulling my leg, surely,' I said.

'Why should I do that? It's true. As I've just told you, you remain in the outside world, marry and lead an ordinary secular life until the call comes. In my father's case he was working in the Hong Kong branch of the Hangkow Bank when he was summoned back to Lantao. My grandfather, the Lama, was dying. He told my father all about this place and invested him as Boddhisatva, that is, spiritual disciple and Sakya Lama elect, and he was then permitted to return to Hong Kong to hand over properly at the bank. He had been married to my mother a little over a year then, and I was on the way. He had become thoroughly Westernized, and the thought of leaving my mother and entering a monastery appalled him—so he skipped to Australia. He went into the import-export business in Sydney, and prospered—became a Christian and a pillar of the Methodist church, mayor of Balmain and worshipful master of his masonic lodge, in short he did all right, but I don't suppose the poor old bugger ever knew a day's peace, because his conscience gnawed the hell out of him, particularly when I, who except in appearance was as Australian as the gum-trees, started to go all Chink at university, and chucked Law in favour of Chinese archaeology. He thought I was being bugged by the spirits of our ancestors and all that sort of thing. He died five years ago and the Western veneer just sloughed off him towards the end. He made me break rice bowls and promise to make amends to the Order on his behalf and to bring him back to be buried here in Lantao, and he passed the secret of this place to me.'

He broke off and went to the embrasure and looked out, and this time I did not interrupt him, and there was silence for some minutes before he came back to the table.

'I did try to keep that promise,' he went on. His voice was flat and expressionless, the Australian accent more pronounced. 'I did my bloody damnedest—but by this time I had

129

been pulled into the Far Eastern Bureau of MI6, and I was under orders and I just didn't have the opportunity. Then I was switched to this mob, with the task of setting up a ratline. The first necessity was a really safe base to work from.' He shrugged again and spread his hands like a Jewish comedian. 'Well—I ask you—where's safer than this? But don't get me wrong, cobber, I still feel it's a shit's trick on the old man's memory, and if there's anything in the afterlife belief he must be spinning like a top in Waverley cemetery.'

'You're working against the Japs though,' I said. 'Surely that would have pleased him.'

'Yeah, maybe you're right, Let's hope so anyway.' He smiled twistedly. 'I suppose you're wondering why all the boyish confidences after I've been giving you the hush-hush, need-to-know tamasha up to now?'

'It does seem a little traumatic,' I admitted. 'But it certainly makes things clearer.'

'It's all part of the technique,' he said. 'You don't trust anybody until you have to; but once you have to and you're committed, you come clean and spill the lot. Half-truths and withheld facts only confuse the bloke you're briefing. You know it all now, for better or worse, and you're on the ratline in a dual capacity. You're the first customer as an evader, and you've been recruited as an agent. You stumbled on to it by chance in the first place and threw the old girls into a hell of a tizzy and they got on to the radio to me for orders, and it threw *me* into a tizzy and I had to improvise fast. You see, the procedure as we laid it down was that people we wanted to get out would be contacted by our agents *in the camps*. They would be wafted over or under the wire as opportunity presented, and guided to the first safe house—Hung Fat, the camphorwood merchant, in Chatham Road—'

'Who the devil appointed *him*?' I demanded. 'He's got a Japanese wife and he's been on the Suspect Traders' List for years.'

He nodded. 'You're right. Little Madam Butterfly, his

130

everloving, runs a bath-house which is a thinly disguised knocking shop—bloody good one too, I've been there. I bet it's full of buckteethed Nip officers now having their backs massaged. Hung himself smuggles considerably more opium into the Colony then he exports camphorwood chests out. He has a factory at Shaukiwan for converting the stuff into morphine base which he sends to San Francisco by safe-hand-of-purser on the *President Lincoln* every trip. It's cooked into ninety-eight per cent pure heroin there, and the purser brings back ten-to-one gold. That means ten ounces of gold for every ounce of heroin. Forty per cent of the gold is paid to the Triad, ten per cent to the police "makee-looksee-other-way" fund, and he's on the remaining fifty. Very rich man—and a damn good agent—the best in that particular sector. Who appointed him? Me. Excuse the conceit. Now, do you mind if I get on with it without you interrupting? Good. Where was I? Oh yes. The next safe house is the Misses Willis', which you know all about. They're the best in *any* sector. The next house after theirs is the police post in Lowu. The Chinese inspector there is violently pro-Jap, so we hope they think. I believe he's a bit suspect though, so I gave orders that you were to be bypassed round that one. The sugar-cane break, which you also know about, is the next, then comes the mill—then here. All clear so far?'

'All clear,' I mumbled, feeling very foolish indeed. 'You apparently know all about Hung Fat, but I still think you're taking a chance on his Japanese wife.'

'One has to take chances in this business,' he answered. 'They've just got to be kept as small as possible, that's all. Actually the wife is a Neisei; that means Hawaiian-born US citizen. They're reckoned to be as fanatically loyal as only converts can be. Well, to continue—I'm sending you forward tonight. In twenty-four hours you should be clear of the Jap belt, which finishes just north of Canton, and you don't run up against them again until you approach the Yangtse, south of Chungking . . .'

131

Another long walk through passages that twisted and jinked unendingly, up flights of worn stone steps, and down others. Sometimes the air was dry and laden with the dust of ages, at others chill and damp. At one stage we came out into a cave as high and wide as a cathedral, and the beam of the torch fell on stalactites of incredible beauty—blue, pink and white, inset with clumps of crystal that danced in the light; at another we skirted a lake, black and sinister, which seemed to be at least a couple of hundred yards across. I tried at first, purely as an exercise, to memorize the route, but it was hopeless. And there were branch passages and offshoots further to bedevil one, but Kwan never hesitated once. He just strode ahead of us with the light, from time to time giving a curt warning over his shoulder at places where the roof came lower. Except for that, the eerie silence was broken only by the occasional dripping of water and the constant scuffing of our feet.

We walked for about an hour, and Kwan's statement that the cave system extended for miles no longer seemed an exaggeration; then, completely without warning, cold, fresh wind was blowing in our faces, and the stars were above us. It was so sudden as to be anticlimactic. One minute we were in the tunnel, the next we had climbed up through a manhole and were standing in the middle of a dense patch of kika thornbush, that natural barbed-wire entanglement that defies even wild goats' efforts to browse and destroy.

'Careful,' Kwan cautioned. 'Step just where I do. If this stuff snags your clothes you're going to finish up stark naked.' Carefully and slowly he guided us out into the open, pushing aside strands of needle-pointed thorns with heavily gloved hands and holding the passage open until all three of us were clear, and I sensed rather than saw that we were on the edge of a sheer drop and I could hear the sound of the river far below us.

'I won't come any further,' he said. 'Just follow this path

down the cliff face. Take it carefully, it's a bit dodgy in places. You'll find two blokes waiting for you at the bottom. So long and good luck.'

He melted back into the darkness and I cursed under my breath because I had several questions I still wanted to put to him, and I guessed that his abrupt departure was because he realized this.

Raucous said reflectively, 'Funny geezer. Looks like a Chink but doesn't talk like one. Nice little dump he had down there. Wouldn't of minded staying a bit longer. Where do we go now, sir?'

'I haven't the faintest idea,' I told him. 'You heard what he said. There are two "blokes" waiting for use down below. Come on.'

We stood huddled together looking about us irresolutely. The two blokes were conspicuous by their absence and this rock was the end of the line unless we were expected to swim.

'The bastard was having us on,' rumbled Raucous. 'What do we do now? I'm not climbing that bloody cliff again—not in the dark, anyhow.'

I tried to frame a curt and compelling officerlike reply, but it tailed off stillborn, because he had expressed my own views exactly.

'We wait,' I said lamely.

'Good old army,' he said. 'When in doubt just sit on your arse until someone comes along and leads you still further into the shit.'

Then the boat arrived, and I saw that it had been moored on a long line fastened to the rock and two dark figures were hauling themselves in on it against the current. One of them stood up in the bows and helped us to embark, chattering directions in Hakka to sit perfectly still amidships, then without warning they cast off and we were whirled away frighteningly and seemingly completely out of control, the sampan spinning round and round in the rapids and shipping water. Raucous and Aggie were yelling in sheer terror, but I maintained a stoic silence, largely because my vocal cords were paralysed. But through it all the two boatmen squatted completely unconcerned, one at each end of the wretched little craft, for what seemed miles, until the one in the bows grunted an order and both took up paddles and, miraculously, brought her steadily on course in midstream; then, after a few more hair-raising minutes, they turned her side on to the current and paddled in to the western bank, and we grounded gently on a sandy shore.

'Bloody clever,' breathed Raucous, 'but next time I'll walk.'

We climbed out on to the bank and the sampan pushed off immediately without a word from its crew, and disappeared into the darkness. Raucous started to give tongue again, but I had now had time to collect my scattered faculties, and I told him sharply to shut up.

'Everything has been arranged,' I said sternly. 'All you have to do, Rawcliffe, is to obey orders and stop bitching. *Understand?*'

Once again it seemed to work. He said, 'Yessir—very good, sir. There's a bloke coming up behind you, sir.'

There were two in fact, dark, faceless figures who materialized wraithlike from the surrounding gloom just as the boatmen had done. One said, surprisingly in pidgin, 'Follow my, one time, chop-chop,' and they set off at a fast clip over the flat sandy ground, the speaker in front of us and the other bringing up the rear.

The night air was crisp and clear, and we had been cooped up for so long that the exercise was, for me at least, sheer joy, but, inevitably, Raucous started to grouse after the first hour. 'We're marching dead north,' he said. 'That's the Pole star up ahead of us. These types are stupid.'

'North happens to be the way we want to go,' I told him with unanswerable logic.

'Then what the hell did we want to come south, down-river, in that damn boat for?' he demanded. 'Why couldn't we of crossed straight away and saved ourselves a few miles? Five or six at least—the wrong way. No sense in it.'

'Oh, shut up, Rawcliffe,' I told him yet again, but I had to admit to myself that he had a point there, particularly when, as the eastern sky started to lighten, I made out the stark cliffs of the Boque level with us the other side of the river. We have covered quite a lot of distance, but we didn't seem to have made much headway.

We halted in the false dawn, on rising ground a few hundred yards from the river, in a hollow where clumps of esparto grass gave us a limited amount of cover.

The linguistic one of the two said, 'Makee stay same place all day. Night-time plentee walk more far.' I regretted this because it afforded Raucous another opportunity to argue, which he seized on immediately.

'That place we come from,' he said, pointing towards the Boque. 'Why for no come straightee way one time? Plentee walk no bloody good, this way that way—damfool.'

You can abuse a Chinaman, impugn his father's honour or his mother's morals, and call him a bastard, but never a damfool, so here I interposed.

'We thank you and admire your skill,' I soothed in Cantonese. 'Sickness has unbridled this soldier's tongue. We ask forgiveness.'

'This soldier will be fortunate to *keep* his tongue,' the guide said, only slightly mollified. 'Long tongues are sometimes shortened—painfully. Please explain to him that no reference must be made to the place one has come from—*ever*, because I fear he is a man of low intelligence.'

'A damfool,' I supplied, and since in addition to a prickly *amour propre* in regard to intellect, most Cantonese have a sense of humour, he grinned grudgingly, and face was restored.

'To cross directly,' he explained, 'would involve travelling up one channel and down the next, many times, sometimes against the current, thereby trebling the distance, and time, we have taken.' And the whole thing fell into focus when the sun came up fully and I saw the network of sandbanks that lay between us and the opposite shore.

135

He insisted on our remaining in the hollow for the rest of the day, keeping well below the level of the grass, and the necessity for this became clear when a small reconnaissance plane came downriver, dragonfly-like, during the morning, and, later on, a grey-painted motor-launch puttered slowly up the nearest channel against the current, and, peering through the grass, we could see men searching the banks through binoculars. But the guides remained comfortingly unperturbed, even when a strong foot patrol of Japs appeared over the skyline from the north and plodded along the path which lay between us and the shore.

'There is nothing to fear while one takes sensible precautions,' the linguist told me. 'If there is a path the Japs will follow it, so one remains off the path, and *still*, in daylight.' He was a cheerful youth, whose precise and pedantic speech in both Cantonese and Mandarin, to which latter he switched when he realized that Aggie did not understand it, bespoke at least a Middle School education, although his short stature, bowed legs and round moon face were those of the typical Kwantung peasant. He would probably be one of the many thousands who would in normal times be applying for clerical jobs with the princely houses of commercial Hong Kong, no doubt my own among them. If he got one he would set to with grim determination to learn 'business' English, as distinct from pidgin, in order to rise from the purely Chinese counting house to the Olympian heights of 'Main Office', where they used electric comptometers in place of the age-old abacus, and typewriters took over from the inkblock and brush, and they called each other 'mister', wore ties and gents' natty suitings, and lost a lot of their sturdy individuality, but gained much 'face'. If they missed out, then they became ready grist to the mill of the Chinese Communist Party, which had been making ground in the Colony hand over clenched fist since the young Mao Tse-tung had begun seriously to challenge Chiang Kai-shek's corrupt Kuomintang. I didn't trust them, in fact I was healthily frightened of them, but at least I knew them to be natural enemies of the Japanese.

I asked this lad his name, and he told me it was John. It was no doubt an operational code name, but it was sufficient to indicate that, like Kwan, he was a Christian, because no unbaptized Chinese would dream of using what they call, with some contempt, a 'Mission boy name', even as a *nom de guerre*.

'I have been baptized,' he informed me, 'but I am not a rice Christian, becoming converted to gain a free education. My father worked himself to death to pay for mine.'

'What do you intend to do when this war is over?' I asked him.

'That depends on which side wins,' he said with refreshing frankness.

'We are going to,' I told him, getting in a propagandial swipe.

'In that case I remain here and apply for a good position in government employ, one where much squeeze-pidgin can be made—police, customs or Department of Finance.'

'But just *suppose* we don't—?"

'I still remain here, and run opium for the Japanese garrison.'

'They don't use it.'

'Neither did we until the British introduced it,' he said simply, and to that I had no answer.

We had a meal at sundown of cold rice and kunji, a revolting but sustaining barley gruel, and then we walked throughout that livelong night until our legs were moving mechanically, mercifully bereft of all feeling while actually moving, though our feet became twin burning hells in the brief halts John called every two hours. Raucous's infantry-hardened feet stood up to it well for most of the way, although even he was showing signs of wear and tear towards the end, but from Aggie, brave soul, there was not a whimper.

I had lost all count of time and distance when we came to the crest of that last slope which overlooks Canton City itself and its suburb of Honan across the river, but looking back we must have covered twenty-five miles in the nine hours between sunset and dawn. I was on familiar ground now because it was here that my grandfather had sent me to serve my apprenticeship, in the Kwangtung branch office, and I had spent three years in the tea, spice and silk godowns that lie along the waterfront. I was nervous because dawn was breaking and I knew that the countryside within the horseshoe of hills which enclose the ancient city walls on three sides was flat, featureless and devoid of cover. There seemed to be a partial blackout over the streets, but here and there it was broken by scattered groups of dim lights and, to the north, outside the walls, the headlights of moving vehicles fell upon serried rows of tents. We halted, and John came back to where I was standing.

'The Japanese camp,' he said, pointing towards the tents. 'It is the last big one. After this there are only outposts, and even these cease fifty miles north of here.'

'Where do we rest?' I asked him uneasily. 'It will be light soon.'

'Small piecee more far,' he answered, lapsing into pidgin, an irritating habit he had when he wanted to avoid further questioning. 'You come—soon good chow—makee sleep.' And with that I had to be content.

He left the road and we followed him across dry and dusty paddies down towards the river, which lay on our left, and my nervousness increased because I knew that this way we could only finish on the praia, a broad esplanade that runs under the outside perimeter walls of the city and along which the thousands of junks and sampans that form a floating metropolis in their own right are moored. Some, the inner lines of them, are permanent fixtures, only moving vertically, as they become waterborne when the floods come downriver, to subside again on to the mud when the rains have ceased. They lie crowded cheek by jowl, ten or twelve deep, along the entire three-mile curve of the praia, and must house at least a million souls who live, eat, sleep, breed and die aboard them without ever coming ashore for longer than it takes them to sell the fish and soft-shelled crabs they garner from the river. Only the outer lines are fully mobile, the large junks trading downriver to Hong Kong and back, the shallower draft sampans either fishing along the Honan mudflats or ferrying farm produce down from the north. At dawn each day the men set out on their lawful and some-times *un*lawful occasions, for, inevitably, most run a sideline in opium, and the women set up their stalls along the praia to sell and barter with their longshore neighbours, and the boats are left to the children and the dogs, and there are literally thousands of both.

My unease was due to the fact that I knew that the praia was always heavily policed during market hours as, although the boatpeople and town-dwellers were dependent upon each other, they were anything but friendly neigh-bours, and fights were frequent, so I assumed that the Japs would be following the same policy. I quickened my pace and hobbled up beside John who was now some yards ahead of us, and voiced my fears, but all I got out of him was an enigmatic grin and that most infuriating of Chinese phrases, 'Ha'magu-a,' clipped and in the higher tone, which is the equivalent of saying to a fractious and rather dim English child. 'Now don't worry, dear. All in good time. Nanny knows best.'

I could have hit him, and Raucous, although he didn't understand the words, guessed their import, because he ranged up the other side and snarled, 'If this little flat-faced son-of-a-whore doesn't call a halt soon, I'm going to clobber him.'

Unfortunately, although 'son-of-a-whore' may have been a little esoteric for John, 'flatface', like 'damfool', is perfectly understood in pidgin, so he riposted with 'dirty Tommy bastard', another endearment common to both languages, and I had my work cut out keeping them apart for the next half-mile until we were actually on the praia. John strode ahead then in dignified silence while I tore furious strips off my military subordinate, with the second guide, whom Raucous had christened Sling Shi Tye, joining in with a well-timed epithet whenever I paused for breath. Only Aggie maintained her dignity in those last wretched minutes. Of course, the whole reason was that we were at the end of a murderous march and exhausted—always a dangerous time, as Kwan had pointed out.

We had reached the praia now, and the light was strengthening by the minute, but still John walked on ahead of us, seemingly oblivious of all danger. The boatpeople were stirring and carrying out planks and trestles busily like ants, chattering shrilly and jostling each other as they set up their stalls along the embankment.

And then I saw a Jap patrol striding purposefully towards us.

There were a dozen of them, in two files with a couple of wretched Chinese in their midst being led along roped together, hands bound behind them and placards round their necks. An NCO marched in front of them, and two flank men wielded bamboo staves clearing a path for them through the crowd, and the people nearest to the edge were dropping their planks and jumping back on to the inner line of boats to avoid being struck. I saw John jump and I followed suit, glancing round quickly to make sure that Raucous and Aggie had grasped the situation. They had, and all three of us were below the stone coping by the time the soldiers passed, and the imperturbable John, three boats away, was grinning broadly and waving to us. I hopped from one deck to another and came up beside him, raging.

'Why have you brought us this way, in daylight?' I demanded, but he only grinned the wider and answered 'Ha'magu-a,' again, and added, 'This way. Five rows of boats out and eleven along,' and he set off like a mountain goat across a griddle. Lean yellow dogs barked and snarled as we followed him, and tiny brown-eyed children looked at us without particular interest, but he was right: there were few adults to mark our passing.

He halted finally on a sampan that differed in no way from the possible ten thousand others that lay all around. Except for a cramped foredeck and a small open cuddy in the stern,

140

it was roofed over with straw matting for its entire length of about thirty feet. We crawled in after him and waited while he fumbled for matches and lit an oil lamp. A seat ran along each side of this long cabin and there was sufficient head-room to sit upright but not to stand. There was a clay cooking place at one end and some neatly stowed quilted bedding rolls at the other, and, although there was a strong odour of dried fish, the whole place was surprisingly clean.

John said, with the smugness of a conjuror who has just pulled a rabbit from a hat before a doubting audience, 'There! I have brought you to a safe place. A good place. Here we will rest for a day and a night.'

My anger had abated, but I was still badly shaken. 'Could we not have come under cover of darkness?' I asked.

He shook his head. 'No,' he said. 'There are but two short periods during the day when one can come to the boats without attracting attention: now, as the women are erecting their stalls, and at sunset, when they dismantle them. Then all are too busy to notice strangers, and there is not enough light to see faces clearly.'

'But those soldiers,' I protested. 'Only by the merest fluke did we miss being taken.'

Again he shook his head. 'There is no danger from that particular squad,' he said. 'The executioners—they come at the same time every day and attend strictly to their own business. They are an added safeguard, because the people watch the show at the end of the praia.'

I shuddered. 'Every day?' I asked.

'Most days,' he amended. 'There were only two this morn-ing. Sometimes there are as many as twenty heads stuck on poles. Curfew-breakers who have been taken overnight, thieves and those who have been denounced for anti-monkey-people activities. There are big rewards for denun-ciations.'

'And yet you say this place is safe?'

'Quite safe, as long as you stay in the boat and do not talk too loudly.'

'But what if somebody looks in by chance?' I pointed to

141

the entrances at each end, which John's silent colleague had now carefully covered with matting curtains.

'That would never happen. The boatpeople have a strict code. No man, woman or child would ever look into the cabin of a neighbour unless invited to do so. To them privacy is sacred.'

'But they have to cross from one boat to another, just as we did,' I insisted.

'There is a code for that also. Right of way is from foredeck to foredeck, and it would be considered a grave discourtesy to pause for a moment. Even the smallest children observe that. The dogs the same. They will let you pass, but if you halt they'll be at your ankles in an instant.'

I began to realize how little we, the European overlords, knew of these people, even though many, like myself, lived their entire lives out here. There were vast colonies of boat-people on our very doorsteps in Hong Kong, Kowloon and Aberdeen, and I knew that they were clannish and had their own tribal customs, like the Romanies, but I had never previously heard of this strict protocol.

Raucous yawned cavernously and looked longingly at the pile of quilts. 'Christ, I'm shagged,' he said. 'Permission to fall out, sir?'

'By all means,' I said. 'But you mustn't let yourself be seen outside the shelter.'

'Suits me,' he grunted, and stretched out on one of the seats, and Aggie, dog-tired though she was, covered him with a quilt and carefully folded another into a pillow. 'Velly good,' he acknowledged graciously. 'Go catchee chow for Number One Master and me, chop-chop.'

I was about to tell him to mind his manners, but at that moment the curtain at the rear was raised and an old woman entered carrying a large copper dixie, followed by a small boy with a miscellany of pots and bowls on a tray. Without a glance at any of us, she went to the cooking place and knelt and blew life into the embers that smouldered there, then

142

made up the fire with charcoal and produced a wok from under the seat and handed it to Aggie, who took it in silence but with a little bobbing bow, and passed it on to the boy who started to clean it with a fistful of sand, then she set about washing rice and chopping vegetables. They know their pecking order in a Chinese kitchen. With the incredible speed and legerdemain of the Cantonese when dealing with food, the two women had a meal of rice, noodles, fish, crab and pork steaming in communal bowls before us, with a variety of side dishes and little porcelain pots of jasmine tea.

Whenever I am tired and hungry to this day, I think of that meal—sitting cross-legged in the gloom with the inner warmth of the food calming and dispelling the exhaustion, fear and alarms and excursions of the previous few days. There was no conversation and nothing broke the silence save the clicking of our chopsticks, the champing of our jaws and the occasional muted belch of sheer appreciation— which is the proper way to enjoy any Oriental meal. We finished with lychees, that superb balancer and aid to the digestion of rich food, bowed right and left to each other, and three times to the cooks, and, for my part at least, drifted off into deep, contented sleep.

I awoke as John shook me gently by the shoulder, and never did man come more reluctantly back to consciousness. There was noise all around us now—voices from other boats, crying children, the rattle of mahjong tiles and the barking of dogs.

'It is time for us to move,' he told me, and added when I groaned, 'It is not far this time, then you can sleep again.'

We had some difficulty in arousing Raucous, who refused to open his eyes until Aggie, well versed in his idiosyncrasies, took the lobe of his ear between finger and thumb and twisted, hard. He surfaced with a roar of rage then and we filed out of the cabin on to the afterdeck. It was dark now except for the chinks of light which filtered through the matting roofs and walls of the surrounding boats.

John said, 'Follow me, putting your feet exactly where I place mine, and don't halt. Please explain this to the soldier. The woman already knows.'

I whispered the translation to Raucous, then we followed John across the lines of boats, not towards the praia as I had expected, but outwards to the open river, until we came to a line of smaller sampans that were obviously being prepared to sail, because men were loading nets, poles, oars and baskets and chattering loudly. As unerringly as he had led us to the first boat, John took us along this outer line until he came to one with only two men in it as against the crew of six or seven which seemed to be the normal complement of the others. He climbed down into it and signed to us to follow; then, when we had all boarded, they cast off and we moved out into the stream with a group of others. The two crewmen and John and his silent partner each took an oar, and within minutes we were pulling against the strong current, headed upriver.

Chapter Five

1

We rowed upstream for five days, always in the hours of darkness, lying up in the undergrowth from dawn until sunset with the sampan hidden under the bank, speaking only when we had to, and then in muted undertones, and I could feel that the strain was telling on Raucous as much as it was on me. Three or four times Jap patrol boats passed up and down the river, and once a party of them footslogged along a path within a few yards of our position only minutes after we had landed to camp for the day. That shook even the seemingly imperturbable Chinese badly.

Then suddenly, on the sixth day, the whole atmosphere changed, and one of the fishermen produced a bottle of murderous rice spirit and passed tots all round.

'No more monkey people', John said happily, in pidgin for Raucous's benefit. 'All gone—no come this side.'

'How can you tell that with certainty?' I asked with some scepticism.

'*I* no tell,' he said. '*They* tell.' He nodded towards the fishermen and tapped himself on the forehead and stomach. 'They tell inside like muntjak or deer in jungle when tiger go away. Soon we come to Silk Road, then plenty walk, many days. All men fliends all time.'

I received this with even more scepticism. The Silk Road, an established fact since pre-Marco Polo days in North China, where it ran along under the shadow of the Great Wall for over two thousand miles, was in these southern areas a matter of constant controversy. He sensed my doubt, and reverted to Mandarin.

'It is true,' he said earnestly. 'It is the ordinary road to Kweilin, and then on to Chungking, unmarked, without signs, in some parts in disrepair—but there is a truce on it, like the Khyber Pass in India, which is another part of the old Silk Road. On it no man fights or interferes with another, even though off it they may be deadly enemies. Communists, Kuomintang, bandits, smugglers—all leave each other in peace to get on with their own affairs.'

'What about the Japanese?' I questioned, and he shrugged.

'I do not know with certainty,' he said. 'Personally I should say that it did not apply in their case. Who could trust the monkey people to keep a bond? The peasants and farmers along the Road certainly do not. They place signs out to warn travellers if Japs are thought to be in the area.'

'What sort of signs?' I asked.

'A fragment of white rag impaled on a kika thornbush, as if torn from the clothes of a passer-by, at the boundary of each man's land—when the road ahead is clear. If danger threatens from the north they change it to blue; if from the south the rag is black. One leaves the Road then and takes cover.'

'How do they know when danger threatens? Telephone or radio?' I asked sarcastically, and he laughed.

'They know,' he said. 'They have known long before the invention of either. Every farm keeps a boy with sharp eyes posted on high ground, all within sight of each other. They signal, and the marks at the roadside are changed accordingly. 'They are not always rags. Sometimes it is a broken potsherd, or a torn branch, or twigs twisted in a certain way. One must learn to read them.'

The fishermen dropped us on the bank later that day, waved cheerily and turned downstream again.

'Don't we reward them in some way?' I asked John, and he shook his head.

'That is attended to by others,' he said. 'They are part of the organization, and who are we to interfere?'

He pointed out some of the marks as we marched—tiny

146

shreds of cloth that could not possibly be noticeable by anybody not actually looking for them, anything up to five miles apart—and they were all white. I felt the tension leaving me for the first time in weeks. We were very tired but our general condition seemed to be improving. We were moving faster and, speaking for myself at least, our feet were holding up to the strain. And my powers of observation were becoming more acute, because it was I who saw the blue rag on a bush first. I called out to John, who had passed it, and pointed to it, and he looked abashed and made the stroking gesture under his chin with his fingertips which signifies loss of face and is the Chinese equivalent of *mea culpa*, and he led the way into a patch of undergrowth on the right-hand side of the road.

'What's the flap?' asked Raucous, mystified.

'Somebody approaching from the north,' I told him. 'We must lie up here out of sight until things are clear.'

'How would you be knowing that?'

'I just know, that's all. Keep your head down, and don't talk so much.'

'Suits me—but how about making a fire and cooking some grub.'

'Shut up, and do as your are told,' I snapped.

'Very good—*sir*,' he said, and subsided. It seemed my powers of command were improving also.

We lay there for over an hour, and first Raucous, then Aggie and finally the Silent One dozed off and I felt myself nodding also, but I sat up with a start when the sound of an approaching motor vehicle came faintly from the distance.

'Japs?' I muttered to John.

He shook his head. 'Not from the north,' he answered, 'unless the whole position has altered. Either General Tai Li's Blueshirts, or Communists. Each as bad as the other as far as we are concerned.'

'Why?' I queried. 'Both are enemies of the Japs.'

'Both would regard us with suspicion and treat us as spies. Their treatment is not gentle.'

147

'So—?'

'So we remain here until the way is clear again.'

'How will we know that?'

But he had no time to answer, because the vehicle came into sight then, round a bend in the road above us. It was a three-ton truck, camouflage-painted and partially covered by a screen of brushwood, with a machine-gun mounted on the roof of the cab. Two steel-helmeted troops stood with their heads protruding through the screen, scanning the road each side. There may have been others squatting under cover, but I couldn't see any.

It rolled slowly past our position, its engine clattering noisily in low gear, and I searched in vain for some sort of distinguishing sign on its side, Rising Sun, Nationalist star, or hammer and sickle. It could have belonged to any of the three protagonists; just a party of armed men shrouded in the anonymity of war, their one common factor being their certain hostility to our small party. I felt very lonely and vulnerable.

'What do we do now?' I asked John as the sound of their passing faded and the dust settled.

'We wait,' he said. It was the sort of answer I would have given Raucous, and, for that reason, it infuriated me.

'I asked you a question,' I said through clenched teeth. 'I want a proper answer.' He smiled benignly and pointed past me and, turning, I saw a man emerge from the scrub the other side of the road, remove the blue fragment of cloth and replace it with a white one, then, without a glance in our direction, he disappeared back the way he had come.

'We wait for that,' John said mildly. 'It is as I informed your excellency earlier. The road is now clear.'

I simmered down, very slowly. The 'your excellency'—the Chinese word is 'ku-an'—could have been fulsomely complimentary or just plain impertinent, like calling somebody 'your lordship' in English, when you really mean 'big-head'. It was undoubtedly the latter in this case.

Raucous said conversationally as we rose and shouldered our packs, 'Them buggers was Nips.'

'They weren't,' I told him positively.

'What then?'

'Either Kuomintang—that's Nationalist—or Communist. Neither like us very much, but they certainly weren't Japs.'

'Looked bloody like 'em to me.'

'I don't give a damn what they looked like to *you. They were not Japs*'

'I didn't say they was. I said they *looked* like Japs.'

'Oh, shut up,' I snarled. 'Look to your front, Private Rawcliffe, and speak when you're spoken to.'

'Yes, *sir*,' he said, making it sound like John's 'your excellency', and thereafter whistled softly through his teeth as we marched, a habit of his when he wanted to irritate me, or so I thought. Of course, it was the usual end-of-the-day syndrome—muscles tired, legs aching, nerves frayed. I must do something about it, I decided. Childish tantrums, venting one's spleen on a subordinate—it was hardly the thing.

We came round a bend in the road, and two small men armed with very long rifles and fixed bayonets stood facing us.

It is funny how tiny, unimportant details can register on the sensitized plates of one's memory in situations like this, and then remain indelibly fixed for all time. I can still see those two. One wore glasses that had been broken and clumsily repaired with black insulating tape; the left big toe of the other stuck through his canvas shoe; both wore dirty camouflaged combat jackets and had absurd bits of leafy twig stuck in the nets covering their overlarge steel helmets; both had whistles in their mouths like babies' comforters, and they started simultaneously to blow a twittering obbligato.

Raucous said, with the smugness of a man who has been proved right in the face of contradiction, 'I told you the bastards was Nips, didn't I?'

Others were emerging from the undergrowth, I counted six, all chattering excitedly, and the characteristic stink I had noticed in my previous brief contacts with them came to me strongly—a compound of dried fish, sour rice and rancid cooking oil blending with that of unwashed bodies and sweat-soaked clothes.

They ringed us with menacing bayonets while an NCO came forward and grabbed our packs and rummaged through them, grunting with satisfaction when he came upon the remnants of our rations. He stuffed the lion's share of the food and a cake of soap into the front of his jacket and tossed the rest over his shoulder to his merry men, and had an immediate dogfight on his hands. This he resolved by laying about him with his rifle butt, and then an officer arrived, who chastened them still further with the flat of his samurai sword—and in the fracas nobody thought to search us before tying our hands behind us, which meant that I still had my pistol under my coolie shirt, when they marched us off the road into a clump of trees, not that I was able to extract any comfort from that fact—they would find it eventually, and that in itself would be my death warrant—and Raucous's, because he was carrying one also. The two boys and Aggie might just possibly get away with it—Aggie, most likely at the cost of a 'fate worse than death,' which shouldn't incommode her unduly, I hoped dully.

It was getting dark and they had a lantern under a brushwood shelter, and two soldiers were working on the disembowelled carcase of a radio which was spread out on a blanket. The officer strode up to them and spat out a question. They cringed apologetically and he kicked them both in the ribs. He turned to us then and started to hector John, who was nearest to him, in bad Cantonese. Who were we? Where had we come from? Where were we going? Who had we seen along the road? How many Hung-hu-tse were there in the neighbourhood? Where was their encampment? The answers didn't seem to matter; the officer wasn't listening. He just called John a liar and punched him alternately in the face and the stomach after each question, and then he seemed to tire of it and turned his attention back to the radio mechanics, and we were hustled across the clearing and cuffed down on to the ground beside a group of four shadowy figures who I realized from the way they were sitting, with their hands behind them, were captives like ourselves. And only then did it come to me. The Japs hadn't recognized Raucous and me as Europeans—yet. It was dusk when they picked us up, we were dirty and our coolie hats shaded our faces still further. We were just a group of Chinese peasants at the moment, unfortunate enough to have run into this party and held for questioning as a matter of routine. We might still get away with it . . .

But that hope died even as it dawned. As soon as they saw Raucous and me in the light the fat would be in the fire—and us with it, literally. If only we could make a break tonight. I flexed my wrists tentatively, testing the binding. The same thought must have struck Raucous, because he said out of the darkness, 'If one of us can get this fucking rope off our mitts we might be able to do a scarper.'

And behind me a man's voice said stiffly in English, 'Just mind your language. We have a lady here.'

'So have we,' Raucous said drily. 'Can't do much with them with your hands tied though, can you?'

'Stop that,' I told him, and turned my head to the others. 'Sorry,' I said. 'Who are you?'

'Mixed bag—British and American—never mind about details at the moment,' the man said. 'As that soldier has just said, if one of us can get loose we might be able to do something.'

'Who said I was a soldier?' Raucous demanded.

'I did,' the other said crisply. 'Now shut up. Who's in charge of your party?'

'I am, I suppose,' I said uncertainly.

'What do you mean—"suppose"?' he said impatiently. 'Either you are or you aren't. I'm a Brigadier. Any advance on that?'

'Second-lieutenant,' I mumbled. 'Yes, I'm in charge.'

151

'That's better. How many of you?'

'Five. Two Chinese men, one woman, and this British soldier, plus myself.'

'What are the Chinese exactly?'

'I'm afraid I can't go into that now,' I said. 'But they are quite reliable.'

'You're sure of that?'

'Completely.'

'Um. Have to take your word for it,' he said doubtfully. 'Right: now listen carefully. We've been here for three days and I've been observing these people. There were sixteen of them originally but four went off in their truck just before dark, so that's twelve present at the moment: lieutenant, couple of NCOs, nine privates, LRPG, R and R—'

'I'm sorry,' I said. 'You'll have to translate that.'

'How long have you been in the army?' he asked suspiciously.

'Not long, I'm afraid,' I said. 'I'm a Hong Kong businessman, very recently commissioned in to the Defence Corps.'

'Oh, part-timer,' he said, as if this explained and excused all my military shortcomings. 'Well, that means they are a Long Range Penetration Group engaged on reconnaissance and reporting, and they don't seem to be terribly good at it. Their truck and their wretched wireless broke down and they ran out of rations, they had a brush with a Communist crowd up the road and the bloody fools have expended nearly all their ammunition. They managed to get the truck running, after a fashion, and they've sent it down the road for more supplies. They hope to get it back by morning.'

'Might I ask how you know all this, sir?' I ventured.

'I happen to speak Japanese, although they don't know it, and they've been blathering like an Irish parliament,' he said. 'The officer is absolutely putrid—hasn't a clue in the wide world. The sergeant is marginally better, but he's gone off with the truck. This son of a pig doesn't even mount a sentry over their arms—bloody great pile of ironmongery in a heap over there by the wireless shelter. Oh God! Oh, for a

152

free pair of hands and one piddling gun and we'd have the bastards cold. All my people are hurt,' he added, lowering his voice.

'I've got a gun,' I told him, lowering mine. 'They didn't search me.'

'*What*?' he almost yelped. 'How are your wrists?'

'Tied,' I said.

'I know they're tied, you damned fool—but have they poured water over them?'

'No.'

'They will. It shrinks the sisal fibre they use and it cuts right to the bone. They've done it to us and we're helpless. Listen—*listen*—you've got to try—'

'Got mine off,' broke in Raucous. 'Most of the bloody skin with it—er—sorry, sir—been skagging it on the root of the tree behind me.'

'You've—?' I thought the Brigadier was about to burst into tears. 'Oh, *good man*! You don't happen to have a knife as well?'

'Yessir. Right here, sir. Be with you in a moment, sir,' said Raucous, who realized that his star was in the ascendant and was plugging it for all he was worth. He wriggled over to me, fumbled for my wrists, slid the blade between them and sawed. I took it from him when they were free and went and released John, the Silent One and Aggie.

'Sit just where you are now, with your hands behind you,' I told them. 'Do nothing more until I tell you.'

I crawled to the group behind us. The Brigadier was nearest, sitting with his back to a tree-trunk, his face a white blur in the darkness. I fumbled for his wrists and shuddered as I felt them, because they were so swollen that the bonds had all but disappeared into the flesh, and it took me a good five minutes to saw through them because the sisal had became as tough and unyielding as steel wire. I certainly admired his fortitude. The agony must have been well nigh unbearable as the circulation came back, but beyond a suppressed groan and a tensing of his muscles he didn't flinch.

153

We moved back to the other figures then. There were three of them, indistinguishable one from the other in the darkness, each with his back to an adjacent tree—*her* back in the case of the middle one. All were asleep, and we wakened them cautiously and cut their wrists free in turn. The Brigadier swore savagely when we dealt with the woman.

'War is war, and you don't play it with pingpong bats,' he said, 'but if I get out of this and have the opportunity of commanding troops in the field again, I promise I'll never take one of these little bastards prisoner.'

One of the men cut loose with a good fullbodied stream of cussing in a rich Texas accent as we sawed through his bonds, but the woman and the other man appeared to be only barely conscious. The former gasped faintly as we chafed a little life back into her almost atrophied arms, and the man asked hoarsely for water.

'In a moment, old boy,' the Brigadier whispered. 'Just hang on a little longer.' He touched me on the arm. 'Let's move away a bit for a council,' he added. 'And bring that excellent chap of yours.'

We shifted into a small hollow on the outskirts of the copse and peered over the edge.

'Well now,' the Brigadier said briskly. 'You've seen the others. All casualties, I'm afraid. Hapgood, that's one of the Americans, has busted a couple of ribs, I think. Harrington, the other, got an almighty crack on the head, and Shivka was knocked out for some time. The other poor devils were killed—'

'How did all this happen?' I asked.

'We crashed—Hapgood was the pilot—never mind about that now. The immediate problem is to get away from here, but we can only move slowly, and these sods will be after us like longdogs, unless—' he paused.

'Unless—?'

'Unless we deal with them first, obviously. Shouldn't be too difficult. Twelve of the animals. They'll snore their heads

154

off until morning, so we have the advantage of surprise on our side. How many rounds in your gun? What is it, by the way?'

'Browning nine millimetre—eight rounds in it but I haven't any spares. But Rawcliffe has a revolver, six-chambered—'

'Better and better—and, of course, we'll collect some more when we've dealt with these people. Now listen to me. We can't just rush in picking them off at random in the dark. We'll merely waste rounds that way, because they'll scatter and some of the quicker-witted of them will pick up their rifles in passing and have at us. See what I mean?'

'Yes,' I said, doubtfully.

'Good. Then the thing to do is to knock out the officer first—quietly. He's no bloody use, but without someone in authority yelling at them and booting them up the arse the troops will just mill round in a bugger's muddle. So we stick the officer. Done any of this sort of thing before?'

'Er—no—' I said.

'That's all right. Don't let it fluster you. Haven't done any myself since the trenches in the last show. The rules are the same, though. Sleeping man, put the muzzle right alongside his earhole, but don't touch him with it or he'll probably move his head and ruin your shot. Standing man, aim straight for the guts—better target than the head in the dark. Right—move forward. Steady—steady—'

We crawled through the damp grass, the faint rustle of our passage sounding in my straining ears like the roar of Niagara. One of us, it might have been me, knelt on a dry twig that cracked like a pistol shot. We froze, and the Brigadier hissed a filthy word. From somewhere to our left came the sound of concerted snoring and I made out a group of forms in the shadow of the arms pile, and then we were in front of the wireless shelter. The Brigadier put a restraining hand on my arm, and Raucous continued on without a second's hesitation and disappeared into the deeper gloom. I could feel cold sweat trickling down my face and neck and finding its way under my shirt and making icy runnels over my chest.

Then, without warning, there was a strangled exclamation in the pitch darkness, and a brief flurry followed by a metallic clang as something was knocked over—and finally came a horrible gurgling sound culminating in a long, sobbing gasp. Then silence, and I wanted to be sick.

The Brigadier was whispering urgently, 'The gun! For Christ's sake don't forget his gun—the gun—don't forget the gun—' and he kept on repeating it until Raucous loomed up beside us again and said, 'Here it is, sir. I brought his ammo pouch an' all.'

'Good boy! good boy!' the Brigadier said fulsomely, as one would to a retriever that had just brought a stick back, and I realized with something of a shock that he was as strained and jumpy as myself. 'Let's have a shufti at it. Ah, one of these Mitsibis things—like a Luger. Splendid, splendid. How did it all go?'

'Didn't like it, but he had to have it, as the bishop said to the barmaid, begging your pardon, sir.' Raucous chuckled breathlessly, and here again I could detect nerves stretched to their utmost.

'Bit of a wag, this feller of yours,' the Brigadier grunted. 'Right, let's get this thing cocked. Fine. Covey of 'em over here to the left. One apiece—quietly—quietly.'

There were four blanket-enshrouded figures that didn't stir, not even when I stumbled over one of them. I felt something like a coconut under my questing hand and I pulled the trigger, and nothing happened, because once again I had forgotten to slip the safety-catch. Two shattering bangs merged into one as the others fired almost simultaneously, and the fourth man sat up with a startled yell while mine was still struggling out of his blanket. The Brigadier said angrily, 'Come on! What the hell's the matter with you?' and I partially redeemed myself by getting both of them. Two more that we hadn't noticed before jumped to their feet close by, and Raucous dealt with. Then the Brigadier accounted for yet another who was crawling away through the shadows. He made a quick count.

'There's four more of them,' he said. 'Come on—quickly. If a single one gets away the whole thing's ruined.'

It was almost an anticlimax, because all four came charging up together at that moment, screaming 'Banzai!' and scrabbled for rifles from the pile, completely ignoring us as we knelt in the dark surrounded by their departed comrades, and we shot them in the back.

The reaction set in then, and we sat for an appreciable time in silence until the Brigadier said in a still, flat voice, 'It can be a dirty business at times, gentlemen, even when dealing with ullage like this—but no omelettes without broken eggs, and all that sort of thing, I suppose. We'd better go back to the others. They'll be wondering what the hell has been happening.'

The American was on his feet, and the woman was trying to rise, but the other man was still unconscious. The former wanted to know, with a plenitude of Texan embellishments, what the hell had been going on, and when the Brigadier told him, he was angry because he hadn't been included in it.

'I didn't think you'd be up to it, old boy,' the Brigadier said mildly.

'I might at least have been given the option,' the other said furiously.

'Had I done that you'd have insisted on coming, and we hadn't a gun for you.'

'You've been trying to freeze me out all along, Brigadier-General—'

'Just Brigadier in our army, old boy.'

'I don't give a shit what you call yourself—'

'Language, old boy. Lady present—and her English happens to be considerably better than yours. But I'm forgetting my manners. This is Captain Hapgood of General Chennault's American Volunteer Group. May I present Second-Lieutenant—er—dammit, I don't know your name.'

'Stafford,' I said, because I couldn't think of anything else at that crowded moment.

'Good. Mine is Cavendish-Feltham, by the way. And this splendid chap—er—what's your name—?'

'Rawcliffe, J. three-nine-two-five-four-eight-three—*sir!*' Raucous snapped, as if on parade.

'Private Rawcliffe—I don't know his regiment, because a well-trained chap like this wouldn't give it in these circumstances—but it has every reason to be proud of him. It was he who got us loose—and he has just slit the throat of our Samurai friend.'

'Hi,' said the captain. 'You guys find any water any place?'

'God! I'd forgotten. I wonder if you chaps would—' The Brigadier broke off and turned to the woman. 'Now sit down again, my dear, you'll tire yourself.' And he lowered her gently to the ground. 'Just rest until we find some water.'

I went back and searched unsuccessfully for some sort of bulk container but the more astute Raucous just shook waterbottles next to his ear until he had accumulated a supply which we took to the others. He muttered to me, 'There's a couple of them Nips still twitching. I'd better go and finish 'em off.'

'No more shooting if you can help it,' I shuddered.

'Christ, no,' he said. 'I've only got one round left anyhow, and I don't suppose any of their stuff will fit my gun,' and he went back into the copse.

The Brigadier and Hapgood were arguing again. 'So we're not much better off than we were before,' the latter grumbled.

'It all depends how one looks at it,' the Brigadier said. 'Personally I didn't much enjoy sitting trussed up like a spatchcocked chicken waiting for somebody to chop my bloody head off—Sorry, Shivka.'

'Don't mind me,' said the woman. 'You've expressed my sentiments exactly.' She had a young voice and her English was completely accentless, both of which surprised me somewhat. I still couldn't see her face, but I had imagined her, with a name like that, to be a Shanghai Russian and, for some totally unknown reason, middle-aged. 'I would like to add my thanks to those of Brigadier Cavendish-Feltham and Captain Hapgood,' she went on, 'both for the rescue and this lovely water—that's if Captain Hapgood *has* thanked you both.'

'He hasn't,' the Brigadier said drily. 'He said he'd just as soon be tied up and parching.'

'Goddammit! I didn't say that at all,' Hapgood howled. 'These guys have been great and I appreciate it. What I said was—'

'Keep it down, old boy, will you. Our friends in there are no longer interested, but the truck will be showing up soon—and that voice of yours carries.' He turned to me. 'Have you any idea of our exact location here?'

'I told you our exact location,' Hapgood snapped. 'We're a couple of hundred miles south-east of Kweilin.'

'You didn't seem too certain of it when you crashed.'

'I didn't crash.'

'I rather thought you had. There was a frightful bump and we were all somewhat shaken up, weren't we?'

'I force-landed, God damn you, because I had run out of gas. I ran out of gas because we were chased by a flock of Jap Zeros and I had to divert south. The Jap Zeros came from a sector which your limey Intelligence had declared absolutely clear—' He paused, choking with rage.

'And now you've run out of breath as well,' the Brigadier said sympathetically.

'Actually Captain Hapgood is right,' I said in an effort to pour a little oil on troubled waters. 'We're about two hundred miles from Kweilin.'

'*Thank* you,' the Brigadier said sweetly. 'It's always comforting to have confirmation—'

'You're trying to get my goat,' Hapgood said, breathing heavily through his nose.

'And succeeding,' said Shivka. 'You're foolish to let him.

Stop it, Brigadier, or these gentlemen will be wondering into what sort of madhouse they've landed. And you haven't introduced *me*, by the way.'

'My dear, I'm sorry,' said the Brigadier. 'May I present Mr Stafford. This is Miss Shivka Ulanov. There are a lot of "ovnas" and "oviches" in between but she prefers not to use them.'

'How do you do?' said the woman. 'And once again, thank you, although that sounds totally inadequate. Stafford?— Stafford? You're not by any chance—?'

'This is Private Rawcliffe,' I said hastily as Raucous rejoined us. He's the one we've all got to thank—' I went on talking at random to head off any further questions—'and the others are Aggie and John and a chap we call the Silent One. Quite a party.'

'Look,' the Brigadier cut in, 'it's time we discussed our next move. How's Harrington, Shivka? Do you think he can walk?'

'I doubt it,' she answered. 'He comes to very woozily for a few moments and then goes off again. He could hardly swallow the water I gave him.'

'So we'll have to carry him,' the Brigadier said.

'Where the hell to?' asked Hapgood. 'You heard what the guy said, even if you doubted *my* word. We're *two hundred miles* from Kweilin.'

'So we carry him two hundred miles if necessary. There are five fit men now—Stafford, Rawcliffe, myself and the two Chinese—'

'What am I—a goddam cripple?'

'Walking wounded at the moment. We'll make a stretcher out of a blanket and a couple of saplings tomorrow. The immediate necessity is to get away from here and into hiding before that truck gets back.'

It was Lao-tze who said, in the *Tao-te Ching*, I think it was, that in the life of every man, however humble, occurs a Golden Moment—one flash of pure, blinding inspiration. Raucous had his then.

'Couldn't we knock the truck off ourselves, sir?' he ventured. 'There was only a couple of blokes in it beside the driver when it passed us.'

'God Almighty,' said the Brigadier in tones of wonder. 'And the chap's still a private. And when you think of some of the riffraff they're giving commissions to nowadays—Yes, my dear Rawcliffe, we *can* knock the truck off. We *will* knock the truck off. Now let me see. The officer told them to go to a place called Teking, where they apparently have an advanced supply dump—I haven't the faintest idea where that is, unfortunately, but he told the sergeant that he'd have the stripes of his arm and the skin off his arse if he wasn't back by first light. Anybody got the time? The devils stole my watch.'

'Just after midnight,' I told him, squinting at mine. 'Teking is a village on the Canton road, south of here. It would be about seventy miles away, assuming we're two hundred from Kweilin.'

'Thank you. First light is about five-thirty. Now let's get our heads together.'

2

We heard the approaching vehicle long before we saw it, because although it was well past sunrise there was a heavy mist in the valley which completely blotted out the road.

'It mightn't be him, of course,' the Brigadier mused. 'Although I haven't heard any other motor traffic the whole time we've been here.'

'It's him all right,' Hapgood said. 'Missing on one cylinder—'

'Like your wretched aeroplane,' said the Brigadier with malice aforethought.

'There was nothing wrong with my goddam airplane,' Hapgood snarled. 'Now look here, once and for all—'

'S-s-s-h!' hissed the Brigadier. 'You really have a voice like

161

a foghorn, Hapgood. Check weapons again, everyone. Stafford, make certain you don't leave your safety-catch on this time. You quite happy with that Jap burpgun, Rawcliffe?'

'Yessir—quite simple. The truck's gone past, sir.'

'Dammit, yes—I believe you're right. Must be another one with a missing cylinder.'

'Half a mo, sir. It's stopped!'

'Reversing,' said Hapgood. 'Missed the turn-off. I told you it was the bastard, didn't I?'

'Now, if he follows his previous wheel tracks he's going to halt directly in front of our position here—'

'Yes, so you've told us—a dozen times. You don't have to be right, though.'

'And I'm telling you again: *keep down*. Fire from the prone position, and only when they have all dismounted. *Quiet!* Here they are. Please, *please* let them follow their wheel tracks,' the Brigadier prayed.

It loomed blackly through the mist and halted alarmingly close to our position under a clump of ti-shrub, its screened headlights gleaming palely in the grey dawn, then they went out, and the engine died in a clatter of pre-ignition, and the driver opened his door and climbed down stiffly, stretched wearily, unbuttoned his pants and stood urinating, and two others jumped down from the back of the vehicle and joined him in the same function, then the passenger door opened and a fourth man got down on the other side and stood with his back towards us, also communing with nature.

'Yours are the three birds on the right, Rawcliffe, but for the Lord's sake don't hit the radiator or the tyres,' the Brigadier whispered. 'Right, you other two—gent on the left. Take aim—all together—Now!'

There were no misses, and so no need for squalid *coups de grâce*, for which I was thankful.

'Drag 'em out of sight,' the Brigadier said briskly. 'Oh, and while you're at it, cover the others back there with blankets before we bring Shivka through. If one of 'em's wearing a rather good Omega watch, it's mine. Come on,

162

Stafford, collect your people and get them aboard. Hapgood, you and I can check the POW.'

'Prisoner of war?' Hapgood said in amazement. 'For Chri'sake, we're not taking *prisoners?*'

'Petrol, oil and water, my dear chap,' the Brigadier smiled. 'Sorry, it's *gas* in your case, of course. The stuff we ran out of in your aeroplane—then the oil in the sump—sorry again, *crankcase*—and the water in the radiator. That's the same in both languages, isn't it?'

'Comical old bugger, ain't he?' Raucous chuckled as we went off. 'Not half taking the piss out of that Yank.'

I went through the copse to where the others were crouching in the hollow. Shivka was supporting the unconscious man's shoulders, holding his head clear of the ground, while Aggie gently kneaded his neck muscles. John and the Silent One watched impassively. The Chinese are a peculiar race—excitable and volatile, in everyday life, but, superficially at least, completely phlegmatic and devoid of emotion under strain. Shivka looked up at me and I saw her face clearly for the first time. It was very dirty, and the hair that escaped from under her woollen cap was black, lank and greasy, but I was struck by her eyes, which were intensely blue, like twin ultramarine lakes in grubby surroundings. The whole effect was disappointing, because I had been quite taken by her voice, which had sounded so attractive in the dark.

She raised her eyebrows inquiring, and the lids, so exposed, looked white against the rest of the grime, like those of an imperfectly blacked Al Jolson. What a pity, I thought.

'Everthing OK,' I told her. 'The others will be here in a moment and we'll carry this chap to the truck.'

'Poor Mr Harrington,' she said. 'I don't know much about nursing, but Aggie says she thinks his skull is fractured and he needs a Chinese pillow—you know, one of those porcelain things that supports the neck and relieves pressure on the affected part.'

'How on earth did she get all that over to you?' I asked.

163

'Quite clearly,' she said, and added in perfect Cantonese to Aggie, 'Tell the gentleman what you have told me about this sick man.'

'A very bad blow,' Aggie said. 'It is on the back of the head, which is dangerous if pressed upon. I have told this missie that we should have a kai-si for his neck—otherwise one of us must support his head clear of the ground at all times.'

'You have heard that,' I said to John and the Silent One. 'All of us must take our turn until we get this master to a doctor. Is that understood?'

They nodded solemnly, and then the Brigadier joined us. 'There is food of a kind in the truck,' he told us. 'Plenty of it, but I think we can find a rather more congenial spot than this to brew up and cook, if you can hold out just a little longer. All right?'

We got under way immediately, with Raucous driving, which he did very well, earning yet further plaudits from the Brigadier, in whose eyes he could do no wrong. He had still further covered himself with glory in that he had found the Brigadier's watch, together with eleven others, three of which he generously bestowed upon those who needed them.

'One of the bastards was wearing four,' he told me. 'Must have been the quartermaster, the thieving sod. Looting. You can get five years in our mob for that.'

We drove off the road up a side track a few miles further on, and Aggie, assisted by Shivka, produced a gargantuan meal of rice, noodles, dried fish and various things from cans in an incredibly short time. We gorged, and some of us, myself among them, were sick through sheer overeating, which brought beams to Aggie's face, for that is the ultimate compliment to any Chinese cook. Then we got under way again, and we drove the whole of that day, relieving each other in watches of two hours at the wheel and on look-out—and apart from an occasional peasant who scuttled under cover at our approach, we saw not a soul.

I was drivng at one period and the Brigadier was sitting

beside me in the cab, the first time we had been together without witnesses.

'One of the cloak-and-dagger boys, aren't you?' he suddenly shot at me without warning, then, when I denied it, he went on, 'That's an unanswerable question anyhow. If you were you'd naturally say no; on the other hand, if you looked cunning and winked knowing-like, you'd undoubtedly be masquerading. Amazing the number of liars out East lately who claim to be working for Intelligence. What *do* you do, by the way?'

'Just business, as I told you,' I said shortly.

'What sort of business? I've got a vested interest in asking.'

'Import, export—bit of this, bit of that. I make a living.'

'Are you a taipan?'

'It all depends what you mean by taipan. I run my own show certainly, so I suppose the answer is yes. Might I ask what your "vested interest" is?'

'Certainly. I'll probably be coming to you, or somebody like you, cap in hand asking for a job when this lot is over, always assuming we win and I come through in one piece.'

'You're thinking of leaving the army, then?'

'The army will be leaving me, I have no doubt. Like last time. I was bowler-hatted at the age of thirty-two—major—no job, no training for anything useful, right in the depth of the Depression. I was damned glad to be called back a couple of years ago.'

'You seem to have done all right this time,' I said. 'Major to Brigadier in two years?'

'Acting rank to give me parity with my American opposite number—paid as a spare-wank lieutenant-colonel,' he growled.

'Where did you learn Japanese?'

'I was junior military attaché in our Tokyo embassy from nineteen-twenty-two to 'twenty-five, before being axed in the economy cuts. Cantonese is my second language. Not as good as yours, though. I've been listening to you.'

There was silence between us for a time and I had the feeling that he was going to assail me with more questions, so I got in first.

'What are you doing in this part of the country, sir?' I said. 'Or is that a rude question?'

'Nothing secret about it, if that's what you mean,' he answered. 'At least, there's nothing cloak-and-dagger about it. Military Mission to Chiang Kai-shek. Training his hairy-arsed gaggle of bandits to fight the Communists originally, but now he and Mao Tse-tung have teamed up against the Japs on the one hand, while keeping a nervous eye cocked at the Russians on the other. The Japs are, of course, allied with the Germans, and the *Red* Russians with us, which *should* make the latter anti-Jap, but there's been no declaration of war as yet. The *White* Russians are naturally up against the *Red* Russians, which makes them a bit pro-German if you can follow me. The net result is that everything is all over the place like a mad dog's dinner at full moon, with only one common factor running through the muddle. That's the dislike all of them have for the British, with the Yanks running us a close second in the unpopularity stakes—which doesn't of necessity make *us* altogether kittens-in-a-basket. You've heard that bugger Hapgood getting at me the whole time?'

'And you at him, sir,' I said, 'if I may say so without disrespect.'

He chuckled. 'Nothing in it really. He's a damned good chap, and a splendid pilot, but it *is* symptomatic of Anglo-American relations at the moment. The Mission is a joint venture but we tend to look a bit wall-eyed at each other in the day-to-day running of things. Take this crash of ours. It wasn't in any way Hapgood's fault, but I just can't resist taking the mike out of him over it.'

'What happened exactly?' I asked.

'The Japs made a breakthrough in strength to the south of our HQ at Chingpo. We evacuated everybody to Kweilin,

166

including a two-hundred-bed hospital, and we, the American Brigadier-general and myself, with our personal staffs, came out in the last plane—fifteen of us with a crew of four. We were buzzed by a whole flight of Jap fighters and Hapgood had to take violent evasive action—in cloud over the mountains. I've never been so frightened in my life—a great lumbering Dakota, and he chucked it all over the sky like a bloody shuttlecock. He was really wonderful. He shook them off, but by this time he was right out of fuel, and he had to make a forced landing. He almost made it—in a pocket handkerchief of a rice paddy, but unfortunately we hit a belt of trees.' He shrugged. 'I often wonder what law, if any, governs these things. There were nineteen of us aboard that aircraft, and three of us crawled out of the wreckage—Hapgood, Shivka and I. We went in again and managed to get Harrington out. He was the co-pilot. There were others still alive—we could hear them calling out, but, as we burrowed in again, the whole damned thing went up in flames. Oh God, it was horrible, but at least it was quick. The poor devils hadn't a chance.'

There was another silence, then he went on in a flat expressionless voice, 'We were still sitting there, stunned and witless, when those bastards came along in their truck. I suppose we were lucky in so far as they were a reconnaissance party, because normal patrols just bayonet prisoners out of hand. I heard the officer tell the sergeant to take good care of us as he wanted to send us down the line for interrogation. And that was it. They bundled us into the truck and took us along. They gave us a drink of water from time to time, and a mouthful of some nauseating sludge or other and kept us, tied up. Right, that's my story. What's yours?'

'Nothing as exciting as yours,' I told him. 'All organized resistance had ceased in Hong Kong and the Japs were swarming through the Colony. I was separated from my unit and I ran into Rawcliffe. His officer had just been bayoneted, and he made a dash for it. We managed to get out of

167

Kowloon, and we just walked, mostly at night, with a substantial lift in a fishing-boat up the Pearl River past Canton—then more walking, until we met up with you.'

'You make it sound very simple. How did you manage for food, and the clothes you're wearing?'

'We were lucky. I had money and we bought and scrounged as we came along.'

'What about the Chinese?'

'The woman, Aggie, is Rawcliffe's girl-friend, "down-homer" I believe is the term. He insisted on picking her up in passing.'

'He would. Good chap, that.'

'The other two—well, we just seemed to accumulate them. They wanted to get out of Jap territory, and they've been very helpful in our scrounging so we're letting them stay with us, certainly as far as Kweilin.'

'I see,' he said. 'And what are your plans after that?'

'We'll have to take it as it comes. I've heard that Chiang's second-in-command isn't particularly friendly towards us—'

'That's an understatement. Tai Li? He hates our guts. He runs a private army of his own—the Blueshirts—absolute villains. Well, we can repay you a little now. We are still an accredited Mission, and however much Tai Li gags at it he can't act openly against us. You'll be under diplomatic protection—part of the Mission, as far as he's concerned—until I get some orders regarding you from our lords and masters.'

'Who are they?'

'A wretched funfair in Chungking calling themselves BTC—British Troops in China. It's run by a brigadier—a real one, I'm only acting, as I told you. I haven't met him yet, but I've had a few acrimonious exchanges with him in despatches. Anyhow, he's my boss, and since you're a British troop and you're certainly in China, presumably he's yours also.' He looked at his watch. 'Hell, we've overshot our time. Pull into the side and let our friend Rawcliffe have

168

another go, and Shivka and—what's her name, the down-homer, Aggie?—can rustle up some tea.'

'One question, sir,' I said as I switched off. 'Shivka. Who and what is she?'

'Just Shivka. She's unique. White Russian. Her father is, or was, a doctor in Shanghai. He was one of the original émigrés from the 1917 revolution. Quite a colony of them in northern China—'

'I know,' I said. 'I've come into contact with a lot of them, but this one sounds so English. Most of them, even the second and third generations, have a pronounced accent.'

'English mother,' he said. 'The old man has made quite a pile in his practice, and Ma insisted on sending Shivka home to be educated. You can't get anything much more English than Roedean. She's a lep—'

'A what?'

'LEP—locally enlisted personnel—my interpreter. She speaks Cantonese, Mandarin, Japanese, French, German and Russian—with a good working knowledge of American—and what in God's name I would do without her, I just do not know. That was the first of my rows with Chungking. They told me to fire her—and I told them to go and screw, so I've got that hanging over me. Fire her? Christ, she's worth that whole damned crowd of chairborne sons of pigs twenty times over.'

'What was their reason?'

'Said she hadn't been peeveed. Sorry to keep bunging these ghastly acronyms at you. PV—that means "positively vetted"—her whole background, parentage, grandparent-age, all her antecedents put under the microscope to see what her political affiliations might be. She hasn't got any. She's just got loyalty—and she's passionately anglophile. Peeveed my arse. It takes about six months, and then it doesn't prove anything one way or the other. I'd trust her with my life.'

She jumped down over the tailboard carrying a kettle as we alighted, smiling at me with a flash of white teeth. She

169

had good teeth. It was as if nature had relented in its parsimony and thrown them in together with her very beautiful eyes in grudging compensation for her other lack of charms. I wished that she could have followed Aggie's example and spruced up a little, because she really was filthy.

'Hi!' she called. 'For this relief, much thanks. I could just do with what Raucous calls a "Mugger char". What a lovely name for the bum. Suits him down to the ground.'

'Who're you calling a bum?' Raucous demanded over the tailboard. 'Cor! Look at yourself—dirty as a Shee-wah amah.'

'That's enough of that,' I said. 'It's your turn to drive, Rawcliffe. Help Miss Shivka to gather a few sticks to boil the kettle first.'

'*Celui-là n'est pas impudent,*' she laughed and winked at me.

'Hear that, sir?' said the unabashed Raucous. 'Speaks Chink as good as Aggie. Did you check the mileage when you stopped?'

'A hundred and twenty,' I told him. 'Eighty-odd to go. You'd better top up with petrol. How much have we left?'

'Four four-gallon cans, sir. I reckon we're doing about twelve to the gallon, so that ought to see us through.' He lowered his voice. 'I don't like the look of the gent who had the bash on the head. He's real poorly—and Mr Hapgood ain't so chipper either, his ribs are giving him hell. The girls have been looking after them both a treat.' He grinned. 'The Russian one's a fair caution. Had me in stitches, she has. Talking as posh as the Colonel's old lady one minute, and telling yarns that'd make a sergeant-major blush the next—in English *and* in Chink. I thought Aggie would bust a gut.'

The Brigadier and I climbed into the truck and looked at the patients. It was as Raucous had said. Harrington seemed to have lapsed from ordinary unconsciousness into a coma. His face was waxen, the eyes half open and staring, and he was hardly breathing. Aggie, supporting his head, looked up at us and shrugged hopelessly. Hapgood appeared to be having difficulty with his breathing also. He sat in a corner with his knees updrawn and both arms wrapped round himself, and I noted with alarm that there was a trickle of blood coming from one corner of his mouth.

John nudged me covertly and whispered, 'There is a village some way ahead, with a makee-flangee—I think about five miles from here.'

'What's that?' the Brigadier asked sharply.

'A village doctor,' I told him. 'Homeopathic, and some of them practise acupuncture. Five miles ahead,' and Hapgood overheard me.

'No sunnervabitch is going to make a goddam pinchusion out of me *or* my sidekick,' he said positively, and the effort made him cough, and more blood came from his mouth.

We swallowed our scalding tea and pushed on, and came to the village as night was falling, because it was considerably more than five miles ahead—and it was deserted. The Brigadier sniffed at the air. 'Notice anything?' he muttered to me, and I nodded miserably as I recognized the sweetish, cloying, sickening stench of death that was beginning to pervade Hong Kong when we left.

'Japs or Reds,' the Brigadier said. 'Nothing for us here. Let's get on.'

'We'll have to let her cool off a bit, sir,' Raucous said. 'She's been boiling her head off for the last few miles.'

He went off with a bucket to find water for the radiator and it was while he was away that Shivka saw the rescript nailed to a door in the village square. She brought it back to me and we pored over the running Mandarin characters in the fading light.

'Neither Japs nor Reds,' I told the Brigadier bitterly. 'Your friends the Kuomintang.'

'Not my friends,' he snapped. 'Just my temporary masters—by order of Whitehall. What have they been doing?'

'The village has been accused of harbouring Hung-hutse—that's bandits—'

'I know what Hung-hu-tse are. What happened?'

' "Collective discipline", is the term they use here. Three days ago.'

'The bastards. That means they've wiped out the entire village, men, women and children. Let's get this damned truck started, and shove off.'

Raucous came back then and we got the radiator cap off with difficulty, and a fountain of scalding rust-coloured water cascaded over the engine block, and then, inevitably, after we had topped up the wretched thing refused to start again. We ran the battery almost flat, and Raucous said resignedly that he would have to take the plugs out and dry the leads. check the points and a string of other technicalities.

'We should take the opportunity of getting another meal on the go, I suppose,' The Brigadier said dubiously, 'but I can't say I feel like eating here. Do you?'

I didn't, so I helped Raucous hamfistedly and after an hour or so we got a sullen cough out of the enginer, and we nursed it back into reluctant life.

'Thank God for that,' said the Brigadier. 'Come on, let's get moving. Your turn to drive again I think, Stafford.'

We had driven for over an hour, and I was having a struggle to keep awake before he broke silence again.

He said, 'I'm going to ask you a question. You can either answer it or tell me to go to hell—but please don't lie, because this is deadly important.'

'Go, on,' I said tentatively.

'Thank you. Are you just another military microcosm—a British officer evading the Japs, blundering along towards Chungking, or are you under definite orders?'

I thought for some moments. This was awkward. I instinctively trusted him, and yet . . .

'What makes you think I might be under orders?' I temporized.

'One of your Chinamen—John, as you call him. He doesn't know it, I hope, but *I* happen to know who he works for.'

'Who?'

'Never mind. Bit of a cheek that, I know. I'm asking you to be frank with me, but I'm holding back on you. He's a courier, a first class one, and I know very well that he wouldn't be wasted on a mere evader. Ergo, either you or Rawcliffe are agents. Possibly both of you are.'

I had had time to think now. 'Neither of us, as far as I know,' I said.

'Which tells me nothing,' he sighed. 'It serves me right— I shouldn't have asked.'

'Then why did you?'

'In your own interests. If you are an agent, then Kweilin is the last place you should be going to. You'll go into the lost, stolen or strayed compound that Chiang has caused to be opened there, and you'll be screened and interrogated and then given some lousy job like mine—training guerrillas, censorship duties, signal monitoring—for the duration, until either we win, or the Japs break through and slaughter us, or the Communists turn on Chiang and do something equally nasty. The point I'm trying to make, very clumsily, is, if you have any pressing reason for wanting to get to Chungking I had better drop you off here, because we're getting close to the first Kweilin checkpoint.'

'Thank you,' I said. 'Just drop me then in that case.'

'I thought so,' he said quietly. 'Pull up, will you. I have one more thing to ask you.'

'No more questions,' I said firmly.

'Not a question—a request. Take Shivka with you.'

'Not a chance. We're too big a party as it is.'

'What if I made it an order?'

'I'd accept your invitation, and tell you to go to hell.'

'It's not an order. I'm not fool enough to give one I couldn't enforce.' His voice was flat and expressionless, and very tired. 'I *am* appealing to you though. Stafford, if I take her in to Kweilin she will undoubtedly be arrested by Tai Li's Blueshirts, and God knows what will happen to her then.'

'But surely that's nonsense,' I said. 'She's a member of your Mission, isn't she?'

173

'She's a Chinese national, as are all White Russian refugees who have been given political asylum here, and she is no longer officially under my protection. I told you, didn't I, that I was ordered to discharge her. The fact that I didn't carry out the order doesn't alter anything. Her papers have been cancelled.'

'But you were taking her to Kweilin yourself, weren't you?'

'We had it worked out. She was going to remain on the aircraft, and Hapgood was going to take off again immediately. That's been knocked on the head now. Stafford—please, I beg you—she's served us well, and handing her over to these people would be a pretty poor return.'

'You don't give me much option, do you?' I grumbled. 'All right—but by God she'd better behave herself. Anyhow, couldn't the same fate be awaiting her in Chungking?'

'No, we've got an embassy there, and they could give her a temporary passport and fly her out to India. I don't know how to thank you, Stafford,' he said simply, and we got down and went round to the back of the the truck.

'Come on, Rawcliffe,' I said sourly into the darkness. 'We walk from here on. Bring the others. That goes for you too, Miss Ulanov. I understand you wish to come with us.'

I heard Rawcliffe grousing sleepily, and Shivka giving Hapgood instructions about the injured man, then they piled over the tailboard and there was a mumbled colloquy between the girl and the Brigadier. He turned to me and held out his hand.

'A scurvy pay-off for everything your party has done for us, Mr Stafford,' he said. 'But I think you'd agree that this was the better course if you knew the whole wretched picture.'

'Since I don't, I can't comment on that,' I said, shaking his hand perfunctorily.

John jerked at my sleeve. 'Ask the Honoured Master for our exact location,' he whispered, and the Brigadier overheard him.

'The Silk Road,' he said in Mandarin. 'The part that is said to be lost—nine miles to the south of Kweilin and two from the first checkpoint.' Then he walked away abruptly and climbed into the cab, started up jerkily and drove off into the gloom.

'We leave the road,' John told me. 'It is a long way across the plain before we come to it again, then there will be food, shelter and safety.'

'How far?' I asked, and he made a quick mental calculation.

'Maybe fifteen miles—perhaps a little more,' he said airily. 'Come, please.'

It had started to rain heavily.

Chapter Six

1

If I had not been hating everything and everybody, myself included, quite so venomously that night I think I would have admired John very much indeed. He never hesitated or put a foot wrong once. He hadn't a thing to guide him, the sky was heavily overcast, the rain fell continuously, and we didn't see a single light anywhere along that whole ghastly route after we left the road. There were no fields or cattle enclosures or even irrigation canals—no signs of human habitation whatsoever that could conceivably have been used as landmarks. It was just a featureless plain broken here and there by clumps of kika-thorn with, underfoot, an overlay of glutinous mud that plucked at our feet and caused us to slither and skid as we trudged in single file.

It came to an end as dawn was breaking. John said, in pidgin for Raucous's benefit, 'Stop along this side, my makee looksee chop-chop,' and he went off through the swirling mist that completely blanketed us on all sides, cutting visibility to little more than arm's length.

'Gawd,' moaned Raucous. 'Like a Chink laundry on a Monday morning, only not so warm. Not even anywhere to sit down without getting wetter arses than we got already.' And I was too weary to check him for his language.

We stood there, drooping like cattle after a long drive, waiting listlessly for whatever an unkindly fate had for us next, and I went to sleep on my feet, literally, and nearly fell flat on my face just as John returned.

'Softlee-softlee,' he whispered. 'Follow my. No makee noise.'

The mist cleared momentarily as we went forward, and I made out the stark outlines of a double-storeyed house before us, steeply roofed and with upward-curving eaves in the traditional Chinese style; just a house and nothing more, no garden or surrounding wall or outbuildings as one would have expected with a normal farmhouse. Two rows of heavily shuttered windows and a massive teakwood door confronted us, and I had never seen anything so depressingly unwelcoming in my life. The door opened in response to John's almost noisless tap, and there was a muttered exchange, then we filed through into darkness that was partially lightened by a guttering clay lamp carried by someone, whether man or woman I couldn't see, who led us up some stairs on to a landing, along a wooden-walled passage and up a second flight through a trap-door into an attic, where there was standing headroom only in the very middle. We followed the lampbearer along the length of this, and came to a second trap with a ladder that led straight down vertically, seemingly into the bowels of the earth. Somehow we managed to descent into a cellar at the bottom, passing our packs down from hand to hand in a human chain. A glaring petromax light stood on a table and I could see that the cellar was high-roofed and commodious, conforming, I should say, to the entire area of the house above it and, amazingly, there was a smouldering wood fire in a stone emplacement, although there seemed to be no windows, doors or any other apperture other than the shaft down which we had come.

John said, 'Please rest while I go to arrange for food. We are quite safe here, but there must be no noise, please, because many people sleep in the inn above us.'

'Inn?' I questioned.

'Safe house,' he explained. 'Truce of the Road, which runs past it the other side, and it is used equally by Kuomintang and Communists. There is no fighting between them while they are actually on the premises, but naturally the place bristles with spies, so it is well to arrive and depart with discretion.'

'I can quite understand that,' I agreed. 'But I would like to know—'

'I go to see about the food,' he said with finality, and disappeared up the shaft. Once again I had apparently received my full meed of information for the moment.

We stayed there for three days, although it seemed much longer because, in the absence of daylight, we could only reckon the passage of time by our watches. John and the Silent One came and went quite freely, but never at the same time. One was always there to watch us, and the confinement was irking me, although the others seemed quite content.

'Can't I come up just once?' I asked him. 'At night. Nobody is likely to notice me in the dark.'

'The night has a thousand eyes,' he said, shaking his head.

'*You* seem to be safe enough,' I said sourly.

'I am just one face among many, as also is my colleague. We know how to make ourselves inconspicuous. With Europeans it would be different.' He grinned impishly. 'All Chinese look alike. Isn't that what the foreign devils say about us?'

But he did at least give me a little information some time later, after a better than usual meal, when we sat comfortably before the fire, smoking manila cheroots that he had bought from a trader in the inn.

'Can she be given some work to do?' he asked, inclining his head in Shivka's direction. 'What I have to say is not for women's ears.'

Shivka jerked upright from her seat beside us on the quilts, and I expected an instant burst of outraged feminine wrath, but to my surprise she bowed with the utmost docility and went and joined Aggie who was darning socks.

'That is better,' John said complacently. 'She is one of

178

much learning, but women are women. They talk. We move at midnight.'

'What is the weather like?' I asked.

'As it was when we came here, raining, and very cold.'

'With the mud that much deeper on the plain,' I said glumly. I wanted to get out of this cellar, but suddenly its warmth and dryness had taken on a new allure.

'We do not travel on the plain,' he said. 'On the road—on foot for five miles, then by truck for the entire distance to Pengshui, which is a mere sixty miles south of Chungking.'

I heaved a deep sigh of relief. 'How long will that take us?' I asked.

'Four hundred and fifty miles. Two days if we are not unfortunate.' A Chinese would never tempt malicious Fate by saying 'if we are fortunate'.

Raucous, half asleep, with his hands folded Buddha-like over his distended stomach, noticed my reaction.

'The flat-faced bugger given you some good news for a change, sir?' he asked hopefully.

'Possibly,' I answered in English. 'Please don't interrupt.'

John appeared to understand the reproof, because he smiled acidly and said, 'You are right to chide him. A good man, and brave, but soldiers, like women, are not strict guardians of their tongues. I often wonder how much of our language he understands.'

'None,' I said flatly. 'Just coolie's pidgin. You can speak freely.'

'Hm,' he said doubtfully. 'The foreign devil who takes a Chinese woman to bed has a sleeping dictionary. It is surprising how much can be learned in those circumstances. Could you ask him, also, to withdraw?'

'Not without causing him to lose face. That would mean bad blood between you. You would not wish that?' While I had little compunction about slapping the ebullient Raucous's ears down myself, I was not going to allow others to do so.

'No, no,' John said hastily. 'Soldiers are men of violence. I

179

would as soon pull a mad dog's tail. All right. I have gathered certain news here. It is known to the Japanese that a big taipan, head of one of the three main business houses of Hong Kong, has escaped them and is on his way to Chungking. That may, or may not, be you?'

'May—or may not,' I agreed cagily.

'Whoever it is, there is a big reward being offered for him.'

'For all Europeans. We have already heard that.'

'But now it is much bigger—and more specific. In gold, to the value of fifty thousand American dollars, paid in Macao.'

'You are telling me nothing new, except that the reward has been increased.'

'I *am* telling you something new. The Japanese know that this taipan was involved in the killing of a party of their soldiers and the stealing of their truck.'

'Nonsense!' I exploded. 'How can they possibly know that? We are all here together and—'

'And three are in Kweilin,' he said quietly.

This was too much. 'One British and two American officers?' I said. 'Are you suggesting that they have given information to the enemy? How dare you even *think* such a thing?'

'I am not suggesting that,' he answered, in no way put out. 'But don't forget that they would have been debriefed, separately, by Kuomintang officers. A word here, a word there, perhaps an unguarded phrase dropped, then contradicted—two of them very sick men, all tired—the place riddled with spies—patriots, politicals and professionals—all playing their own hands, and all very skilled. Those gentlemen, entirely honourable and above suspicion, could quite easily have disclosed a great deal without knowing it.'

'Oh God,' I said wearily. 'What a filthy game this is. Is there nobody one can trust entirely?'

'Nobody—entirely,' John said. 'That is why we are trained to say as little as possible, even to each other, particularly at the end of a march, or when one is relaxed, as we are now.'

Kwan's words were coming back to me, and I was beginning to see the deadly necessity of caution at all times. 'Need to know'—'Tell as little as possible'—'Never use your own name'. How silly and childish it had all seemed at the time.

John was leaning forward, looking into the fire. 'There is one other thing,' he said. 'Something that worried me that night, but which I hesitated to mention, because I was a humble Chinese civilian among warriors. It would have been an impertinence.'

'What?'

'You have an English phrase for it among fishermen who joke after their sport—"the one that got away". Are we certain that all those Japanese died? Could not one have feigned death in the darkness?'

I nodded slowly. 'Two of 'em still twitching,' Raucous had said, and had gone back to deal with them. There might well have been others.

'There could have been,' I nodded. 'I would prefer to believe that than the other.'

'We consider it advisable to cut the throats of wounded in those circumstances,' John said simply. 'Our own as well as the enemy if it is not practical to take them with us.' He might have been discussing the disposal of weeds in a cottage garden. I tried unsuccessfully to repress a shudder, and hoped he hadn't notice it.

'Yes, I see what you mean,' I said with pseudo briskness. 'We'll have to watch that in future. So, we move at midnight, do we?'

'Yes. As I said, we have to walk to where the truck will pick us up.'

'The road is safe?'

'From all save the Japanese. They do not observe the Truce—but as far as our Intelligence can tell us, there are no Japanese between here and Pengshui. There may be a few penetration patrols after that, like the one we have already encountered, but I should have reports in time if that is the case.'

'The Truce?' I said. 'Does that mean we will be on the Silk

Road?' I knew that I was laying myself open to yet another snub, but this time it did not come.

'Yes,' he confirmed. 'We were on it before, as I told you, but it ends south of Kweilin, at that village, and starts again here, at the Inn of the Five Dragons, and runs without a break to the Yangtse.'

Raucous, who had dozed off, woke with a start at this point. 'What's the buzz, sir, if it's not a rude question?'

'All questions are rude to these people,' I told him. 'One must learn not to ask them. I can tell you in this case, however, that we start out from here at midnight, walk a fairly short distance, then ride by truck nearly all the way to Chungking.'

He stretched and yawned. 'Thank Gawd for that. This place is getting on my wick, good grub and warm kip notwithstanding.'

2

It was as if Fate had relented at last. The rain had stopped, the night was clear and cold, and the walk to the pick-up point was positively exhilarating. The truck, a big German diesel, for which, ironically, my company had been importers and agents in pre-war days, was drawn up at the side of the road with an assortment of others in varying stages of dilapidation, seven in all, and their crews were squatting round a fire nearby. Nobody took the slightest notice of us as we approached through the darkness and climbed up into the back of the vehicle. It was empty except for a pile of the ubiquitous padded cotton quilts which are the Chinese peasants' sole concession to sybaritism. These looked, and smelt, as if they had been used by successions of travellers over a very long time, but we burrowed into them thankfully, because the night was growing colder by the hour.

We seemed to have passed yet another of these unseen

points at which tension slackened and the general atmosphere became easier, and John was quite loquacious without any prompting from me.

'This is a returning supply column,' he explained. 'Food, munitions, fuel and general war materials are flown into Chungking from India over the Himalayas, and then distributed to Chiang's various outposts by road, where in theory, they are shared with the Communists.'

'And they let us travel without question?'

'If the individual or party is carrying the right chop.'

'And you are?'

'All three. Chiang's, Mao's and Tso Lin's.'

A 'chop' is nothing more nor less than the equivalent of our rubber stamp, but in China it is of transcending importance—a seal of one or more intertwined characters carved in jade or ivory or sometimes the hardened root of the bamboo plant, without the impression of which no document, bond, cheque or *laissez-passer* is valid.

'Who is Tso Lin?' I asked. The former two needed no explanation.

'He is the Grand Master of the Triad in this province, so we are protected from Kuomintang, Communists and bandits, from all except the Japanese, but, as I have already told you, there are no Japanese in this area—yet.'

'I wish you had a chop against small creatures,' Shivka said out of the darkness. 'These quilts are lousy.'

'Confucius says that a woman's ears should be attuned only to the voice of conscience and that of her lord and master,' John informed her with dignity.

'Wretched hypocritical rice-Christian,' Shivka said to me in English. 'If he wants to take me on about Confucius I'll blind the little beast.' But to him, in Mandarin, she replied meekly, 'A merited rebuke should be received as a pearl, graciously. Also Confucius. I thank you.'

The vehicles started up then, and we ran steadily through the remaining hours of darkness, and the whole day that followed, halting only once to refuel at a camouflaged dump and to stretch our cramped limbs. Convoys similar to our own passed us on occasion, going south, piled with crates and oil drums, and once we had to pull into the side to allow passage for a mile-long column of jaded, very second-water Kuomintang troops trudging by on foot.

'Gorblimey!' Raucous said, surveying them with a jaundiced professional eye. 'Call themselves soldiers? Not on our side, are they?'

'Nominally,' I told him.

'They'd be more use on the other. It'd take a battalion or two of ours to keep that hairy-arsed shower in the line,' he grunted.

We had reached the ultimate depth of misery by the time we arrived in Pengshui. It was raining heavily and we were soaked, shivering and famished. We drove under a crumbling archway into a courtyard that was enclosed by buildings on all sides, making the place a well of darkness that was deepened rather than relieved by a dim light showing through the cracks of a wooden shutter covering a ground-floor window. John climbed over the tailboard and dropped to the ground.

'Wait, please,' he said to me. 'I go for orders.'

'Make it quick,' I told him tersely, and settled back squelchingly into the sodden quilts which were no longer giving even an illusion of warmth.

I saw a narrow beam of light reflect back off the wet ground as a door was opened. It closed and I resigned myself to the inevitable wait that precedes any transaction whatsoever in the East, but it opened again almost immediately and I heard footsteps approaching rapidly, and John's head reappeared over the tailboard.

'All fix chop-chop vellee ni',' he said happily. 'You come please.'

We climbed down stiffly and trooped through the mud after him to the door. The room we came into was softly lighted by two shaded porcelain lamps and a bright wood fire that crackled on an open hearth, and the atmosphere was blessedly warm and relaxed. It was akin to sailing out of a stormy sea into a snug harbour. The lamps made twin pools of light, leaving the rest of the space in comparative darkness, so that I was unable to make out any details of a figure that advanced towards us as we entered, other than that two hands were outstretched in welcome, which in itself was unusual in this part of the world, because Chinese thrust hands into opposite sleeves, and kowtow on greeting. They certainly never enfold one in a bearhug and use terms of affectionate abuse. This one did both. She called me a bum, and seemed to have difficulty in controlling her voice and I could feel her trembling.

I said, '*Mom!*' which restored the status quo, because it was a term of address that always infuriated her.

'Don't you call me that, you lug,' she snapped, then disengaged and passed on to Shivka, who was standing immediately behind me. 'Welcome back, honey,' she said. 'What in God's name have you got on your hair?'

'Lamp-black and butter,' Shivka said. 'It'll wash out.'

'I hope so. Holy sailor! Don't you stink! You'll find a bath through that door, and I've brought you some clothes along,' my mother said, and turned to Aggie. 'You are welcome in my filthy and unworthy house,' she said in Chinese and smiled.

'I thank the very old and wise grandmother,' Aggie replied respectfully, and kowtowed.

I had ceased to wonder any more. I just stood in a haze of dumb bewilderment as she went on to greet Raucous, John and the Silent One, switching from English to faultless Mandarin and back again. I spotted a bottle of scotch on a low table by the fire and I poured myself a good half tumblerful and was about to include the others, but Abigail intervened.

'There are drinks, baths, food and beds for the boys next door,' she explained to me in a quick aside as she ushered them out. 'You sit down right there. You use my room next door, Shivka.'

The whisky, the warmth and the comfort of the chair were taking effect by the time she returned. I came to with a start to find her standing over me. I tried to get to my feet, but she pushed me back.

'Relax,' she said. 'You're just about all in, aren't you?'

'Not any more than the others,' I said. 'I *am* in a bit of a whirl, though. How the devil did you find you way to this place? What are you *doing* here?'

'Nothing puzzling about it. I got out of Shanghai the day Pearl Harbor was bombed. I sent you a note—'

'I got it.'

'I sold the Hotel Kempton to Lars Bründahl, my manager, for one dollar.'

I laughed. 'Of course! He's Swedish and neutral. You wily old lady.'

'Not so much of the "old". It may be complimentary in Chinese, but I'm damned if it is in English. I don't *feel* old.'

'Or look it, my love,' I assured her truthfully. She had been a noted beauty in her day, red-haired, green-eyed, with a peerless complexion, and the years had treated her kindly. I was nearing forty, so she had to be something over sixty,. but few outsiders would have guessed it. 'So you sold out to Bründahl? Against the day we win and push the Japs out of Shanghai again? What if he refuses to sell it back to you—for one dollar?'

'Can you imagine anybody pulling anything as raw as that on *me*—and getting away with it?'

'Hardly'.

'Then why ask damfool questions? Actually the deed of transfer was drawn up over a year ago by three of the best international lawyers in town, and it covers every contingency. All it needed was one date and two signatures to put it into operation. Then I hightailed it for Chungking and the Cathay Palace.'

'Have you a deed of transfer and another handy Swede standing by for that also?"

186

'No. It wouldn't mean anything anyhow. If we lose Chungking we'll have lost the war.'

'I'm inclined to believe you. All right then: next question.'

'I'll allow you one only, then for Pete's sake go away and bath before dinner. You smell even worse than Shivka. Ask away.'

'You were obviously expecting us here. How? And where had you met Shivka before?'

'That's two questions. How did I know you were on your way here? Radio, for God's sake. How else? I've had tabs on your movements ever since you came out through Kowloon. Shivka? If you'd come up to Shanghai and visited your old Maw occasionally you'd have met her. She has been my chief receptionist, secretary and woman-of-all-work for the last three years at the Kempton. Worth her weight in diamonds. I was furious when the Army grabbed her. Co-opted was the word they used. They couldn't conscript her because she's not a British subject. What do you think of her?'

'Heart of gold, no doubt,' I said. 'But I thought reception-ists in five-star international hotels had to have a little glamour as well.'

'Don't you think she has?'

'If she has it's certainly eluded *my* notice.'

'Oh well, no accounting for differing tastes, I suppose. Which brings us to the subject of Helen and the kids.' She couldn't abide my wife, but adored the children. 'You got them out in time, I gather?'

'Only just. On the last boat to Australia.'

'Why on earth did you leave it so late?'

I shrugged, and unintentionally played into her hands. 'You know Helen,' I said. 'She thought her place was with me. I had a hell of a job to make her go.'

'Yes,' Abigail said drily. 'It was the same with lots of dutiful little wifies in Shanghai, the stupid cows. They hung on and fouled things up for their husbands, who might

187

otherwise have put up a better fight if they hadn't been looking back over their shoulders most of the darned time. The concentration camps along the Whangpo are full of them—starving and wailing their heads off.'

Stung, I said, 'Then why didn't *you* get out?'

'Because I'm a different kettle of fish altogether,' she answered levelly. 'I had work to do. Not like them, sitting on their rumps playing bridge, drinking gin slings and hopping in and out of bed with their friends' husbands.'

'You're a spiteful old woman,' I told her. 'English old—not Chinese.'

'Maybe, but I've got the measure of some of your Colonial wives, my son.'

'You're a hell of a one to talk. Some of the stories I've heard from Aunt Anne—! And you a missionary's daughter!'

She smiled disarmingly. 'Your Aunt Anne, eh? That's one dyed-in-the-wool limey I always made an exception for, rest her soul. But she wasn't a Colonial wife, was she? Just an unconsidered old maid who worked herself into the ground looking after male Staffords—first that old sunnervabitch of a grandfather of yours, then your father and uncles, then you.'

'Exactly,' I agreed. 'Picking up the pieces that you and my grandmother, the famous Mrs Kempton, left behind when you scooted.'

'Time!' she said. 'First round a draw. Let's drop it—before I whip in a couple of mean ones about the Princely House of Stafford & McMurtrie, and what they tried to do to your father, the *real* prince of the whole boiling, before he and I teamed up and got the better of that old rooster.' She was still smiling, but I could see an incipient glint of tears there now.

'It beats me how you managed to get radio news of us,' I said, to get off dangerous ground. 'I mean—well, I know you're a very important lady in Chungking and all that, but I'm just a military evader—second-lieutenant, lowest form of animal life—so why the special treatment?'

'Wheels within wheels,' she answered vaguely. 'We'll

have a long talk about everything when we get to Chung-king.'

'When will that be? And how do we travel?' I asked.

'We'll rest here overnight and arrive there late tomorrow afternoon if there are no air raids to hold us up,' she said. 'I have a couple of jeeps here. I'd like you to drive one and your soldier the other. My two drivers can come back by truck later.' She rose, then bent over and kissed me on each cheek. 'Now go and clean up. You'll find everything you want there—no, not that door you fool. The unglamorous Shivka is scrubbing off there. Now don't be too long, because there's going to be quite a dinner when you've finished. One of the drivers is moonlighting. He's my second chef in real life.'

I squeezed her hand and smiled at her. 'We'll do it justice,' I said. 'I'm sorry about the spat. I started it. I won't make any more snide remarks—Mom.'

'*Abigail*, you bastard,' she said. 'You nearly were, you know. I'll tell you about it some day. My God, that was two wars back—the one that took your father, and the South African, Now we're up to our eyes in a third. When the hell are we going to gain a little wisdom—and compassion?'

I went out through the second door into a small annexe where a coolie was emptying buckets of nearly boiling water into a big wooden tub. A charcoal brazier made the place delightfully warm, and on a table I could see some neatly folded clothes and a pile of soft white towels. A burst of laughter came to me from a room the other side of the annexe as I started to strip my filthy garments from me, and I applied my eye to a crack in the dividing partition. Raucous, Aggie, John and the Silent One were sitting round a laden table scrubbed clean and comfortably at ease, with chopsticks busy. I felt a wave of affection for all of them. They were an uncomplaining and dependable crew, Raucous's old sweat's bellyaching notwithstanding, and I was tempted to go in and thank them, but I felt that it might appear pretentious and patronizing.

A sustained hammering on the other wall brought me

reluctantly out of that glorious bath. I towelled vigorously, dressed and went back, and stopped short in the doorway because there was another woman there, standing in front of the fire talking to Abigail. I thought she was Chinese, because she was wearing a jade green cheongsam, that most subtly flattering of garments, high-necked and slit-skirted, which fitted her to perfection, but then she moved forward into the light and I saw that she was an almost Nordic blonde.

She said, 'Good Lord! This is the first time I've seen him clean. He just misses being handsome, doesn't he?'

'Um, yes, I suppose so,' Abigail agreed dubiously. 'Of course, his father was very good-looking, and he gets a certain amount of it from me as well, but the Stafford strain has come out in him strongly, I'm afraid. They all tend to look like dyspeptic Presbyterian deacons as they get older.'

'You're a pair of bitches,' I told them when I found my voice. 'Yes, it's remarkable what a little soap and water will do, even for you, my dear Shivka—in a dim and kindly light like this.'

'Well, that's something,' said my mother. 'He said he thought you were distinctly unglamorous earlier.'

'Did he now?' said Shivka. 'Oh well, I'll forgive him for that. I'm most grateful to him—really—sincerely. For everything.'

She came forward and held out both her hands in a natural and totally unaffected gesture and smiled up at me, and I felt my throat muscles constricting, because I had never, before or since, seen anything as beautiful as that face. I took her hands and mumbled something about having done nothing, and dropped them hastily as I caught Abigail's enigmatic eye on us both.

I don't remember much about that meal, except that it was a very good one. I suppose I was in a mild state of shock. It was a Grimm's fairy tale—an ugly and dirty slattern turning at the touch of a wand into something as lovely as this, and I was completely bowled over—for the first time in my life. I asked her at one stage why she had so enthusiastically over-egged the pudding in the matter of her disguise.

'For the same reason as the Chinese call their children cock-eyed and bandy, I suppose,' she laughed. 'So the gods wouldn't want me. Lascivious Chinese generals in my case. Most of them are ambidextrous—oriental or occidental, sling 'em on the bed unless they're really too, too repulsive. Incidentally, Abigail, we can keep Aggie, can't we?'

'I don't know,' my mother temporised.

'She'd be very handy round the hotel—' Shivka coaxed.

My mother brought her palm hard down on the table with a loud slam.

'Too damned handy,' she said. 'She's a soldiers' tart. One can see that with half an eye. It's hard enough keeping a hotel respectable in wartime China without having home comforts on tap.'

'She's an absolute dear,' Shivka said stoutly. 'And who made her a tart?'

'Oh Christ,' sighed Abigail. 'Here we go again. Workers of the world unite—you're supposed to be a *White* Russ, not a Red.' She turned to me. 'This goddam girl had half the waifs and strays of Shanghai feeding their heads off at my expense, yellow, white and brindle. All right, all right, just this one—and I mean that.'

'Just this one—cross my heart.' Shivka winked at me. 'You're a darling.'

'From all of which I gather you two are joining forces again?' I said.

'That's in the lap of the gods, Abigail sighed. 'The gods in this case being Chiang's Foreign Department. Shivka, unfortunately, can be pushed around by any little jerk who wants to demonstrate his own importance. You've got to have a permit just to breathe in Chungking at the moment.'

'That's all right,' I said in my innocence. 'The British Embassy will look after her there.'

'You don't say?' Abigail said gravely. 'And who told you that?'

I floundered. It wasn't that I didn't trust my mother, but this wretched 'need-to-know-don't-talk-to-anybody-on-arrival' nonsense was bothering me again. 'Oh, nobody actually. I mean—well, I assumed that . . .' I tailed off awkwardly as I saw the others exchange quick glances.

'It doesn't matter,' Abigail said kindly, and I felt like a small boy who had butted into a conversation between elders and was being politely put in his place. 'I'm afraid things are a little more complicated than that. Shivka is a stateless person, you see. You, of course, will be reporting to the military attaché at the Embassy on arrival, and I think it would be better if you didn't mention her—not at this stage, anyhow.'

And now I was really worrying, because I could feel myself getting into deep water. It seemed that I was being counselled to hold back important information from our own people.

'Yes, but apparently somebody is going to debrief me when I get there,' I began.

'Exactly,' said Abigail. 'Then you tell all, my son, because some guy who knows his job will be putting you through the mangle. You'll be in the hot seat and you'll be scraping through the recesses in your memory giving him the lot—who you met up with on this trip, and where, what you talked about, what you saw, timings, descriptions of the places you've been in, every last little seemingly unimportant detail. That's at the *debriefing*. I'm referring to what you talk about in the outer office—to junior officers, both British and Chinese, when there are civilian clerks and interpreters around, Russkies of both colours, people like Lola the beautiful spy here.' She jerked her head at Shivka. '*I* happen to know that this one is OK, but you don't—not yet. If it comes to that, you don't know if *I'm* OK.'

'Oh, come off it,' I protested. 'There must be a limit to this absurdity at some point.'

She shook her head. 'No limit,' she said flatly. 'War itself is the ultimate negation of reason—Nietzsche—which is why you can't afford to let up for a moment. Oh, don't worry. You're doing all right. You've told me nothing you shouldn't have. Just keep it that way.'

'And he shied away from me along the road as if I were a leper,' Shivka put in, coming to my aid.

'Maybe because you looked like one,' Abigail said drily. 'It might have been a different story if you'd been looking and smelling, like you do now. Go on, beat it to bed, both of you—you through there, and you through there, and if I hear any tiny footsteps in the night I'll be round you both with a hickory.'

'Charming old Abigail,' yawned Shivka. 'Mind like a sewer.'

'You bet,' said my mother. 'I had a good moral upbringing. And no so much of the "old".'

3

If there is a more depressing place than Chungking, then God preserve me from it. It stands on a rocky promontory that rises two hundred sheer feet about the Yangtse-kiang where it is joined by the Kialing River, the two in summer making a mile-wide maelstrom of tumbling brown water that sweeps eastwards to the China Sea a thousand miles away. In the winter, as it was now, it shrinks to two much narrower streams, exposing a mile-long sandbank in between which serves as the city's nearest approach to an air landing ground. The river is the main thoroughfare, and from the docks along the banks rises a flight of nearly five hundred worn stone steps to the main town. From first light until sundown every day of the year, summer and winter, an endless chain of laden coolies toil up and down—laden both ways, because Chungking is the main entrepôt for the whole of Central China, and the tide of its trade flows reciprocally. When darkness falls the steps are lighted dimly by guttering oil lamps on poles, and beggars, footpads and whores emerge like cockroaches from the shanties which cling to the rocky face of the almost vertical cliffs on either side. The whole place is perpetually shrouded in fog, which in summer is thick and damp, in winter, impenetrable and drenching. Its apologists assure one that the winter temperature never drops below freezing point, but for all that there are many bundles of rags that do not move when the police clear the steps each dawn of their overnight denizens. Deaths from exposure are not quite so numerous in summer, but heatstroke tends to balance the score then, so the daily tally of corpses floating downriver remains fairly constant the year round.

We left the jeeps at the police post on the south bank and crossed the river in a sampan, round the western end of the sandbank, and landed at the bottom of the steps as the first lamps were being lit, and a yelling crowd of huakan coolies descended on us. The huakan is a sedan chair when it is on the steps but becomes a rickshaw when its wheels are lowered on the limited level ground in the town at the top. It is said that the expectation of life for the average puller/carrier is thirty years, unless he is an opium smoker, when it drops to twenty-five. I pushed through them and started to climb, and Shivka caught up with me.

'Not riding?' I asked her.

'No,' she answered. 'This is a penance for days of sitting and overeating. Have you been to this place before?'

'Several times,' I told her. 'And liked it less on each occasion.'

My mother overtook us in a huakan, the four coolies grunting in unison as their bare feet slapped the wet flagstones.

'All right, you self-righteous humanitarians,' she called. 'But if nobody employs them the poor bums starve.'

'Go ahead,' Shivka said. 'At your age you're entitled to a little comfort.'

'You bitch,' Abigail said sweetly. 'There'll be cars at the

194

top. You can use those without bleeding.' Then she urged the carriers on with a blast of blistering Hakka.

'A strange mixture, my mama,' I said as the huakan went ahead into the gloom. 'Ministering angel and longshore slavedriver.'

'A bit pragmatic at times,' Shivka agreed, 'although she's pretty logical with it. She curses the coolies in heaps, but pays them tenfold. She wouldn't give one of these beggars a copper cash, but she spends thousands on soup and rice kitchens for them.'

'You surely don't call that logical, do you?' I said.

'Very. She knows that the beggars are controlled by their Triad guild, and they have to hand over half of everything they collect in the way of money—but what they put into their bellies is theirs. If she gave the huakan coolies money for nothing she would be reducing them to beggary, but by hiring them she is helping them to preserve their self-respect.' I was conscious of her looking sideways at me as we climbed. 'You don't like her, do you?' she said. 'A pity. She loves you very much.'

'Piffle,' I said brusquely. 'We hardly know each other. I was brought up by my father's family while she has spent ninety per cent of her time up north here running her business.'

'Nevertheless, she does love you.'

'How on earth could you possibly know that? You didn't know who I was until yesterday.'

'Oh yes I did. I knew who you were from the moment we met.'

'How?'

'Does it matter?'

'Yes—if only to prove that you're talking nonsense.'

'Because she has told me about you, shown me photos of you, and your wife and the children—'

'Nothing to the credit of any of us, I'll bet. She can't stand my wife, and she knows less about my children that she does of me.'

195

'You'd be surprised—'

'I doubt it. You're talking too much. Save your breath for the steps.'

We climbed on in silence, stepping over huddled bundles and shaking off supplicating hands that reached out from the darkness and clawed at us in passing. Behind us I could hear Raucous cursing in a continuous rumbling undertone that was exacerbating my already frayed nerves still further, and I turned and shouted at him to shut up.

'Don't raise your voice,' Shivka said sharply. 'Certainly not in English.'

'What the devil has it to do with you?' I asked angrily.

'Please,' she said. 'You never know who's listening on these steps.'

My common sense told me that she was right, but I was childishly angry and beyond all reason now, and I kept on arguing with her until she quickened her pace and went on ahead of me, and when I tried to catch up with her I knocked out whatever wind that was left in my labouring lungs and my legs turned to lead.

We reached the top at last and I turned and looked back. The fog, in its erratic fashion, had momentarily cleared, and I could see the river far below us in the moonlight, a broad ribbon, dull silver between black hills as it emerged from the Szechuan gorges to the west and started on its long course across the plains to the sea. Two cars stood waiting at the beginning of the muddy street that runs from the top of the steps in a straight line and bisects Chungking into two polarized worlds—the pseudo-modern business section to the south, with the packed and pullulating shanty town facing it the other side. There was a police post here where in normal times passports were demanded from new arrivals, day or night, and I had been expecting some sort of check and wondered how Abigail would cope with it, but, although there was a light showing through a small and dirty window, the door remained closed as we passed it.

'You and Shivka into the first car,' she directed. 'The

others into the second one. You poor dears, you must be just about pooped after those damned stairs. It won't be long now.' She climbed in after us and we started up, squelching and squattering through what I knew from past experience was almost axledeep liquid mud at this time of the year with a corresponding depth of choking dust in summer. 'What are you looking for?' she asked as I leant forward and cleared the moisture from a side window.

'The gates you're supposed to have pinched from the Summer Palace in Hangkow,' I answered.

'I didn't pinch them,' she laughed. 'I won them from old Robert Po Lee, the tobacco king, in a poker game two years ago. There they are—what's left of them.' She pointed as the masked headlights swept over a pile of fallen masonry. 'I lost out on the deal. The damned things weren't insured against war and civil strife.'

'What happened to them?' I asked.

'Bombed flat—what else? This place used to be plastered every second night. They've left us alone since Pearl Harbor. Too busy fighting a real war down south now.'

'But the hotel itself? Wasn't that hit?'

'And how! High explosives and incendiaries. It's a burnt-out shell. You'll be able to see it in the morning.' She chuckled. 'That *was* insured—all risks.'

'But we didn't hear anything about that in Hong Kong,' I said.

'You never heard anything that didn't immediately affect your profit and loss accounts in that ivory tower of yours,' she retorted.

'So where are we going now?' I asked.

'To fresh woods and pastures new,' she said. 'It's a bit further out of town, but a darned sight healthier. Chengtu, the Old City. It's of no strategic importance, so it's never been bombed, touch wood.'

We drove on for another hour, leaving Chungking proper behind us and coming out into mountainous country through which a rutted narrow road ran along a line of cliffs

197

parallel with the main river but two or three hundred feet above it, and I felt my hair standing on end because the driver, once clear of the cluttered town put his foot hard down and fairly screamed round hairpin bends on a track that I swear was not much wider than perhaps a car's width and a half.

'Here's the gate,' Abigail said calmly when I had reached a point when I could take no more. 'This one's genuine. Po Lee's was a fake.'

We turned sharp left off the road through an archway which I was only able to catch a glimpse of before coming on to an avenue which seemed twice as broad as the so-called road we had left. There were lights ahead of us, lots of them, and I had an impression of a long verandah on to which french windows opened, then we were back into darkness, skirting round a cluster of buildings. We pulled up and the driver switched off the engine, and I thought I was suffering from delusions because from somewhere in the distance I could hear the Blue Danube being played by what seemed to be a full orchestra.

'Welcome to the Cathay Palace, Mark Two,' Abigail said.

'It looks like a Shinto temple,' I said, because I could make out curved eaves and pagoda towers against the night sky. 'Although Shinto is Japanese.'

'Clever of you,' she said. 'Shen-tao, actually, which is the Chinese branch of it, and officially banned as a religion since 1937. That's why I was able to buy it cheap and desecrate it into a pub. Come on, this way.'

'Where's that music coming from?' I asked her.

'Courtesy of the band of the Twenty-second Route Regiment. Chiang must be dining here tonight,' she told me. 'He's a heller for Western Music—so long as it's The Blue Danube, Lead, Kindly Light or Marching Through Georgia. It can get a bit wearing if he's here for more than three hours.'

We followed her in through a door, stumbling in the darkness because she would allow no lights until we were all inside.

'Knock twice and ask for Alice, as your father used to say, whatever that means,' she said. 'I'm sorry to sound conspiratorial, but one never knows who is hanging about, and I'd rather nobody knew you're here until I've reported you in.'

'Reported me to whom?' I asked.

'Oh, the Embassy people,' she said vaguely. 'Now, let's see about getting you bedded down.'

She certainly was a hotelière *par excellence*, because, with the aid of a smiling, soft-footed little *valet de chambre* who appeared from nowhere, she had us allotted to rooms, hot baths were laid on and drinks and supper trays appeared by magic. For myself I remember nothing more until sunshine through a latticed window and the twittering of birds in a garden awakened me very agreeably a considerable number of hours later. I stretched luxuriously and heard the completely inimitable 'z-e-e-p' of silk pyjamas against silk sheets, which was not as decadent as it might seem, because silk in Szechuan is cheaper than cotton in most other places.

The bedside telephone sounded softly and I came out of my laze with reluctance.

My mother said, 'Sorry, dear, but the mountain has come to Mahommed. Two of them. I'll stall them off if you don't feel up to it yet.'

'Who are they?'

'Backroom boys—preliminary debriefing. They'd rather do it here than down at the Embassy.'

I ran a hurried eye round the room. 'Somebody's pinched my clothes,' I complained.

'And burnt them—they were lousy. You'll find a robe at the foot of your bed.'

'You mean the black silk confection splurged with golden dragons? Good God! They'll think I'm Noël Coward.'

'Don't worry about that. It's all very palsy-walsy at this stage. All right, I'll send them up, with some coffee.'

'Hey, wait a minute,' I started to protest, but she had hung up, and I only had time to stick my head under the cold tap in the bathroom before there was a tap at the door.

199

I let them in, two of them, followed by the room boy carrying a silver tray. They waited while he set it down on a low table and then left, which gave me a few moments in which to study them—a full colonel, wrong side of fifty, thin and sun-dried with a clipped grey moustache and beady little monkey eyes, and a captain, younger, fuller and taller, both anonymous in not very well fitting battledress, web belts and holstered pistols.

The colonel nodded pleasantly and put out his hand. 'Good morning, Sir Vincent,' he said. I must have grimaced, because he grinned and went on, 'You'd rather not use the handle at the moment, eh? Perhaps that's wiser. Congratulations all the same. Very well deserved, I'm sure. Gathercole.' He introduced himself and palmed an identity card towards me. 'Junior military attaché—very junior, in fact, this dogs-body, Captain Robert Wickham and one Chinese typist are the only ones in our HQ I can pull rank on. Show the gentleman your card, Robert, let's keep it businesslike.' He looked at the tray and sniffed appreciatively. 'Three cups—and real coffee at that. Your mother's an angel. Pour out, Robert, and remember your manners. I bet you haven't been in a bedroom like this since your last visit to Madame Eileen's in Calcutta. Good. Shall we sit down?'

I may be classed as humourless, but I cannot stand heartiness before breakfast at any price, and I found myself disliking this type very much indeed. I sat down and took the cup that Wickham handed me.

'I take it you have some questions for me, sir?' I said rather stiffly.

'*George*,' he said archly. 'Formality on parade *only*, in our little assembly. Last parade I was on was Proclamation Day in Shanghai in 1928. Chairborne type, me. No, no questions. Just let it run ripplelike—everything you can remember since, say, Christmas Eve, when the Sons of Heaven marched in on you, and you took it on the lam, as the Americans say. Right, your own words. Take your time. Shoot.'

200

'I had a couple of hours' leave to go to my house to collect some clothes for my wife and children, who were being evacuated,' I began, and I was surprised at how easily it all flowed thereafter. I finished half an hour later, hurrying a little towards the end because I wanted my breakfast. And never once did Gathercole interrupt me.

'First class,' he said approvingly when I finally petered out. 'Nothing like a good debriefing, unless it's a dose of brimstone and treacle. Almost a physical relief, isn't it?' He turned to the captain. 'Any questions, Robert?'

'Nothing from me,' Wickham answered. 'He went a bit off track with dates once or twice, but the sequence is correct.' Only then did I realize that he had a tiny notepad in the palm of his hand and that he had obviously been checking my story.

'Nothing from me, either,' Gathercole twinkled. 'Absolutely bang on. Once again, congratulations. You're the first rabbit to come the whole way through. There have been five on your heels, but they've all been scuppered, poor chaps. Do you think you could find your way back along the line?' he added casually.

I felt the skin of my scalp tautening. 'I hope to God I wouldn't be expected to,' I said.

'You probably won't be,' he said. 'But *could* you? The question is not entirely hypothetical.'

'If I *had* to, I suppose—yes—but I'd have to have the passwords to the safe houses and all that sort of thing,' I said reluctantly.

'Naturally. That would all be laid on.'

'And I'd need a reliable Chinese courier. Someone like this chap John—'

'Make a note of that, Robert,' Gathercole said. 'Shan Lee is to be assigned to Stafford if—I stress *if*—he should be required to do a reciprocal at any time in the future.' He smirked. 'I can't promise you the company of Shivka again, though. She's wanted up here. Gorgeous piece of crackling, isn't she?'

201

'I hadn't noticed, *sir*,' I said very coldly indeed, and he cackled with mirth.

'Bloody liar,' he said. 'She certainly gives *me* a rush of blood to the fork, and I'm much longer in the tooth than you. He, he, he—hear that, Robert? "I hadn't noticed, *sir*." Vincent—may I call you Vincent?—you'll be the death of me.'

'Call me what your bloody well like,' I said savagely. 'I don't consider your remarks about that lady in the best of taste.'

'It's no good, Stafford,' said Wickham. 'The old bastard is unsnubbable.'

'There, what did I tell you?' Gathercole chuckled. 'We're only formal on parade—and we never go on parade. Well, that's that for the moment.' He rose. 'I'm afraid we'll have to ask you to stay under wraps here pending further orders. Abigail managed things beautifully last night and as far as we know the Blueshirts don't know you've arrived.'

'Who *are* the Blueshirts exactly?' I asked. 'And how do they concern me?'

'Chiang's private army—strictly irregular,' he answered. 'Funny how all "shirts" are shits, isn't it? Ossie Mosley's and Musso's blackshirts, De Valera's greenshirts, and Hitler's brownshirts. I'd like to launder the lot—with a Vickers gun. Well, so long, and thanks again. We'll be in touch. Come on, Robert, I'm going to touch Madame up for a double Napoleon brandy before tackling that bloody road back to Chunkers.' And they went out.

I was still fulminating when Abigail arrived with breakfast some little time later. 'Who the hell is that damned old military geriatric?' I demanded.

'One of the most dangerous men in China,' she answered airily. 'I would have thought you'd have known him. Stafford & McMurtrie have their own shamuses, don't they?'

'If by "shamus" you mean spies, the answer is no,' I said.

'You surprise me. That devious old devil of a grandfather of yours most certainly had a network.'

'Well, I haven't—and I don't know Colonel Gather-cole—or want to. If he's typical of the British Army in China, no wonder we're on the dirty end of things.'

'He's not typical,' Abigail said. 'He's not British Army, either—except as a wartime co-optee. Shanghai Conces-sional Police—Chief Superintendent.'

'What's dangerous about him?'

'Perhaps I should have said *potentially* dangerous. He knows so much about everybody.'

'That's a policeman's job, surely?'

'To know criminals and their machinations maybe—but our Colonel Gathercole—incidentally that was originally Gallacolin—knows a hell of a lot about the respectable and near-respectable also.'

'Does that mean he blackmails people?'

Abigail shrugged. 'Your guess is as good as mine,' she said. 'He'd certainly be in a position to if he was crooked.'

'Gallacolin?' I said. 'Russian?'

'Georgian. Same as Stalin.'

'Damned funny type to be in British Intelligence, isn't he?'

'Not at all. A pretty obvious choice, I should say.'

'But his politics? Is he Red or White?'

'Neither. The real professionals have no politics. They're loyal to their paymasters. The British are his.'

'But it has been known for some of them to have two paymasters, I believe.'

She shrugged again. 'Double spies? Could be, I suppose. I wouldn't be knowing. Not my business to. There is one thing certain about Gathercole, though—that's his implacable hatred of the Japs. His daughter, whom he idolized, was raped and murdered by them in 1937. She was a nurse in Soochong. Now get on with your breakfast before it gets cold.'

'All right, but could you do something for me?'

'That all depends what it is. I can't get you any clothes. I've been told to keep you incommunicado until orders come through for you.'

'That suits me for the monent,' I said, applying myself to ham, eggs and kidneys. 'No, I just want some news of Helen and the children if it's possible.'

'I'll do my best,' she promised. 'Radio communications are pretty snarled up at the moment and personal inquiries are bottom priority, but the Swiss are running a refugee information centre in Calcutta. I'll have a letter sent over.'

'Thanks,' I said. 'How are the others, by the way?'

'Fine. Some sleeping, some eating. You pack as much away of both as you can while you've got the chance. I have an idea that those bums down at the Embassy are going to find you a job before long.' With a gesture so unusual that it was awkward to the point of embarrassment, she bent over and kissed me on the top of my head. 'Take care, son', she said. 'Do take care,' and she went out.

4

'Three options,' Gathercole said. 'Lucky old you. I didn't get *one*. I was drafted out of a nice air-conditioned office in the Bund police station to a dump in Woosung Barracks with no roof. I went up two steps in rank and dropped back four in pay and pickings.'

'What are the options?' I asked.

'Ministry of Supply, Far Eastern Division. That's the one I'd advise you to take. Rank of major to start with. Lord Louis Mountbatten's headquarters in New Delhi when it's opened. Lovely grub. Grab it, Vincent, grab it by the short and curlies and hang on tight.'

'Why on earth are they offering me that?'

'Tin, rubber and copal, I believe. They reckon that there are lots of pockets scattered around the East in the hands of the Swedes and other neutrals, and you would be the lad to know where.'

'Absolute nonsense. Those are commodities my company never dealt in.'

'Maybe, but once you were in the job there'd be nothing they could do about it except promote you.'

'What are the others?'

'Jungle Training Centre in India. Place called Ranchi. Six months' sore feet, curry-and-rice and bug bites, then you'd be available for posting up the line somewhere as a competent infantry officer. Wouldn't touch it if I were you, not at thirty-nine. That's for the keen and young in heart.'

'And the third?'

'Wouldn't touch that either. Sucker's choice. You fly over to Calcutta and report to some feller in Barrackpore who'll tell you all about it and probably send you back here—or somewhere.'

'Doing what?'

'Take the first one, Vincent. Bloody fine job, with a more than ten-to-one chance of finishing the war in one piece—win, lose or draw.'

'I'd still like to know something about the third.'

'Can't tell you.'

'Can't or won't?'

'Both.'

'I'll take it.'

'The third?' I nodded and he cackled drily. 'That's what I like to see. A feller that'll chance his arm and take a flier at the unknown just for the hell of it. Do you know what would have happened if you'd picked one of the others?'

'No?'

'You'd still have got this one. Drafted—like me. This way they can say you volunteered for it if you finish in the shit, which you're more than likely to. Absolves them of moral responsibility, see? Caps off, stiff upper lip—"He's volunteered for it. He knew the risks but he never faltered. Let us honour a brave man, gentlemen—blah, blah, blah!" Bullshit. Well, I did my best to make you pick one of the others, and thereby force me to detail you for this one. If you'd been longer in the army you'd have seen the ploy. Take my advice in future, son: Never volunteer for anything.'

205

'You're a humorous sod, aren't you?' I said sourly.

'Life and soul of the party, to the world at large,' he said. 'To those under my direct command—just a sod. You *are* under my command now, so pay attention. Are you well known in Calcutta?'

'Not as far as I know. I've passed through it once or twice. The last time about four years ago.'

'Any social contacts? Sign the book at Government House? Honorary membership of the Bengal Club or anything like that?'

'No, I've never stayed long enough for that. An hour or two at the most.'

'What about your local office staff?'

'I'm afraid I know very little about them. Our Indian branch is under the direct control of the London head office. The manager is a chap called—just a moment—yes, Price, I think. I've never met him. Why do you ask?'

'Just answer my questions, will you. You can ask yours at the end. This is a briefing. So, dressed up as a captain, of say the RASC, you could be Hieronymus Bosch in Calcutta, apart from a chance encounter with someone from the past who happens to be there?'

'Yes, I suppose so.'

'Good. Actually you'll be Captain James Andrew Maxton. It won't affect your pay, but you're so stinking rich that I don't suppose that'll worry you. You'll be sorry to hear that Second-lieutenant Sir Vincent Stafford is missing believed killed, by the way.'

'Who the hell started that one?' I demanded, really angry.

'Not us, but it suits us well enough,' he said. 'The Swiss Red Cross have had time now to make out lists of both civil and military Europeans known to have been in Hong Kong at the time of the fall, and check with the people in the Jap prison camps. Those unaccounted for are MBK, like I said.'

'Then you'd better put out a disclaimer, damned quick,' I told him. 'If my wife, wherever she is, sees that—'

'She's going to think she's a widow. Sorry about that, but

206

think how happy she'll be when she knows she isn't. No, things stay as they are, Vincent, and you ought to be darned glad of it.'

'But why?'

'Because you're top of the Jap wanted list, that's why. They want you for the same reason as our own Ministry of Supply and also, as a very desirable incidental you're supposed to be one of the consortium of taipans who knows where the boodle is buried. A mere couple of hundred tons of gold bars or something, isn't it?'

'How the hell do I know? Another of the wild rumours that were floating round Hong Kong, I should imagine.'

'Rumour or not, the Nips are convinced it's true, and they'd give a lot to get their hands on you. They've put the screws on half a dozen merchant bankers already, two British and four Chinese. Two of the latter have died under interrogation. You wouldn't want anything like that to happen, would you? No, you stay dead for the nonce, laddie. You're safer that way.' He rose. 'All right, that's enough for today. Robert will be along later with a photographer for your identity card and a cover story.'

'Look,' I said. 'I've been stuck in this room for three days now except for a walk in the garden at night. How much longer is this nonsense going on for?'

'Lucky man,' he sighed. 'Damned nice room. I'm pigging it in a Nissen hut in the Embassy compound. Why don't you get Shivka along to keep you company sometime?' He winked. 'Tell you what: I'll invite Ma out to the Chinese opera one night to give you a clear run. No, don't throw that lamp. Mutiny is punishable by death in wartime.'

Chapter Seven

1

I felt like a school-leaver going out to his first job—
excitement tempered by self-consciousness—glad to be free
of the old authority but apprehensive of the new, awkward in the scratchy serge battledress that stank of moth-
balls, and horribly aware of the three worsted pips of my
spurious rank which Abigail had sewn on to each epaulette
the night before. My boots, straight from an Ordnance crate,
had defied even Raucous's expertise in trying to impart a
shine to them, and my cap was half a size too small. Oh yes, I
felt, and no doubt looked, a very new boy indeed, and the
lunch-basket that Abigail insisted on bestowing on me gave
things the finishing touch. I had surreptitiously pushed it
under the bed, but she spotted it and ran out to the car with it
just as we were leaving.

'Kind of you,' I mumbled, 'But I'm loaded with bits and
pieces already.'

'Take it,' Wickham advised. 'You'll be glad of it later. I
know what this damned trip is like.' So I was stuck with it.

I had desperately wanted to say goodbye to Shivka, but I
dreaded the quizzical look that I knew Abigail would have
given me had I mentioned it, so in the event I left without
even a farewell message to her.

'Look after yourself,' my mother said for about the twent-
ieth time. 'Write when they'll let you.'

'Christ,' I said irritably, 'I'm not going to prison—I hope.'

'No, of course not,' she gabbled. 'But *do* look after yourself.
Don't take any silly chances—'

'On what?' I asked.

'We'd better be moving,' Wickham said. 'You've got to be at the bottom of the steps by six.' And then, mercifully, we were speeding round that ghastly road through the pre-dawn mist.

'Right,' Wickham said. 'Let's run over things once more. Barring accidents you should be landing at Dum-Dum, the Calcutta airport, sometime this evening. What happens then?'

'I'll be met by some comedian who'll say, "Hello, old boy. Decent trip? I hope it wasn't too bumpy over Lashio," and I've got to answer, "Reasonably smooth, thanks, except for a bit of turbulence over Magwe," and he'll then take me off somewhere.'

'Good. And then?'

'Some other clot will want to hear my cover story.'

'Which is?'

'God Almighty, not again? You yourself told me I was word perfect.'

'Again, please.'

'Captain James Andrew Maxton, Royal Army Service Corps. Not a Regular. I managed a meat-canning plant in Buenos Aires before the war. I've been sent from England to explore the possibility of starting one out here to feed the troops—'

'And in the unlikely event of your running into a meat-canning expert from Buenos Aires, and he starts to talk technicalities and ask questions?'

'Laugh like hell and say, "That's the Army for you, old boy. They got my papers mixed up with someone else's"—and break things off.'

'Good.'

'Good be damned,' I said. 'Any fool could wriggle out of a situation like that with a stranger in a club or a mess. It's meeting somebody from Hong Kong that worries me, some-body who really knows me and comes up and says, "Staf-ford! For God's sake! How are you? What are your doing here?" Go on, tell me. How the hell do I bat that one off?'

209

'In the first place,' he said quietly, 'you won't be coffee-housing in clubs or messes. You'll be "under wraps" as we call it. You might, of course, bump into somebody who knows you in the street. In that case you brass-neck it. "Sorry, I think you've made a mistake", quite pleasantly—smile and walk on. You've got a moustache now—bit incipient at the moment but it's growing fast. You'll wear sunglasses constantly. Your mother says you're a darned sight skinnier than you ever were as a chairborne taipan; and people who don't normally wear uniform look vastly different when they do. The bloke concerned will, ten chances to one, stammer an apology and move on quickly, feeling foolish.'

'I'm the one who's feeling foolish at the moment,' I grumbled. 'I hate this cloak-and-dagger attitudinizing of you people. I'm not cut out for it. I wish to God I'd insisted on one of the other options.'

'There weren't any. George has told you that already,' he said. 'You have a potential for a certain job, and that's the job you're being given.'

'Well, tell me what the job is. Just give me a hint,' I begged.

'I haven't the faintest idea.'

'Bloody liar.'

'Aren't we all?'

'Not me—from choice anyway.'

'Then I'd advise you to start practising hard. Nothing like a good, unblinking thumper properly told when you're in a tight corner.' The car had stopped at the top of the steps. He opened the door and stepped out into the swirling mist. 'Wait here. I've got to clear things at the police post, and I'd rather they didn't see you.'

He came back after a few minutes and handed ne a folded paper. 'Right, here's your chop. You'll be taking off in an hour for Kunming, where you change aircraft for the flight over the Hump. There's a boat waiting for you at the bottom. Good luck.' He shook hands perfunctorily, climbed back into the car and was off.

I walked down the steps. It was like the descent into hell, because the fog thickened and it got darker the further one went. A sampan was moored at the slimy mudcoated landing-place and a coolie came forward and took my bag and then we puttered across the few hundred yards on an outboard motor and I landed on the hard sand of Shuang Hu Pa, where another coolie waited. He took me to a rickety bamboo shelter and I sat and shivered with half a dozen muffled figures, all Chinese, while mechanics fussed around a small humpbacked aircraft, the twin engines of which resolutely refused to start for a long time, and when they did it was with a hesitatnt and horribly uncertain note. I dislike flying at any time; now I was loathing the prospect, the more so when two Americans arrived, gloomily discussing the weather outlook and the likelihood of the sonsabitching motors clapping out once again, not to mention a report of Jap fighter activity en route. I hoped with all my heart that the three prognostications combined would be sufficient for them to call the whole thing off, but the hope faded when they herded us aboard and assured us cheerfully in pidgin that everything was velly ni', no tlouble—but if we did come down unexpectedly, to punch the emergency panels clear and beat it the hell out of it chop-chop before she went up in flames. It was only as they helped us to fasten our seat-belts that they realized that I was British and had probably overheard and understood them earlier.

'Don't worry, bud,' one of them said then. 'We were only kidding each other. Everything's going to be dandy—just dandy.' But it did nothing to reassure me.

In the event the two-hour flight was quite smooth, even enjoyable. We followed the broad sweep of the Yangtse-kiang west for some miles through the Szechuan hills, then bent to the south, and through the starboard windows I could make out a white thread in the distant blue haze that I knew was the snowcapped summit of the main Himalaya range itself.

Kunming airport was a different proposition from that of Chungking. It had been the headquarters of General Claire

L. Chennault's American Volunteer Group, who had been fighting Chiang Kai-shek's air battles against the Japs for the better part of five years; it was accordingly magnificently organized and maintained, and now it was seething with activity. There was a properly equipped control tower and meteorological station here, concrete-protected fuel storage tanks and even a transit hostel for passengers and aircrew, and the whole complex was ringed with both light and heavy anti-aircraft gun emplacements, with fighter aircraft standing at the ready under camouflaged netting over a wide dispersal area. I remember reflecting how different the story might have been had we had these resources in Hong Kong just a few short weeks previously.

I walked to the transit section and showed my chop and identity card to a young sergeant sitting at a desk.

'Captain Maxton?' he said, and consulted a list. 'Yeah, you're lucky, sir, Priority two—that'll get you on to the next one out, in about an hour. You can get some chow through there in the mess hall. Your name will be called over the tannoy.'

I tailed on to a line of denim-clad airmen who were filing past a vast hotplate, and received a flat compartmentalized tray with cereal, ham and eggs and hotcakes lavishly slapped on to it, together with a glass of ice-cold orange juice and a large mug of coffee, which cheered me considerably. If this army was going to fly on its stomach, the war was won already.I sat by a window and did ample justice to this so American meal, dispensed with such typical openhandedness, and watched the activity outside. One plane, a lumbering Dakota, had recently landed and was being unloaded with speed and efficiency: forty-gallon drums of gasoline, ammunition boxes, crates and gunny-wrapped bundles. Another plane was being towed from under camouflage nets, and mechanics were swarming all over it. This I guessed, was mine. It looked safe, big, dependable, and my spirits lifted still further.

I looked round the mess hall. Groups of Americans,

212

officers and enlisted men, sat at serried rows of plastic-topped tables, with here and there a smartly uniformed Kuomintang officer coping awkwardly with Western knives and forks. There seemed to be only one other European there, a civilian in a scratch collection of clothes topped by an army greatcoat hung cloaklike over his shoulders. He sat at a table with his back toward me, some distance away, wholly concerned with his food, which he was tackling with gusto, and I only saw his face in profile once when he turned sideways when the tannoy cracked into life to call for 'Top-sergeant Kulik—on the double to deepo three-A.' I wondered idly who the man was—if, in fact, he *was* a European, or perhaps an American technician sensibly dressed for whatever his job was. I think the warm food with its comforting bulk under my belt must have taken effect about then because I dozed off.

I came to with a start to hear the tail end of the call over the tannoy, '—Captain Ping Loy, Lieutenant Pao Shang, Sergeant Riley, Captain Maxton and Major Lobo to assembly point, please—assembly point, please—' I sat blinking stupidly for a moment or so, not yet used to my recently acquired name and rank, then as I saw people getting up and collecting their hand baggage, the penny dropped, and I picked up my haversack and duffel bag, and moved towards the door. I felt a tap on my shoulder and I turned. A young American said, 'I think you left this, sir.' It was the damned lunch-basket which, in view of my magnificent breakfast, I had pushed under the table and had intended to leave. I thanked him and took it, feeling like the Ancient Mariner on having his albatross kindly restored to him. The 'European' was immediately behind me and our eyes met—and recognition was instant and mutual.

He smiled delightedly and held out his hand and I could see the greeting forming on his lips—and I looked right through him and turned my back. It was the first time I had ever deliberately cut another person in my life, and I didn't like doing it one little bit, but what option had I?

Outside the door an American captain was checking us off from a list, and I had to put my luggage down while I got my identity card from my breast pocket.

'Captain James Andrew Maxton, British Service—Priority two,' he said. 'OK, fine. Follow on to that airplane ahead out there, please. No smoking until after take-off. Good trip and happy landing. Next, please.' Then, as I picked up the luggage again, I heard him checking the man on my heels, 'Mr Frederick Seymour Stewart, British civilian—Priority two. Right, straight ahead, sir.'

I walked across the tarmac raging inwardly. The clever, cocksure *bastards*. They knew it all, didn't they? Like hell. 'Just brass-neck it, old boy. Look at him and smile pleasantly and say you think he's making a mistake. He'll slink off feeling foolish—etc. etc.' Not this one. Not Freddie Stewart, manager of the Shanghai branch of the London, Peking and General Bank—the LPG, as it was known universally through the Far East. They handled the bulk of our foreign exchange business and I invariably spent an hour or so closeted with him in his palatial office on the Bund each time I visited Shanghai. I had dined at his house and lunched with him at the Club. We had played golf together. A warm, friendly soul—and I had gratuitously insulted him. And now we would be cheek by jowl in an aircraft for hours. What the hell was I to say if he spoke to me, as he undoubtedly would? Insult him again—or lay a conspiratorial finger across my lips and look mysterious—and foolish? Pretend to be sleeping? I could hardly keep it up for six or seven hours. Disregard their nonsense and take him into my confidence—tell him I was doing some confidential work and rely on his discretion? That would be the most rational course. I'd find myself in breach of the Mumbo-jumbo Act and in front of a court martial if they ever found out, no doubt, but Freddie wasn't the type of man to talk loosely and spill the beans. Yes, I'd do that at the first opportunity, when I was certain I would not be overheard.

I had reached the plane and I followed the Chinese officer

ahead of me up the awkward little ladder and into its cavernous aluminium belly. It was empty except for some discarded packing material untidily heaped in the middle of the floor, and there were no seats as such, just a narrow tin shelf running along each side under a line of dirty little square windows. Outside the air was cold and bracing. Here it was colder but flat and stale, and it stank of slopped petrol and glycol. I glanced sideways and saw Freddie place his duffel bag on the shelf immediately opposite the door, so I moved ahead and chose a place on the same side so that, at least, we were some distance apart and wouldn't be looking at each other. I counted the others. There were twenty-four of us on our feet, and two stretcher cases in charge of a Chinese medic—twenty-seven altogether plus a sergeant crewmember whom the others addressed as 'loadmaster'. He and the medic lashed the stretchers to ringbolts in the floor, and then passed straps round the blanket-swathed patients. Four American officers arrived then, fresh-shaved and incredibly clean and smart in short, fur-collared leather flying jackets and peaked caps. They paused at the door leading through to the flight cabin and grinned amiably at us.

'Morning, gentlemen. Welcome aboard,' one of them, a lean, fair young man said. 'I'd like you-all to pack in tight up forrard here. These ducks are a bit heavy in the ass on take-off. When we're airborne you can spread out a bit and make yourselves as comfortable as conditions allow. Lashio, the other side of the Hump, first stop—if the Nips aren't there ahead of us. If they are we keep going to Imphal on the Indian side. We don't expect any trouble, though maybe it'll be a mite bumpy over the mountains. We're not pressurized, but there are oxygen masks on the airline behind you. The loadmaster will show you how to use them if you feel a bit chokey at any time. The john's down aft in the tail section. Puke bags under the seats.'

They went through and the door slammed behind them with that awful note of finality that always gave me a vacuous feeling at the pit of my stomach, then the loadmaster

215

closed and clamped the massive side door, the big twin Pratt & Witney engines spat, backfired, then roared into life and we bumped over the tarmac to the startpoint. The roar increased, died to a whisper, then rose again and the whole fabric shook and vibrated, and we were racing down the runway. The tail lifted and the bumping ceased, and we were airborne. I resumed breathing.

We spread out then and relaxed, and to my relief Freddie showed no inclination to join me from his place nearer to the tail. What was he doing in this part of the world, I wondered? I remembered vaguely hearing that he, in company with many other businessmen who had stayed at their posts, had been rounded up into the notorious Jap concentration camp for civilians known as the Gatehouse, long before Pearl Harbor. I studied him covertly. The heaters in the aircraft were now working off the engines, and the temperature had risen sharply so he had shed his heavy greatcoat, and I saw that he was wearing a shabby tweed jacket with a sailor's sweater and faded jeans, and his heavy army boots were cracked and down-at-heel. He looked up and our eyes met again, and I felt my face reddening, but this time he showed no sign of recognition. Damn it all, I thought angrily, I must clear this with him sometime in the future. Our association had been almost entirely in the line of business, but he was still a friend and a most likeable character, and I had slighted him for no valid reason, or so it must have appeared to him.

The plane suddenly lurched and seemed to drop like a stone but I felt my stomach had stayed in its original position. The Chinese officer sitting opposite me looked pale and strained and I could see that his knuckles were showing white as he gripped the seat each side of him, and I realized that I was doing the same—and no doubt looked the same. We smiled at each other in a pathetic attempt at non-chalance, and then our whole wretched tin world seemed to be gripped in a giant hand that was shaking it as a terrier shakes a rag doll. Through the window opposite I could see a

216

snowclad crestline through which outcroppings of black stone thrust upwards like jagged teeth, then we plunged into cloud and I could see no further that the wing tip, which was no comfort at all because it was shuddering and whipping up and down in a way that I was certain no metal could stand for long. Then we came out of the cloud, like a surfer getting his head out of the breakers for barely long enough to take one breath before being overwhelmed again, and I saw that either we had descended or the mountains had increased in height, because now the crestline was far above us, on both sides and we were, in fact, flying through a pass.

There is a saturation level of terror, and I think I reached mine at that point. The extreme turbulence continued unabated for over two hours, long enough, in fact, for me to achieve a state of stoicism where nothing more mattered. I just sat there, envying the aplomb of three American sergeants and a Chinese lieutenant who played hand after hand of stud poker throughout the whole horrible nightmare, finishing only when one of the sergeants had cleaned the others out.

Then, as suddenly as it had all started, we came out of it, emerging from the snowbound and rocky pass and flying into blessedly still air over a limitless carpet of solidly green jungle, broken here and there by the silver thread of a stream. The pilot came back then and grinned disarmingly. Through the open door I could hear the staccato chatter of the radio on morse.

'Kinda shook up, gentlemen?' he said. 'The medics say its good for the liver. Mine must be real healthy. We won't be dropping into Lashio. The little sonsabitches are coming up the Irrawaddy from Rangoon, fast, so we're heading for Imphal. Weather outlook fine, no enemy aerial activity reported and we got a tail wind. Chowringhee tonight for sure.'

The loadmaster dispensed coffee in paper cups. I looked at the lunch-basket longingly, but decided that there wouldn't be enough to share out between nearly thirty, and I couldn't

217

indulge myself alone, so I interred it finally under the loose packing material and applied myself to the tasteless K-rations that the loadmaster handed out in rectangular cardboard boxes. Then I slept my way across the entire width of Burma and down into Assam.

2

It was dark when we landed at Dum-Dum, that anteroom to Hades that is Calcutta's apology for an airport, and when the doors of the Dakota were opened the fetid heat of the Bengal night hit one like the slap of a wet and dirty turkish bath towel. Shepherded by Indian military police, we stumbled over potholed, weedgrown tarmac towards a large, dimly lit quanset hut, but I never entered it, because just as I reached the door a hand came out of the darkness and touched me on the arm and somebody said, 'Hello, old boy. Decent trip? I hope it wasn't too bumpy over Lashio.'

I started to say that we hadn't called there, then remembered and told him that it had been reasonably smooth except for turbulence over Magwe, and I was drawn out the straggling line and steered towards a waiting staff car.

'Well, that's one of you,' said my conductor in relieved tones, and wiped his face with a large handkerchief. 'You didn't happen to have an English civvie on the plane with you, by any chance?'

'Yes, there was one chap,' I said.

'Did you get his name?'

'I didn't need to—I knew it already.'

'What?'

'Stewart.'

'Oh Christ,' groaned the other. 'A proper cock-up. Does he know *you*?'

'Of course he knows me,' I said irritably. 'We're business associates.'

'Oh, shit,' he said glumly. '*I'll* take the can back for this lot, you see—and it's not my fault. American bastards—they'll never do as they're asked. He was supposed to have been on yesterday's plane. What did you talk about?'

'We didn't talk about anything.' I was hot and prickly in my heavy battledress and I could feel myself getting angry. 'I pretended not to know him—and a right damned fool I felt. Who's in charge of this absurd charade? You?'

'Not me, old boy. I'm only the handrag—the silly bugger who gets it in the neck when things get screwed up, which is most of the time.' I could now make him out in the murky light that filtered from the badly blacked-out windows of the hut. He was a tubby little lieutenant with a disproportionately large and ginger moustache that made him look like a frightened but well-nourished mouse peeping out of a haystack. 'Well, nothing for it,' he said, after a period of agonizing indecision. 'He'll have to come back with us, or God knows where he'll finish up in this madhouse. Hang on.'

He shot into the hut and emerged holding Freddie firmly by the arm. 'Look,' he gabbled desperately. 'I know you know each other—the captain has just told me—but you're not supposed to, see? You were supposed to come in on different planes. Don't drop me in the cart, for Christ's sake. Look surprised and all that when you meet properly. My name is Sidney Ford-Adams, by the way—unfortunate initials. I'm always called Sweet FA. See what I mean?'

'More or less,' I said wearily. 'Hello, Freddie. Sorry about all this nonsense. I haven't the faintest idea what it's supposed to mean. I was just told not to know anybody.'

'That's all right, so was I,' he laughed as we shook hands. 'How are you, Vincent?'

'Ahem,' I coughed. 'The name's Maxton—James Andrew of that ilk.'

'I'll try not to put my foot in it,' he promised, 'But I'm darned certain that I will. Maxton—Maxton—I must remember that. They didn't give me an alias, thank God. I'm still plain F.S. Stewart—escaper.'

219

We climbed into the car, Freddie and I in the back, and the lieutenant beside the Indian driver, and carried on our conversation in an undertone.

'Escaper or evader?' I asked, and added knowledgeably, 'There's a distinction, you know.'

'So I'm told. They shoot you for one and behead you for the other if you're caught—but I'm not sure which is which. Anyhow, I'm an escaper.'

'Where from?'

'The Gatehouse, Shanghai. Five of us made a break on our third night behind the wire. You probably know some of the others—Dwerryhouse, China Maritime Customs; Pentreath, one of my assistants at the bank; Crosswhaite, of the Harbin & General Company, and Beedham, the secretary of the Jockey Club; all civilians. We swam the Whangpo—at least, four of us did. Dwerryhouse, poor chap, didn't make it. We lost him in the dark half way across. The rest of us crawled out on the opposite bank and just set out to walk westward alongside the Yangtse, with the vague hope of making it to Chungking.'

'Eight hundred miles,' I said. 'I can sympathize with you.'

'Oh, we didn't do it all on foot. We were extraordinarily lucky—luckier than we deserved. We were carrying over five thousand dollars between us. We hadn't been searched on entering the camp—there were too many of us—two thousand at least, and things were very confused that first day. The Japs screened us all in batches eventually, of course, stripped us to the skin and confiscated everything we were carrying, but we'd had time to bury the money by this and we dug it up again before leaving. We fell in with some boatmen a few miles upriver and they carried us almost as far as Hangkow for five hundred dollars. We never saw a sign of a Jap for the first three days after getting outside the Shanghai area, but then we were chased by a gunboat and only got away by the skin of our teeth—we dropped into the river on the blind side and made it to the bank—then a bunch of hairy gents, absolute bandits, picked us up. I think

220

the general idea was to hold us for ransom if anybody was interested, or cut our throats for our money and boots if they weren't. Fortunately I heard them discussing it, and we slipped away in the night—'

'Of course, I'd forgotten,' I said. 'Your Chinese is pretty good—and Japanese, if I remember rightly.'

'Language proficiency was the only way to gain promotion with our concern,' he said. 'I got stuck into both as a youngster when first I came out. Look, I'm not boring you I hope?'

'Anything but,' I assured him. 'Please go on.'

'Actually there's not much more to it,' he said modestly. 'We ran into a patrol of Kuomintang then and they took us to Chungking and we were screened after we'd had a few days' rest in hospital, and our Embassy asked what we'd like to do. We all plumped for the army, of course. They were a bit dubious in my case as I'm forty-five but they jumped at the others. They said they'd probably be able to use me in some quiet job—censorship or the interpreters' pool or something equally repulsive, then the chief inquisitor, a copper I knew in Shanghai, now a colonel—'

'Gathercole?'

'That's right—said he thought he could fit me into something useful and reasonably interesting down here, so here I am. But tell me about yourself. Helen and the children? I hope—'

'Yes, safe,' I told him. 'I got them out at the last minute.'

'Thank God for that. You know, for the first time in my life I've been thankful to be a confirmed bachelor. Oh, I'm not queer or anything like that—I hope. It's just that I've always been too busy trying to make my way up a very slippery ladder without much in the shape of initial advantages. It didn't leave a lot of time to go a-courting. There was a girl once, but—' He broke off and laughed. 'What the hell am I talking about? Yes, I was glad I had no family ties in those last bloody awful days,' he went on. 'You know, it was comparatively easy to get out of the bag. The Nips just

221

haven't the manpower to guard the camps properly, but a married man couldn't risk breaking out if he was leaving a wife and kids behind him, even though the sexes are segregated. The little swine have lists. They know who's who and they've actually said that if a married man got away his wife would pay the price.' He was silent for a time, then he spat, 'Bastards, bastards, *bastards*! God, I've seen some awful things, Vincent—sorry—What do I call you, captain, *sir*?'

'Anything you like so long as it isn't Vincent Stafford. It had better be James, although I probably won't answer to it until I get used to it myself,' I said.

'You lucky bugger,' he said enviously. 'You're obviously doing something interesting. Oh, don't worry, I'm not going to ask you what it is.'

'That's just as well. I haven't the faintest idea myself yet,' I told him.

'I hope they give me something really useful,' he said. 'They ought to. God, I'm as fit as a flea. I was the oldest by far of our party—the others were absolute kids, all in their twenties, except Dwerryhouse, but I could outwalk them, outswim them and keep going when they were sitting on their backsides whimpering over their sore feet. That's a bit unfair. Actually they were damned good boys. They're all due for the Jungle Warfare School when they're completely fit again. But here I am, still waffling about myself. What about you? Escaper or evader? And where from?'

'Hong Kong,' I said. 'Evader—I wasn't captured. I was separated from my unit—the Hong Kong Volunteer Force—when the surrender came, and I headed out of town and kept walking. My experiences were far less hair-raising than yours, but basically our stories are much the same. I was helped by people along the road—boatmen, coolies and so forth—until eventually I reached Chungking.'

'All on your own? And you call *my* little promenade hair-raising! I think to tackle a walk like that solo really takes some guts and resolution. Of course, your Chinese is first class, isn't it?'

222

The car stopped with a jerk, and through the window I could see the glimmer of a guard lamp and a turbaned head silhouetted against the night sky. The lieutenant flashed an identity card, there was a mumbled exchange, a barrier was raised and we drove on. 'Barrackpore, gentlemen,' he said over his shoulder. 'Accommodation has been arranged for you, but in different messes, I'm afraid. I'll drop you first, Mr Stewart. His Nibs will be seeing you tomorrow morning.'

We turned in through a gateway, and I had an impression of palm trees fringing an open space, then we stopped under a portico and somebody came out of the shadows and opened the car door.

Freddie said, 'Well, this looks like it. Au revoir, I hope, Vince—dammit—James. Best of luck, old boy.'

'And you,' I said as we shook hands again. He followed the lieutenant into the darkness and I sat and waited with a curious feeling almost of bereftness. This brief encounter had been a bridge back over the chaos in which we were floundering, to the safe, sane workaday world of yesterday—the business world built by the industry, acumen and sheer sweat of three generations, which was now being swept away on a wave of madness and destruction.

3

But 'His Nibs' didn't see us that day, nor indeed the next or the next. He was in New Delhi, Ford-Adams informed me apologetically—'Conference. Top Secret. Burn before reading, and all that, old boy. A bit of luck for me. He's not likely to ask questions about which plane, or planes, you each arrived on now.'

'And I've got to stew in this damned room until the wretched man returns, have I?' I asked acidly.

'Oh no,' he said blandly. 'There's no objection to your

walking in the compound. Just so long as you aren't seen in public.'

'Do you mean that I'm "under wraps", as you call it, for the duration?'

'Good Lord no,' he giggled. 'We don't know how long the war's going to last, do we? It may go on for ages. I shouldn't say that, of course. Defeatist talk.'

'What about Stewart? Is he incommunicado also?'

'Tight as a trout's bottom, old boy—and not nearly as comfortable as you, poor chap, He's in the junior mess, with me. Three to a room, and no electric fans. You sybarites up here have no idea how the other half has to pig it.'

The bungalows, as these massive stonebuilt mansions were inappropriately termed, dated from pre-Mutiny days, each standing in gardens—'compounds' in India—of about an acre which sloped gently down to the Hooghli, that arm of the Ganges that wends its malodorous course through the centre of Calcutta, fifteen miles to the south. I had a strong feeling of *déjà vu* the whole time I was in Barrackpore because old Ross, my grandfather, had been stationed here during part of his service with the East India Company army the better part of a hundred years previously, and I had listened spellbound as a small boy to his tales of alarms and excursions, brigandage, rapine, and the story, which varied in detail with each telling, of his wholly illegal acquisition of the Midnight Gun which now stood in its specially constructed emplacement on the lawn at Annandale. I wondered what the Japs had made of it, because it was still operative, and we had fired a last salute from it on the old boy's death.

I was sitting on a moss-covered stone seat on the third evening, looking across the river at the sun sinking behind the palms on the opposite bank, fighting down a rising tide of impotent fury at the sheer futility of the whole inept conduct of the war as fought by the chairborne warriors of Calcutta, when Ford-Adams appeared, nose and inadequate chin twitching spasmodically.

'He's back,' he quavered. 'He wants to see you right away.'

'Thank God for that,' I said, getting up from the bench.

'He *knows*,' he went on, his voice rising plaintively. 'Some interfering, mischief-making swab has tipped him off that you arrived together, and he's after my blood.'

'Too bad,' I said unsympathetically. 'At least it lets me off having to prevaricate on your behalf. Come on, let's get it over.'

In silence, save for muted moans from my guide, we walked down the peepul-shaded Mall to another bungalow, past double sentries, to a desk inside the main door where an Indian babu made an impressive display of checking our credentials, until Ford-Adams said shrilly, 'Come on, Chatterjee, for Christ's sake—you know bloody well who we are. The burra sahib is waiting.'

'I am knowing *you*, yes, Mister Ford-Adams sahib, but not this gentleman,' the Indian replied. 'Identity card, please, then it is necessary to be signing this chit showing time of arrival, leaving space for time of departure, for record purposes in Visitors' Log. There is password of day to be given also—'

'Oh, bollocks!' said Ford-Adams. 'Come on, Maxton, this way.'

'That is not word,' the Indian said severely as we swept past him. 'It is "Belladonna".'

We came to a door at the end of a long corridor, and Ford-Adams took a deep breath and tapped softly. A grunt sounded the other side, and we went in.

'Captain Maxton, sir,' Ford-Adams said reverentially, and saluted smartly. I followed suit, sloppily.

'Sit down,' a man the other side of a wide desk said, and added to Ford-Adams, 'And you get the other chap, and wait outside until I send for you.'

I sat as the lieutenant shot out of the door. There was a shaded reading lamp on the desk which cast a pool of light downward, throwing the rest of the room into partial darkness so that I couldn't make out much of the other man at first, and even less as his hand came out and tilted the shade so that the full beam of light fell on me.

He chuckled. 'Dirty trick that, isn't it?' he said. 'I saw it in an American movie. The police do it when they're putting a client through the third degree. Now, would you mind telling me who you are and where you have come from?'

'Captain Maxton, J.A., sir', I parroted. 'RASC. I'm supposed to be an authority on the subject of meat canning, and I've been sent out here in an advisory capacity—'

'Good, good,' he interrupted. 'I do apologize for all this silly buggaboo. I know who you are, of course, but I'm trying to impart the first kindergarten principles of security into these Indian Army people. Splendid chaps, first class when it comes to chasing hairy-arsed Pathans up the Khyber, but a little naive in matters pertaining to modern Intelligence procedures. Take your arrival here, for instance. A complete box-up—'

'If I may be permitted, sir,' I ventured. 'I'd like to put a word in for Ford-Adams. It was hardly his fault. The—er—other chap and I just happened to find ourselves on the same plane.'

'Oh yes, I know that,' he said. 'But the lesson must be emphasized. It's a natural thing for a pup to pee on the floor, and he'll continue to do it until you rub his nose in it. Don't worry about Sweet FA. His head isn't going to roll—this time. He'll know in future not to book two agents who are not supposed to meet prematurely, at the same time.'

I felt the homily was for my own future guidance rather than Ford-Adam's. There's a Confucian proverb that deals with this sort of situation; 'Beat the post in order that the wall may hear and learn therefrom, and so not lose face.' It was a policy I followed in my own business, but it irritated me to have it levelled at myself.

'Right,' he went on. 'No harm done in this case as you'll possibly both be doing your training together—the first part, at least. You know Stewart, of course, don't you? Really know him, I mean?'

226

'Quite well,' I confirmed, 'although we didn't meet very frequently. I saw him on business matters whenever I visited Shanghai, or he came to Hong Kong, and we usually lunched or dined together at least once on each occasion.'

'You've played golf with him, haven't you?' he said sharply, almost accusingly.

'Good God!' I said involuntarily. 'Have I been under surveillance?'

'No more than another dozen or so of you top businessmen in China. "Taipans" is the term, isn't it?' Again came the throaty chuckle. 'Oh, please don't get any wrong ideas. Nothing sinister about it, I assure you. It's a thing called the "Y" List—a register of people in potential theatres of war, men *and* women, who can be called upon for jobs if and when the need arises. To be really effective every damned last little thing about them has to be known—temperament, tastes, backgrounds, likely reactions in any given set of circumstances. There's only one way to gain that type of information, that's by observation over a long period.'

'I thought we were fighting a war against that sort of thing,' I said coldly.

'Don't talk like a bloody fool,' he snorted. ' "That sort of thing", as you call it, has been going on since the seige of Troy, and before. Every government follows the same practice. Rather a compliment to be "Y" listed by one's country, I think.'

'It's still spying on the individual,' I argued. 'I regard that as distasteful and unnecessary. If you wanted to know anything about me you had only to ask.'

'So you've never made inquiries about an applicant before offering him a job?'

'Of course I have—of the man himself. We have a proforma which he is asked to fill in.'

He didn't chuckle this time. He roared.

'Sorry,' he said. 'I was just wondering what a chap's reactions would be to the sort of questions we would be asking if *we* used pro-formas. "Do you talk too freely when you have a few drinks under your belt?"—"Have you a mistress or mistresses? If so, please give nationalities of same, etc, etc." No, no pro-formas—not that we'd have any moral scruples about them, but purely because we don't need them. We have all that type of information before the person concerned is ever considered for the list.'

'I'm glad of that,' I said, 'Because I couldn't supply the answers as far as Stewart is concerned—nor would I even if I knew them.' I rose. 'I suggest you ask Stewart about *me*, although he will probably give you the same omnibus answer as mine, which is, "Go to hell—*sir*".'

'Good,' he said, in no way put out. 'Actually that tells me more than your blasted pro-forma. Staunch type, in your opinion, eh? Straight as a die. Would go to the stake for a pal. Tells me a bit more about *you* at the same time. Sit down, my dear chap. You worry me, standing there quivering with righteous indignation.'

'With your permission I'd prefer to terminate this interview,' I said.

'Sit down!' he barked. 'Where the hell do you think you are? In your managerial office? You're in *mine*, and subject to military discipline. Do you understand?'

I said I did, and sat.

'That's better,' he said in milder tones. 'Where was I? Oh yes, information about you both. We have reams of it, and I can assure you that there's not a single derogatory entry in either of your dossiers. Qualifications? My God! Between you you have the lot—organizing and administrative ability of the highest order, languages, encyclopedic knowledge of the country, integrity beyond question, and as far as courage, initiative and endurance are concerned old George Gathercole has been positively lyrical. You've each put up a wonderful show in getting out—you from Hong Kong and Stewart from Shanghai. So why am I putting you through the hoop again?'

He broke off and was silent for some time, as if weighing his next words, then he went on, ruminatively, seeming to be thinking aloud rather than addressing me.

'Compatibility,' he mused. 'That's what I'm trying to assess—your ability to get on with each other when you're out in the blue, away from superior authority. One of you has to be in charge, of course. Can't have two prima donnas. It's difference in background and upbringing that worries me slightly—I stress *slightly*, but it *does* worry me. You have been rather silver-spooned, haven't you? The young master trained from the cradle to take over the whole enormous show. Unquestioned authority from a very early age. Not altogether a good thing—even has the thundering gall to tell a brigadier to go to hell—in his own office!' That was the first indication I had of his rank, because I still couldn't see him clearly behind the light, and I confess in retrospect that I went hot and cold at his point, but the chuckle, repeated again, reassured me a little. 'Now take Stewart—different start in life. Leeds—never quite rid himself of that slight Yorkshire accent—none the worse for that, however. No public school behind him. Father a provincial journalist. Kyleton Grammar school, took every prize and scholarship they had to offer, including a Carnegie Award which gave him two years at the Harvard Business School—very prestigious—after a phenomenally early Cambridge Honours degree, then into the London office of the bank for a year before being posted to Shanghai. Went up like a house on fire after that—managing the whole show five years later. What was he like to do business with?'

'First class,' I said.

'And to play golf with?'

'Average. I'm no Henry Cotton, but I could usually beat him. Cricket was his game.'

'Yes, so it says here.' I heard papers rustle the other side of the desk. 'Good all-rounder, sixty-three not out against the Navy in 1934, medium-paced bowler, captained the English Club eleven in '36—that was the year they won the McIraith Cup. Quite a record. Right, so here's the sixty-four-thousand dollar question. How would you feel like working under him on an extremely sticky job back in China—if circumstances so dictated?'

'I would rather work under him than a lot of other people I can think of,' I said with complete sincerity.

'Good,' he said. I thought he sounded relieved. 'Of course, it might quite easily be the other way round. Anyhow, I'll be asking him the same question, and I hope I'll get the same answer. All right, Maxton, thank you for your cooperation, and do please forgive me for putting you on the rack. There *is* a purpose behind it all. We're trying to obviate the possibility of round pegs in square holes, with your necks at risk if we get it wrong. Send the others in, please.'

I saluted clumsily and went out. Stewart and Sweet FA sat on a bench in the hall looking apprehensive. 'What was it like?' the former muttered as I joined them. He looked stiff and uncomfortable in the jungle-green uniform which was now replacing khaki drill in the Far East, and like me, he was wearing a captain's three pips.

'Hairy,' I told him. 'Don't cheek him—he's a brigadier.'

'My God!' squeaked Sweet FA. '*You* didn't cheek him, did you? Do be careful, Stewart. *I* take the can back if he gets his balls in a knot.'

I watched them go into the office. Sweet FA rejoined me almost immediately, mopping his damp brow. 'I should have warned you,' he said apologetically. 'He can be a bit of a rasper at times. One has to be so careful—'

'I'm sure *you* are,' I said. 'Can you tell me what the hell is happening to us? *He* certainly didn't.'

'I'm afraid I can't,' he wailed, 'so please don't ask me. Oh dear—that bloody fool Stewart saluted without a hat when we went in.'

'We've lost the war,' I said hollowly.

'It's all very well for you to joke about it,' he said tartly. 'It's not you who gets it in the neck—'

'There seems to be quite a preoccupation with necks in this place,' I said. 'Don't mention them again, or I'll be doing something unmilitary—like bopping a brother officer.'

'Very funny,' he said, and smiled with malicious pleasure.

230

'Actually I *can* give you a bit of news if you'll promise not to tell anybody. You're both going on a training course.'

'Oh, I knew that,' I said airily. 'Your boss told me himself.'

'Did he tell you that it involved parachuting among other things?' he asked. 'I'm afraid necks do come into that—and I'm bloody glad mine's not one of them. Oh, here's *Captain* Stewart coming back. *He* wasn't kept long. With all this promotion kicking around I think one or other, or possibly both you, ought to buy me a drink.'

4

The parachuting came first—a pre-jump course over the tailboard of a speeding truck on to iron-hard ground, then a couple of descents from a captive balloon, and finally six from a Dakota, two of them by night. I was terrified the whole time, but Freddie seemed positively to enjoy it. We both qualified but we were not presented with the little blue-winged emblem that the rest of our mixed bag course of British and Gurkhas received on the final parade, and Freddie was as indignant as a boy scout dispoiled of his badges, but Sweet FA, who accompanied us everywhere, even to the landing grounds where, to do him justice, he unfailingly waited for us each day with a hip flask of whisky, was adamant.

'Sorry,' he commiserated. 'Boss's orders—nothing permitted that is likely to attract attention. Pair of captains, one General Service Corps, the other in the Galloping Grocers, are just dogsbodies, and nobody is likely to spare you a second glance. Parachute wings? Ah, that's different—particularly since you're both a bit long in the tooth. People would ask questions.'

'Have it your own way, you little louse,' Freddie said.

231

'We're going to celebrate though, both of us. We're going into Calcutta to have dinner at Firpo's, and we're going to get as drunk as skunks.'

'You're not, you know,' said our shadow. 'You're leaving immediately for the Jungle School at Ranchi—and me with you. Explosives and sabotage, infiltration and communications, six weeks of it. Very interesting, they tell me.'

And there was not a thing we could do about it. We did try once or twice to elude him and go into town to sample the limited fleshpots of the Ranchi Club, but he was unshakeable. 'Don't put me in an impossible position, chaps,' he begged almost tearfully. 'If you come out from under the wraps without permission I have strict orders to report you to the Boss immediately.'

So, still incommunicado with the outside world, we came back to Barrackpore at the end of two months in the clinical isolation of the SOE Mess, and paraded before the 'Boss' again, this time together in daylight and without trick lamps. He was so true to type that it was banal. He reminded me strongly of C. Aubrey Smith, an English actor much in demand in Hollywood for British Army roles.

He shook hands with us, then gestured us to chairs before dismissing Sweet FA with a curt jerk of his head.

'I apologize for the Delphic oracle act last time, gentlemen,' he said. 'That was, of course, to preserve my incognito in case you didn't make the grade and were posted elsewhere. You *have* made the grade, handsomely, according to your reports, but whether that is a cause for congratulation or condolence you will have to judge for yourselves. As far as I am concerned you are both eminently suitable for certain highly specialized duties back in your respective territories. Maxton, you will be returning immediately. That is jumping the gun rather, but Sir Vincent Stafford has been reported officially "missing believed killed", and we cannot risk your being seen by anybody back here who knows you—'

232

'My wife—' I began to protest, but he cut me short.

'I'm sorry,' he said. 'We'll enlighten her as soon as we can with safety, but it will have to stand at least until this first mission is completed.' He rose and crossed to a large map spread out on a trestle table. 'Come here—both of you, because you might have to go in later, Stewart, if Maxton doesn't make it.'

The map was a one-inch to the mile Ordnance Survey edition, with the English placenames overprinted with Chinese characters. He pointed to a spot ringed faintly in pencil. 'The Inn of the Seven Dragons,' he said. 'Remember it?'

'The safe house with the cellar, near Kweilin,' I acknowledged. 'Very well indeed. We spent three or four nights there on the way out.'

He nodded. 'Exactly. You're to be dropped there from an American bomber twenty-four hours from now—two miles from the inn itself, due south—' He tapped the map again. 'Memorize that in case the Chinese reception committee make a box-up of it and are not in position when you land—*two miles due south of the inn*. The six-figure coordinates of the inn itself are 543298 on Sheet 26. Check with the pilot and navigator that you and they are both in agreement before you exit, for God's sake. Got it?'

I nodded dumbly, with a cold feeling at the base of my belly.

'You'll be meeting somebody in the cellar. His codename is Rollo—yours, for this job, is Tantrum. You'll use that as a password and identity sign also. Rollo will give you your final briefing there, so there's no need for me to clutter you up with further instructions at this stage.' He held out his hand again. 'Good trip, my dear chap, and I look forward to seeing you back here in a few weeks' time. Ford-Adams is taking you up to the American base at Nirsa. Stewart, you can relax for a few hours. I hope you won't be needed to go in this time, but you will hold yourself in readiness.'

I don't remember much of that last crowded hour. Fred-

233

die, hiding his disappointment sportingly, asked if he could come with us for the fifty-mile run to Nirsa, but Sweet FA turned him down flatly.

'No, you relax, like the Boss said, old boy,' he advised, 'and for heaven's sake if not mine, don't take advantage of my absence to go on the scoot to Calcutta. I'd get it in the neck horribly if you were seen in Madam Eileen's or anywhere like that.'

So we parted with hollow cheerfulness, and I had to endure the braying of our constant shadow alone for the rest of that long night, until he handed me over to the Americans and departed. I sweated it out for a further two days 'under wraps' in a cramped bedroom, because the weather had clamped down over the Hump; then, when I felt I couldn't take another hour of it, Sweet FA turned up again.

'ABC,' he grinned fatuously. 'That means "all been changed"—usual bloody thing these days. You go back to Chungking again. This caper has been cancelled.'

'Freddie?' I asked, feeling like a condemned man reprieved at the last minute.

'Sent on another job,' he said. 'Don't ask me why. Because I wouldn't tell you even if I knew.'

'He hasn't been sent in place of me, has he?' I asked, relief fighting with shame.

'Oh no, nothing like that,' he told me. 'Just a change in policy. Come on, your plane takes off in fifteen minutes, and the Americans hate being kept waiting.'

It was a horrible flight, worse than the one out, and I had a two-day wait in Kunming for an onward plane to Chungking—but Shivka and Raucous met me at the foot of the steps, and Abigail had the best room in the house and a perfect dinner awaiting my arrival, which compensated in some measure for a few further days 'under wraps'.

Gathercole came round a week later. 'That's my boy,' he beamed. 'You did fine. They're very pleased with you.'

'What did I do fine?' I said sourly. 'And who the hell are "they"?'

He shrugged vaguely. 'Oh, the top brass generally. Freddie sent you a message, by the way.'

'When will he be here?' I asked.

'He won't be,' Gathercole said. 'The message was, "Best of luck. You can't win 'em all." He was damn right. He certainly didn't win the last one—the one that counts.'

'What on earth are you talking about?' I said irritably.

'Freddie. I said he wouldn't be coming here—'

'Why not? Where has he been posted?' I was conscious of his beady little black eyes regarding me obliquely, as if waiting for a reaction.

'Posted?' He shrugged again. 'Couldn't tell you that, not being an ecclesiastical type. He was court-martialled in camera, then they shot the bastard in the forecourt of the Trimulgherry Military Prison on Tuesday morning. Hey!—You've spilt your drink.'

Chapter Eight

1

Abigail said, 'You'd better face up to it. They're too polite to tell you so, but you're over age for infantry—in a junior rank at any rate. Why not be sensible and settle for Censorship? You'll rate major then.'

'Because the job they've offered me is in New Delhi, still "under wraps", damn them,' I told her. 'I want to get right out of this racket, and use my own name again, as a private soldier if necessary. I feel I've been wallowing in a sewer. You know what they made me do, don't you?'

'No, and I'd rather you didn't tell me,' she answered quickly.

'You're tarred with the same brush as the rest of them,' I said bitterly. ' "Need to know", "Knock twice and ask for Alice", "Trust nobody"—passwords and countersigns. You love it, don't you? All of you playing secret societies in darkened rooms. Well, I *don't* love it. I want out.'

'In your case I should say that it would involve about six months' debriefing, posting to a non-sensitive area, which means right out of the Far East, and then an Official Secrets writ on you for the duration and seven years thereafter.' She shook her head. 'I can't see you being very happy under those restrictions.'

'Happiness doesn't come into it. I just want to forget that I ever touched this business. They made a Judas Iscariot out of me,' I said.

'Too bad,' my mother said. 'I'll cry tomorrow. George Gathercole is coming tonight.'

'I won't see him.'

'You will. Either here in comfort or down at the Embassy, standing in front of his desk. Don't make difficulties for yourself, lovey. This is official.'

He arrived early enough to mooch a first-class dinner on the house, and then came up to my room. He stood in the doorway and looked around appreciatively.

'Achilles in his tent, eh?' he said, grinning broadly. 'Nice comfortable place to sulk in. Better than a real tent in the Embassy compound. Like to hear a few facts?'

'Not from a professional liar,' I said.

'Nasty,' he said reproachfully. 'You're going to, all the same. It *might* save you some snivelling.' He twisted a chair round and sat astride it, his arms resting on the back, facing me. 'Frederick Seymour Stewart,' he went on without further preamble. 'Born in 1897 in Harbin, Manchuria, of Irene Sulvarov, widow of Stefan Sulvarov, an escaper from Siberia. There was a constant trickle of them in those days; the tough ones made it the whole way to Shanghai, but for every one that did, six left their bones in the Gobi. "Runcons" they called them—short for "running convicts"—and you must never confuse them with "Migs", which is a contraction of "Emigres"—*they* came later, as a result of the 1917 Revolution. I'm a descendant of the former, the lovely Shivka of the latter.'

'I don't know where all this is leading,' I began, 'but—'

'Bear with me,' he said. 'The Runcons were largely proletariat, with a sprinkling of bourgeois liberals and intellectuals, all at variance with the Tsarist regime. The Migs, on the other hand, were ci-devant aristocracy, ex-officers and professional people, with a ragtag-and-bobtail assortment of hangers-on, running from the Bolsheviks. The two lots, naturally, never mixed, even in the International Concession orphanages, where many of the children, Freddie among them, finished up. But he was lucky. He was adopted by an English couple—Reginald Stewart, a feature writer and sub-editor on the *Shanghai Mercury*, and his wife Elizabeth—and he went Home with them before he was five,

237

and became a thoroughpaced little Englishman. He did brilliantly at school and even better at Cambridge, where he was first recruited by Lenin's talent scouts, indoctrinated and trained and kept under wraps, then infiltrated into that capitalist holy of holies, the LPG Bank, after post-graduating from the Harvard Business School. Impeccable background—British *and* American. He was what is known in this business as a "sleeper", that's an agent who remains inert, sometimes for years, until activated by his Control. We first knew of him in 1935—'

'And yet you did nothing about it?' I said indignantly.

'Damn right we did nothing,' he agreed. 'Why should we? He wasn't working against *us*—not then he wasn't. It was much more profitable just to watch him until he did something interesting—normal procedure. And he *did* do something interesting—in 1940. He doubled to the Japs, and we had him by the short and curlies from that moment, because he used to send his stuff through the LPG private mailbag, and we had a man planted in their Tokyo office who used to extract it, photograph it and have it back to us within forty-eight hours. We never stopped any of it, because it was all fairly innocuous—commercial intelligence mostly, in a very breakable code. Actually they were only training him in communication procedures. Then came Pearl Harbor and the round-up of all British and American nationals in Shanghai, Freddie among them, naturally, and being a bloke of courage and initiative he organized his own escape together with four other men, one of whom was an employee of his own bank, Pentreath, a moonlighter we'd planted on him three years previously. It was all very clever and authentic—an ingenious ploy by the Japs to get him into India, and a job where he'd be *really* useful to them. I debriefed his party when they arrived here. "What do you want to do?" I asked Freddie. "Have a go at those little yellow bastards—the sooner the better," he said, really savage. "I may be getting a bit long in the tooth, but I'm tough—" etc. etc. "Sorry," I told him, as solemn as an owl, "nothing do-and-dare for you, my lad. You're far too valuable to waste. You're going into Intelligence." He sent up an awful squawk—infantry—parachutes, even—*please*—He wasn't cut out for cloak-and-dagger. No, we said, very kindly but very firmly, you must go where you'll be the most use—and we sent him down the road he and his masters had planned. Very obliging of us.'

'But if you knew all about him why didn't you deal with him here?' I demanded. 'Why this cat and mouse business? Why send him all the way to India? And above all, why involve *me*?'

'Oh, come off it,' Gathercole said, pained. 'You don't throw a lemon away half squeezed. There was one very important bit of info we wanted from him first. The line of communication he would be using from India back to his control. The best way to get that was to feed him a red-hot tip and watch what he did with it—hence your supposed move to Kweilin. He couldn't delay with that one because you were leaving immediately, so he thought. He coded it as soon as you left for Nirsa, and shot off to Calcutta with it like a long dog. He was tailed to a Bengali silk shop in Lower Circular Road, *then* knocked off, bang to rights, *in flagrante delicto* with the message on him—and the bonus we got was a high-power radio installation on a river boat that the direction-finders had been unable to fix previously—a straight link with Jap HQ in Singapore.'

'But *why*?' I asked. 'I don't know what the bank paid him, but he must have been on a very high salary—he was a bachelor and he didn't live lavishly. *Why* was he doing it?'

'There's probably a dozen answers to that, and all of them partly right,' Gathercole said. 'The short one, I think, is that there's something atavistic about it. Scratch the hide of any Russian, Red, White, Blue or Pink, and you'll find a potential spy underneath. The "innate Slavic predilection to clandestinity" as a college-educated chief of mine once called it.'

'But Stewart was brought up in England, as an Englishman, you say—'

'A duck will still swim, given the opportunity, even if it

was hatched in the middle of the Sahara. In Freddie's case he was a bit pre-conditioned anyhow. Old Reggie Stewart and his missus were both card-carrying Party members, jobs on Right Wing papers notwithstanding.'

Deliberately, with calculated malice, I said, 'You're Russian too, aren't you?'

'I am indeed,' he admitted, in no way put out. 'Ethnically anyhow. *I* was an orphanage brat also—stateless. In my case I was given the chance to enlist as a boy piper in the Royal Scots, who were stationed in Woosung at the time. I was fourteen then, so at eighteen I became entitled to a British passport. I transferred to the police four years later—opium control department at first, then they gave me a trial in Special Branch, so I was able to indulge my "Slavic clandestinity" legitimately. I'm a hundred per cent British in outlook and loyalty though, if that's what you're getting at. Passionately, *boringly* so—like a convert to Catholicism. That's what being stateless as a kid does to one. If you've come in out of the cold you don't lightly risk being booted back into it.'

'I wasn't getting at anything,' I protested insincerely.

'Of course you weren't.' He smiled blandly. 'But let's get back to Freddie. He was a Red sleeper originally, so logically he was anti-German and therefore ipso facto anti-Jap. How come he was spying for them then? Money? He didn't particularly need any, though as a banker he certainly didn't despise it. Was he being blackmailed? Not as far as we know—no record of perversion or other peculiar habits on our files, and I can assure you that we really investigated that possibility. Political change of heart? I don't think so. He wasn't a political animal, in spite of his early indoctrination. So what?'

'So what?' I repeated. I was becoming interested, like a kibitzer overlooking somebody else's jigsaw puzzle.

'So we come back to the original premise—Slavic predilection to clandestinity. I have no doubt whatsoever in my own mind that he was bored stiff with being a sleeper. He

240

could see this fascinating game being played out here and his talents weren't being used. He was like a pinch-hitter sitting in the bleachers, firmly convinced that he could do a bloody sight better than any of the players on the field, frustrated to the point where he finally says, "Right, you stupid bastards, if you don't want me, there's plenty that do"—so he goes double, as we call it in the business.'

'I find that hard to believe,' I said.

'Because you don't understand the "business"—yet. Field agents going double is a constant occupational hazard that gives poor devils of spymasters on both sides the screaming willies. You never know where the hell you are with them. Like I just said, some do it for the money, some are black-mailed and some, like Freddie, for the sheer hell of feeling the adrenalin running. It's good insurance, too—like backing a horse both ways. When the battle's o'er, you stay with the winners.' He cocked an eye at the well stocked tray of drinks Abigail had sent in. 'May I? You look as if you could do with one too.'

He poured scotch into two glasses and offered one to me. I shook my head, and he looked hurt.

'Oh, come,' he said reproachfully. 'You're not still sore at me, are you?'

'What the devil do you expect me to be?' I said. 'You made a complete fool of me.'

He shook his head. 'No, not that,' he said seriously. 'I used you, yes, and I make no apology for it. Suppose I'd taken you into my confidence before sending you off—what would have happened? You'd either have turned the job down, or you'd have been so nervous that you'd have cocked it up.'

'But to make me lead a man to his death—' I began, and he cut me short impatiently, thrusting the glass towards me.

'Here, drink this, for Christ's sake,' he snapped, 'before we all burst into tears. You didn't lead anybody to his death, for the simple reason you didn't know what was going on. If you'd had the advantage of a good Irish Mick orphanage education, like me, you'd know that where there's no intent,

241

there's no sin—and if doing the dirty on old Freddie is worrying you, what the hell was he doing to you, *with* intent? He had the whole thing set up very professionally indeed—the time to expect you, map coordinates of the inn, the lot. If that had been a genuine mission and the message had gone out, you'd have been dropped right into the arms of a Jap welcoming committee.'

I took the scotch and swallowed it in one.

'That's better,' he said approvingly. 'Now listen to me. If this has really upset you, then go back to India where they'll no doubt find something for you to do. On the other hand, if you can get it into its proper perspective and accept the fact that this is a job like any other, maybe a little smellier than many, but a very, *very* necessary one, then I can most certainly use you here. The choice is entirely yours, but if you do decide to stay there must be no more horrified vapours if you're called upon to do something really unpleasant at any time—like cutting your Ma's throat or selling your best pal downriver. You just do it, then put it out of your mind—or try to.'

'I'll stay,' I mumbled, and held my glass out for a refill.

2

But on the heels of that Napoleonic decision came anti-climax, and in Chungking we followed a policy of masterly inactivity for the rest of that dreary winter and most of the even more ghastly summer that followed. We watched the stream of war material come in over the Hump—fuel, ammunition, food, clothing and medicines, the lifeblood of an army—knowing that more than fifty per cent of every Dakota cargo went underground as soon as the Kuomintang got their paws upon it, to be stockpiled against the day when the uneasy alliance between them and Mao Tse-tung's forces ended, and civil war succeeded the present bogged-

242

down conflict, and there were times, many of them, when I begged Gathercole to release me and let me go to India and take up some sort of job, in the army or out of it. But I begged in vain, because although he never turned me down flatly, he was adept at putting me off.

'Yes, yes, I know,' he would say sympathetically. 'It's absolute hell for a feller that's been used to being up and doing. I know just how you feel. As a copper I never had a moment to call my own, and I thrived on it. Here, I would feel I'd been dumped in the discards, forgotten, overlooked, if I didn't know for absolute certain that there was something big coming off—really big—something they had up their sleeves that they'd be wanting *us* to handle and us alone. See what I mean?'

'No, I bloody well don't,' I snarled at him once. 'Tell me who "they" are and I might. Or let me go and put my case to them if you haven't the authority to release me.'

He looked worried. 'Well, I can't do that—not exactly. It's one of those things, you know—' he tailed off vaguely.

'One of what things?' I persisted.

'Er—I tell you what I'll do. I'll go and see them and put it to them straight. I'll tell 'em that it's not fair to be keeping an officer of your special talents and ability under wraps for so long. I'll tell 'em that you've got to be given a job, a really important, *significant* job, and given it soon.' He beamed at me as benignly as a fond father promising his favourite son a pony for Christmas. 'Yes, that's what I'll do—you see if I don't. I'll put a firecracker under their asses that'll lift a few of them through the ceiling. Just hang on a few days longer.'

But nothing came of it, and I sat those weary months out watching on paper the tide of war ebbing and flowing, with most of the former heartbreakingly on our side, leaving us high, dry and impotent. We were cocooned in our drab fortress, with the Japs holding the entire China coast from Mongolia in the north to the Siamese frontier in the south-west, three thousand miles of it, slowly but steadily eroding their way into the troubled heartland of this vast territory.

243

They had reached, captured and held Ichang, the big deepwater port on the Yangtse-kiang a mere three hundred miles downriver from us, and they had thrust over the border into Burma in two long pincer movements, taking Rangoon in the south and reaching and crossing the Indian border near Imphal in the north. Slim's 'forgotten' Fourteenth Army was holding them now, with Vinegar Joe Stilwell at the head of a mixed force of Kuomintang troops and semi-bandit irregulars harassing their right flank and disrupting their lines of communication, but we knew, sickeningly, that we had not stopped them, and nowhere had we forced them into retreat.

Things were not made easier by the knowledge that Shivka was operative, while I sat twiddling my thumbs. As a White Russian she was technically neutral as far as the Japs were concerned, and, in fact, her father was still in Shanghai, not only at liberty, but running his practice in the neutral community, which included Swedes, Swiss, Portuguese and, of course, other White Russians, and no less than three times she had, to my knowledge, dropped downriver and crossed the Jap advance lines near Ichang and made her way into the city. I tackled my mother about this, and got nowhere. She just looked blank and shrugged. She herself was also working, ostensibly with refugees who continued to come through in a trickle, and here at least I was graciously permitted to help, because all of them had to be searchingly and rigorously debriefed.

'Right up your alley,' Gathercole told me, 'your Chinese being so polite and educated. Mine's all right for coolies and criminals, but it rubs the mandarin classes up the wrong way. Remarkable how like us the Chinks are in many ways. Snobbish. I remember pulling an Old Etonian con man in once in my early days, and I used a bit of soldier's language. He looked down his nose at me and said, 'I know perfectly well that you've got me bang to rights, my dear chap, but I refuse to discuss the matter with a yahoo. Take me before a *gentleman* and I don't mind making a statement.' Yes, be nice and smooth with 'em, but get it all. We don't want any more Freddie Stewarts slipping through, do we?'

I did my best with them, but I don't know how successful or otherwise I was, because although he always thanked me fulsomely when I handed my reports in, I noticed that he invariably questioned the clients further himself, and I have no doubt that he garnered much that I had missed. His denigration of his own mastery of the language was nonsense; he was the only European I have ever met whose vocabulary, grammar and tonal range was better than my own. I hated him, but I respected him and, although I was loath to admit it to myself, I feared him. His tentacles were everywhere.

I took up the matter of Helen with him more than once. 'I insist that my wife is told that I am safe and well,' I said. 'She needn't be told where I am or what I'm *supposed* to be doing. Damn it all, what difference could it possibly make to your blasted war effort?'

'You're absolutely right,' he agreed solemnly. 'Just leave it with me. I'll clear it with 'em. Tell 'em straight, I will.'

But I didn't trust him, and one day I slipped a Red Cross postcard into the diplomatic bag that used to be flown out to India twice a week. I was careful not to breach security, so I merely wrote, 'V. Stafford—alive—well—will communicate when able,' and addressed it to Helen care of our Sydney office, with the request to forward it if necessary. It was something we did whenever authenticated news of a prisoner, escaper or evader reached us, and on this particular occasion there were a dozen or so such postcards going out to next-of-kin.

Gathercole came into the dog kennel of an office they had given me for my censorship duties next morning, and flicked the card on to the table in front of me. 'Don't do that again,' he said quietly, and walked out before I could find enough breath to curse him.

It would have been difficult to define my real feelings at that period. I was not excessively fired by patriot zeal, in

245

fact, if anything, I was almost as resentful of the bungling British tactics as I was revolted by those of the enemy, and while not, I hope, altogether a physical coward, I was certainly no fire-eater—but to have got out of that enervating backwater I think I would have volunteered to storm the very gates of hell. Reports of the appalling conditions suffered by our prisoners kept coming through, and here I was living in the lap of luxury in my mother's hotel, eating the bread of idleness spread with Beluga caviar, and not even allowed to work for it. I would willingly have changed places with Raucous, who, now a sergeant, was running the Embassy road link between Kunming and these headquarters, efficiently and well, with even a spice of danger to make it the more attractive to one of his temperament. Shivka, when she was not cloak-and-daggering for Gathercole, was more than earning her keep helping Abigail, both in managing the hotel and with the refugees. And Abigail herself? God knows what *she* was really doing. I 'didn't need to know'—therefore I was not told.

But at last it came.

3

Gathercole said, 'There's a chap in Hong Kong I'd like you to meet. How do you feel about it?'

'You're the boss,' I shrugged. 'When does he arrive?'

'He doesn't, unfortunately. You'll have to go there.' He was pretending to study a map on the table in front of him, but I could feel his beady little taktoo lizard eyes watching for my reaction obliquely, so I tried to play it as casually as he, but the old familiar empty feeling at the pit of my stomach was back.

'More walking?' I said. 'It will probably do me good. I'm as deskbound and corpulent as the rest of you up here on Olympus.'

'Not such a hell of a lot. We'll set you down at the Inn of the Seven Stars by Silent Lizzie this time.'

'Who's she?'

'*She's* a Westland Lysander aircraft—little fart of a thing that can land on a handkerchief and take off again, in the dark, that they're using a lot for agent-dropping in Europe. Too many broken necks and ankles by parachute apparently.' He looked up at me directly for the first time, wide-eyed and innocent. 'You've been asking for a more up and doing job for such a long time that I thought you'd like this. You don't have to take it, of course.'

'I'll take it,' I said. What option had I? 'Who and what is the chap?'

'Code name Angelo, which is all you need know at the moment. He's a stay-behind.'

'A what?'

'A stay-behind. You've heard of them, haven't you?' I shook my head, so he went on. 'One of that small, select band of lunatics that volunteer to stay put in enemy-occupied territory to filter out Intelligence and do a little useful sabotage from time to time. Sooner them than me. I'd rather play Russian roulette. Anyhow, this fellow Angelo has quite a lot of useful stuff that we'd like to see up here, but communications have broken down. He's got a receiver, so we can talk to him, but he can't transmit to us. You can collect the gen from him and bring it back here. Simple as that.'

'It shouldn't be too difficult,' I agreed. The initial shock was abating a little by now. 'We fix up a rendezvous on the outskirts, I take it—?'

'I shouldn't have said "as simple as that",' He smiled gently. 'In fact it *could* be a bit complicato. You see, he's in the bag.'

'You mean he's a PoW—in a *camp*?' I stared at him and he nodded gravely. 'For Christ's sake!' I exploded. 'You expect me to get into Hong Kong itself, then into a camp—and then find my way out again?' I choked on the words.

247

'Like I said.' He nodded gravely. 'A bit complicato—but then you needn't take it on if you have any qualms—'

'Qualms be damned!' I shouted. 'Listen, Gathercole—' but he checked me with upraised hand.

'Watch it,' he said sharply. 'I've told you about that before. "George" if we're being pally, "Colonel" or "Sir" if we're not. All right, so you've turned it down. I'm not blaming you for that, but don't come yammering to me for a do-and-dare job again. Dismiss.'

'I'm sorry,' I mumbled. 'I'm not turning it down, but—well, one can't help seeing the difficulties—'

'Oh, I can see the difficulties all right.' He was being gentle again. 'Yes, plenty of difficulties, but maybe they're not as hair-raising as they might seem at first blush. You see, work parties of prisoners are coming and going out of the camps constantly, and it's not difficult for an intelligent chap to merge into one. In fact, we've done that more than once and the stuff has come out over the hills to Kwan, who has radioed it on to us. Unfortunately the last runner was intercepted in the New Territories with the dope on him. Whether they busted the code or not we're not sure. The runner, a Hakka fisherman, was tortured as a matter of course, but thank God they weren't successful in tracing it back to Angelo. All the Hakka could tell them was that he received the stuff from a Chinaman in Nathan Road and he got payment when he handed it on to the next relay on the Border—but the Nips now know that there's a Mister Big somewhere in Hong Kong sending information out, and they're on their toes trying to find him. In other words the line is broken, and likely to stay broken as there are no more runners forthcoming, certainly not at the moment, so a lot of gen that we really need up here has accumulated in Angelo's hands. With me so far?'

I nodded gloomily. 'Yes, I understand that, but the point that puzzles me is the Mister Big, as you call him, being a prisoner. What use is he to you inside the wire?'

'Good question,' he nodded. 'Actually he was outside the

248

wire for over a year, accommodated in different safe houses, but he was nearly caught one night breaking the curfew and only got away with it by mixing in with a squad of prisoners cleaning drains next day, and going back with them into Shamsuipo POW camp. He's been damned ill for a long time, unfit to go out with parties, but he's carried on collecting gen from intelligent NCOs who *are* going out. He's taken a dead man's identity and apparently he is unsuspected by the Nips. To them he's just another living skeleton starving to death like the others—a private soldier inside the wire while they are looking for an officer on the loose outside, but you can appreciate the clamp he's in. One false move and that's *it*. He's under wraps and his real identity is known only to one sergeant and a sergeant-major. You'll be told at your full briefing how to contact one or other of them once you're inside, and then it will be up to you—when they're satisfied who you are. Any questions?'

'Only a couple of dozen or so—' I gulped.

'Save 'em for the briefing,' he said. 'You'll go in the same way as you came out, that is from the Seven Stars. There'll be guides and couriers the same as last time, as far as Kwan's hideout. Getting you into Hong Kong from there will be in his hands.'

'Will I be alone?' I asked.

'That, also, is a matter for the briefing. They'll most probably allot you one back-up man. Anybody in mind?'

'Rawcliffe,' I said. 'He has been over the ground. That's if he's willing, of course.'

Gathercole smiled grimly. 'If he's got any sense he *won't* be willing. I'll mention it to them, but I can't make any promises at this stage. All right, Vince: you've accepted it, but you won't be held to it if you change your mind after you've had time to think it over. I'll see you again this time tomorrow. I don't have to warn you, of course—' He tapped himself on the lips. 'Not a hint, particularly to your Ma—or Shivka.'

'No, you don't have to warn me,' I snapped, and marched

249

out stiffly. Behind me I could hear him chuckling throatily, mockingly.

Fear and abnegation had merged into self-pity by the time I reached the hotel, and I was whimpering inwardly. What had I done to deserve this? Why were they making a sacrificial goat of me? Damn them! Why should I fall for it? I'd tell them—tell them honestly that I just wasn't up to it. But I knew that I hadn't the guts to do that. Perhaps if I did let it slip to Abigail she might have enough on Gathercole to make him drop the whole stupid, suicidal nonsense—because that's what it was. Go into the lion's mouth to pick his teeth? Who the hell ever heard of such a crazy, half-baked idea?

But Abigail wasn't at home. She had gone off to screen a party of refugees somewhere, and Shivka had been down-river for some weeks—probably in as great, or greater, danger than I'd be if I couldn't dodge this thing. I'd at least do the decent thing by Raucous though, or so I told myself. I'd let them know at the briefing that I'd changed my mind on that point, and I no longer wanted him with me.

But I knew I wouldn't do that either. If I had to go down that lonely road I certainly would want that solid, dependable bulk between my shivering self and danger.

But he was at the briefing when I arrived the following afternoon, and the fool was actually grateful.

'Gaw! Lovely,' he burbled. 'Thanks for asking for me. I could do with a holiday.'

'Don't talk like a bloody idiot,' I snarled. 'You know what it's like—the walking—no food most of the time—and you know what they'd do to us if we were caught.'

'Still a holiday,' he grinned. 'It's Aggie, you see—backed up by your Ma and Miss Shivka. Wedding rings, for Chri'sake. They want me to marry her proper, to get her a passport and a pension if I cop out sometime. Not me. I got plans for when this lot's over, and she just don't fit into any of them.'

'Turn it down, Raucous,' I begged insincerely. 'They won't think any the worse of you.'

250

'But I would of meself,' he said solemnly, and I could have hit him. 'No, sir, if you're going, *I'm* going. I *want* to.'

He didn't come in with me. He waited in the outer office while the G-One (Operations), Gathercole, and an SOE man who had flown in over the Hump, and who seemed to have as much specialized knowledge of the Hong Kong hinterland as I had of the South Pole, briefed and rebriefed me until my tired brain was a mass of mixed-up, garbled map references, safe houses, pick-up points, drops, blocks, cut-offs and dead letter-boxes, because I was not allowed to make notes. Then, while I was still weltering in all this, they gave me the passwords and countersigns, and then we went off to draw our clothes—black peasant pongees, like those we had arrived in—and pistols. A squadron-leader took us over then, and we drove out to some open ground a few miles to the north of the city—open only insofar as there were no trees there, merely a patch of dried paddy no more than a hundred and fifty yards long, where a small and horribly fragile-looking aircraft waited humped like a miniature pterodactyl in the gloomy twilight.

The pilot, who looked about sixteen and didn't impress me at all, eyed our admittedly bulky packs sourly and muttered that with the extra fuel he was obliged to carry for the round trip he was already overloaded, so we were obliged to shed the few creature comforts in the shape of canned food that Raucous had gathered together.

But things improved somewhat when, in the inky blackness below, our infant prodigy picked up the faint pinpoints of light that marked our landing ground—just three flickering oil lanterns in the form of a triangle—and he landed unerringly, guided solely by what seemed to me a very rudimentary system of signals from a flashlight. Then, without a word, four shadowy figures lifted the tail of the aircraft and swung it in a half circle and he had taken off again almost as soon as Raucous and I had jumped out. There was a stumbling walk of about an hour then, led by the silent reception committee, and dawn was just beginning to streak the sky as we reached the inn. Yes, they certainly had streamlined the organization since we had passed through on our way north, and I experienced in spite of myself a distinct lift of spirit.

We rested in the comfortable cellar for twenty-four hours, then set out again over the previous route, guided by two couriers who, like the rest of the staff at that strange hostelry, seemed to know their job, and we passed through the valley, where we had fought our first battle, three days later, and were picked up by Kwan's fishermen at the rendezvous punctually to the minute and were wafted silently downriver past the Canton waterfront on the fifth night. It had all gone like well-oiled clockwork.

Kwan came straight to the point without preamble on our first meeting.

'I suppose you know the general idea behind all this?' I asked him.

'The *general* idea, yes. There's nothing definitely settled yet. That's why they want this information from Angelo. Reoccupation—a seaborne attack on Hong Kong, the soft underbelly of Asia, like Churchill's landings in Italy. I think it would fail, but I'm only the postboy, passing information both ways, and nobody's asked my opinion.' There was a distinctly querulous note in his voice, and I sensed that the strain was telling on him, because he had aged far beyond the three years since we had last met.

'Why do you think it would fail?' I asked.

'They're jumping the gun by six months.'

'Why six months?'

'There'll be a better balance then. The Japs are pulling out troops to plug holes in other parts of their front, which now extends to just short of five thousand miles, from Japan itself to the Indian frontier. They took Hong Kong with twenty thousand men; they're holding it now with seven thousand, the sick and the lame, old men and potwallopers—the scrapings of the barrel.'

'So it shouldn't be so difficult—' I began, but he cut me short with an impatient gesture.

252

'That's the sort of response I'd have expected from a *soldier*.' He literally spat the last word.'A real do-or-dier, with his arse in an office chair a few hundred miles back from the front.'

Stung, I said, 'I know I'm not a soldier. What I meant was—'

'Sorry, no offence meant to you personally. I was merely breaking wind in the direction of the top brass.' He gestured hopelessly. 'Vince, *it will fail*—their way, by sea. Gallipoli in the last war all over again—Dieppe in this one—thousands of men thrown away for *nothing*. Won't the bastards ever learn?'

'I don't know,' I said, my spirits starting to plummet again. 'Like you, I'm just a postboy. I have very definite orders and I suppose I'll have to carry them out—or try to. You're going to get me into Kowloon, I understand?'

'That's easy enough,' he said surprisingly. 'I've been in myself, a dozen times, flatly in the face of their orders up there, so I'd ask you to keep that to yourself.'

'Easy enough for *you*,' I said. 'You're Chinese, ethnically at least. So why the hell have they sent me?'

'Oh, there's a reason for that. I can get into Kowloon, and out again, without difficulty, but Chinese are forbidden to enter the camps—and they want to contact Angelo. There's a second reason also. This place is important, and if I were caught and put through the mangle I might blow it.'

'So might I.'

'Not quite such a risk, according to their thinking. The Japs suspect I've been constantly in this area and would undoubtedly put two and two together. They wouldn't of necessity connect you with it if you stuck to your brief that you'd come straight down through the New Territories.'

'I see,' I said glumly. The old hollow was back in my stomach. 'So in your opinion it's all pretty hopeless—not to mention *useless*?'

'*Their* way,' he said quietly. 'Even if the landing was successful it would take four divisions at least, with full

253

artillery support plus air cover to hold it. Thirty thousand men to supply and feed—not to mention twelve thousand prisoners already dying of starvation.'

'What the hell are they thinking of?' I said desperately.

'The Grand Strategy,' he said, smiling twistedly. 'This place taken and held, in spite of appalling losses, would mean that the Japs would have to strip other parts of their front to retake it—to prevent our advancing into the interior and getting behind them and presenting them with two fronts. And then we'd put in other landings on the parts so weakened—and eventually the inevitable would happen and they would have to bring troops from the heartland—the Japanese Islands themselves, and our *real* attack would go in—Tokyo or bust—the thing they dread most of all.'

'So what you're saying is that Hong Kong is the cheese in the mousetrap?'

He shrugged. 'Only theory, and pessimistic theory at that, on my part. You needn't take my word for it. I could well be wrong. The thing that is galling the hide off me is that there *is* another way—a way that could bring all that about with negligible losses.'

'What is that?' I asked, snatching at straws.

'An attack by air—parachutists—gliders—five thousand men, first-class assault troops—dropped without warning—no preliminary bombing—just a strike at dawn—key posts seized and the whole Jap garrison wiped out before they knew what had hit them. With full surprise *it could be done*.'

'But we'd still need the four divisions to hold it,' I objected.

'That's just the point. We wouldn't attempt to hold it. We'd put the whole place to the torch, particularly the dockyard which they rely on so heavily to keep both their naval and supply ships serviced, and then get out again. Every damned thing sabotaged—power stations, water supplies, food stocks, ammunition dumps. The place wouldn't be worth a hoot in hell to them after that, and we could land dry-shod and unopposed later, at a time of our own choosing.'

254

'You've forgotten something, haven't you?' I said. 'The prisoners? What happens to *them*?'

'I hadn't forgotten them. They come out with the attacking force.'

'How, for God's sake?'

'By air, naturally.'

'Twelve thousand of them?' I shook my head. His enthusiasm had begun to communicate itself to me, now I could feel it vitiating. This was just a pipe dream.

'Two hundred Dakotas would do it—two flights each—a seventy-five minute turn-round to a previously prepared landing-ground north of Kweilin, outside the Jap-held zone, with Chiang's hitherto useless army to screen it while we ferried them out to safe territory.' He took a sheet of paper from a drawer of the table in front of him. 'Have a look at these figures if you have any doubts.'

'But where would the two hundred Daks come from?'

'They have over a thousand in full operational service in India at the moment, supplying Slim's Fourteenth Army in Burma and Chiang's circus in the north. Two hundred diverted for a mere twenty-four hours would be a fleabite!'

I could feel the enthusiasm creeping back, but I had learnt my lesson now and I suppressed it. It was still a pipedream. 'Have you put this up to the brass?' I asked him.

'Of course. To Gathercole, on the occasion of my one visit to Chungking.'

'What did he say?'

'Pretended to see possibilities in it and said he'd put it up to New Delhi. Whether he ever did or not, I can't say. I certainly have heard nothing since, other than a "negative—no repeat no" in morse when I sent him a reminder—also in morse. No, that one is dead—strangled before birth.'

'I wish you hadn't told me,' I said regretfully. 'I've still got to go in to make contact with Angelo, but it all seems so pointless now.'

'Oh, I wasn't making a Wailing Wall out of you just for the

sake of clearing my liver,' he said. 'What I was hoping was that *you* might try a resurrection exercise up there when you get back.'

'Christ! If they've turned *you* down they're hardly likely to listen to me.'

'On the contrary. Yours is a name to conjure with—Sir Vincent Stafford, taipan, acknowledged authority on Hong Kong, and what is far more important, you will have seen the Colony for yourself—the state of its weakened defences and the general feeling of the place. They haven't. Oh, they'd listen to you all right.'

'But you've seen it. You've been in and out of the place, you tell me—'

'But I couldn't admit that. As I told you, I've been forbidden to go there, and even threatened with arrest if I did.'

'I see,' I said slowly. 'All right, I'll certainly mention it—*if* I get back.'

'You'll do that all right.'

'I wish I shared your optimism. Frankly, the whole crazy business of getting in and out again scares me stiff.'

'You'll be quite safe as long as you keep your wits about you and do as Long John Silberstein tells you,' he said, and I felt he was watching me closely for my reaction. If he expected me to be astonished he was not disappointed.

'*Silberstein?*' I stared at him. 'You can't possibly mean that *crook?*'

'I certainly do. I've been trying to have him enlisted officially, but Gathercole blew his stack when I suggested it and gave me a direct order to have nothing to do with him. You seem to have heard of him.' He grinned mordantly.

'You bet I've heard of him,' I said. 'The Americans have been trying to have him extradited to Hawaii for years. Damn it, I was on the last board of magistrates that dealt with the case. That lawyer of his, Chang Yuen, has beaten us every time—'

'That's right—Charlie Silberstein. The "Long John" is because of his one leg.'

'Yes, yes, I know all that and more—opium, brothels, gambling—every crooked activity—He's into the lot.'

'The gambling wasn't crooked.' Kwan smiled reminiscently. 'He ran the best poker school in the Colony—twenty-four hours a day. I *know*. Poker, with the Americans, is a much loved game; with us Australians it's a religion. I won three thousand dollars in that back room of his one night—and dropped six the following week.'

'But how on earth does he come into this business? Where is he, anyhow?'

'It's a long story.'

'And as I've just told you, I know it. He broke out of prison in Honolulu, before the war—'

'I don't think you *do* know it. Not all of it. In the first place it wasn't prison exactly, it was the Stockade—the detention barracks where they send Service offenders. He was a petty officer in the US Navy, and he had struck a *commissioned* officer and been court-martialled, busted and sentenced to five years' imprisonment. He escaped and made it to Tahiti. While there he saved a small Chinese boy from a shark—and lost his leg in the process. He was lucky, if you can call it that, in so far as the boy was the son of Chen Ming, the local Triad tong chief. Some people say that it's a myth, but actually it's true—if you do that sort of service for any Chinese worth a damn, he is indebted to you for life. The Americans had fixed up an extradition warrant with the French, and an escort was on its way for him, but Chen Ming got him out of Tahiti to Shanghai, where Gathercole, then a cop, was on his tail, fast. He came on here then, and the Triad staked him to his café. It was just a front for all his other nefarious activities I'm afraid, but—'

'Look, come to the point, Kwan,' I butted in impatiently. 'Where is he, and what makes you think he could be trusted? From what I know of him I wouldn't be at all surprised to hear that he was wholeheartedly collaborating with the enemy.'

'Then you'd be wrong. Oh, Long John is a bad egg, all right—but not *that* sort of bad. As a matter of fact the Japs want him a darned sight more than the Americans ever did. He makee them losee face plentee too muchee—'

'How?'

'Very rudely and vulgarly. He stood his ground when they took over Hong Kong—business as usual. It wasn't *his* war, he said. He wasn't much use to anybody with one leg, and even if he did get a sudden rush of patriotism to the skull, and made his way back to the Yanks, they'd only stick him into the Stockade again. A Jap take-over party arrived at his café the day after the formal surrender, to assess and commandeer his stocks of food and drink—twelve men under a fat-gutted supply officer, the type who is fiercer and more military than their real fighting men. Long John was quite philosophical and cooperative at first—all he wanted to do was to survive—but he's inclined to be a little short-tempered on occasion, which is what had landed him in trouble originally. The officer was rather drunk and very bellicose, and he started to wave his sword in Long John's face. Long John asked him not to, but the officer seemed to be enjoying it, so Long John apparently lost his temper and told him that if he didn't stop it he'd push the sword up him, or words to that effect. Anyhow, the officer didn't stop, so Long John carried out his threat, literally. One leg or not, he's as strong as an ox—and the sword went right up to the hilt. The troops were dancing around, not able to fire for fear of hitting their own officer, and in the fracas one of them dropped his sub-machine-gun, and the quick-thinking Mr Silberstein pounced on it and tailored the bloody lot of them, in one long sustained burst from the hip.'

'Good God,' I said, very impressed indeed. 'What happened then?'

'Another golden inscription was earned on the monument we ought to put up to the whores of Hong Kong when this is

258

over. Long John hadn't come out of it scatheless, but a couple of his sing-sing girlees whisked him along various back alleys and under cover. He's been leading a very precarious existence ever since. You can't disarm an Imperial Nipponese Son of Heaven, shove his sacred Samurai sword up his arse, and expect to be loved, especially if you're one-legged. That's something that can only be wiped out by blood, fire and spiritual expiation, as they call the Kempitei torture routine. What they'd do to him if they ever got their hands on him defies contemplation. He knows that, but still he has volunteered.'

'For what?'

'For the one thing that could, if not *guarantee* the success of the Hong Kong raid, at least give it a sporting chance—which it hasn't as things stand at the moment. A transmitter inside the city that can give us accurate up-to-date information—hour by hour sitreps.'

'I understand we've tried repeatedly to set one up but have failed each time,' I said. 'So how can Silberstein help?'

'We've failed because nearly every time we've tried to smuggle a set in it's been discovered by their rummaging squads, and the fishermen and opium runners concerned have paid the price in flaying and beheadings, so nobody will try now, however much we offer to pay. Two actually made it—one eighteen months ago, one only last July. The first one lasted two weeks before their direction-finders uncovered him, the second was caught while making his very first transmission. Their DFs have improved tremendously—'

'I still don't understand how Silberstein comes into it,' I said.

'Silberstein was a Chief Radio Technician and operator in the Navy before his fall from grace. He has a transmitter almost complete, built from parts I've been smuggling in to him over the last year.' Kwan took a deep breath. 'I'm laying my own head on the block now, because what I've been doing is in direct disobedience of Chungking's orders. He put up the idea to me when I first visited him and since then he has sent his requirements out, item by item, on tiny scraps of rice paper. I've got the parts for him from various places. He's almost ready to go into business—we've only been held up by a semi-diode-conductor-rectifier or some such bloody thing—I'm no technician.' He took a small square box from the drawer in the table between us. 'Anyhow, I managed to get one for him eventually, through Macao. This is it. Now, do you see the point? The information Angelo, and possibly others, collects could go to him and be sent through to me immediately.'

'But the Direction Finders?' I objected. 'You say they caught the others straight away.'

'Correct, but Long John is a vastly different proposition. The two operators who were caught were just that—operators. Brave men, but not very skilled—the product of a six-month course as against years of highly specialized training and experience. To get a fix on a transmitter you have to have two bearings. The average semi-skilled operator sends for a maximum of three minutes, then changes his position, which as we know from bitter experience is not much protection against *fully*-skilled DFs backed by adequate covering squads. I mean, you can't shut off in the middle of a message and run through crowded streets carrying a heavy transmitter, then set up immediately in another building, without attracting a certain amount of unwelcome attention. The real adept is versed in varying his frequencies and picking locations where he knows the detector vans can't go—hillsides, blanked-off valleys, all that sort of thing. Oh no, given the chance Long John could stay in business for a very long time.'

He was convincing me, but some remaining small points worried me. I said, 'All right, I agree: all this seems pretty feasible, so why is Gathercole objecting to it?'

'Because Gathercole is a cop and Silberstein is a criminal. It's as basic as that. Gathercole could no more credit Silberstein with even *partially* honest motives, let alone burning patriotism, than a lamb could trust a Bengal tiger. He has told me that in so many words.'

'You do think it is burning patriotism?'

'Yes. Are you a religious man?'

'Not particularly. Why?'

'I was wondering if you knew the story of Lucifer, that's all.'

'Oh, I know that, all right—'

'Well, there you have it. The man who has been cast out through his own misdeeds—too proud to ask for forgiveness, but eating his heart out to regain that which he has lost. His country at war, the Service that he genuinely loved fighting for its very existence, and he a cripple skulking in the shadows. Man, I tell you he'd gladly be torn to pieces for the chance to serve again.'

'How do you know all this?' I asked. 'I mean, if your only communication with him is on scraps of rice paper—'

'I have known him very well indeed for some years.' Kwan sat in silence with his head bowed and his clenched fists drumming on his knees, a picture of pent-up frustration.

'But *how* do you know him very well?' I persisted. 'Your world and his are pretty far apart, I should think.'

'Not so far,' he answered. 'We're both gamblers—he a professional, I a very keen amateur. And we're both archeologists, with the statuses reversed. He was building a bungalow at Shatin, and his workmen came across some very interesting tiling as they dug the foundations—terracotta, early Ming period. He told me about it one night when I was playing poker in his back room, and I went out next day to have a look at it. He didn't know the first thing about archeology, Chinese or otherwise, until that day, but we talked, and he got bitten by the bug, and I lent him books and he attended some lectures I was giving at the time. That was the start of it. I don't think I've ever met a more interesting character in my life, or a more complex one, with the good and the bad seemingly so inextricably mixed, but with the good, I am certain, predominating. He is loyal, generous and has the guts of a lion—and he doesn't whine or make excuses for himself.'

'I see,' I said slowly. 'What's behind it all?'

'Behind what?'

'Behind what you have been telling me. I don't think you've been talking just to hear your own voice.'

'You're damn right. Here it is, laid on the line. Will you take over here and relieve me for forty-eight hours?'

'No,' I said flatly.

'You haven't heard my reason yet—'

'I don't need to, because I know quite well what it is. You want to go into Hong Kong and set this thing up yourself, don't you?'

'Exactly. Don't you see what it could mean? A constant stream of up-to-date Intelligence, even if our air strike didn't come off.'

'You're probably right,' I conceded. 'But you'll have to set it up without my connivance. I have my orders and I intend to carry them out.'

'Oh God,' he groaned. '*You've* gone all military too, have you? I thought I was dealing with a man of judgement, with a mind of his own, not a heel-clicking robot.'

'I'm sorry,' I said, 'but I don't think it would work out. Not your way. Disobedience of a direct order by *one* man is *one* thing. Disobedience by two or more in concert is quite another thing—*mutiny*, it's called. I'm not an expert in law, either civil or military, but I know that that can be a capital offence in wartime.'

'You don't mean to tell me that you'd be scared of that, do you?'

'You bet I'd be scared,' I told him. 'Whatever your opinion of their competence may be, I can tell you that those people up there are not playing games. I know of one officer who has been shot—in fact, I was involved in the case.'

'What was that?'

'Never mind. Now listen to me. I think you might well have something here—and I'm willing to help to this extent. I'll go on into Hong Kong and carry out the instructions I have been given to the best of my ability, and in addition if

262

you wish, I'll take this diode-thingummybob with me and see Silberstein—'

'You know what would happen if you were caught with it?'

'From what I've heard I'd be up the creek anyhow, if I were caught, so it wouldn't make much difference one way or the other. The thing is *not* to be caught.' It sounded splendid in my own ears, but I was squirming inside and regretting the offer even as I spoke, but I ploughed on. 'That way nobody is disobeying anybody, and if the link is set up it can be presented to them as a *fait accompli*, with bouquets all round.'

'They can shove the bouquets where Silberstein shoved the sword,' he said. 'All I'm concerned with is getting this thing set up, and I know that I have a ten times better chance of getting into Hong Kong, and out again, than you have. Christ! It's obvious, isn't it? I'm Chinese, you're European—'

'You've been impressing on me that you're Australian,' I said.

'Oh, don't be bloody clever, Stafford,' he snapped. 'You know goddam well what I mean. Ethnically. There's another aspect to it, also: it's taken me a very long time to establish a full rapport with Silberstein. He trusts me, and I'm damned certain that he wouldn't trust you. It stands to reason. You're one of *Them*—one of the comfortable, smug buggers on the Bench that tried to send him back to the Stockade. He *loves* your sort.'

'We'll cross that bridge when we come to it,' I said. 'He probably won't even remember me.'

'And one last thing,' Kwan went on. 'The Japs want you even more than they want Long John—'

'That's nonsense,' I said. 'I know I was on their taipan list originally, but that was a blanket thing that applied to a lot of businessmen they couldn't account for—well over two years ago. I've been under wraps, don't forget. I'm probably labelled "missing believed dead" by now.'

263

'Not so,' he said gravely. 'Look, don't think I'm just raking up more objections out of thin air, but this is something you really ought to know. When your name came through for this mission I was on to that morse key like a scalded dingo. I told them I thought it was madness to send you—but they told me to belt up and forbade me to mention it to you in case it punctured your panache. The Japs know you're alive all right, and what is more, they know that you were one of the party that zapped a truckload of their troops on your way out—'

That startled me. I had told the whole story at my debriefing, of course, but I knew enough of the workings of the system by now to be positive that it wouldn't have been broadcast by Chungking, so how did Kwan know?

'Who told you that?' I asked him.

'It leaked. My dear good bloke, you can't keep that sort of thing dark,' he told me. 'They had it back in the camps here in a matter of days—a real morale-booster. You didn't kill them all, unfortunately, and one of them recognized John, the little Hakka joker who took you on from here, remember? Anyhow, he was captured and put through it. You can't blame him. He held out much longer than I could have done—but the Kempitei get it all out of you in the end when they're really trying—*everything*. Old Cavendish-Feltham had his throat cut one night by one of Tai Li's undercover Blueshirts, and the Americans, who are a damned sight more sensible than our mob, evacuated the two pilots who were with you to another theatre, and we should have done the same with you and the Russian girl.'

And now my stomach was really turning over. They knew us all—and yet I had been sent back here and, even more terrifying, they were shuttling Shivka in and out of Shanghai. It was almost as if they wanted us to be taken.

I said, 'Kwan, what do you know about Gathercole? *Really* know about him?'

'Probably no more than you do,' he answered. 'A re-vamped Russkie—a cop, very good at his job—as a cop, I mean.

264

As a senior Intelligence officer?' He shrugged. 'Well, they seem to think a lot of him.'

'Who are "they"?'

'The British Military Mission at Chungking. Chiang Kai-shek's crowd don't like him, but I would say that's a point in his favour.'

'Do you trust him?'

He shrugged again. 'No more than he trusts me, or you, or anybody else in this business. That's a lesson that you should have learned by now. You trust nobody more than you absolutely have to. If you're asking me if I think he might be doubling, no, I *don't* think so. I believe him to be a genuine Jap hater for purely personal reasons. He's clever, *very* clever, but he can be incredibly pigheaded at times—witness Silberstein, witness yourself being sent down here. So now, having sown seeds of doubt and mistrust in you, how about minding the store while I go in to Hong Kong?'

I shook my head. 'No, sorry,' I said. 'I'm going myself.'

He drew his breath in sharply in exasperation. 'I've told you the position and given you a sensible alternative. What the hell are you trying to do? Play Daniel in the lions' den?'

'I think *you're* playing your own hand,' I told him. 'In other words, *I* don't trust *you*.'

He stared at me in outraged indignation, then his face cracked in a grudging grin and we both laughed—a rather thin and brittle laugh, but it served to break the tension.

'Touché', he sighed. 'All right, I'd better tell you how to make contact with Long John.'

Chapter Nine

1

We went on the next day. Once Kwan accepted the fact that I wouldn't relieve him at his post here, he was fully though grudgingly cooperative.

'I have another rat-run into town,' he told me. 'I haven't let Chungking know because they'd want me to overwork it, and this is one that I'd prefer to keep up my sleeve. The two old ladies aren't reliable any more—no reflection on them, they're as sound as a pair of bells themselves, but they're ace high with the Nips because of the chrysanthemums they give the cruds, and some of the locals think they're collaborating, so they've put the hex on them. I still use them for escapers *out*, but try and avoid them for agents *in*.'

'Which way does this one run?'

'Boat all the way—right into the harbour.'

'That sounds a bit hairy. What about spot checks?'

'There aren't any once you're inside the submarine booms.' he explained. 'They can't afford the manpower, so they've plugged every entrance except the deepwater one at Li Mun, where they have a guardship anchored, and the one at Sulphur Channel at the west end of the island, which is left open for the fish and vegetable junks each morning. Officially everything entering or leaving is searched there, but the sergeant, bless him, is a hophead.'

'Opium addict?'

'Much better. He rides the dragon. That means heroin rolled in a scrap of tinfoil, burned over a candleflame and then the fumes are gulped straight down. It has a bigger wallop than mainline injection, and it doesn't leave incriminating puncture marks. Junk has become such a problem in the Nip army that they've made it a capital offence. Anyhow, we've got this drongo so hooked that he waits for this one sampan of mine every third morning, snotty-nosed, runny-eyed and shaking like a gum-tree in a gale. I let him have just enough to keep him keen and eager, and he knows damned well that an anonymous chit to his boss will get him the big chop, so he's our man.'

'You can count on his always being there?'

'Pretty well. It's a permanent posting because he speaks Cantonese, Hakka, pidgin and Portuguese. Of course there's a drill in case he's absent for any reason. If there's a wicker fishing basket hanging on a hook on the left side of the guardroom door, he's on duty and in business. If there's no basket and my boat is carrying something that it shouldn't, it just stands off and tries again later.'

'How on earth have you managed to lay all this on?' I asked.

'Not me—Long John. That bugger knows more ways of corrupting the innocent than I've had hot dinners. Scotch for the General, chocolate for his concubines, French lingerie for the Town Major, who's a poof, junk for the sergeant and cigarettes for the troops. Things are getting pretty tight in there.'

'Where does Long John get it all from?'

'From me. Who else? I get it from Macao—and it's costing the earth, and those miserable sods in Chungking keep querying my expense sheets.'

'I see,' I said thoughtfully. 'Well, you'd better tell me how I get in touch with him when I arrive, hadn't you?'

He said, 'Yes, I suppose so, but he's going to be furious about it. He's told me never to ring anybody else in on this. For the last time, will you let me go in your place?'

I shook my head firmly. 'Absolutely not,' I told him. 'Look, Kwan my brief is to get in to see Angelo, and you have said yourself that Chinese are not allowed into the camps. So there you are. It's as simple as that.'

'All right,' he sighed, and capitulated. 'The fish and vegetable boats go through the boom in single file at dawn. Sergeant Hawaka will be watching for you because our sampan will be carrying a little yellow paper lantern at the masthead, which means that we've got some sweeties for the son-of-a-bitch. The boatboy will slip him the packet, and you'll be nodded through. They'll land you at Shek Tong Tsui. Do you know that part?'

'Near the University? Yes, quite well.'

'You'll hardly recognize it now—it's been bombed flat and it's completely deserted, a real no-go area. You'll have to hurry because it will be getting light by this time. Go up what's left of Belcher Point Road until you reach the burntout pumping station, about half a mile from the waterfront. There's a path on the left, pretty steep and it peters out after a bit. Keep going on your original line, with the Peak radio mast dead ahead and above you. You'll come to a little ledge overgrown with ti-tree scrub at the top. Just sit down and whistle softly. If it's safe, he'll show up. If he hasn't done so in five minutes don't wait—come away and carry on with your business. The sampan will call at the landing-place at the same time every third day, so wait there under cover when you're ready to come out—same procedure in reverse. Don't take Rawcliffe up the path. Long John won't show up if there are two of you. Got all that?'

'More or less,' I said with some uncertainty.

2

We were the last boat in a string of twelve. Peering out from under a net of assorted vegetables that stank to high heaven of the night-soil in which they had been nurtured, I could see a knot of Jap soldiers dimly in the light of a hurricane lantern at the end of the guardroom jetty. Two of them jumped on to our deck as we bumped alongside, and I could hear them trying to mooch cigarettes from the boatboys and threatening to put us through a rigorous going-over if they weren't forthcoming, then, when I was really breaking into a sweat, there was a bellow from the shore, and the troops hopped back on to the jetty with alacrity, and a third man boarded us. I couldn't make out any badges of rank on him in the darkness, but there was no mistaking his authority as he cuffed the others and sent them scuttling off.

'Where is it? Give it to me,' I heard him say urgently in Hakka, then, when something was apparently handed over he added furiously, 'Is this all? You thieving bastards! You're keeping some back.'

'There is another similar packet to be picked up in Kowloon,' the boy answered smoothly. 'That will be handed to the sergeant-san on our way out.'

'Go on—move, you filthy bat-droppings,' the other snarled, 'and be back before high water tonight, or I'll have the leprous hide off you.'

The boys bent to their sweeps and we glided on through the channel into the harbour.

'Gawd!' breathed Raucous. 'I thought we were going to be tickled up with them bayonets for sure.'

It was getting perilously light as we landed on the sea wall at Shek Tong Tsui and crept up the narrow main street. To the left I could see the roofless ruins of the central university buildings and to our right and ahead of us, the lunar spread of what was left of Kennedy Town, but to my relief there was no sign of life whatsoever. We walked in silence until we were clear of the former densely built-up area and had come out on to the lower slopes of the Peak, and the gaunt skeleton of the pumping station was before us. The filter beds that surrounded it were overgrown and weed-choked, but traces of the path that led off along their concrete verge were still visible in the half light.

I said to Raucous, 'You'd better get under cover here. I'll be back as soon as I can.'

'Oh Jesus,' he said. 'Can't I come with you?'

269

'Sorry,' I told him. 'I'm strictly under orders from here on. I have to go alone.'

He looked as wistful as a dog that has to be left behind when he wants to follow, but he didn't argue, so I set off. The slope was gentle at first, through thick undergrowth, but then it got steeper and all vegetation ceased except for patches of scrub scattered at irregular intervals over the mountainside, although there was none at all that I could see in the line I was following until I was a good two-thirds of the way up to the crest; then, over a slight hump that hid it from below, I came to it—a shelf, just as Kwan had described, thickly shrouded in ti-tree undergrowth. It was no more than four feet wide, and then the vertical wall rose again behind it.

I sat down, my heart and lungs pumping and pounding, soaked in sweat and sick with vertigo, and it was some minutes before I was able to get the view into focus, but when I did, it was breathtaking. The whole sweep of the city of Victoria was below and to the right of me, with the mile-wide harbour beyond it, and, across the other side, the sprawl of Kowloon and its backdrop of mountains, with the airfield at Kai Tak far to the east, and Castle Peak balancing it to the west. The Pearl River, down which we had come in the night, was hidden in the morning mist. Somewhere, away to my right was my home at Annandale, but it was masked by a bend in the range. Somehow I felt strangely glad I couldn't see it. I didn't want to—not under these conditions. There was some movement in the city—a little motor traffic, and I could even see lumbering trams, and quite a number of junks were threading through the harbour, but for all that, the pulsing heart of Hong Kong was, if not quite dead, certainly in a state of catalepsy. The soul had gone out of it, and the scars of aerial bombing and artillery fire looked like the sores on a leper's corpse. I could have wept.

A man's voice behind me said, 'Take that hat off and put your hands up. Don't turn and don't try anything or I'll blow your goddam head off.'

'How do you do, Mr Silberstein?' I said, politely. 'I was

270

just about to start whistling "Marching Through Georgia".'

'Don't try soft-softing me, you lousy, limey sunner-vabitch,' he said. 'Who the hell are you, and who sent you?'

'Kwan, actually—' I began, but he cut me short.

'O-o-o-h—Kwen, ectually, old cheppie,' he parodied. 'Did he now? Well, do you know what I think?'

'I don't know what you think, but I assure you that's the truth,' I said, and turned to face him.

'I said not to turn,' he roared, and then I saw him—just an impression of a face behind a screen of leaves, and something snapped inside my brain.

'I don't give a fuck what you said,' I roared back. 'I risk my neck to bring you something from Kwan and this is the reception I get.' I pulled the box containing the diode out of the front of my jacket. 'Here, take it you ill-mannered oaf.'

'Keep your hands up,' he warned.

'Who the hell do you think you are?' I gibed. 'The sheriff of Deadman's Gulch?' I threw the box on the ground. 'It's a diode or something that you said you wanted for your radio,' I went on. 'If you do manage to fix it and get through to Kwan, you might tell him that you've seem me—the name is Mister Jones—and that I am now going about my own business—'

'Which is?' he said, and his tone was considerably milder.

'Just what I said,' I answered. '*My* business. I suggest you mind your own.'

'Okay, okay,' he said placatingly. 'No need to get your knackers in a knot just because a guy wants to know who you are.'

'A guy who called me a lousy, limey something or other,' I said stiffly.

'What the hell did you call *me*?' he said indignantly. 'Aw, forget it.' He rose from behind the scrub, stuffing an automatic into the waistband of his tattered trousers, and hopped forward, and I saw a huge, barrel-chested man, built like the type of water buffalo they used for ploughing in the New

271

Territories. He had practically no neck, his bullet head seeming to rest straight on his shoulders which were themselves a pad of bulging muscle. His face had seen much wear and tear—a great beak of a nose that had been broken, probably more than once, and had finally set with a pronounced list to starboard, beetling brows and under them a pair of small, twinkling and, surprisingly, very blue eyes. He was clean-shaven, not only his face but his head also, but to restore the balance, his bare chest was a matted jungle of black hair. His right trouser leg was pinned up and one could see that the leg itself had been amputated above the knee. But one-legged or not, I would have preferred to tangle with a wild boar. 'Long John' suited him. Only the parrot was missing. Actually, although he had been in the Colony for about five years, I had never seen him as near as this before. He stood rock steady on his one leg, studying me closely for some moments, then suddenly he thrust forward a hand that was in absurd contrast to the thickness of his muscular wrist and forearm, because it was small and well-formed—the hand of a surgeon, musician or perhaps a craftsman in precious metals. There was delicacy there, but, like the rest of him, strength in every line of it. We shook hands, and he grinned, and the whole atmosphere changed in that instant, because the menace had now gone and in its place was warmth and humour.

'Sorry about that, *Mister Jones*,' he said, 'but a guy just can't afford to take chances nowadays. Those little yellow bastards have got Krauts and Russkies working for them and you could have been either. What have you got for us this time? Another ticket back to Uncle Sam's Waikiki hotel?' which told me that he had recognized me, but beyond that quip he made no further reference to my real identity.

'No, just that,' I said, and bent to pick up the box, but he forestalled me and pounced on it without even steadying himself with his free hand. He opened it and gave a yelp of pure joy when he saw the, to me, insignificant metal and Bakelite item inside.

272

'Hellsapoppin!' he crooned. 'Kwan! The clever little sunnerva! He *got* me one! Boy, we're in business!' He peered down the slope. 'The guy who was with you? Who's he?' he asked.

'A soldier,' I said. 'I can answer for him. He's been with me in one capacity or another for three years.'

'Okay, I'll have him sent up,' Silberstein said. 'He pulled a gun on my guys but they got it off him before any damage was done. Can't blame him for that.'

I stared at him in unbelief. 'How do you know that?' I asked. 'I only left him an hour ago, and you've been up here out of sight.'

He laughed deep down in his belly. 'No sweat,' he said. 'Telephone. Here, you better talk to him yourself in case he thinks he's being hornswoggled. Just a minute.' He flipped down on to his behind and pulled an ordinary office telephone out from the bushes and jiggled the receiver hook, and spoke in ungrammatical but fluent Hakka to somebody the other end. 'Fut Sui,' he said. 'It is well. The longnose with you is a friend. Put him on the telephone so that he may speak to his master.' He handed the instrument to me. 'Okay, tell him to come up with my joes, will you. It will take a bit longer than the way you came as it's too light to use the front door now.'

Still dazed, I said, 'Is that you, Raucous?'

'Yeah—it's me all right,' came the answer, 'but what the bloody hell goes on? Where are you, sir?' He was obviously as dazed as I.

'I'm up here. Never mind details now. Everything is quite—' I searched for an expression which would give the message authenticity—'tickety boo. Come up with those chaps and do just as they tell you. All right?'

'I suppose so,' he said doubtfully. 'That's unless I wake up in a minute and find I'm dreaming. Okay, sir.'

I handed the telephone back to Silberstein. 'Thank you,' I said. 'My chap seemed a little surprised—and he isn't on his own in that. A *telephone*—'

273

'You ain't seen nothing yet,' he chuckled. 'Come on, we better be getting inboard. Chow'll be up soon—I guess you can do with it. How is old Kwan making out?' He turned without waiting for an answer, dived, then wriggled through the undergrowth. 'Just follow me. It's a bit of a squeeze, but it gets easier inside.'

I had ceased to wonder at anything by this, and I followed as instinctively and unquestioningly as Alice down the burrow after the White Rabbit. It was merely a shallow cave behind the bushes at first, then it funnelled into a sort of natural drainpipe something less than two feet in diameter, and it ran for some yards, bending at right-angles twice so that all daylight from behind was cut off and we were moving in pitch darkness; then without warning we were out in the open again, or comparative open, for there was an overhanging ceiling of rock above us, but the mouth of the huge cave we had come into looked straight down the sheer-sided valley that ran between Victoria Peak and what I recognized as Mount Austin with its coronet of ruined barracks on its summit.

Silberstein jumped nimbly to his foot and hopped across the floor of the cave to the entrance to a second tunnel, one just as narrow as the first, but head-height, so we were able to move along it without stooping. This in turn opened into yet another and even bigger cave, with a mouth that faced due east along the range towards Li Mun—and Annandale—in the far distance.

'Caves in the *Peak*,' I murmured in wonderment. 'I've lived here all my life, but I had no idea—'

'No, nor anybody else,' Silberstein said, 'except guys like Kwan—and they kept it to themselves. It's part of the same system that runs through his hills up at the Boque. The island was joined on to the Kowloon Peninsula one time, but he figures it got broken off by an earthquake a coupla million years or so back. Gee! The things that fella knows. It's a real education just to talk to him. Oh yes, there's caves in the Peak all right. Some of these passages run right down to sea

274

level—and below. I've been living here nearly three years now, and I still don't know the half of it.'

We had reached a third cave, again one with a natural 'window', and it was furnished comfortably, if incongruously, with modern European easy chairs and couches, coffee tables, bookcases and the inevitable hideous carved teak-wood cocktail cabinet that one found in every taipan's drawing-room in the Colony.

He looked at me and grinned. 'Don't be surprised if you find some of your own property here, Mister Jones', he said. 'My joes have ratted stuff from one end of Hong Kong to the other. Knocking gear off is a religion with 'em.'

'If there *is* any of my property here you're welcome to it,' I said cordially. 'I'd far rather you had it than the Japs. The thing that puzzles me is how on earth you've managed to carry furniture as heavy as this up the slopes without being seen.'

'Nothing to it,' he shrugged. 'Like I told you, these passages run every which-way-and-what. You could carry a load of junk into a house in Catt or Icehouse Streets down there in the city, and unload it up here in one of these caves without it every seeing the light of day in between. Shit! We've emptied half the warehouses and godowns the whole length of De Voeux Road—canned goods, booze, sugar, tea, tobacco, coffee—you name it. I tell you, we live high on the hog here, while the Nips are starving.'

'How many of you?' I said. 'Or shouldn't I ask?'

'Ask away,' he invited. 'Anything I don't want to answer, I won't. I got thirty-two here altogether. Twenty-three guys, nine gals—not all of them broads—some are married number-one-plopper-fashion to some of the guys.'

'And all reliable?' I asked, and I could have kicked myself immediately afterwards.

'Yes, all reliable, Mister Jones,' he said very softly, and the menace had returned. 'If they weren't they'd be dead.'

'Forgive me, Mr Silberstein,' I said. 'That was a silly question.'

'My friends call me Long John,' he said, and put out his hand again with a certain gesture that I recognized. I took it, and he gave a slight nod. 'All reliable,' he repeated. 'You know what I mean now. There are Lodges and Lodges—maybe some aren't quite as respectable and law-abiding as others—but one rule runs through them all. Omertà it's called in some parts of the world, Khamosh in others; different languages, same meaning: you keep your trap shut no matter what the hell they do to you—cops, Gestapo, Kempetei or rival gangs. You just button it, *tight*. Actually three of my joes have been taken. I know what they went through before they died, but they didn't talk. *Shema Yisrael*—some of those bastards are going to pay for that before *I* die.'

A telephone shrilled in the corner. He crossed to it and answered, then listened for a moment before turning to me. 'Your guy has arrived topsides here. What do you call him?'

'Raucous.'

'Rorkus? What's that? Greek or Polack?'

'Cockney crossed on Yorkshire in his case.'

'Enlisted man?'

'Of course.'

'And you're an officer?'

'Well, yes, sort of. Why are you asking?'

'I was just wondering about chow—I mean, you limeys are a bit—well, sort of rank-conscious, aren't you? Does he eat with you or with the hired help?'

'With me,' I said solemnly. 'We've had a special warrant from the King passed through the Houses of Parliament to regularize it.'

'That so?' he said, visibly impressed, then he saw my face. 'You're ribbing me, you sunnervabitch. Okay, so we have him in here. It's perhaps just as well. He kicked my straw-boss in the balls during the ruckus, and there might be a bit of hard feelings at first.'

Raucous came in through the tunnel then, still in a state of semi-shock. He looked relieved when he saw me.

276

'This is Mr Silberstein,' I said.

'Hi, Raucous,' said the other, shaking hands. 'Welcome aboard. Forget the "mister"—the name's Long John.'

'Sorry about the do down there,' Raucous said awkwardly. 'Your blokes jumped me from behind. I didn't know who they were, so I just got stuck in sort of naturally.'

'Think nothing to it,' said Long John handsomely. 'The lugs could do with a bit of a workout. They eat too well up here. And talking about eats—' He rang a little brass handbell.

'I'm still wondering about these telephones of yours,' I said. 'How the devil have you arranged it all?'

'Oh, there's a ton of that sort of stuff lying around in derelict houses,' he answered. 'It was just a matter of collecting it. There's miles of wire strewn along the roads, so I've laid out permanently manned observation posts along the only three ways you can get here from the outside, and connected them up. I've got all the juice I need from a tap-in to the Nips' main power supply-line up to the Peak. We've got electric fires for when it gets chilly at night, lighting, and we even cook by it—'

'Lighting?' I said in amazement. 'But can't they see that from down below in the city?'

'No, I haven't been dumb enough to install it in any cave that could be seen from the outside. I won't even allow smoking in those places.'

'But the caves themselves—the "windows"—can't *they* be seen?'

'No. You'll understand when you've had a look round. The "windows", part by nature and a lot by design, are all located in crevices. We face north here, so they are always in deep shadow and, even more important, they are all on the vertical face of the rock. It would be pretty well unclimbable even for a mountaineering buff with proper tackle. I don't want to sound over-confident, but no Nip is going to try it on the off-chance. You don't generate a hell of a lot of energy on a half-ration of rats, cats and frogs. There are no dogs left

277

here, and only the officers get a bit of fish occasionally. I tell you, they've got it tough and it's made them vicious but lazy.'

'But from down below? You say there are ways in through houses?'

'Sure. They found one once—through the cellars of Fat Choy's.'

'The fireworks manufacturer?'

'Right. We had a tip-off about that one through our listening-posts.'

'What happened?'

'Plenty. Fat Choy had about four tons of raw materials stored there—sulphur, saltpetre, phosphorus and God knows what-all. We souped it up with a few sticks of dynamite that I had stashed away, and I touched it off by remote control from up here when they were well inside. They still don't know what caused it, but they didn't like it. They've gone clean off exploring.'

Breakfast arrived then, and it was a good one—fried ham with pineapple and sweet corn, all from cans, and eggs fresh from the General's chicken-house. 'There's a manhole comes up inside it,' Long John explained. 'The dumb bastards have been trying everything to make those chickens lay more, even had a Shinto priest praying over them. The General likes eggs—when he can get 'em.'

Raucous and I slept for the rest of that day, and when we emerged, bathed and in clean clothes, Long John had got his set working, had made his first rather weak contact with Kwan, and was jubilant.

'A few bugs to sort out yet,' he said, 'but all in all it's going to be dandy.'

'What about DF?' I asked, largely to display my expertise.

'They're going to have one hell of a job to pick this baby up,' he said. 'I've got about twenty different spots I can transmit from—and there's another angle I am going to play—a frequency just a mite above or below theirs, then we transmit at the same time as them. You got to have a pair of real smart operators for that bezazus, though.'

'And have you?' I asked innocently.

'Sure have,' he answered without false modesty. 'Kwan's damn near as good as me. He ought to be—I taught him.'

We had another huge meal in the evening which rather took the fine edge off any enthusiasm I might otherwise have had for the long and exhaustive tour Long John took Raucous and me on afterwards. Besides the entrance through which I had come, and which he designated West One, there were two others, known as North Two and Peak High respectively, all natural faults in the rock face, hidden by clumps of ti-tree, and they were closed from the inside when not in use by meticulously quarried boulders. I believed him when he said, 'Unless some sunnervabitch actually sees you hopping in or out like a jackrabbit, ain't nobody's going to know there's a hole there. With enough food I reckon you could stay inside forever without coming out.'

'Water?' I queried.

'No problem. The whole of the top of the Peak is a catchment area for the reservoirs on the lower levels, so no matter which direction the rain is coming from it's got to find its way down through the rocks, so we've got half a dozen natural springs here. We already got mushrooms growing, and Kwan's been trying to get me some sunlamps so we can raise hydroponic vegetables. Crazy, isn't it?'

'Sewage? That must be a problem for thirty-odd people?'

'Sort of underground stream takes it all away. I don't know where to, but it doesn't worry us none up here.'

His 'joes', as he called his henchmen, lived in a spacious series of caves right inside the lower system, where also were located the kitchens, storerooms and a magnificently equipped workshop which would have been a craftsman's dream, because here he had a full range of electric power tools, a forge and a small kiln. He didn't use a crutch or even a walking stick and it was hard to realize that he was traversing all this on one leg, because he had a series of handholds along the passages that enabled him to move smoothly and quickly without appearing to hop. I noticed that he had changed from his earlier tattered garments into a clean white shirt, flannels and smart blue blazer. 'Evening Divisions,' he explained. 'I always shift into clean gear before inspecting the joes going on night duty, unless, of course, I'm going with them. The rest of the time I dress comfortably, like a bum.'

'Night duty?'

'Sure. The listening-posts down below in Kennedy Town, the one that picked you up, and a coupla others I got scattered around, and three sentry posts up on this level. Then I send out a snatch squad whenever a Jap ship arrives with quartermaster's supplies. We got a rat-run into the back of the big army godown in Murray Barracks. That's the squad I go with when I've got to get a bit of air and space around me or go nuts. That can happen, you know.'

I couldn't believe my ears. 'You mean you risk going into *Murray Barracks?*' I said. 'But that's in the middle of town?'

'That's right,' he answered casually. 'Not dressed like this, of course—black ponjee and a Hakka hat at night. No risk as long as you're not caught out after curfew. That's ten o'clock now.'

'But—but—for God's sake!' I spluttered. 'I understood they were looking for you. That you were—'

'A hot number?' He grinned. 'Sure am—but they're looking for a one-legged longnose, which is what they call Westerners. A Chink shuffling along on *two*, head down, hands up his sleeves, meek and mild, minding his own business, that doesn't attract any attention at all. There's half a million other guys look just like me then.'

'Two legs?' I said awkwardly.

'That's right,' he said. 'Wait here for a while.'

He went out of the workshop, leaving me completely bewildered, to return a few minutes later walking normally on two legs except for a barely perceptible limp. 'Pretty good, eh?' he said with some pride. 'I don't wear it round here because I can get about just as good—better—without it.'

'But I never remember you wearing an artificial leg in the old days,' I said.

280

'I had six of the damned things,' he said, 'made by some of the best prosthetic ginks in the business, but I couldn't get on with any of them. Either the balance was wrong, or they were too heavy, or they hurt. It was like my old momma with her dentures. So I just settled for crutches like you might remember. But I've had plenty of time and a good workshop up here, so I sent the joes down to fossick around what was left of my house for the old ones, then I went to work on 'em—bit out of this one, bit out of that, cannibalizing, trying, discarding—until I got it just right.'

'Congratulations,' I said. 'But I still think you're taking an awful risk—and an unnecessary one.'

'That's the cussedness of it,' he said. 'If it was necessary I'd probably duck it. Anyway, what are you doing yourself?'

'Certainly not taking risks for the hell of it.'

'You mean you were ordered on this mission—just like that? "Mister Jones, you'll get yourself into occupied Hong Kong and you'll do this, and this and this"? Bullshit.'

'Well, not exactly that—'

'You're telling *me* it wasn't exactly that. You volunteered for it—so don't look down your snitch at me, brother.'

'I'm not.'

'Good. Fine. So now you're here, what exactly can I do for you?'

'I want to get into the camps.'

'That's easy enough, provided you're dressed right. A G-string, a pair of sandals made out of old motor tyre and a good thick coating of sweat and dirt. You'll be wanting to come out again, I take it?'

'Naturally. I'm told that it's best arranged through working parties.'

'That's right, but you've got to know which working parties, or you might find yourself being marched down to the Kowloon.docks without warning one day, and straight on to a ship for Japan. They've been sending a lot of slave labour east lately. They select fit men for that, and they're getting mighty scarce.'

281

'Thanks for the warning.'

'A warning in itself won't help you a bit. When it comes, it's straight out of the blue. Right face, forward march and up the goddam gangplank. No, what you want is a squad that is on a fairly permanent detail, like building bridges out in the New Territories, or something like that; or better still, sanitary gang—road sweepers—that sort of thing. You get left alone quite a lot on that, without a Nip guard breathing down your neck the whole time.'

'It sounds just the ticket,' I said.

'Okay, so I'll see what I can find out. I'll have the information for you by this time tomorrow. I take it you know that the two main military prison camps are over the other side, in Kowloon?'

'Shamsuipo and Argyle Street? Yes, I know that. And civilians over here in Stanley? That right?'

'Right.'

'So crossing the harbour is going to be difficult?'

He shook his head. 'Not at all. Sergeant Hawaka will fix that—or go without his candy until he's really steamed up.'

'Good God!' I said. 'Do you mean to say that you've got that sort of hold over him?'

'Got him tighter than a bull's ass in the month of May. He'd have the twitches pretty bad after twenty-four hours without a fix. After forty-eight you could make him spit in the Emperor's eye. Now look, I don't want to horn in on anything, so don't tell me if you don't want to—but it would help if I knew roughly what your objective was in the camps.'

I thought for a few moments, and then plunged. 'It's pretty open-ended,' I told him. 'I've got to contact a certain man who has to set up collecting points in each camp.'

'Collecting what?'

'Intelligence—sitreps.'

'Sit-*whats*?'

'Sorry. It's an abbreviation we use for "situation reports".'

'Huh, I see what you mean,' he said, rubbing his chin

thoughtfully. 'Hell of a place to collect 'em, isn't it—inside the camps? What do they do with them then? The sitreps, I mean?'

'That's what my brief is: to work out some sort of line to get the stuff back to Kwan, who then radios it on to Chungking.'

'Dumbest thing I ever heard of—collect it *outside*, take it *inside*, then bring it out again. Dangerous—and slow.'

'There has to be some sort of channel,' I said defensively, although I was now more than inclined to agree with him. 'The people who will be gathering it in the first place will be soldiers on working parties. Personal observation and coolies' hearsay. A lot of the stuff they will be picking up will be pretty low-grade. On the other hand some of it can easily be vital. There will have to be a filtering system where the grain can be sorted from the chaff. Unfortunately we have nobody of that grade outside the camps.'

'What about Kwan?'

'They won't move him from his present location. He's a very important linchpin where he is now.'

'So how's about me?'

'Well, I didn't know about you,' I said awkwardly. 'I will most certainly put the suggestion to them up there.'

'The suggestion has already been put to them,' he said flatly. 'That sunnervabitch Gathercole has thrown it out.'

'I wouldn't know about that.'

'If you weren't a real nice guy I'd call you a goddam liar.'

'And if you had two legs I'd knock you off them,' I retorted.

He smiled twistedly. 'Don't let that stop you. I'd beat you to the punch every time. No, seriously—it *is* Gathercole, I know. I suppose you can't blame a cop for thinking and acting like a cop, no matter how many stars you hang on him in the army. In his book I'm a hood, and evermore shall be. Okay, maybe he's right. Maybe *you* think the same—'

'I don't,' I cut in quickly.

'You mean you'd trust me?' His eyes were searching my face.

'Completely,' I said.

He looked at me for a long moment, then he nodded slowly. 'That's all I wanted to know,' he said quietly. 'Right—so suppose I put a proposition to you?'

'Go ahead. I can't make any promises in advance, but I'll certainly listen.'

'Go back to Gathercole and get yourself assigned here. I'm no strategist, or even tactician. I'm a *tech*nician—communications—and there's nobody in this whole cockeyed hunk of rice-country who's anywhere near my league. You've seen some of what I've set up already. Go back and talk to him. The best salesman in the world couldn't sell a deal in morse—that's where Kwan fell down on it. Get a carte blanche from Gathercole and inside a month I'll guarantee to have a network of secret telephones set up—I've got six already; say another twelve—in ruined houses, cellars, caves, with reliable, *absolutely reliable*, legmen and couriers collecting, carrying and reporting, round the clock. A lot of it would come direct to us up here, but at the same time you needn't cut the top brass out inside the camps. Do you see what I'm driving at?' The words had come tumbling out. He paused now to take breath.

'Yes, I see,' I told him. 'You're preaching to the converted. Well, shall we say three-quarter-converted?'

'What's the hang-up?'

'The "absolutely reliable legmen and couriers". That frightens me. When an organization gets that big, the risk of leakage increases proportionately. A really bad leak could lead back into the camps—reprisals, punishments, beheadings. We can't risk that.'

'The risk has always been there, and it will remain there whether you run it your way or mine,' he said.

'A smaller risk our way. We'd be dealing only with British and American servicemen and officers. Your people would be—what?'

'Signed, attested, fully paid-up Triad members in good standing,' he answered. 'Criminals, like I was talking about earlier, complete bastards who live by stealing and murdering, as nasty a bunch of no-good guys as you'd meet in fifty years out East. They only have one thing to commend them: *they do not talk*. If I were taken by the Kempitei and they really went to work on me, *I would*. So would you. So would anybody I know, except a Triad member. Don't ask me how they do it, because I don't know. It certainly has nothing to do with loyalty or bravery. There's only one thing could possibly knock them off the gold standard—that's heroin. No junkie denied his fix can ever be relied on. That's why there aren't any in the Brotherhood.'

'How can you or anybody else be certain of that?' I asked him.

'Simple.' He shrugged. 'Immediately one was found to have picked up a habit he would be chopped—just like the Nip army are doing now, only they've left it too late. Triad have always done it.'

'What about the secret addict?'

'Mister Jones, *please*,' he derided. 'You mean to tell me you can't pick a hophead at a hundred yards—even a part-timer? How long have you been out here?'

'All my life. Oh yes—*I* can pick them,' I said. 'But not everybody can.'

'I can,' he said drily, 'and so can the tong masters, and that's all that matters. Don't worry—nobody rides dragons in this mob.'

'Can I ask you a question?'

'Go ahead.'

'Are you a Triad member?'

'If I was I certainly wouldn't admit it, except to a Brother—and a Brother wouldn't need to ask. He'd know already. No, only Chinese can belong fully. I'm mei'tai—'

'The "favoured one"?' I said, translating the Mandarin term.

'That's right, sort of honorary membership. I can call on them for a hundred per cent assistance, but I'd never be admitted to the real inside Lodge.' He looked at his watch.

285

'You've had a hard day,' he said. 'You ought to climb into the sack. I got a few things to fix up. If everything goes all right I should be able to put you ashore on the Kowloon side the day after tomorrow.'

'Good Lord,' I said, startled. 'As quickly as that?'

'Too soon for you?'

'No, the quicker I can get into the camps, the quicker I can get back.'

'Okay then. You're taking Raucous with you?'

'I don't know,' I said doubtfully.

'I would, if I were you. Two POWs attract less attention than one guy on his own, particularly if they're carrying something between them, like a basket slung on a shoulder pole.'

'Hell of a good idea,' I said. 'You think of everything.'

'Most of,' he said modestly. 'So what do you think of my plan?'

'We're going to do it, Long John,' I promised, and put out my hand again. 'If that son-of-a-bitch Gathercole turns it down, we'll go it alone—you, Kwan and I.'

He didn't answer, but I've never seen a man look more quietly happy.

3

Long John surveyed us critically as we came out of the tunnel on to the shelf. 'You both look a bit too fat and healthy for genu-wine POWs,' he mused. 'Still, you're smart guys who have been working in the Dairy Farm vegetable plots, so you've been able to mooch extra food there. Maybe a lick or two more mud and cowshit mixture on Raucous would help.'

'Not bloody likely,' growled Raucous. 'I feel a big enough berk as it is.'

'Okay. So what have you got to remember?'

'Slouch, and drag our feet,' I said. 'And salute all Japs, irrespective of rank.'

'Yes, for Cri-sake don't forget that. It can mean anything from a boot up the ass to a poke with a bayonet or a slash with a Samurai sword if you miss one of the love-children. Hawaka will meet you by the filter beds and brief you fully. Give him this.' Long John handed me a tiny ricepaper packet. 'That will keep him happy for the rest of the day. He gets another when you're back safely. Now where do you go on return?'

'No. 327 Fok Lam Lane.'

'That's right. Fifth house on the left before you reach the burnt-out police post down below. That's permanently manned by my joes. Good luck, boys.' He turned abruptly and dived back into the tunnel, and I felt like following him.

The early morning mist was masking the valley below us as we started the descent, but it lifted as we got to the pumping station, layering wispily and distorting stunted trees and clumps of scrub into grotesque shapes that added to our jumpiness. Raucous was muttering again, putting into words the things I was trying not to think, and I turned on him and snapped, 'Go back if you've got the wind up,' and he lapsed into sullen silence, which was worse than the muttering, and too late I remembered a precept from an otherwise forgotten lecture at the Defence Force HQ. 'While the British soldier grouses there's hope. To stop him is tantamount to screwing down on the safety-valve,' so I tried to make tardy amends.

'Long John knows what he's about,' I said. 'He wouldn't have laid this on if he thought there was any real risk.'

'Maybe not,' he grunted. 'But meeting a bunch of these bastards in cold blood, well—it's a bit sort of goosepimply isn't it?'

'Only *one* bastard in the first instance. By the time we meet them in quantity we'll have got used to them.' I tried to laugh light-heartedly. I wasn't successful.

We saw him then, and I felt my throat muscles contract and my mouth go dry. He was standing by the crumbling wall of the police post, his camouflaged green jungle jacket merging him into the background—tall for a Jap, thin-faced and wearing the Charlie Chan type of moustache that always heightens the sinister expression of an Oriental face. I hadn't seen him properly when he jumped aboard our sampan, so I was not absolutely certain that this was our man, but I reacted perfectly and gave a faultless portrayal of a thoroughly cowed prisoner—and I didn't have to try very hard. I just froze in my tracks, and felt Raucous, a pace behind me, do the same. Then I remembered, and I gave the bobbing little bow that Long John had so carefully shown us, and followed it with a sloppy salute, and again I didn't have to try hard. It was sloppy all right, and I could plainly see the irritation and contempt in his eyes, the typically pupil-contracted eyes of the addict. He cleared his throat comprehensively and spat phlegm and a Hakka dismissal simultaneously, and I though he was telling us to go, but the 'Oom'ya!' was directed to two coolie women, squatting unseen until now behind the wall. They rose, bobbed and bowed as we had done, and scuttled off into the mist, and he gestured to use to come forward—with the sub-machine-gun he was carrying, which gave both of us a nasty start.

He held out his hand and said, 'Give.' I handed him the packet, and, as previously, the smallness of it didn't please him. He scowled and grunted, then surveyed us closely, and didn't appear to like what he saw, for which one could hardly blame him. We wore the irreducibly minimum G-string, rough, homemade rubber sandals and the battered remains of Hakka hats with the brims cut off, and nothing else except a thick layer of dirt. Neither of us had shaved for some days, and Long John had butchered our matted hair with a pair of shears. The sergeant pointed over the wall to a large basket of vegetables which had apparently been left there by the women. It was about three feet across and half that in depth, and it had cord loops through which ran a long thick bamboo pole.

He said gratingly, 'You take. You come follow,' and

turned on his heel and strode off down the valley towards Kennedy Town. We picked up the basket, slung the pole over our shoulders and trotted after him coolie fashion. It wasn't easy, because Raucous, who was in the rear position, kept instinctively in step with me, which two men mustn't do when carrying the better part of a hundredweight on a semi-flexible pole between them, because the load swings rhythmically like a pendulum then and can sweep the front man off his feet. I tried to tell him this over my shoulder, and the sergeant turned his head and snapped, 'No talko, benjo!'

We came down through Kennedy Town to the sea wall where we had landed previously, and there was a walla-walla moored there—one of the outboard-motored sampans that ply as water-taxis on the harbour in normal times—with an undersized Jap soldier sitting hunched in the stern. The sergeant motioned us aboard and took his seat amidships with his back to us, and the soldier jerked the starter cord and we headed out towards Kowloon. The mist had cleared completely now and I could see the whole sweep of the range behind us, dominated by the two-thousand-feet-high Peak from which I guessed Long John would have his powerful binoculars on us, so I risked a covert wave and a thumbs-up sign, with an insouciance I was certainly not feeling.

The desolation that I had observed from up there was even more evident at sea level. The tide was out and I could see the masts, funnels and upper-works of the dozens of ships that had been sunk during the battle and the preliminary bombardment—some by them, but mostly scuttled by us to block the fairways in our mistaken anticipation of the seaborne invasion that never came. Those ships, I thought bitterly, could have saved us from abject surrender. Properly used, they could have taken the troops off, as at Dunkirk, to live and fight another day, instead of delivering them into the hell of Japanese captivity. Oh God, if only this inchoate plan of ours could be successfully carried out, this place held for a mere day or so while a nose to tail succession of Dakotas lifted off what was left of them—

The walla-walla had arrived at the Star Ferry wharf on the Kowloon side. The sergeant jumped out and signed to us to get the basket ashore, then he jabbered to the soldier and watched him back off and head out into the harbour again. He turned to us then and pointed in the direction of Nathan Road. 'Shamsuipo,' he barked. 'You walko. I follow,' and he left us.

'Bloody hell!' wailed Raucous. 'Carrying this lot? That's five miles!'

'A bit under two, actually,' I told him. 'And for Christ's sake break the step this time. You nearly had me off my feet back there.'

'What'll we do if somebody stops us and asks questions?' he asked nervously.

'Act just the same as you are at the moment,' I said. 'Like a dumb soldier. It's only if you show a little intelligence that you're likely to arouse suspicion.'

'Good,' he said, taking up his end of the pole. 'We know where we stand now. One dumb swaddy and one officer-and-gent, knowing between 'em point zero-zero sweet-bugger-all. Situation normal.'

'We're both privates, you damned fool,' I said. 'Officers don't work.'

'You telling me,' he sniffed.

Our nervousness left us almost as soon as we came out of the Ferry building and crossed the square to the Peninsular Hotel, because a squad of POWs was clearing rubble in front of the station, and several other lone men were sweeping the road, all looking exactly like us and all, as far as we could see, completely unguarded and without supervision except for one somnolent Japanese soldier sitting at a table outside the Jasmine Tea Rooms on the corner of Nathan Road. Not one of them took the slightest notice of us, each living skeleton seemingly cocooned in a vacuum of his own misery.

'Gaw, bloody blimey!' I heard Raucous swearing behind me. 'Just look at the poor bastards.'

'Don't,' I told him, 'any more than they are looking at us. We're just part of the scenery now.'

'I wish you'd let me bring a bit of grub and a few cigarettes to slip 'em,' he said angrily.

'A drop in the ocean,' I said. 'It would have been worse than useless, because it would have drawn attention to us.'

He lapsed into a moody silence.

Sergeant Hawaka overtook us after a time, in a rickshaw. I think he had been off somewhere to fix in privacy, because he waved to us airily and said, 'Quicko, quicko—not far now,' and even essayed what for him was no doubt a friendly smile, and thereafter he slowed the rickshaw coolie down to a walk, which kept them just ahead of us.

'Quicko, quicko, my arse,' growled Raucous. 'What's this "o" business on the end of everything the bastard says?'

'It's the same as the "ee" that Chinese put on various English words, when they're speaking pidgin,' I explained. 'It doesn't mean anything to us, but it does to them. Try to avoid speaking to this particular bastard, but if you have to, remember to address him as "sergeant-san". "San" is a term of respect.'

'Short for "sanitary orderly" in my book,' he said. 'I'd volunteer for another hitch out here after the war if I could keep my stripes and have this berk and a few of his pals under me. Tough, are they? Boy! I'd have 'em twitching feebly and calling for their bloody mothers inside the first hour.'

'Good,' I promised. 'Keep your wits about you, Raucous my boy, and that could very well happen.'

And then, without warning, we were at the gate of the camp, because it was a foul excrescence that had grown since we had last seen Hong Kong. It was a large open space that lay behind a frontal screen of derelict houses, surrounded by a high double fence of barbed wire, with bamboo watch-towers at intervals round the perimeter and, inside, rows of thatched wooden huts. Not a tree, shrub or as much as a single blade of grass relieved the starkness of the place, and the only shade was that cast by the buildings.

A sentry came to attention as Hawaka climbed out of the rickshaw and walked to the gate. He called out something in Japanese and another sergeant came out from the guardroom, and there was much mutual bowing, handshaking and flashing of buck teeth as they greeted each other. Evidently our Sergeant Hawaka was very much *persona grata* in Shamsuipo. He turned and beckoned us to come forward with our load. We laid it in front of him and then stepped back, and he bellowed, 'Saluto, benjo!' and we hurriedly repaired the omission. He delved under the vegetables and pulled out a couple of packets of Macao-made Algarve Prima cigarettes, which he presented to the other sergeant, together with a small net of potatoes and onions, and there was a fresh spate of bowing. Then we took up our burden again and followed him in through the gate.

We crossed the compound, passing a squad of prisoners coming the other way carrying some baulks of timber, and the man in charge of them—he was dressed, or undressed, like the rest of us, and bore no badges of rank—gave an 'Eyes right!', a bow and a salute, and Hawaka acknowledged it with a languid flick of his fingers. There was an undamaged house the other side of the wire, with a wicket gate opening into the compound. We went through this and humped the basket up on to the verandah, and then Hawaka waved us away and told us to go back through the gate and sitto until he returnoed. We did so, and watched as a potbellied little Jap officer came out, wearing, as they all did, a huge samurai sword, and the roles were reversed, because now it was Hawaka who was doing the kowtowing, but it was quite evident from the officer's cordiality that the former was still a very popular man in this new milieu. He called for a couple of orderlies and the basket was carried inside, and the others followed, so pally that they were almost arm in arm.

'The wall-eyed, flatfaced son-of-a-whore,' Raucous rumbled as we squatted in the sun. 'What does benjo mean?'

'Literally lavatory,' I told him. 'But they use it very much as we do—well, certain of us, shall we say—when they wish to be particularly rude.'

'Calling us shithouses, is he?' Raucous said. '*He* goes to the top of the list.'

'What list is that?'

'*My* list—one I've carried in my bleeding head for years—certain of our own officers and NCOs I intended looking up when I come out of the army. Wiped clean now, though. No room on it for anybody but Nips. I wonder what else they got in that basket?'

'I can tell you, Long John arranged it—two bottles of Macao rum, fifty cigarettes and a half-pound slab of chocolate, and, of course, the vegetables themselves are worth a great deal. Hawaka is apparently greasing up for promotion to sergeant-major. He also wants leave to visit the regimental brothel tonight, which means he can leave us here and pick us up in the morning. Long John arranged that also so I can make certain contacts.'

'Seems they run their army the same as ours,' said Raucous, the eternal cynic. 'Fancy him being able to fix things like that, sitting up there in the clouds, living like a lord. Fair caution, ain't he?'

'Yes, quite a character,' I said. 'Careful, our chap is coming back. Remember to salute.'

He stood in front of us as we kowtowed, evidently pleased with himself and the world in general, 'high on the dragon's back' as the addicts call it.

'Aw ri',' he said. 'You benjo—you heah this prace this time tomorro'.' He pointed to eight on the face of his beautiful gold wristwatch, then remembering that we weren't so opulently equipped, he pointed to the sun, 'When sun theah, ovah fragpo' rike now. No rate or I smacko hardo—Haw, haw, haw!' The Chinese pronounce r as l when they speak pidgin; the Japanese exactly reverse this. I bowed my understanding and he waved us off in the direction of the huts and strode back to the main gate.

We moved in to the shade of a hut and sat drowsing, shifting round it as the sun got higher and hotter. This part of the camp was very quiet and appeared to be unoccupied except for groups of men obviously too sick to be out with working parties, who we could see through the slatted sides

293

of the huts lying listlessly on roughly made plank beds. There was a second, and smaller, compound the other side of the Commandant's house, with a high double barbed-wire fence separating it from ours. There seemed to be more activity in this one, and I could see men moving about the huts, the nearest of which was daubed with a large red cross. I strolled casually towards the dividing fence about mid-morning, but a warning shout halted me some yards short of it. I turned and saw a prisoner shuffling towards me, and recognized him as the one who had been in charge of the timber carriers.

'What the hell do you think you're doing, you bloody fool?' he demanded angrily. 'Do you want to start a beat-up?'

'I'm sorry,' I said meekly. 'What was I doing wrong?'

'You know the orders as well as I do—' He broke off and peered into my face. 'Oh, you're a new bloke, are you? Where have you come from?' he barked.

'From the other side,' I told him. 'We were on a carrying party.'

'I see.' He nodded. 'Well, you're in Shamsuipo now—the lousiest of the lot. That's the hospital next door and we're not allowed to go up to the wire. If the Nip on sentry-go at the main gate had noticed you he'd have taken a shot at you, then they'd have set about the rest of us. Have you got a ration chop?'

I could see difficulties immediately ahead, so I played for safety. 'I'm afraid not,' I said, and he looked exasperated.

'Christ! How often must I be telling you men that you *must get your tally chopped every time you're moved from one camp to another?*' he said.

'We're only here until tomorrow,' I said apologetically.

'It doesn't matter for how long—rations is rations. God, you don't need telling that, do you? How many of you are there?'

'Only me and my mate,' I told him and he looked slightly mollified.

'That's still two mouths,' he snapped. 'All right, tail on to

Number Three squad at grub time. Tell Corporal Wilmott I said so if he binds about it.'

'I'd better have your name in that case, hadn't I?' I said, and he looked at me in pained amazement.

'Me?' he said. 'I'm Company Sarnt-major Painter, Camp Leader—and while we're on the subject, who are *you*?'

'Private Jones J,' I said, hoping frantically that he wouldn't ask which unit, because for the life of me I couldn't think of a likely one at that moment.

'Oh, Private Jones, J, are we?' he said with heavy sarcasm. 'Well just run through the pockets of the breeches you aren't wearing, Private Jones, and see if you haven't overlooked a couple of "sirs", somewhere, will you?'

'Sorry, sir,' I said humbly.

'That's better,' he conceded grudgingly. 'Just remember that in future, Private Jones. We may be pigs-in-shit as far as these people are concerned, but we're *still in the British Army as far as I'm concerned*—and *you're concerned*. Do you understand *that*, Private Jones?' he finished on a roar.

'Yessir,' I said smartly, standing stiffly to attention. His expression softened the merest mite.

'Yes, a bit difficult, I know, with none of us wearing badges of rank—but do your best to remember what you were, and I was, once—and will be again. And try to muck in on a razor blade occasionally.' He pointed to my chin. 'Some of us do, you know. A bit of a wash now and then wouldn't hurt you either. No excuse for letting go, Jones. You look fit enough—a damn sight fitter than a lot of them that are slogging their guts out on that breakwater. Hang on, lad—*Hang on*. This is not going to last forever.'

'Yessir,' I said again, and inspiration came to me at that moment. 'Permission to speak, sir?' I asked, and he inclined his head graciously, like an emperor conferring a boon on a supplicant. 'I have a message for—' I dropped my voice—'Angelo.'

I would like to think it *was* inspiration, but honesty bids me admit now that it was a sheer instinctive shot in the dark, and it came off. His expression and tone didn't alter in the slightest as he went on with his paternal pep talk, and I thought for a moment that he hadn't heard me.

'Yes, hang on, Jones. Get a grip on yourself and for Chri'sake try and get a decent haircut latrine over to your right midnight. *Understand?*' he barked.

'Yes, I understand, sir,' I said humbly, and added through clenched teeth, 'But I haven't got a watch.'

'So don't let me have to pull you up again they strike the hours on the guardroom gong. Carry on.' He turned and stalked off.

'Bloody old Jingle Painter,' Raucous grinned when I rejoined him. 'What did he grab you for? Dirty buttons?'

'You know him, do you?' I said. 'You'd better keep out of his way in case he starts asking some more awkward questions.'

'I always keep out of sergeant-majors' ways,' he said, and shivered. 'Blimey, I'm hungry. I hope that "benjo" bastard turns up again, or we'll be in here for the duration. We better find ourselves bedspaces in one of these huts, hadn't we?'

'Yes,' I agreed. 'As near to that latrine as possible.'

'Guts playing you up?' he asked, and since this seemed a readymade alibi, I nodded glumly and we moved into the shadow of the end hut and sat through the rest of that seemingly endless, dragging day until the work parties returned at sundown.

There were about twenty squads of them, each of approximately two hundred living skeletons, dressed like us in G-strings with the majority without even the partial protection of sandals—mudcaked and filthy, carrying picks, shovels and Chinese mattocks, and on the barked order of a Jap NCO each file of three men had to bow deeply to the sentry as they came in through the gate. Then they were formed up in front of the huts while a travesty of counting and checking was carried out, a farce which took a full hour with much saluting, kowtowing and bellowing, during which several men quietly collapsed and sank to the ground, only to be kicked back on to their feet by the escort.

The parade was finally dismissed an hour later, after three recounts, each of which apparently resulted in a different tally, and the prisoners wearily dragged themselves into the huts, to reappear with battered mess tins and form into long lines before the three cookhouses, and yet a further hour passed before the last of them had drawn their pitifully small ration.

'Look at that,' Raucous muttered as a man passed us close by, bearing his meal like a crock of gold. 'A fistful of mouldy rice and a dollop of something like boiled seaweed. And it stinks.'

'You had better go and tag on to the line, hadn't you?' I suggested.

What about you?' he asked.

'I can wait,' I told him.

'So can I,' he grunted. He seemed to be having difficulty with his voice. 'A drop in the ocean, I suppose, but even two rations would make a difference. Oh, Nips, you bastards, you'll pay for this.'

4

Guided by my nose I crawled through the darkness towards the latrine as the guardhouse gong struck twelve, leaving Raucous snoring on his bamboo-slatted shelf. A dark figure emerged as I reached it, and I was about to speak, but he was apparently a genuine user of the facility because he passed me without a word. It was just an open pit, unroofed or walled, but with a pile of earth behind it that made a low wall, obviously the original spoil from the pit itself rather than as a concession to privacy. I paused uncertainly as I reached it, and a voice said out of the darkness. 'All right—that will do. Follow me,' and I made out a figure lying prone behind the wall.

He rose to a crouch and moved back past the huts and halted in the middle of the open space, and I became aware of another man behind me. I turned my head, and felt a cord pass like lightning round my neck and my arms were grabbed and held tightly in the small of my back. I started to struggle in blind panic and someone said, 'Hold it! You haven't a chance. Just a question or two. Right answers—nothing to worry about. Wrong ones, and you finish at the bottom of the latrine pit, with a couple of others. I want the date of your wife's birthday. Come on—*quick*!'

'Second of January,' I gasped.

'Where were you at school in nineteen-fifteen?'

'I wasn't—there was a war on—private tutor out here—Mr Martin Kemble, MA—' I think it was Dr Johnson who said that nothing concentrated a man's mind like the prospect of being hanged in the morning. He was right.

'That will do,' said the second man, and I felt the cord slacken—just a little. 'Sorry about this. We were expecting someone, but we can't afford to take chances. They've already tried to ring a ferret in on us. Right, let the gentleman's arms go. Pass your message, please.'

It was a pity in a way, because with the release I went to pieces and started to flounder.

'Not a message . . . not exactly . . . some questions . . .' I gabbled. 'Give me a moment . . . I'm a bit shaken . . .'

'Naturally,' the other said, and I heard him chuckle drily. 'Take your time, although we haven't too much of it. Try taking a few deep breaths to start with.'

I peered at him through the darkness but could make out nothing but a black bulk, and there seemed to be others present now—one beside this man, and possibly a further two behind me—five altogether. No, as he had said, they took no chances.

'First question,' I said, as my jangled nerves slowly settled. 'Communications? How well are you receiving us?'

'Remarkably clearly, all things considered. Decoding completed and the set dismantled and under cover again within thirty minutes of reception,' he answered. 'The thing that breaks my heart is getting it out to you people. Look,

298

you could ask me practically any specific question you liked about this place, over the air, and I'd have the answer coded and in the dead letter-box in Kowloon within twenty-four hours, but I know that there it would stay, ticking away like a time bomb, waiting for a courier to pick it up and relay it on, until the information is useless or, worse, it is blown, and then there's a Kempitei round-up—torturing—beheadings. Can you blame the couriers for shying away?' He was silent for a time and I tried to formulate my next question, but then he went on flatly, tonelessly, 'My chaps are good. They use their eyes and ears—they're collecting the stuff, and I collate it and send it out again—but what the hell's the use? Oh God, what wouldn't I give for one, just *one*, effective transmitter outside the wire—'

'We *have* tried to put some in, you know,' I said defensively.

'I know. I saw one of the operators, or what was left of the poor devil, in the prison hospital here,' he said. 'They put a stoolpigeon in the next bed—an English-speaking German. His accent may have seemed all right to the Nips, but we rumbled him immediately, and the boys dealt with him one night. Oh, I'm not blaming any of you, and I certainly appreciate your getting in here to make contact. That in itself is quite a morale-lifter. No, it's just malign fate—the hopelessness of it all that I'm girding against. But you'd better be putting your questions to me, hadn't you?'

'Yes,' I said briskly, trying to keep the despair out of my voice. 'They have to do with coastwise defences mostly—the shore batteries, minefields, what sort of watch they keep on the beaches—wiring, underwater obstacles—'

'With a view to a seaborne landing, I take it?'

'Yes.'

'But damn it all, they've put that to me twice—and I've given them my evaluation of it each time. I suppose that's in the choked pipeline. We, the prisoners, are not terribly enthusiastic about it.'

'Why not?'

'Because we wouldn't be here to swell the cheering even if it succeeded. The Japs have made that quite clear. In the event of an attack on this place they'd massacre us. Did you notice the machine-guns as you came in here?'

'You mean in the watchtowers? Yes.'

'No, those are just light weapons to deal with a single man trying to make a run for it through the wire, if he was fool enough. It's the heavy stuff I'm talking about, in emplacements on the perimeter each side of the main gate. They are positioned to be able to sweep the whole area—bamboo huts—not an inch of cover. It would be all over in five minutes.'

'So you think it's a non-starter?'

'As a rescue attempt I do. Of course, if there's some bigger objective behind it—' He sighed. 'Well, who are we to reason why? I'd better give you what I can remember of the reports I've already sent in.'

And in that moment a divine madness descended upon me, and I threw caution to the winds.

'No,' I said sharply. 'Forget it. Forget the whole crazy thing. Of course it's a non-starter. Consider this instead. An airborne attack. Parachutists out of the blue without warning, when the working parties are out and the camps are practically empty—just the guards to deal with while the main attack goes in on the key points.'

I heard his quick intake of breath, and even in that pitch darkness I felt the change of atmosphere.

'Now you're bloody talking,' one of the others murmured.

'Go on,' the man before me said very quietly.

'I can't,' I told him. 'This is something that has come up since I've been here in Hong Kong. I've got to get clearance from up there—but I *can*—I *will*. Will you trust me?'

'Of course,' he answered. 'But can't you give us a little more—just in the broadest outline?'

'I can't,' I said regretfully. 'I've broken every canon of security already. I haven't the authority to give you details

300

yet. There aren't any, but this operation *will go through*, I give you my word on that. The prisoners will be evacuated and this whole damned place rendered untenable. You will get a full briefing over the air, and what is more a transmitter that will fox their DFs is being set up at this minute, and there'll be a reliable courier service between you and it. Now please don't ask me any more—not at this stage.'

'I won't,' he agreed, and I felt his hand come forward. I grasped it, and he said, 'We'd better have a code name for it, hadn't we? Something to indicate a transmission direct from you to me, to distinguish it from the mush of other stuff that comes through.'

'Yes. What do you suggest?'

'Vivienne,' he said slowly and reverently. 'A woman who is seldom out of my thoughts these days.'

'Your wife?'

'Not exactly. She ran a small restaurant in the Canebière. I can see her now, all eighteen stone of her, sweating like a June bride over a huge black stove. Christ! Could she cook a coq-au-vin! Yes, let's make it "Vivienne".'

'Vivienne,' I repeated. 'I'll stand you your first dinner there when this is over. I'd better get back to the hut now or my partner will be wondering what has happened to me. Au revoir, old boy.'

'Au revoir,' he answered, and as I crawled away through the darkness I heard him murmur dreamily, '—with truffles and pâté croutons.'

Raucous was still snoring when I got back. I envied him because, although I felt exhausted both physically and mentally, I could not sleep. My mind was in a turmoil and I could no longer think coherently, and had it not been for Raucous's inherent old soldier's craftiness we would both have been press-ganged into working parties when the Jap guards came storming through the huts at first light, bellowing, shrieking and laying about us with lengths of bamboo. He seemed to sense that I was, temporarily at all events, a broken reed, because he took charge and pulled me from one patch of shelter to another until Hawaka arrived and claimed us again.

We trotted behind his rickshaw back to the waterfront and crossed the harbour once more to Shek Tong Tsui. One of Long John's joes emerged from nowhere and handed him another of the now familiar tiny packages, and he dismissed us with a grunt and we followed the other man up through the ruins and into the caves.

I find it difficult even now to recall details of that last twenty-four hours with Long John. We got a rough plan down on to paper, then read it over and condensed it, and condensed it again, with the American putting in a suggestion here, and a rejection there—polishing and pruning, until we had a practicable framework worked out that we felt, given a modicum of luck, could be brought off.

'Don't let 'em take this one over,' he pleaded. 'We got it, boy—we *got* it dead right. Your guy Angelo collects the stuff from his men; I've got a Portuguese Red Cross worker who has a pass into the Shamsuipo hospital. He brings it out and passes to one of my runners, and I'll have it over to Kwan within the hour. The set's working fine—we had a breakthrough last night.'

'No chance of them getting a fix on you?' I asked anxiously.

'Not unless they've got shite-hawks fitted out with DF flying up and down the face of the rock. No, don't you worry your ass about communications. You'll have your sitreps in with your morning coffee every day.' he assured me. 'But try and get back here yourself. With you and me running things this end and Kwan up at the Boque, we've got the world by the tail. This is the run-up to the end, Mister Jones. I tell you, I got a feeling.'

The exit went so smoothly that there were times that I almost had an illogical half-wish that some minor snag would occur. The vegetable sampan picked us up at the sea wall dead to the second and we were waved through the boom by Hawaka himself, and a few hours later we were with a deliriously excited Kwan again. He wanted us to rest for a couple of days, but I was now in such a fever to get to Chungking that I waved his urging aside, and he passed us up through Canton the same night, and on the fifth day we came once more to the valley of the Silk Road.

That was my mistake, and I take full responsibility for what happened thereafter. We should have rested—and taken things more cautiously.

Chapter Ten

1

We must have covered the better part of thirty miles that first day, walking steadily from where the sampan had dropped us, an hour before dawn, at the landing-place in the reeds, until the sun was high overhead at midday and we were sweating like working buffaloes. We rested then through the worst part of the heat and set off again after sunset, and marched for a further four hours.

'How are your feet?' I asked Raucous.

'Fine,' he answered sturdily. 'This pair of rubber sneakers Long John gave me are just the job. How are yours?'

'All right,' I said. 'We mustn't overdo it, though. Nine hours I make it, at three and a half miles: that's over thirty.'

'Knock the half off,' he said. 'There was a lot of uphill bits. I'd make the average just about three. Twenty-five to twenty-seven miles. Let's keep it up a little longer while the going's good.'

'The rag wisps,' I said doubtfully. 'I haven't been able to see them clearly for the last hour.'

'They've been white all along since we started.'

'I know, but they could have been changed. Come on, off the road and under cover. It's time we ate something anyhow.'

But, as invariably happens under these conditions, the stretch of road we were on at that time was highly unsuitable for a halt. There was a steeply rising cliff on the one side, and an equally sheer drop into a valley on the other, and we needed somewhere near water, because we had emptied our canteens by this. So on we plodded, and that first fine careless rapture had dulled, and its place was being taken by fatigue and its attendant unreasoning peevishness, and we started to bicker. It was my fault entirely. I should have taken firm charge much earlier and stopped before the light had finally faded.

It was childish no doubt, but I suppose it was only to be expected from two men who had foolishly pushed themselves far beyond their physical and nervous limits.

We came to a spot where the cliff bent back a little, forming a shallow alcove that had apparently been used by roadmenders, because there was a heap of broken stone at one end and we could hear water dripping somewhere in the darkness. There was absolutely no cover there, but that didn't matter as we only intended resting for a while before going on to find a more suitable place. The trickle of water that came down the cliff face was clear and cold, and it blended magnificently with the bottle of scotch that had been Long John's parting gift. We only had one reasonably strong peg each, but it put new life into us and dispelled our earlier ill-humour. We ate then—sparingly at first because we had another three days before we could be certain of further rations—but I was suddenly aware of wolfish hunger and I gorged on cold rice and noodles and urged Raucous to do the same. I remember saying to him, 'We might as well carry it inside us as on our backs,' and being answered by a thundering belch. But that is *all* I remember of that night.

I was dreaming that somebody was prodding me in the ribs and addressing me by name—complete with the absurd title that I had practically forgotten. Then I awoke, and found that I was not dreaming. I sat bolt upright, and the man standing over me smiled and said, 'Easy—easy now, Sir Vincent.'

He had the burp gun with which he had been prodding me in one hand, and our bottle of scotch in the other. He regarded the latter fondly. 'A sight for sore eyes,' he said. 'You know, I haven't seen a bottle of the real McCoy since

the Occupation. The Nips guzzle any that finds its way in.'
He held it out behind him at arm's length, and somebody
came forward and took it from him, and I saw the others for
the first time, about a dozen of them in a half-circle round
him, staring down at us, and my first reaction was one of
overwhelming relief that they were not Japanese, until I
noticed their shirts. 'Wild silk' they call the stuff, as coarsely
woven as sailcloth, and roughly dyed with raw indigo, and
my spirits plummeted. I looked up at the man again.
Thin-faced and sun-blackened, dark eyes, black military
moustache, but unmistakably European. His English was
fluent and idiomatic, but there was a faint trace of accent
that was familiar. I'd seen him before, and I was searching
my memory when he spoke again.

'Kordakov,' he introduced himself. 'Formerly Hong Kong
Police. You probably wouldn't remember me, but I know
you, Sir Vincent. This *is* a surprise—and a very pleasant one.
Would you mind standing up? Hands on top of your head,
please.' Then, when I was slow to comply, he said sharply,
'*Up*, Sir Vincent,' and emphasized the command with
another poke in the ribs with his gun.

I got to my feet feeling sick, and he barked in Cantonese,
'Search him—thoroughly—and the other one,' and one of
his men came forward and jerked my jacket down over my
elbows and frisked me from head to foot, laying my automatic and spare clips of ammunition on the ground at the
other's feet. I looked sideways as I heard Raucous calling
somebody a wall-eyed bastard in English, and Kordakov
smiled and said, 'Just as well they don't understand him.
He's right, you know? Funny how so many of them down this
end *are* wall-eyed. Further north they tend to squint. Right,
sit down again by all means, if you wish.' Then he said in
Cantonese to the two who had searched me, 'Take the other
man out of earshot while I speak to this one. Move!'

Raucous started to struggle as they grabbed him, and I
called out, 'It's no good, Raucous, you'll only get hurt. Do as
they say.'

They passed me as they took him on to the road and he shot me a look that was a compound of bewilderment and entreaty. Kordakov said with bland approval, 'Now that's very sensible. If we can manage to keep things on that footing, nobody need be hurt.'

'Then please see that your people don't attempt to manhandle him,' I said. 'He is a soldier and he would react instinctively.'

'And quite right too,' Kordakov said. 'But don't worry about *my* people. They'll do as they are told. If you'll just see that your chap does the same I'd be obliged. Now, to revert to ourselves. Might I ask where you've come from, and where you are going.?'

'There's nothing to stop your asking, Mr Kordakov,' I said. 'I would want to know a little more about your authority before answering, though.'

The smile was back. He was a very ready smiler. He tapped his burp gun lightly. 'That's rather academic, isn't it, Sir Vincent?' he said in mild reproof. 'I mean to say—well, wouldn't you call this authority enough?'

'I'd call it *force majeure*.'

'The same in my book.' The tone was a shade sharper. 'We're wasting time, Sir Vincent. Where have you come from?'

'Macao,' I told him, and he nodded slowly.

'Macao? That's interesting. How long have you been there?'

'Ever since I escaped from Hong Kong, a long time ago.' This was our cover story in the event of capture by the enemy. These people were officially allies, but I certainly didn't trust this particular individual.

'I see. And you're making for?'

'Kweilin. Generalissimo Chiang Kai-shek is expecting me.'

It appeared to impress him. He nodded ponderously. 'I see,' he said again. 'And where exactly were you to meet him?'

307

'I haven't the faintest idea. I was merely told to make my way to Kweilin to start with.'

'You received these instructions in Macao?'

'That is right.'

'Um, now I wonder why I wasn't told? I happen to be the area commander for this part of the district, and normally I'd be responsible for your safe conduct through it.'

'It's all very confidential.'

'Oh, I'm sure of that—*certain* of it—so certain, in fact, that I don't believe a bloody word of it.' And now the smile had gone. 'Come on, Sir Vincent, you'll have to do better than that. We have an up-to-date list of all escapers and evaders who are, or ever have been, in Macao, and I can assure you that you're not on it. Big man like you, *Ho Cli!*—they couldn't keep *you* under wraps for all that time.' A thought appeared to strike him. 'Ha! I wonder if that little term isn't the key to the whole puzzle? "Under wraps"? Could be—but then, of course, we'd want to know *whose* wraps, wouldn't we? So who are you going to whisper it to, Sir Vincent? To me, sensibly, and then be helped on your way to Kweilin, or to someone else under, shall we say, rather more urgent suasion—and not be helped anywhere thereafter except into the life to come?'

'Are you threatening me?' I asked. I tried to inject cold menace into the question, but it didn't scare him in the slightest.

He shook his head and sighed. 'No. I was merely trying to talk a little sense into you, in the short time at my disposal,' he said. He pulled back his sleeve and looked at his watch. '*Very* short time, I'm afraid. I must be off, Sir Vincent, but I'll be back later. Just think things over until I return.' He rose and signed to one of his men to cover me with his burp gun, and strode off and I saw him giving instructions to another one, a big pockmarked Northerner. This character came over to me and grabbed me by the shoulder and spun me round. I resisted instinctively and got a hard smack across the mouth, and then another man joined him and together they upended me and dumped me face downward on the ground and tied my hands behind me.

They hauled me to my feet then, and I saw Raucous, similarly trussed, being hustled towards me. He started to roar when he saw me, and the Northerner struck him full in the face. I said, 'Don't be a chump, Raucous—shut up or they'll just make a punchbag out of you,' and I received a further smack myself for my pains.

The Northerner grinned amiably and said in pidgin, 'You talkee I beatee, same like, chop-chop.' They roped us together and prodded us along the road for some distance, then we turned off up a path running through thick under-growth to a terraced rice paddy above. We crossed this and continued to climb up the steep slope for what must have been nearly an hour, one man in front and the Northerner behind us poking us with the muzzle of his gun whenever we slipped, which was frequently because the path was very narrow and we were yoked side by side and were therefore stumbling over the rough ground either side of it. Each time this happened Raucous hurled curses at him and got us both a thumping, until I was as furious with him as I was with our captors.

We came at last to a ruined farmhouse in an overgrown compound, just four partially collapsed mud walls and the remains of a sagging thatched roof above. They shoved us into this and kicked our legs from under us and went out again, jabbering in Hakka. One was saying that Longnose wouldn't be back until after dark and that he personally intended to sleep all day as, undoubtedly, they would once more be marching all night, and he was advising his partner to do the same. The partner, a more cautious type, was dubious. If they were both asleep when Longnose returned there would be trouble. They had better have a nap in turns. They were making no attempt to lower their voices and I realized that they, in common with the bulk of the popula-tion of China, were assuming that we, as Europeans, neither spoke nor understood a word of any of their dialects other than pidgin.

This was interesting. 'Longnose' was undoubtedly Kordakov—and he would be back at sundown. I passed this on to Raucous in an undertone, and went on listening, but I heard nothing further of any import, the main subject of their further conversation being the relative merits of Kweilin brothels as distinct from those of Canton.

'Who the hell *are* these sods?' Raucous asked.

'The Blueshirts. You've heard of them, haven't you?'

'Part of the Chink army, aren't they?'

'Only when it suits them. They are really a self-contained unit raised and commanded by Tai Li, Chiang Kai-shek's second-in-command. Tai Li himself is known to be anti-British and American most of the time, and pro-Jap for some of it. The only thing he is at *all* times is pro-Tai Li. Not a very nice man.'

'I suppose you recognized the bloke down there—the copper?'

'Kordakov? Oh yes, I recognized him all right.'

'Where does *he* fit in, I wonder?'

'Obviously working for Tai Li at the moment.'

'What are they going to do with us?'

'Kordakov will want us to talk, naturally. I told him we had evaded capture in Hong Kong for some time after the surrender and had managed to get across to Macao, where we'd been holed up ever since. Now we were making our way to Kweilin to meet Chiang Kai-shek.'

'Did he swallow it?'

'Not a word. He's certain I'm working for Intelligence and he's hinted at a deal if I'll tell him everything, or an unpleasant time if I don't.'

'What are you going to do?'

'Hang on as long as I can, naturally—but I'm no hero. As far as you're concerned you're a soldier under orders. You've been with me all the time but you know nothing. We must both stick to that, do you understand?'

310

'That's easy enough,' Raucous said wryly. 'It happens to be the truth.'

'Yes, more or less,' I agreed. 'The point I'm trying to make is that if they really do put us through it we must tell the same story—and under no circumstances must we let anythin ˅ slip about Kwan, Long John, Hawaka or the two old ladies. Just try to empty your mind about those people. *They never existed.* Now have you got that, Raucous?'

'Yes, yes, yes,' he said impatiently. 'Like you just said, I know nothing. Look at them bastards. Do you see what they've got?'

I turned my head. The two Blueshirts were sitting very much at their ease in the shade a few yards away, having shed their heavy jackets, boots and equipment, and they were giggling like naughty schoolboys over a stolen pot of jam, and taking alternate swigs at a bottle.

'The flat-faced, yellow-hided, wall-eyed something-something-somethings—' he rumbled. '*Our* bloody scotch! Swiped it off the copper, the thieving bastards.'

I felt a glimmer of hope. 'We may have a chance if they finish the lot,' I said. 'Chinese can drink their own booze without effect, but one or two shots of European liquor can sometimes put them flat on their backs. Come on—stop talking and let's see what we can do about these ropes.'

They were made of deresen grass, like the last lot, but this time they had omitted to pour water over the binding, as the Japs had done, which meant that there was still a limited amount of give in it. Even so, it took us practically the whole of the afternoon to make any impression on it. I succeeded first and managed to get one hand loose, but by this time my fingernails were torn and bleeding and the fingers themselves badly swollen, and since we hadn't a knife it took a further hour to get Raucous's bonds off him.

The two Blueshirts had slept through it all. In any other context it would have been amusing to listen to them. They had started by each taking a modest mouthful, conscious of the fact that Longnose would undoubtedly demand a reckoning on return. The first mouthful naturally led to a second, then the Northerner had the bright idea of topping the level up with water—which justified a further and much longer pull at the bottle. Then they became pot-valiant and reckless, and finished the lot. Now they were snoring their heads off, out to the wide.

'Get their guns first, then give them each a bloody good bonk on the bean to hold 'em for a few hours longer,' Raucous said authoritatively. 'Better leave it to me. You might be a bit gentlemanly about it,' and for some reason it annoyed me.

'You stay right where you are, Sergeant,' I told him acidly and moved cautiously towards them.

They were lying side by side and I could see their guns and equipment on the ground between them, and I was still a few yards short of them when the further man stirred and sat up. I froze. He moaned and felt his head, then fumbled for his waterbottle and raised it to his mouth, and in doing so saw me for the first time. There was no reaction for a moment or so. He just gawped at me muzzily, then it registered and he shouted and dived for his gun, but I reached it first and pinned him down with a foot on his neck. The second man woke and grabbed my ankles and almost had me over. I jabbed at his face with the butt of the gun, then managed to reverse it and slip the safety-catch, and I divided a long burst between them.

Raucous came up and surveyed the two still twitching bodies with an expert eye. 'Not bad,' he pronounced. 'But you should've clobbered 'em with a rock first. They nearly had you, between 'em, then.'

'Aw—shut up!' I spat at him, then, as a searing pain shot up my leg I sat flat down on my backside.

'Look what you done,' Raucous said, pointing to my left foot. 'Shot your bloody toe off. A real recruit's trick that is.'

I hadn't, quite. One round had grazed my ankle and then gone through the fleshy part of the side of the foot, and it was bleeding freely and hurting like hell.

'Take that grin off your face, and get me some water, you bloody oaf,' I swore at him, and he reached for one of their waterbottles. He did try to do something about the grin, but he wasn't altogether successful, and I could gladly have turned the gun on him also.

The wound wasn't serious, and we stopped the bleeding and bandaged it with our two soaked handkerchiefs. Raucous made helpful suggestions for the treatment of open wounds in tropical climates in the absence of proper dressings. They all came down heavily in favour of cauterisation. 'You just make the blade of a knife red hot, then stick it on the spot. Kills the germs,' he said, sucking his teeth.

'—off, or I'll kill *you*,' I snarled. I dislike coarse and intemperate language normally, but I was sorely tried that day.

'Yessir,' he answered smartly. 'Pity they drunk all the whisky. That does the trick sometimes. You pour it over the wound. Seems a bit of a waste though, doesn't it?'

We dragged the bodies into the scrub, but by this time I was too deeply preoccupied with our immediate problems to listen to him. Sundown, they had said. That was little more than an hour off, I judged. There didn't seem to be any way out of this eyrie other than the path up which we had come. They would probably arrive back and Kordakov would send somebody up to bring us down, in which case we could quite easily run into them. It was a risk, but one we would have to take. We kept their guns—they were British Stens, no doubt brought over the Hump at the cost of American lives—and I detached the spare magazines and the waterbottles from the two sets of equipment before tossing the rest of it into the bushes, then we started the descent.

Darkness was finally closing in when we reached the bottom. The descent had taken us half an hour, slipping and sliding over boulders and loose scree, and we were hot, tired and thirsty.

I said as we filled our waterbottles, 'We ought to push on for at least ten miles before getting under cover,' and Raucous groaned.

313

How about a stand-easy for half an hour first?' he begged, but I was adamant.

'We can't risk it,' I said. 'They might come sneaking up in the dark at any minute. Come on, up on your feet.'

He checked me with an upraised hand. 'Hang on a sec,' he said. 'Listen.'

I thought for a moment that it was a trick of the night breeze in the treetops, or the distant croaking of frogs in the deep valley below us, but then, as I strained my ears it came to me unmistakably. It was the sound of an approaching motor vehicle.

Now who the hell can this be?' I mused.

'Nobody that loves us, that's for sure,' Raucous said. 'Good job we heard them now or we would have got caught flatfooted on the road like last time. What'll we do?'

'Get out of sight and let them get past,' I said. I darted across the road and looked over the edge, but it was a sheer drop and I couldn't tell in the dark how far down the bottom was. I came back. 'Up the path again,' I told him.

It started as a narrow defile between two huge boulders, and when we came to the top of it we had, as I remembered, a choice of coming out on to an open rice paddy, or turning left on to the top of the nearer boulder. I chose the latter because it gave us a view over the road immediately below, and we lay on our bellies on the still sun-warmed rock.

The noise was getting louder and one could tell that the vehicle was moving slowly in low gear, then far down the road we saw the twin pinpoints of its masked headlights. and someone appeared to be walking in front of it flashing a torch on to the side of the road as if searching for something.

'My God!' Raucous said suddenly. 'It's us they're looking for. Nips. They must have seen us sliding down.'

'How on earth could they?' I scoffed, but I admit, more to reassure myself than him. 'It was pitch dark.'

'Not the first part. And if they was watching through glasses and just caught a bit of movement—' He was putting my own doubts into words, and it wasn't comforting, but it was too late to do anything about it now.

314

'Keep still and shut up,' I told him tersely. 'They'll pass in a moment, whoever they are.'

But they didn't. The torchbearer arrived immediately beneath our position and halted, flashing his light back towards the vehicle, and he yelled in Hakka, 'This is the place! There is the path and here is the spring.'

The vehicle pulled in to the side of the road, and I made out the bulk of a large army truck, so close that we could almost have stepped down on to its canvas tilt, and dark figures piled out over the tailboard, chattering, crowding round the spring, urinating, lighting cigarettes and behaving, in short, like all troops at a vehicle halt.

Somebody called out sharply, 'Quiet! All of you! Chang, go up and bring the prisoners and escort down—quickly!' It was Kordakov's voice.

'The copper again,' Raucous muttered. 'Where'd he get the truck, the lucky bastard?'

Somebody else called out then. I recognized the language as Japanese, but I couldn't understand the words. They got a small fire going a little further along the road, and in its light we saw that Kordakov's party had now been augmented by a number of Japanese in camouflaged jungle kit. There seemed to be about a dozen of them, and I could see by the absurd samurai sword they always wore that one at least was an officer. He and the Russian sat on the running-board of the truck and lit cigarettes.

The Jap said in bad but fluent Hakka, 'When will the prisoner be here?'

'A little more than one hour,' Kordakov answered. 'It is a long way up.'

'I wish to start back as soon as they arrive,' the Jap said. 'The General-san will be in Canton at daylight and he does not like to be kept waiting.'

'I ask the Lieutenant-san for the last time—let me take the taipan to Kweilin first,' Kordakov said, and there was a note of desperation in his voice. 'You can come with me, and bring him back with you once Tai Li has seen him.'

'That will take too long. As soon as your message was

315

received I had my orders from my Commander himself. "Go with Kordakov-san and bring back this man Star-for immediately." I cannot disobey that.'

'The reward?'

'Will be paid as promised.'

'But to whom?'

'Your General-san, Tai Li, naturally.'

'Exactly—and then where am *I*? I who recognized him and captured him? There are many sticky fingers in Kweilin. What will come to me? *Nothing*.'

'That is a matter for discussion between you and your General-san.'

'That would be pissing against the typhoon. He would discuss nothing with me. He would pocket the reward—all of it.'

'If he is that sort of man what difference would taking Star-for to see him make? He would still pocket the money.'

'It is a matter of face. If we both go before Tai Li with Star-for, and you say, "Kordakov has captured this man and we are very pleased and would like him to have the reward" I would gain much face and he would have to pay me at least some of it, or *he* would lose face.'

'I am sorry. I have my orders.'

'Then could you not pay me part of the reward *now*?'

The Jap laughed shortly. '*I*? I am a soldier. I do not carry large sums of money—and even if I did, I certainly would not pay you anything at all until I knew for certain that this prisoner *is* Star-for.'

'I tell you there is no doubt about it. I know him.'

'But *I* don't. He could be any longnose. You all look alike to me.'

'Do you doubt my word?'

'No, but I don't take chances either.'

'What if I refuse to let you take him?'

'I would think you very unwise. I have soldiers here—*Japanese* soldiers.'

'I have soldiers too.'

'Bandits,' said the Jap contemptuously. 'But we should not quarrel. Let us go and have some tea before those pigs drink it all Everything will come right, then we shall *all* gain face, much face.'

They walked towards the fire where the troops had a camp kettle slung above the flames.

Raucous said, 'How much of that did you get?'

'All of it,' I said. 'I know what a prize bull in the sale ring feels like now. Come on, we'd better be off before they find we've flown the coop.'

'Which way?'

'We'll move along up here, parallel to the road for a few hundred yards, then come down on to it and go like hell.'

It was nerve-racking because the hillside was bare rock, and we had to pass the place where they had their fire, and for some yards we were horribly exposed, but fortunately they were all too intent on guzzling tea to be looking in our direction. We sidled crablike along a ledge for some distance, then we ran up against a dense thorn-thicket and although we were still within the light cast by the fire there was nothing for it but to slide down on to the road.

The slope ended in a sharp drop. I went first, and landed at the feet of a Jap soldier.

He had an armful of firewood and he chattered angrily as my sudden arrival caused him to drop it. He stooped to retrieve it, then some instinct caused him to pause. It was rather like the double-take that one sometimes sees in movies. He straightened slowly and looked into my face closely as I gabbled an apology and bent to help him pick up the wood, trying to shield my face with my straw hat, but it was too late—he had obviously seen that I was a European and I saw his mouth open as he took in breath ready to shout. I jumped towards him jabbing at his face with the butt of my Sten, but he jumped backwards. Then Raucous arrived. He landed between us and clasped his hands round the back of the Jap's head and jerked it forward, butting him in the face with his own head. There was a horrible crunching thud,

317

followed by a muted gurgling sound as Raucous switched his grip to the other's throat. The Jap kicked and struggled for a few moments, then went still.

'Grab his legs,' Raucous hissed. 'Across the road—quick.'

We swung him over the edge like a sack, then I started to run, but Raucous hesitated and it was some seconds before he overtook me. 'Must be a hell of a way down,' he panted. 'I listened but I never heard him land. Not his day—a Liverpool kiss, a twisted neck and a bloody long drop. That's another one for the blokes in the camps.'

We slowed to a brisk walk after a mile or so. 'What do you reckon they'll do when they find we've gone?' Raucous asked.

'Come looking for us,' I said. 'I shouldn't imagine they would start out before first light, though.'

'Why not?'

'Well, put yourself in their place. Would you mount a search in the dark?'

'No. See what you mean.'

'We've still got the better part of an hour before they find out, and four or five before dawn. We'll keep going until we can see where we are, then we'll get under cover and watch the road until they pass us.'

'Where are we making for now?'

'The inn. We can get a signal off from there.'

'How far is that?'

'You've been over the ground before—twice,' I said irritably. 'I reckon it to be about a hundred miles from where we are at this moment.'

'And no grub,' he said dolorously. The prospect depressed him. 'We haven't eaten since the day before yesterday.'

'Don't talk so much,' I told him. 'And keep your ears open in case they do decide to come on in the truck before daylight.' And thereafter he maintained a moody silence—which was at least something.

We pushed on until the first streaks of dawn appeared, and then we took to the bush. The country here was more

318

promising as the road ran through a gorge with thickly wooded sides, so we refilled our waterbottles at a stream and started to climb, and we finally settled in a cleft between boulders under a thick tangle of she-oak as the sun appeared over the hills to the east. It was a good choice because from here we could see far up and down the road, which lay well below us.

I said, 'Get some sleep, Raucous. I'll take first watch,' hoping to mollify him a little, but he was still on his dignity. He muttered something about being ready to eat a dosshouse mattress without salt, and in a matter of minutes he was snoring.

2

By mid-morning I had half persuaded myself that they had given up the search and I was once more debating the relative merits of marching on by day or by night, and glooming over my foot, which was giving me hell. The wound itself was slight, but quite obviously it was turning septic, and the flesh below the ankle was blue and swollen and I had difficulty in getting my boot back on. Raucous shook his head portentously and reverted to the subject of cauterization, and I snarled at him, and once again a miffish silence reigned.

Then we saw them. A solitary figure appeared far in the distance, walking in the middle of the road. 'A Nip,' pronounced Raucous. 'I bet he's doing point.'

'Doing what?'

'Point. He'll be the leading bloke in arrowhead formation. There you are—what did I tell you? There's his two flankers. See? One each side of him a few yards back, on the edge of the road. There'll be two more behind them again, further out, pushing through the scrub, and then some more. Yes, see them bushes shaking on the left? It's a hell of a job for the ones right out on the wings. I've had some. Oh, it's a search-and-sweep, all right. If he's doing it proper he'll have a couple of picquets out each side on the high ground as well.'

'As high as this?' I asked quickly.

'All depends how many men he's got.' There was nothing he liked better than to play the military expert. 'There was about twelve of 'em, wasn't there? One in the middle—that leaves ten or eleven—five each side. Say fifty yards interval. No, I don't think they'll come this high. We should be safe enough here.'

'There were twelve Blueshirts also,' I reminded him.

'Hairy-arsed civilians,' he snorted. 'You got to have *soldiers* for a job like this—trained men.' He sounded like the Jap officer.

The truck came into view then, moving at walking pace some hundred yards behind 'point'. Raucous was delighted. 'Just exactly like I said,' he crowed. 'The officer will be in that. Directing operations, they call it—with a few bottles of cold beer and a posh picnic basket, if their army is anything like ours.'

They were nearer now, close enough to catch glimpses of men pushing through the matted undergrowth, and to distinguish between camouflaged combat jackets and blue shirts. 'Hairy-arsed or not,' I said, 'he seems to be using the civilians. There are only two men besides the driver in the truck. On your reckoning that could mean ten or twelve each side, couldn't it?'

Some of the cocksureness went. 'Um, yes, maybe,' he said uneasily. 'Perhaps we'd better be getting further back.'

But it was already too late, because we heard crashing immediately below our position, and a Blueshirt emerged from a thick belt of undergrowth and moved obliquely upwards across a clearing directly towards us. We cowered down into the cleft and I felt Raucous fumbling for his Sten.

'Don't fire,' I whispered urgently.

'I wasn't going to,' he mumbled. 'I'm getting ready to

crown him—' Then there was a sound from behind and, turning my head, I saw a Jap above us, actually standing on the boulder under which we were crouching, but Raucous, his whole attention riveted on the first man was unaware of this newcomer and I thought he was about to speak again, so I hissed, '*Freeze!*' in his ear, and thank God he did.

The Blueshirt halted then, no more than five yards short of us, and took out a cigarette and matches and lit up, and the Jap chattered unintelligibly, then broke into pidgin.

'Sig'ret, cumshaw, give,' he begged, and the Blueshirt spat and said, 'You go shit.'

The Jap let out a squeal of rage and jumped down from the boulder, landing in front of us so close that we could have grabbed him by the ankles. The Blueshirt was trying frantically to unsling his Sten, but the Jap got in first with a kick to the groin. He snatched up the dropped cigarette and made off downhill, with the shrieking Hakka hobbling after him—and we breathed again.

The truck had passed beneath us by now and was out of sight round a bend in the road. Raucous expelled air in a long-drawn sigh. 'Saved by a kick in the cods,' he said. 'At least we know where they are now. All we got to do is keep behind them until we get to the head of the valley.'

'At the speed they're moving now that's going to take two or three days at least,' I said. 'And we've got to find food somewhere—'

'They can't keep up a sweep-search at night,' he said. 'They'll camp, and they'll have a fire going, like they did back there. We can go round them and then belt along hell-for-leather in open country.'

'We can't risk moving on the road,' I said.

'Why not? They've swept this part. They're not likely to come back along it.'

'Maybe not. But what's to stop them leaving an ambush somewhere? A couple of men a mile or so short of where they camp, just in case we're still behind them? I know that's what I'd do if I were in their place.'

His face dropped. 'Yes—see what you mean,' he said. 'What's the answer then?'

'Keep moving behind them, as you said, but up here on the ridge parallel to the road. We can see what they're doing then.'

'It'll be slow going.'

'No slower than they're moving now, and when we're certain they've halted for the night we can get back on to the road a couple of miles ahead of them and make up for lost time.'

He thought that was brilliant. So did I, until I got up and put some weight on my foot. The pain ran from the tips of my toes upward to the knee, burning, searing, as if I had dipped the leg in a bucket of corrosive acid. I clung to a sapling and groaned, and Raucous looked at me in dismay and said, 'Oh Christ! What do we do now?'

'Walk,' I said through clenched teeth. There was no heroism involved in the declaration, it was purely because I had no option. I shook off Raucous's proffered assistance and reached for a handhold on another sapling, then another, and another, hopping like Long John and, surprisingly, making quite reasonable progress. It was only when I attempted to walk normally that the pain became completely unbearable.

We overtook the searchers late in the afternoon, still in their arrowhead formation with the wing man on our side roughly in line with us, a bare two hundred yards ahead. They were frightening in their sheer, antlike pertinacity, because looking for us in this jungle was akin to trying to find a couple of needles in a haystack, and none but Japs—or perhaps Germans—would have kept it up as long as this. We could see the truck as the merest speck far below us, and as the sun finally dipped behind the western crestline it pulled into the side of the road and its headlights flashed three times and the searchers closed in, crashing down the hillside through the scrub.

'Lucky bastards going down for their evening scoff,' said

Raucous enviously. He shook his canteen by his ear. 'And we haven't even got a dribble of water left between us.'

'We had better not stop,' I said, knowing that if I sat down now I wouldn't be able to get up again. 'Let's push on for another mile at least, and then go down and look for water.'

But we struck a small atoll in our sea of misfortune before we had gone far, in the form of a tiny spring that trickled out from under an outcropping of rocks, and we lay on our bellies and drank to bursting point, then we filled our canteens and started out again, but the pain, which had become a dull nagging ache while we had been moving, now flared up afresh to a level where I became completely disorientated and kept missing my handholds on the saplings and falling flat on my face.

Raucous said, 'I'll have to give you a piggyback,' and tried to lift me.

'Don't be a fool,' I said ungraciously. 'It's no good, Raucous. I can't go any further—not tonight anyhow,' and keeled over.

3

It was milk, to which I have held a total aversion since earliest childhood, and I was slobbering it over my chin, and Raucous was cursing me.

'Take it easy,' he was saying. 'This cost us fifty Hong Kong dollars. Get it down you and try and hold it.'

I was lying in long grass, looking up through a canopy of leaves, and the sun was high above. Raucous was supporting my head and holding a pannikin to my mouth.

'Where did you get it?' I croaked.

'A Chink farm. I got rice and eggs and some fruit too, but you better get some more of this milk in you first,' he answered.

I made a better fist of it then and managed to swallow

several mouthfuls. He sat back on his heels, looking pleased with himself.

'What happened?' I asked.

'Nothing much,' he said. 'We just walked, and walked—and walked—all night, because I knew that if we stopped and you sat down you'd never get up on your feet again. You was chunnering away in English and Chink most of the time, making a hell of a racket. When morning came I saw where we were—on this hillside looking down into the clearing where we had that first do with the Nips. Remember?'

'Yes, of course. We must have been moving faster than I thought.'

'The convoy arrived down below then—sweep-and-search right to the end. They seemed to give up then, though. They had a pow-pow and the Nips went back the way they came, and the Blueshirts kept on going. Then I saw the smoke.'

'What smoke?'

'From the farm. You couldn't see it from the road, but you can just spot the roof from here. I thought it over for a bit, then decided to risk it. I took a hundred bucks out of your shoe and went over, leaving you sparked out. There's an old josser and a couple of women and some kids there. Scared rigid they were when I went in. I could have taken anything I wanted, but I reckoned it would be best to pay for it. I mean, with that sort of money in their sky-rockets they'd be more likely to keep their traps shut if anybody came along asking questions. Don't you think so?'

'You're absolutely right,' I agreed. It sounded horribly condescending, the more so when I added, 'Well done, Raucous,' but what else was there to say?

'I couldn't get anything for your foot, though,' he said sorrowfully.

'Oh, it will be all right,' I said cheerfully.

'Take a look at it,' he said. 'I had to take your shoe off to get at the money, and if you can get it back on again you're a better man than I, Gunga Pooch.'

324

I looked down at it. It was swollen to twice its normal size and had turned an angry puce, and, ominously, the colour was creeping up the leg.

'Not too clever, is it?' he said.

'Not too clever,' I affirmed glumly.

'So?'

'So you'll have to go on alone.'

'Good, that's what I was thinking. Let's see if we can settle this without chewing the fat and arguing. How long will it take me to get to the inn?'

'Three days, really pressing it,' I told him.

'*Two*. I'll show you what the infantry can do when they're really trying,' he said. 'Two there and the same back, with some coolies and one of those carry-me-charlie-chair things they cart their old women round in. Can you stick it out here for four days.?'

'I'll have to, won't I? Yes, you get on, Raucous. Don't worry about me.'

'Good. I'll move you down the hill to our old battle-ground. There's more shelter there and it's nearer to water—' His voice was fading, and my next relatively clear recollection is of his gently shaking me. 'Milk in this jar and boiled rice and stuff in the other one—right here alongside you—and a full waterbottle—and the spring is close by. Look, for Christ's sake try and understand me,' he was saying desperately, and I surfaced again momentarily.

'I'll be all *right*,' I told him peevishly. 'Push off. You're wasting time.'

'That's better. I did think of trying to get you into the farm, but you'll be safer here as long as you keep under cover—they don't know about you, see? Look, maybe it might be better if I stayed with you for a couple of days more. I don't like leaving you—I mean—' And so he went on in an agony of indecision, until I rallied again sufficiently to blast him into positive action.

I remember watching him recede into the gathering dusk across the clearing, and after that I lost all sense of time. Sometimes it was night, at others the sun beat down on me through the undergrowth, and once there was a heavy rainstorm that soaked me to the skin and relieved for a short time the burning fever that was consuming me. I had short periods of lucidity, in one of which I found myself lying out in the open in full view of the road when a truck rumbled past. My foot no longer hurt, in fact there was no feeling there at all. It was just an amorphous excrescence at the end of my leg that weighed a ton. Sanity returned for long enough for me to drag myself back to my lair in the clearing, and it was shortly afterwards that Shivka appeared. Her arrival occasioned me no surprise because I had been visited by Abigail, Gathercole, Long John and even Freddie Stewart, who seemed to bear me no animus, and a host of others from the past including old Grandfather Ross. None of them ever stayed long, and seldom spoke. She did both.

She told me crisply to stop using filthy language when she jabbed needles into my foot, which I didn't feel, and my arm, which I did. Then she forced some stuff down my throat, and, after a titanic struggle, got me into the back of a truck and under some blankets.

It was night again, and she was supporting my head and pouring something more down my throat. I felt as weak as a kitten but I was conscious for the first time that the fever seemed to have left me.

I said, 'I don't believe it You'll disappear, like the others.'

'I will, if you don't swallow this and then shut up,' she answered.

'How did you get here?'

'In this truck.'

'Don't play the fool. You know what I mean. What happened?'

'We're about an hour from the inn. You can ask all the questions you like there.'

'Raucous—what happened—*please*,' I begged.

'He ran into a Blueshirt patrol. He managed to give them the slip but there was some shooting, and he was hit in the stomach. He reached the inn and they got

326

through to us on the radio and he was lifted out in the Lysander.'

'How is he now?'

'All right, I promise you, but it was only in hospital that he came round sufficiently to tell us about you—so I came down, also by Lysander.'

'But why *you*?' I raged. 'Why did they let you take that sort of risk? Are they all stark, staring bloody mad?'

'Pipe down!' she commanded sharply. 'Use what little savvee you have left. I knew the place—he was just able to mumble "where we met you the first time and had that do with the Nips". They wanted me to pick it out on the map so someone else could come, but it was hopeless. It *had* to be me.'

'But why on your own? Why didn't they send somebody with you, for God's sake?'

'For the simple reason that the Lysander will only carry two beside the pilot when it's fitted with long-range fuel tanks.' She started to tuck the blankets round me again. 'Now go to sleep again. We'll be there soon.'

I struggled. 'Let me ride in front with you,' I whimpered pitifully. 'It's cold here.'

'You're better lying down.'

'No—please. I'm stiff and sore on these boards—'

'All right, but you've got to keep quiet, do you understand?'

Amazingly I was able to walk without pain. She helped me round to the passenger's seat and draped a blanket over my shoulders and we got going again.

She relented after a while and gave me some more news. 'We had a minor prang on landing,' she told me. 'An undercarriage strut was broken, but they're sending another down from Chungking. It should be there by now, and Terry is going to replace it.'

'Who's Terry?'

'The pilot—'

'The Boy Wonder who brought us down? Looks about fifteen?'

'That's right. He's our only Silent Lizzie driver, as they call them, and they're working him to exhaustion. One long-distance flight after another, and no proper rest in between because he does all his own maintenance and repairs.'

'My heart bleeds for him,' I said sourly, and I felt her glance at me sharply. 'He can't be so hot if he busts a strut on ground he knows well.'

'What a nasty thing to say,' she reproved. 'The boy is absolutely magnificent. You've had one of these night landings yourself so you must know what it entails. I've flown with him a dozen times and it always amazes me—'

'All right, magnificent if you like, but not unique if someone else is bringing his spare part down,' I countered.

'They're dropping it by parachute,' she said coldly. 'What on earth's the matter with you?'

'Sorry,' I mumbled. 'Sore head as well as a sore foot. It did strike me, however, that he might have come down the road with you in this truck. I'm only now beginning to realize the chance you've taken on your own and it's making my hair stand on end.'

'Nonsense,' she laughed. 'The risk is no greater for one than for two. Actually he wanted to come, but I thought it better for him to get on with the job.' Her hand came out through the darkness and covered mine. 'You're tired, Vince. No more talking, please.'

I'm jealous, I realized with a feeling of self-contempt—me, a staid, middle-aged father of a family, jealous of a mere boy. Thank God Abigail hadn't witnessed that exchange. I could see that quizzical look of hers, and I cringed inwardly like a snail with salt on it. I must have dropped off then.

The truck pulled up with a jerk, and I heard Shivka say, 'Oh my God!' in tones of stark horror. In front of us something was glowing incandescently in the darkness and there was a pall of smoke swirling round the truck. 'It's burnt out—the inn—burnt—' She opened her door and jumped out, and without thinking I did the same on my side, and felt my leg buckle under me. Through the haze I could see her running forward towards the smoking ruins, and I stumbled after her.

'Shivka! Shivka, for God's sake come back—they may be still around,' I implored, and tried to pull her back.

'The cellar,' she sobbed. 'Some of them might still be down there.'

'Not a chance,' I said, and pointed to where the ground floor had collapsed into a glowing pit. 'Come on—back to the truck and let's get out of it while we still have a chance.'

But she would have none of it. 'The plane,' she said. 'He'd had it pulled round into the cane break at the back and covered with camouflage nets,' and nothing I could say would deter her from making a complete circuit of the whole compound, so I limped miserably after her.

The aircraft was a twisted metal skeleton, and there were bodies in the yard behind the main building, stripped and so hacked that it was impossible to tell who or what they had been—male or female, Chinese or Occidental.

I got her back to the truck and tried to climb into the driving seat, but she had recovered slightly by this, and she pushed me to one side.

'You can't use that foot on the pedals,' she said dully. 'God knows what you must have done to it, traipsing through that mud. Come on, let's get on up the road as far as our petrol will take us.'

'How much have we?' I asked, and she made a mental calculation.

'About another thirty miles I should say. With luck we ought to be able to get more at the first staging section. We're on the Silk Road again now, and reasonably safe.'

'It didn't protect them back there,' I said bitterly.

'That would have been a Jap raiding party,' she said. 'No Chinese, not even Blueshirts, would destroy a safe house. They depend on them too heavily.'

'They may be still around in that case,' I said uneasily.

329

'I doubt it. They get out of the area as quickly as possible after a hit-run attack,' and I extracted what small grain of comfort I could from that.

But the first staging-post was deserted, although she insisted on halting and changing the dressings on my foot. I was amazed to find it almost back to normal. The pain had certainly gone and the angry colour had paled.

'This new drug,' she explained. 'Penicillin. No wonder one small capsule fetches five hundred dollars on the black market. It is more valuable than heroin.' She smiled wanly. 'You must be worth quite a lot on the hoof at the present moment. I've shot you full of it. Incidentally, we bought this truck and fifty gallons of petrol for twelve capsules and a carton of Lucky Strike.'

'You can trade *me* for petrol when this lot runs out,' I said. 'Well, whatever it is, it certainly seems to have done the trick. Look, let me drive. You are just about all in.'

'All right,' she agreed reluctantly. 'It can't be for much farther, unfortunately.'

We ran back on to the road, and, glancing sideways, I saw that she had at last thrown in the towel and had fallen asleep. One-handed, I arranged the blanket around her, and drove on sedately, determined to get the last yard out of this ancient vehicle before she coughed and died, but that melancholy moment was long in coming, because we were still rolling when dawn broke—and I ran into the road block.

I braked violently, and the sleeping Shivka shot forward and hit the windshield.

There were about a dozen of them, armed to the teeth with a miscellany of weapons that ranged from sub-machine-guns to villainous muzzle-loaders, and, curiously, my first feeling was one of relief when I saw that they were neither Japanese nor Blueshirts. They had a line of big stones across the road, and had I seen them earlier I might have been able to make a rush for it and nudge them aside, but it was too late now.

'I'm sorry,' I said wretchedly to Shivka as one of them jumped on the running-board and shoved a pistol in my ear.

'It's not your fault,' she said, as she ran an experienced eye over them. 'Communists or Hung-hu-tse. Let's hope the former. They usually have a Russian-speaking commissar with them and I might have a chance of blinding him with dialectical materialism. You'd better whistle the Internationale and give clenched fist salutes at strategic intervals while I'm trying. Silent bunch, aren't they?'

They were. They stood in a half-circle round us and nobody uttered a word.

'The inferior speaks first in this sort of encounter,' I told her. 'He kowtows, tells the other of his lowliness and then supplicates. What's our story when somebody does open the bidding?'

'Evaders from Hong Kong,' she muttered. 'No affiliations with either side—just trying to get clear of the Japanese—husband and wife—Here's somebody coming.'

A man came out from behind a clump of bamboo and strode up to the truck. He was dressed like the others in dusty black peasant smock and trousers, with ammunition bandoliers crossing his broad chest, and a Luger pistol thrust into his belt, but his authority was evident in the way the others stood aside for him. The man holding the gun to my head said, 'Longnoses—spies, *tovarich*, shall I shoot them?' He spoke in the Shanghai dialect, which I knew Shivka was more fluent in than I, but I wondered if she had caught the one Russian word for 'comrade'. If she had, she gave no sign.

The newcomer shook his head and said, 'Not yet,' and looked at us both closely. He had a remarkably steady pair of eyes, small, black and piercing, and totally at variance with the rest of his face, which was round and rather moonlike. I had an uncomfortable feeling that I had seen him before.

He said in Mandarin, 'Where are you going?' and the implication, slight though it was, that we were to be allowed to proceed, heartened me a little.

'To the north,' I said. 'Away from the Japanese.'

'Do you know Kweiyang?' he asked. I nodded. It was the next town of any size north of Kweilin on the Chungking road.

'Then perhaps you will render me a great service?' he said.

331

It was a request, courteously phrased, and my relief was such that I couldn't speak immediately. I bowed my assent.

'The mission hospital from Hengyan,' he went on. 'It has moved ahead of the Japanese advance. It is now in Kweiyang, that is two hundred miles north-west of here. Will you take a sick man there?'

'Willingly,' I said, 'but we have no petrol left.'

'That will be attended to,' he told me. 'Have you food?'

'A little.'

'That also will be attended to. Thank you.' He put out his hand, Western style, and I felt mine grasped firmly. 'The road is clear at present, but the Japanese are advancing swiftly from Changsha,' he went on. 'They will be at this place within two days, so you must not delay.' He handed me a small carved bone chop—a seal in the form of a bird rising on outstretched wings. 'Show this to any who might stop you. Good fortune go with you. I am grateful.' He bowed, then turned abruptly and went back through the bamboo, and I heard him giving instructions to some people unseen the other side, and two forty-gallon drums were manhandled out to us, our tanks were filled and the remainder was lifted on to the back of the truck, together with a wicker basket of rice and fruit, and an earthenware water container. Then they brought out a blanket-covered form on a rough litter and loaded it aboard, and an old man took his seat beside it, and the silent guards moved the stones and waved us on. I drove forward in a daze.

Shivka said in a hushed voice, 'There's the whole wide world between him and my people, and I hate all he represents, but no wonder they worship him. That devil will take this whole country over in the end—if he is allowed to live.'

'But who is he?' I asked. 'And how on earth do you know him?'

'My God! You're a blinkered lot in that money-grubbing citadel of yours down there,' she said impatiently. 'Fancy not recognizing that face. Mao Tse-tung, you fool. He knew *you*.'

332

Then, and only then, did I remember the face that had been on a thousand posters in Hong Kong five or six years previously when he had led the Long March from Kiangsi to Shensi—six thousand miles on foot—an army of thirty thousand.

'Of course,' I said. 'But why should he know me—a blinkered money-grubber from Hong Kong, I think you said?'

' "Know your enemy",' she answered. 'That's the first precept in their sort of war.'

'But he's not an enemy, we're allies,' I said, and she snorted.

'So is Uncle Joe Stalin at the moment—but just wait until this lot is over, my bonny boy. Mao and his mob will have you off that rock down there just whenever it suits him.'

'Wretched Russians,' I said angrily. 'Red, white or pink, you're all the same. If there's nothing brewing at any given time you'll soon stir something up. Listen, my bonny *girl*, Hong Kong was built, *made*, by people like my grandfather. It has stood there, stable and rockfast, for over a hundred years in its present form—'

'And it took a race of monkeys, as you call them, four days to throw you out—people your stupid Empire backed in the Russian-Japanese war, and set on their present road. It serves you damned well right,' she spat at me, and I saw the crucified Canadian major, and the slaughtered nurses, and the pitiful remnants of a beaten army in the camp at Shamsuipo, and I turned and struck her in the face.

I slammed on the brakes and stared at her. 'Oh Christ!' I whispered. 'Shivka—please—I'm sorry. Please, my dear—'

She opened the door on her side and got down, taking her haversack with her. 'I'll ride in the back,' she said and went round to the tailboard.

I ran after her and took her by the arm. 'Please, *please*, Shivka, listen to me,' I babbled. 'Oh God, I'm sorry. I don't know what came over me—*please*'

'It's all right,' she said in a flat voice. 'I want to look at the

333

patient anyway.' And she climbed into the back. I stood looking up at her for a time, then I slunk back to the cab and drove on.

We only stopped twice in that two hundred miles, each time when she hammered on the roof of the cab, in order to attend to the patient.

'He's Mao's chief of staff,' she told me. 'Broken leg—compound fracture—and it's turned septic, much the same as your foot. It's lucky I have some penicillin left.'

She seemed in no way resentful, and she included me in the conversation as she and the old medical orderly prepared a quick meal after renewing dressings, injecting the ghastly swollen leg and generally making the semi-conscious man comfortable. But something had died between us—something that only now I was realizing had been growing over the years since we had met, or, if I *had* realized it, I had been refusing to recognize. Perhaps, horrible though the incident had been, it was better for it to die before either of us was too far committed. That was the sensible view to take of things. But I wasn't feeling sensible. I was more suicidally miserable than I had ever been in my whole life before.

We came to the hospital late in the evening. They had taken over the old mandarin's yamen a mile or so short of the town's outskirts, and a Red Cross flag hung over the gateway. It was not a mission in the accepted sense of the word, but rather a monastic medical order, staffed by Nestorian monks, Syrians for the most part, and therefore technically neutral, but they were cautiously taking no chances with the Japanese advance. They accepted the patient without question and were almost speechless with gratitude for the remainder of the penicillin that we gave them. They allowed me to park the truck and the priceless petrol inside the compound, and they mounted two hefty lay brothers to guard it. They laid on a meal for us and hospitably put their official guesthouse at my disposal.

But there was one thing which, with the deepest regret, they could not depart from—the rule of their Order which

334

forbade the entry of women to any part of the monastery. There was a gatehouse, however, they informed me—a single-roomed building outside the compound wall, and they gladly had it swept and cleaned, and sent out huge cans of hot water and a tin bathtub, bedding and everything else a solitary female guest would be likely to require for an overnight stay.

Shivka and I ate together out there. There was no more awkwardness. We were once more two sane, reasonable people—so much so that when I tried again to beg her forgiveness, she brushed it all aside and told me to forget it. It had never happened, she said. Anyhow, it wasn't half as hefty a wallop as I had handed her in between singing dirty hymns and howling curses the night she found me.

And on that note I started to leave. I turned at the door and looked back at her. She was standing in the light of the one church candle the good brothers had kindly let her have. She looked very lovely.

I said, 'You'll be quite safe here. There's a monk on guard by the gate.'

'Then tell him to go away and say his vespers somewhere else, you bloody fool,' she said, and held her arms out. 'Oh, Vince, you perfectly proper, ever so correct British-cum-Hong Kong solid chunk of unimaginative stuffed shirt business taipan, how I loved you when you let the mask slip, just once.'

And the official guesthouse remained unoccupied that night.

Chapter Eleven

1

We left the truck, crossed the river and shuddered as we looked up at the four hundred and eighty steps to Chungking, which was, itself, still lost in the pre-dawn mist, but then Abigail called from the darkness and told us that she had a boat further along the bank.

'That louse Gathercole has his minions laying for you both at the top,' she said venomously. 'Him and his damned debriefing. You're coming home first, for baths, food and a long sleep.' And she wouldn't take no for an answer, so we were rowed up-river for five miles and were carried up a three-hundred-feet climb in huakans, which may have been a pusillanimous ending to an odyssey, but one we were too tired to argue with.

But it was only a passing surcease, and I awoke at mid-afternoon to hear Gathercole arguing with my mother outside my room, or, to be more accurate, he was cajoling and she was cursing. I pulled on a gown and went to the door. He looked at me and beamed and said, 'That's my boy—won't keep you long—just a chat, and you can roll back into bed.'

'You're a fool,' Abigail said to me. 'This little jerk will put his own words into your mouth when you're tired. Tell him to go to hell until tomorrow.'

'And that's my *girl*,' he said, the beam widening. 'If anybody else called me out of my name I'd be hurt, but from Abigail, it's a compliment yet.'

'Sak me'i tao!' she snarled at him, which would have been rude from a Hakka fishwife. From a *lady*, it was devastating. 'You can stay for ten minutes—and don't you dare go anywhere near Shivka when you leave this room or I'll have you thrown out.'

His manner changed as the door closed behind her, and there was no more waggishness. 'Right,' he said as he dropped into a chair. 'You can skip the trip down, although I'll want it in detail when you write your report, and just tell me what happened after you got into Hong Kong itself.'

'Kwan put me in touch with a man called Silberstein,' I began.

'Who, if he's still running true to form, tried to sell you a proposition?'

'Not exactly—'

'Then he's *not* running true to form.'

'I don't know much about his form, but—'

'*I* can tell you that. He's a professional criminal, a wanted person under the fugitive offenders' act, he's in opium, heroin, prostitution, gambling, tied up with Triad, chief liaison man for Mafia out here—'

'You seem to know it all,' I cut in. 'So why grill *me*?'

'Sorry,' he said with a wintry grin. 'That's the copper in me Go ahead with the proposition—I won't interrupt again.'

'A courier service through the camps,' I told him. 'Up-to-date information collected by the working parties and channelled through to him. He will then relay it on to Kwan in the form of a daily sitrep—'

'Nothing new, in other words. Kwan has been putting that one up to me for the last twelve months.'

'And you've turned it down flat—yes, they told me that. What puzzles me is why you sent me down there. The idea of a seaborne landing and the evacuation of prisoners is a non-starter in Angelo's opinion and I agree with him. I know I'm only a layman, but anybody familiar with that coastline will tell you—'

'Yes, yes, yes, I know that too. A fleet of coastwise shipping big enough to take them all off in one go would be bombed out of the water before, during and after the actual landing.'

'And yet *you* told me to investigate that possibility. That was my sole mission—the only briefing you gave me,' I raged at him.

'Exactly. If I had told you about their alternative scheme—the one you haven't mentioned to me yet, but which I'm darned certain they discussed with you—I'd have been pre-empting them. I wanted you to take a fresh mind to it—to have it sprung on you—and then to get your immediate reaction, your honest opinion. So go ahead, Stafford. Quit spitballing around and tell me—two hundred Dakotas, nose to tail, in, out and away smartly. What about it? Can it be done?' His eyes were searching my face and I felt that he was waiting for the slightest equivocation or hesitation to commit myself, so I plunged.

'It can,' I said shortly. 'That's if you people up here give them the necessary support, and stop being enigmatic.'

'Good,' he said. 'That's all I wanted to know.'

'Then why the hell have you been cat-and-mousing with Kwan?' I demanded. 'I can understand your attitude towards Silberstein, you've explained that yourself—the policeman's distrust of the crook—but Kwan's a different proposition altogether, yet you've treated him abominably and—'

'If you'll shut up for a moment I'll tell you why I've been giving him a rough ride,' he said. 'In the first place I'll admit that the whole idea of a mass rescue by air seemed pure cloud-cuckoo-land to me, so I squashed it at this level, but then, as I went into things more carefully, I began to see its possibilities, so I put it before my boss here—you know who I mean—and half convinced him. He put it up to New Delhi, to the Supreme High God Almighty himself, only to have it shot down in flames. No, it was said, if it was to be done at all it would be done by sea. Yo-ho-ho! and a bottle of rum! Up the Navy! You know how things are being run up there nowadays—or do you? Well, it doesn't matter. An airdrop and a quick snatch is *out*, they said. The cock-up at Arnhem scared the living be-Jesus out of the top brass. One more like

338

that, Churchill has said, and heads will roll—not a decoration, a promotion, possibly a higher title, and then a discreet retirement, but a straight out, honest-to-God firing. None of 'em are going to risk *that*. So there's your answer.'

'I still don't understand,' I said. 'All right, you've failed to get it off the ground, but why take it out on Kwan? He feels you don't trust him, that you doubt his ability, judgement and even his integrity.'

He shrugged. 'Well, all I can say to that is that I'm sorry. I certainly didn't mean to give him that impression. I was given orders to kill the project, and I've done just that. I'm certainly not going to whine to my subordinates when I pass orders on to them—"I'm sorry—*I* believe in the idea but my boss doesn't—not my fault, etcetera, etcetera." No, to hell with that. But that's not the point. *You* believe it can be done?'

'I've just said so, but I'm not a soldier—'

'Thank God. As Lloyd George or somebody once said, "War is too serious a matter to be left to soldiers." No, you're not a soldier by *their* standards, but you *are* a businessman with a better knowledge of Hong Kong and the people who live there, and the people who are occupying it at the moment, than anybody I know.' He held up his hand and checked me as I was about to interrupt again. 'You know how to evaluate chances, when to take a risk, when to box crafty. You know how to get the *feel* of things. In other words, you're a top business taipan. The regular soldiers may smile kindly and patronizingly on your breed, but behind their polite masks they have a pretty healthy awe of you—'

'I don't believe that—'

'Believe what you like. I'm telling you what *is*—what I've learned over the years from my coign of vantage, which is dead half way between those two worlds, the Army and Big Business. You've got the added gimmick of a DSO, which puts you among the dons on their side of the fence.'

'You're getting me mixed up with somebody else.'

'I'm not. The recommendation has been approved—and

339

a DCM for your fellow Rawcliffe. In short, you've got enough weight to get you a hearing in New Delhi—'

'I'm not going back to India,' I told him flatly.

'You'll go where you're sent,' he snapped. 'God damn it, man—you've been belly-aching for a break for your pal Kwan, not to mention Silberstein, and now you're coming the prima donna. Get up there and sell them the deal.'

'Why don't *you* go?'

'I wouldn't make first base with the top brass. Can't you hear them? I can. "Gathercole? That's that policeman fellow from Shanghai, isn't it? Masquerading as a colonel. Russian, isn't he? Get rid of him, somebody," and I'd be fobbed off by a Staff Captain or an ADC. No, *Sir Vincent, you* go, and lay it on the line. I've got you a seat on tonight's plane.'

'I want to see Rawcliffe first,' I said.

'You can, as you go through Calcutta. He was evacuated to the Military Hospital there a couple of days ago.'

It was that which swung it. I nodded.

I have never seen Abigail angrier. She came storming into the room as Gathercole left. 'Where's your guts?' she fulminated. 'God, I wish I'd stayed in here with you. I'd have told him just where he got off.'

'You could probably get away with it,' I said. 'I'm "a person subject to Military Law". It was an order.'

'What do you think he could have done if you'd chucked it into his teeth?'

'I don't know, Mother dear, neither do you, so suppose you be a good girl and pack me some clean gear for India. How's Shivka?'

'Ask her yourself,' she flashed. 'She's gone. I only found out ten minutes ago.'

'Gone where?'

'To Shanghai, that's where.' She stepped up to me, her face a grim mask. 'This is the third time the pitcher has gone to that particular well. She was nearly caught last trip, and I think her cover might have been blown—'

The room was spinning round me. 'But they still let her go?' I gasped.

'*Let* her? They *sent* her, for God's sake. I begged of Gather-cole not to, because I know the danger. It's my ratline they're using, so I had to be told. "Vital mission" they said. She was already under orders for it when word came through about you. She jibbed then, for the first time, and refused to go unless they let her fly down to Kweilin to get you off the hook first. A devil's bargain, and they've held her to it. She hardly had time for a meal before she was on a sampan, heading downriver. Don't go, Vincent. Refuse to do another thing for them until they've got that girl back here safely. Another devil's bargain. That's the way things are run in this cesspit.' Her eyes were searching my face, and I was trying to avoid them. She turned away. 'What's the good?' she finished bitterly. 'You'll go. You're as hooked as the rest. They jerk the strings up there and you starry-eyed fools dance to their tune.'

'I've got to go' I said wearily. 'There are others to be considered, back there in Hong Kong. I promised to do my best—I'd be letting them down if I didn't at least try.'

2

We landed at Dum-Dum late in the evening of May 8, as the news of the German surrender in Europe was coming through, and it made as much impact on me as a wet sponge hitting a sodden haystack. That was another world—another war. Ours would still drag on, and the prisoners in a hundred festering camps in Hong Kong, Singapore and the Philippines would continue to die like flies until Japan itself was crushed—and Shivka would follow her lonely and hideously dangerous path until the Kempitei or Blueshirts caught up with her, because I had no faith whatsoever in Gathercole's last promise to me as he saw me off at the steps, that he would have her lifted out in a matter of days.

I fought my way through mafficking British troops and American airmen in Chowringhee to the Military Hospital

341

overlooking the Maidan. Raucous was an amorphous shape under white sheets, with ghastly tubes protruding from his belly. He grinned delightedly when he saw me, and whispered that he wanted to come out, back to Chungking, and I promised insincerely that I would collect him on my return.

'It's Aggie, you see,' he went on. 'I've had time to think here. Got to look after her. She done a lot for us.'

'You mustn't worry, Raucous,' I tried to reassure him. 'My mother's looking after her. She's quite safe.'

'Yes—yes—thanks. And Miss Shivka? How is she?'

'She's fine, fine,' I mumbled. 'She sends her love. I'll tell you all about everything when I get back.' And then, mercifully, the sister told me it was time to go.

I went on to New Delhi then, and found myself up against an unsurmountable barrier of bland, polite officialdom. I hawked my story round to a dozen junior and middle-piece staff officers, all of whom were most interested. They told me to put it in writing, and to draw maps and make recommendations, and they promised to give it their urgent consideration when one or two rather more pressing matters had been dealt with. In the meantime I'd better remain here, they said, and I found myself shunted into a deadly dull job in censorship, and at last it dawned on me that I was once more 'under wraps' and completely incommunicado, because, try as I did with might and main, I was unable to get word to or from Chungking, and when I pleaded with them to send me back there they shook their collective heads. No, I was needed here—sorry. I even lost touch with Raucous. He had been evacuated again, to a convalescent depot near Bombay.

I did, however, get my first letter from Helen, dated four months previously, from Sydney. She had just received official notification of my survival and was obviously in a state of mild shock when she wrote. She was overjoyed, of course, and the children were wildly excited. They were in school in the Blue Mountains, and she herself was working with the Red Cross—and so on. Two or three other letters followed, all as stilted and awkwardly phrased, as, no doubt, were my replies. I think we were both doing our best, but we were like people with broken limbs trying to adjust after the plaster casts had been removed. Things were not going to be easy in the years ahead, I reflected.

And so the days dragged on, ninety-two of them to be precise, until at dawn on the morning of August 8 the Bomb was dropped on Hiroshima. They relented a little then.

'We couldn't risk it, old boy,' an apologetic colonel told me. 'It has been the war's best kept secret, but you were on a very short list of people who might, conceivably, have picked up a hint of it, and you had to be kept away from any chance of capture. We hadn't an inkling of things to come when you went into Hong Kong, or you'd never have been sent.'

'Can I go back to Chungking now?' I asked.

'Afraid not. Chiang Kai-shek has taken over again, and the Mission is being closed. He's very grateful and all that, but he wants us out. Anyhow, Hong Kong has been liberated and they are screaming for you back there. War Rehabilitation or something.'

That was better than nothing, but even so it took me a further two weeks to make it, and then only by bribing my way on to an overloaded Red Cross plane. A red-capped but rather white-faced military police sergeant was first up the steps of the Dakota when we landed at Kai Tak.

'Saw your name on the Arrivals signal,' he babbled joyously. 'Your Ma's out at Annandale—got Aggie with her—they're trying to get the place mucked out—Jesus! What a job—I'll drive you out there—got me own jeep—'

'Raucous! How the hell did you get here?' I gasped when I found my voice.

'Volunteered for it back in India—only job I could get—some of me mates would turn in their graves, poor buggers, if they could see me in this rig—'

Talking incessantly, he steered me through mountains of stores being unloaded from strings of transport planes by Japanese prisoners, their roles now reversed—and I couldn't get a word in edgeways.

'All sorts of things happening, you wouldn't believe it. Pinched Kordakov the other days—yes, me personally—trying to grease his way on to a plane for Formosa, the cheeky bastard. Old Long John is back in business—first restaurant to open, only place in town you can buy a drink. Oh, and Professor Kwan wants me to let him know when you get in—'

'Raucous, for God's sake shut up for just one moment,' I begged. 'Miss Shivka? Have you heard anything of her?'

'Yes, sure. She came down from Chungking with your Ma and Aggie,' he said.

'Where is she now?' I asked quickly.

'I don't know at the moment, but your Ma will. Oh, and I got out to see the old ladies—bright as buttons, they are—' But I no longer heard him.

She was safe. That was all that mattered—immediately.

But Abigail was no help when we arrived at the Augean stable that Annandale had become.

'I won't tell you,' she said firmly. 'She doesn't want me to, and that's good enough for me. She's getting out as soon as they can allot her a passage.'

'I only want to *see* her,' I raged.

'Leave things as they are,' she advised. 'Don't make it any harder for her. Have you been to your office yet?'

'Damn my bloody office,' I spat at her. 'I want to know where Shivka is.'

'All right, damn your bloody office if you like, but they're set up in temporary premises near Murray Barracks, and they tell me that they've managed to fix air passages for Helen and the kids on a Red Cross plane. Sheer damned nepotism. They will be here any day now. There's a letter from her there on the table. It came up from the office yesterday.'

I picked it up mechanically. It hardly seemed worth opening. It would differ not one iota in tone and content from the previous ones—stilted, formal and trite—like our lives. But I did open it. This had to be faced. There were pieces to be

344

picked up and fitted together into something that would pass for a pattern of life. What had happened was in no way *her* fault.

The words danced before my eyes, and just didn't make sense for a long time.

> ... I don't ask for forgiveness, just a little understanding . . . missing believed dead, and I'd accepted the latter when the months and years went by without a word. . . He's an American air force officer . . . helped me through those awful days . . . the children are fond of him, and he of them . . . many such cases, and the authorities are sympathetic and they go through the courts quickly, so if your lawyer could get in touch with mine here in Sydney . . .'

I handed the letter to Abigail. She moved to the window, fumbling for her glasses, and I saw her lips moving as she read. She looked across at me when she came to the end.

'Holy sailor,' she said in tones of deep wonder. '*She's* dear Johnned *you*. Good for her—I didn't think she had it in her. My, oh my! aren't you male Staffords unlucky in marriage—or lucky, depending which way you look at it.'

'*Now* will you tell me where Shivka is?' I shouted.

'No, I darned well won't,' she retorted flatly. 'I'll go and see her. If she wants to see you, I'll bring her back. If she doesn't, that's final. Raucous,' she called. 'Can you give me a ride in that jeep of yours?'

3

The mist was layering over the Li Mun Channel. I sat on the weed-choked emplacement of old Ross's brass cannon and looked down to the city, where paper lanterns and naphtha flares were pinpointing through the darkness. Across in Kowloon they already had the electricity connected up. The lighthouse on the Po Tois was flashing once more. Soon the

345

Peak, behind me, would be necklaced again with its arc lights. Hong Kong was breathing, rising phoenixlike from the ashes. It was the Hour of the Dog, when darkness descends, but not, to the Chinese, a Götterdämmerung—a time of dying—but rather of rest, peace, before the travail of tomorrow.

I heard the jeep coming up the ruined drive to the house. Its lights swept the lawn for a moment and then snapped out, and darkness was complete. I sat on, eyes tightly closed and fists clenched, with the nails biting into the palms. Then I heard her call, and she was running across the grass towards me.